"Do you deny ever having chained your sister up, for any purpose whatsoever?" Sullivan demanded. "With your hand on the scanner, Mr. Kirushenko!"

Dmitri refused to be intimidated, but knew he had to answer. If he didn't, they'd force him, or worse yet, separate him even more from Sarah, and that would only upset her further. For better or worse, they'd been a team for almost seven years. Yes, at times their relationship had strained to the very last thread, but that frayed thread had held. He couldn't let this break them apart, either. Sarah understood the risk.

He eyed the scanner with distrust. He knew how those things worked. They couldn't read minds, only biometric reactions. His blood pressure was already high, his heart revved, his palms slimy with nervous perspiration.

Good! Let them be!

With a self-righteous air, Dmitri squashed his palm firmly on the plate, increasing the contact. He held his breath while the scanner adjusted to his biometrics, and replied, "No, I haven't."

When the Moons turn against you, who will you trust?

The **Best Intentions** series

Best Intentions
Best Efforts
Broken Trusts

Also available in e-book format

Broken Trusts

Susan Staneslow Olesen

This is an original work of fiction. Names, characters, places and politics are the work of the author's imagination. Any similarity to persons living or dead is entirely coincidental.

Artwork enhancement by
Bob Staneslow

For my dear friend Pony Peake,
fellow writer and confidant,
who held my hand and talked me through it

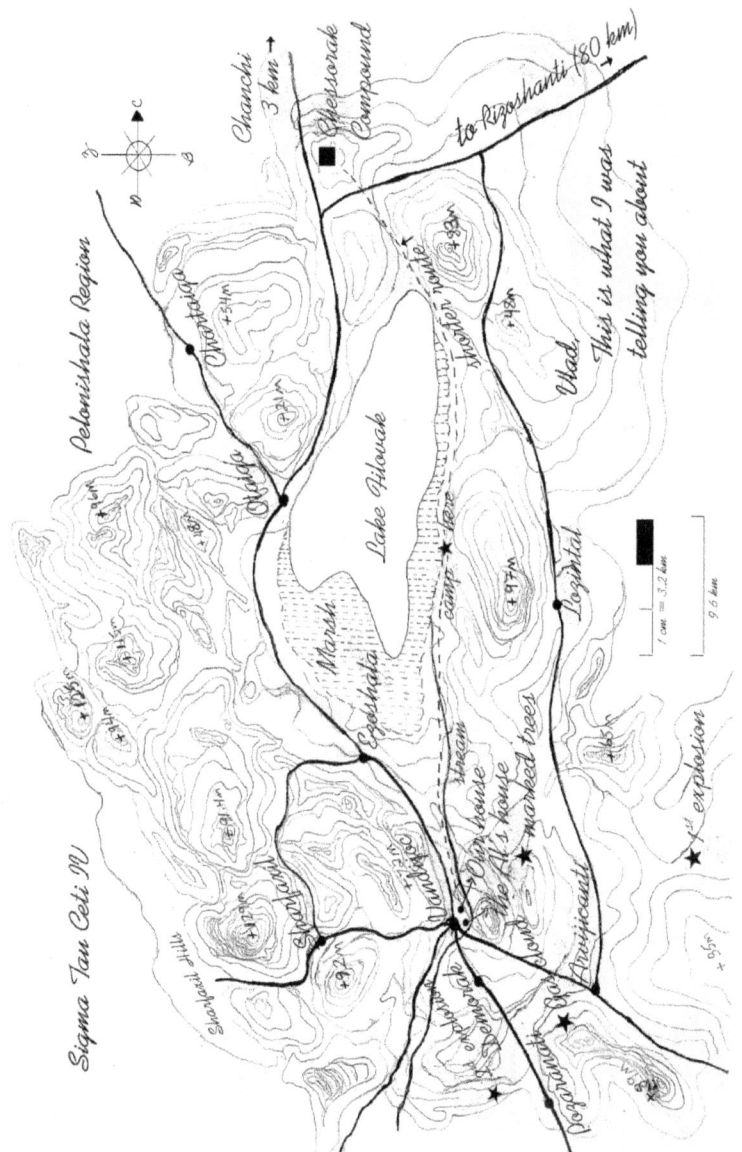

Sigma Tau Ceti IV

Pelonishala Region

Sigma Tau Ceti IV
Epsilon Quadrant
Earthdate: Spring, 2270

*S*he knelt before the safe on the floor of her brother's closet and opened the folded papers on the ground before her. Row upon row upon row of two-digit number sequences covered the pages in tiny perfect print, each already tried and discarded. The longer time went on, the more determined she was to break the combination on the lock. She didn't even care what he kept in there; it was just something to **do**. For someone who grew up with replicators and Davies Warp ships and matter-energy transportation, being stuck on a technologically primitive planet for the last four years had become unbearable. Oh, what she'd do for a holocinema, or a museum, or chocolate! She dabbled in different science projects, always on the lookout for a new insect to catalogue or an animal to follow back to its young, but mostly she was just bored. This planet had only so much to offer someone of Sarah's intense level of curiosity.

Dmitri's safe became her crusade a month after he brought it home. Knowing her too well, he showed her what he was storing in it: all the notes and papers yet to be turned in on their next visit to the Alliance Research Compound, their rule books and by-laws and agreement contracts for remaining on the planet, some of his own treasured possessions. Nothing exciting, nothing interesting, nothing worth bothering.

"You want me to put anything of yours in here?" he asked.

"Like what? All I've got is books, and I use those all the time. I suppose I could keep my pictures in there. How do you open it?"

"Hah! Like I'd ever tell you! Too bad I can't keep YOU in there."

Anything off limits to Sarah became an immediate challenge.

She knew the last number for certain: he'd forgotten to turn the dial after the last time he'd opened it; that cut the magnitude of the challenge by a full third. She'd tried sets of numbers, both random and in order, knowing the likelihood of coming across the right sequence before she was fifty was next to zero. Still, every time Dmitri left the cabin for at least an hour, she scurried to rule out the next series of numbers. It was a challenge, a puzzle, a game to keep her mind busy, and it was, of course, forbidden, which added to the fun.

No. Write it down. A turn of the dial to the right, a number to the left,

9

around to the right. Tug. No. Write it down. Next. No. Write. Next. No. Write. Another. Next. If the house hadn't been so deathly silent, she never would have heard the soft metallic click of metal rods sliding back.

No way! Could it – ! Was that **it**? *Sarah held her breath. She stretched out three fingers and gave a tentative tug on the handle. The door swung toward her with a faint sucking sound.*

She circled the numbers on the paper and studied the door, open just a centimeter, weighing her choices. She'd accomplished her mission; she'd broken the code. The decent, honest, proper thing to do was to close the door, spin the dial, close the closet, and find something else to do.

Find something else? *She'd spent almost a year and a half on this! To have accomplished it was strangely disappointing.*

Sarah crossed over the landing to her room and leaned out the window to check the paths. All clear. She sped back and opened the door all the way.

She knelt to get a better look, memorizing the exact position and location of every item. Dmitri wasn't that observant, but old habits died hard. Once upon a time, Father liked to drink, and when he drank, he often became violent. If you dared mess with something, you had to be damned *sure it was put back so exactly Father wouldn't notice. Father might forget where he was or how to fasten his pants, but he always knew when something had moved. Mother was such a perfectionist, so proud of her finer things, that she knew almost by instinct if there was a crack or craze where there shouldn't have been, and the* gavno *would really hit the ceiling fans if she let the defect slip to Father. Unless you liked pain, you left things* exactly *as you found them.*

One by one, she took items out and lined them up nearby, positioned the precise way they'd been inside. Three bottles of local alcoholic brew – how hard she wished she could dispose of them! Allied Fleet papers and manuals for the Compound – boring, she'd already read them. Something flat brushed her fingers; Sarah turned it over and gave a hard shudder. A locally made, grainy grey photograph of Dmitri and Jaycee, the girl he wanted to live happily-ever-after with. Some memories, like broken hearts, were best left undisturbed. Another shudder as she removed a square of cream-colored paper. In her perfect penmanship she'd written:

I, Sarah-Irina Kirushenko, do voluntarily give ownership of my immortal soul to my brother, Dmitri-Mikhail Kirushenko, as partial payment for the terrible wrongs I have wrought him, until he declares the debt

10

repaid and returns it to me.

    She couldn't think of any other way to make him believe the sincerity in her apologies. Two years had passed since he'd accepted her peace offering, and he was certainly in no hurry to release her. She placed it aside with the utmost of care.

    Only one item remained in the dark recesses, and she had to stretch to reach it. She untied the small cloth bag and dumped out a smooth metallic object, as long as her hand and two fingers thick.

    Son of a **bitch***! She'd forgotten all about that!* <!Shojen ki Chaven!> *she swore in the local fashion – a backward planet with three moons garnered a lot of lunar superstitions. She turned it over and over in her hands, not just a little in awe.*

    It was a Type-A, Allied Fleet-issue EPSAR weapon.

The judge reviewed his computer screen before speaking. "This hearing is called to review the petition for parole by Alexander Grigorevitch Kirushenko. Mr. Kirushenko, please rise."

One of two men at the center of the room stood up. The motion seemed slow; at five centimeters past two meters, it took time for him to unfold. His chiseled head was large, the knobby hands thick, his feet ridiculously big if studied by themselves. He was an imposing figure, so much so his 131 kilos looked underweight on the giant frame. The cropped hair was still dark, as was the thick beard, but up close they were peppered with silver, lending an undeniable reality to his fifty-four years. He wore the bright yellow coverall of a penal rehabilitation inmate, the double blue stripe on the shoulder signifying he was a working professional, someone who had served enough time, survived enough hours of psychodynamic therapies to have gained back some respect and responsibility.

The strong, deadly hands clasped in front of him as he stood straight, displaying the red tattoo of prisoner's numbers across the back. The code would be removed before his final release. Likewise, the tiny security locator chip at the back of his head would also be removed at that time.

His eyes darted toward the seven-person board of review, eyes dark as starless night, two black holes dragging with a gravity all their own. Eyes that were a bit sad, a bit shy, a bit hopeful-but-afraid-to-hope. Eyes that held immense pain, and the silent resolution to bear it. Eyes not as impassive as he desired.

"Mr. Kirushenko, your sentence was seven to fifteen years for battery of a juvenile and negligent homicide in the death of your daughter, Elizabyeta Kirushenko. What makes you feel you deserve parole after serving only the minimum sentence?"

The bottomless eyes cast downward. The big man raised his head after a moment of thoughtful silence and spoke in accented Standard, his voice deep and slow.

"What happened to my daughter was an accident I truly regret. I believe I am now a stronger person, with more self-awareness, and more self-control. I have undergone genetic therapy to eliminate my risk for alcohol dependency, and completed the prescribed program for those with chemical susceptibility. I have submitted to chemopharmaceutical,

12

behavioral, and psychodynamic therapies for chronic depression. I have completed intensive retraining for anger management. To the best of my knowledge, my incarceration has been without incident. I can only hope my efforts vouch for themselves."

The judge eyed the man with the boredom of seasoned hardness. "Nearly everyone in this penitentiary enters this room feeling their actions here prove their reform, Mr. Kirushenko. If you were released today, what means would you have to support yourself?"

"I was a Professor of Archaeology and Antiquities at various universities on Earth and Navara," Kirushenko replied with more confidence. "I retained my certifications, so I can still apply for teaching positions. As part of my vocational rehabilitation, I have been teaching general studies to those inmates whose programs require further education. I am able to give guest lectures, and last year, at the suggestion of a therapist, I wrote and published a small paper in a lesser journal. Just a review of literature, but it was accepted and published. I could apply for grants to do research, or put together an expedition of my own. There is a twentieth-century site on Earth that is undergoing exploration, and the team is still looking for qualified candidates. And I am working on an old offer to write a book on one of my more major discoveries."

The judge gave a nod. "Very good. We don't often see candidates with so many options. You demonstrate an ability to handle time wisely. Financial stability is only one prerequisite for early release, however. Personal support is another. Are there any friends or family who would be willing to supervise your transition back into the community-at-large?"

The dark head dropped. "My wife died seven years ago. I was hoping perhaps to contact my sister, on Earth. She has always helped me, whenever I have asked."

The judge touched a line of text on his viewscreen. "That would be... Anastasia Groliak? We will contact her for confirmation, if necessary. Mr. Barwyck." The judge addressed the other man in the center. "Have you conducted surveys as to the position of the victim's family regarding their stance to the subject's parole?"

The court-appointed lawyer stood up, scratching an ear. "I did, your Honor, but the case is a little complicated due to the fact that the victim's family and the incarcerated's are the same. Mr. Kirushenko's wife is deceased. He had thirteen children, minus the victim, leaves twelve children. Of those twelve, eight are legal adults of at least seventeen years of age."

The lawyer approached with several loose documents. "I have here the results of that survey. Of eight adult children, the eldest son could not be located, the second eldest son is deceased, the third eldest son is living on an undeveloped planet and could not be reached for comment. One son is simply, quote, 'unopposed to his father's release,' while one survey was returned unopened with the phrase, uh – this is a direct quote – 'wrong goddamned address, don't fucking look here,' unquote, scrawled on it. Of Mr. Kirushenko's elder daughters, one response has not been received, but two responses profusely petition the court to allow the prisoner to be released as soon as possible, and promise aid in any feasible way."

"Two out of eight in strong favor." The judge sighed, pursing his lips. "That's not particularly encouraging. As a convicted child batterer, you cannot regain custody of the remaining four children, but visitations are permissible if both parties wish it. Do you wish to reestablish ties with your children, Mr. Kirushenko?"

"I – I don't know," Kirushenko stammered, unsure of anything at this point. The thought of being incarcerated had terrified him; he was just as frightened at the thought of being released. No doubt his children hated him for the way he'd treated them over the years; he hated himself for having done it. Perhaps facing them would be the real punishment, the soul-crushing branding iron of shame that would burn against the weight of guilt seven years of therapies had been unable to eradicate. "I won't blame them if they don't wish to speak to me, but, I think my wife would want me to make the attempt."

The judge scanned the hearing room from habit. "Are there any representatives of your family present here today, to speak for or against you?"

The rear seats were empty except for a lone, thirty-something woman sitting just inside the door. A brown Venusian-silk scarf encircled her neck; the sheer cloth deepened the hazel of her eyes and complemented the dark gold of her wavy hair. Pretty, but not stunning. She stood up, revealing long, shapely legs. She was tall, very tall. Not as tall as the prisoner, but certainly as tall as, or taller, than any other man in the room.

"Yes, your Honor."

The prisoner twisted to see the speaker, disbelief crossing the haggard features.

The judge seemed surprised as well. "Please, come forward."

The woman walked forward confidently until she stood opposite the lawyer. "You are …?"

14

"Valeria-Lyn Alexandrovna Kirushenko, your Honor, eldest of the Kirushenko children. You have my written statement in your hand."

The judge flipped through the pages the lawyer had given him, skimming his eyes over one. "You are aware what a pledge of support entails?"

"Yes, sir. I am well aware of the responsibilities involved. I am an attorney for the Ivanov Corporation on Earth. I have both the flexibility of schedule and the financial resources available to me to help guarantee success. You hold a document signed by my sister Galina, also pledging assistance. My sister Ekaterina – she did not return her survey, but I have her permission to speak for her – Katerina has family concerns of her own that currently take precedence. She cannot pledge full support at this time, but will help if necessary.

"I – I feel somewhat responsible for my father's incarceration. I was partially at fault for allowing the circumstances to occur that resulted in the death of my sister, and for allowing the circus that was my father's trial. The man before you now is not the man who was arrested seven years ago. He is more like himself twenty years ago, someone able to successfully juggle the responsibilities of employment, education, and rearing numerous children, all at the same time. I am the legal guardian of my youngest brother and sister. Marina was an infant; she has no memory of her father at all. Nikolai's only memory of his father is of a nameless, faceless man being dragged from our home in restraints. It would be in their best interest to be reunited with him as soon as possible. Every day they are apart, unable to learn from each other, is a day that can never be replaced. I beg you to release him on parole *this* year, to heal the pain we have already suffered, and reunite this man with his family."

"You have a valid argument, Miss Kirushenko. So noted." The judge tapped the loose papers together and placed them on the table. "Your testimony and the written statements will be taken into account by the Board of Review. The Board will render its decision within twenty-four hours. Regardless of outcome, in light of the aforementioned circumstances, I feel it would be worthwhile to order Mr. Kirushenko be provided with the services of a family reintegration counselor. Should parole be granted, the conditions for release will already be in progress. If parole is denied, then the process will leave Mr. Kirushenko in an excellent position for release upon review next year. Case dismissed, pending decision of the Board of Review."

The woman stepped forward and hugged the man in yellow before the guards could remove him. Sasha Kirushenko returned the gesture with a marked sense of reserve, the look of nervous uncertainty never leaving his face.

Один ~ *One* ~ *Oben*

Constellation-class Star Explorer
Alliance Fleet Ship Triumph
Epsilon Region
Unified Date: 637570
Earth date: Late November, 2270

It was dark outside.

It was always dark outside the ship, as little visible light crossed the vast emptiness of interstellar space. The ship itself had running lights, cute little colored blips on the outside skin to highlight where the edges lay, but they did little against the absolute black. Floodlights shone across the wedge-shaped main hull to illuminate the name and registration number, but they had little effect unless the ship ran on sub-light power or stood still. Once the enormous Davies Drive engines kicked in and slipped the ship into the warped bubble of space/time that made it seem to travel "faster" than light, light couldn't follow and all was black again. Since most of their travel time was spent in warped space, the hundreds of port holes and observation windows were virtually pointless. Nonetheless, their effect on morale during planetary orbits made up for the engineering difficulties they presented.

It was dark outside, and for another five seconds Jack Sullivan's quarters remained dark, too. The computer gave a soft but insistent chime, and the lights came up to quarter-power. Sullivan opened his eyes quarter-power to match.

Four hours.

He'd slept four hours, and his eyes didn't want to open any farther. Backlogged with reports and daily follow-up after the last mission, he'd shorted himself on sleep for the past two days to catch up.

"Alarm off."

With extraordinary self-discipline, Sullivan rolled to a sitting position, stretched and stood. He finished his triple-S routine in the small washroom, and checked the mirror out of habit. Forty-three, and not a trace of gray in his brown locks, though the front looked annoyingly thin. Didn't matter much; he no longer had enough time to play the lady's man, and captains were forbidden from fraternizing with the women on their own ships. He pulled on a clean blue-and-gold uniform and hit the call switch on his room's interface.

"Mr. Raines, ship's status?"

The dark-skinned face of the *Triumph's* first officer grinned across the captain's vidscreen. "G'morning, Captain! Ship's status normal, all departments reporting no problems, sir. Proceeding to Sigma Tau Ceti IV at Davies Power six, sir, as per orders."

"Thank you, Commander. I'll see you in a half hour. Sullivan out." He cut the interface and headed for the mess hall.

The *Triumph* was a big ship, 862 crew strong, one of ten swift star explorers commissioned twenty-five years previous by the United Planetary Alliance. As it sped through the darkness, toying with the laws of quantum physics, Jack Sullivan walked the dull corridors to the officers' mess. He scrolled the electronic menu until he found something appealing, then touched the screen. Twenty seconds later the replication unit gave a chirp. He swung the front panel to remove his breakfast, then stopped at the beverage bar to retrieve real coffee for his artificial milk. Across the room another officer waved, and Sullivan carried his tray over.

"'Morning, Jack." Kyle Granger motioned to the seat across from him, and Sullivan took up the offer. Granger looked over the captain's tray. "I thought you gave up on the big breakfasts?"

"I did," Sullivan said. He poured salt over his imitation ham and eggs. "After three days, I was ready to eat the stuffing out of the command chair." He buttered his toast, spread it with jelly, and took a hungry bite, washing it down with a slurp of coffee. "I need the energy for today's briefing."

"Mm. You'd get more if you ate some fruit with that. What's up with the meeting? I read your note. If it's a tech investigation, why are you involving medical?"

"Radiation," Sullivan replied between mouthfuls. "The two biggest explosions were loaded with radiation. There isn't any type of medical care in the area we're looking at; if I have to be in an irradiated area, I want a qualified doc with me."

"A dangerous, possibly deadly situation, so you immediately thought of me," Granger said dryly. "Thank you so very much. I signed on this ship to treat patients, not risk my life traipsing across planets chasing after adventurers."

"As Chief Medical Officer, you do have the right to assign someone else to the task. I didn't realize there was that much difference between traipsing across planets and traipsing through canyons on horseback."

Kyle pointed his fork at the Captain. "You leave my horses out of this! I've never met a horse yet that would walk into danger like you do. I'd trust a horse before half the kids on this ship."

Sullivan's blue eyes laughed. "And in the almost twenty years I've known you, Doc, you've never once kept your nose out of trouble, either. That's why I picked you for my crew."

"That shoots down the theory of my good looks, now, doesn't it." At fifty-one, Kyle Granger was lean and tough, kept strong by the six weeks' leave he spent every year at his family's horse ranch in Wyoming. Gray had worked into his hair, arthritis into his bones, but, like his friend and captain, Kyle still pushed himself like he was twenty. "Four years as captain of the *Triumph*, a star of the fleet, and you only stop to remember me six weeks ago. So much for knowing people in high places."

"It's not my fault you signed up for a five-year mission before I made captaincy, Kyle. It's not like I could have pulled you off the *Covenant*. I grabbed you the minute you came available."

"I guess I'm supposed to be thankful for that." Granger drained the last of his coffee. "Physical science isn't going, is it?"

"Well, considering it's a scientific investigation of a physical nature, I kind of figured he might. Haven't you made peace yet?"

Granger dropped his voice low. "Come on, Jack! You know my feelings on Navarans. You knew them before you invited me aboard. I've got half a mind to put a tack on his chair, see if he flinches."

"Do it, and I'll write up your reprimand myself," Sullivan said with a look that dared to be challenged. "Your problems with Navarans aren't funny anymore, Kyle. That was thirty years ago. Get over it."

"That's easy for you to say! You've never had a dozen of them for supervisors! Six months in that furnace with those arrogant bastards, sweating out every damned electrolyte I could produce. I had the best damned grades of any resident in the program, and they still had the nerve to give me a poor recommendation. You bet your bridge I hold a grudge."

Sullivan wasn't impressed. "Ti'onam's more than qualified for any number of positions on this ship, including mine. We're talking one Navaran, Kyle, not a battalion, and not your supervisor. I expect every one of my officers to work with everyone else on my ship, whether they like it or not. If it bothers you that much, Doctor, maybe this isn't the best ship for you."

Granger gathered up his empty tray. "No, no problem, *Captain*. See you in half an hour."

Sullivan finished his breakfast in peace and headed for the conference room. It was barely sunup in the artificial day and he was exhausted, but only death or a direct medical order was supposed to keep a captain from his duty, and even those clauses were negotiable. The last mission had been a diplomatic one, a week of listening to two committees growl over a trade dispute. He filed it under the category of Boring and Aggravating. The current mission had a chance at being interesting: a scientific investigation of an anomaly on a low-tech planet. A mystery was good for the crew; it made them think, and often involved several departments at once, socializing crewmembers and encouraging cooperation. It was a chance to let his crew shine at what they did best. And a few weeks' work in a wilderness setting was almost as good as shore leave.

The doors of the meeting room slid open and Sullivan found his physical sciences officer already waiting. Two hundred forty-three non-human officers resided aboard ship; Firinar nal Ti'onam was the only Navaran. Sullivan didn't tolerate prejudice on his ship; it interfered with functioning and was bad for morale, but he could understand his medical officer's long-standing frustration. Navarans – especially those on the homeworld – too often fell under the category of Boring and Aggravating as well.

Ti'onam rose as Sullivan entered, his feathery blue-black hair and leathered tan skin contrasting his uniform. His ears were smaller than a human's, set higher on the skull, and they rippled around the pinna, reminding Sullivan of misplaced scallop shells.

"Good morning, Mr. Ti'onam. At ease."

"Good morning, Captain," Ti'onam replied from habit, though the idiom was lost on him. Navara's intensely analytical mindset made for excellent scientists, economists, mathematicians, and precision engineers and craftsmen, but diplomacy among the more excitable races – such as Terrans – proved a most difficult cultural challenge.

"Looking forward to our next mission, Commander?"

"A new planet often brings new opportunities for learning. Although Sigma Tau Ceti IV has been mapped geographically, less than a quarter has been explored in any detail. It is possible we may discover a unique and previously uncatalogued phenomenon." If it wasn't for the occasional blink or ponderous twist of his head, on first glance Ti'onam might have been mistaken for a frilly android.

"I'm confident you won't be disappointed. Our next mission could be a lengthy one. Do you have any objections to being off ship for several weeks?"

The Navaran's deep-set gray eyes blazed with interest for a brief moment. "If you feel my expertise would best serve on the planet, Captain, then I cannot object."

"Good. Your skills will no doubt prove an asset. Please review any necessary data on radioactive energies and their sources, and consider yourself on the team."

* * *

"Sigma Tau Ceti IV, fourth of seven orbital planets. First catalogued 2258 by Scout Vessel *AFS Quindal*, first exploration 2260 by *AFS Meritorius*. Class M, gravity 0.96 that of Earth, 26 standard hour day, 346 standard day year. Most climate types represented, temperate forest being the most wide-spread. Inhabited on three of four continents by intelligent humanoid lifeforms, technology rating of G on the Mimba Scale, approximating that of the last half of Earth's nineteenth century. Due to technology status, the law of Independent Destiny is in full effect," Commander Raines recited with a flourish. "No mod tech allowed."

"Current status of exploration?" Sullivan glanced at the chronometer glowing in the corner of the room's wallscreen. Twenty minutes, and one officer still hadn't bothered to show.

Raines thumbed another toggle, and the screen image changed to a long-range video of forest, interspersed with small farms and communities.

"There are three Alliance research and observation stations. Their mission is to gather as much information as possible and record it for future use. Three commanders are in charge of the compounds, overseeing approximately one hundred eighteen various scientists, anthropologists and archivists, as well as another twenty associate personnel who live within the planetary communities themselves."

"Thank you, Jupiter." The doors to the meeting room opened, and Kyle Granger slid into an empty seat.

"Doctor Granger, nice of you to join us," Sullivan said. "I believe my memo said 0700."

"Sorry, Captain – last minute emergency in the officers' mess I had to tend to."

"Anything serious?"

"An ensign collided with a lieutenant holding a fresh cup of coffee. Just some minor burns. They'll both be fine in twelve hours or so."

"Good. Anything to add to our discussion on the population of Sigma Tau Ceti?"

"Not a whole lot, I'm afraid. Due to technology restrictions, it's very difficult to get a decent analysis. You can't just post a notice asking for volunteers." Granger paused, sliding a data slip into the interface. A narrow-focus video appeared on the wallscreen, made by a tiny hidden camera. Bipedal humanoids in drab, dirt-streaked native costumes populated a rustic village. A heavy cart drove by, hitched to a hairy, long-necked creature.

"They're of a fairly common humanoid stock, on average seven centimeters shorter than Earth types for both men and women. There are no known extremes in racial characteristics – no Negroid or Nordic types – a fairly homogeneous population of moderate skin and hair coloring, but a predominance of green, hazel, brown, and even dark gold or rust-colored eyes. There are some variations in organ systems, and an unexplained low rate of fertility, which helps account for the slow population growth. The most noticeable differences are in body chemistry – antigens, blood factors, enzymes and such – nothing immediately obvious. Don't expect a blood transfusion from them. We'd be more or less able to blend in, physically. With notable exceptions," Granger added under his breath. His gaze slid to the Navaran.

Sullivan caught the tone. "Who wouldn't you recommend go planetside? I assume you have valid reasons."

"I, uh... Of course, Captain," Granger stuttered. "As I said, there are no racial extremes. There are any number of crew on board who could put an exploration party on the defensive. Commander Raines, for one. Doctor Bakari. Nurse Sundback. Mr. Ti'onam. The Inusians in communications. Lieutenant Xiki in engineering, for another. Anyone over 175 centimeters tall. In the interest of program integrity, it has been officially recommended that such extremes be avoided if at all possible."

Sullivan threw his medical officer a razor-edged glare. "In that case, I will take that into consideration when making my choices for the team. Mr. Andreiev, the Chessorak research compound has reported two major radioactive explosions, as well as intermittent bursts of energy that match no common weapon frequency. Attempts were made to explore the area, but radioactive contamination prevented all but the briefest of observations. Speculation, Lieutenant, as to what could cause such phenomena on a planet with no knowledge of nuclear weapons or particle beams?"

"Being the Epsilon quadrant, this is a very recently explored area of space, so our information may not be complete," Danil Andreiev spoke. An ambitious lieutenant of twenty-five, he was already a qualified weapons specialist, and the number two officer in the weaponry and defense department.

"Native weapons are primitive; hunting weapons, depending on region, include refined knives, clubs, spears, snares, traps, and crossbows. There are a few projectile weapons in use using an explosive propellant, but they are used mostly by certain militias. Accuracy is limited to 150 meters. Some explosives are used in mining industries, but none are known to emit radiation.

"The Alliance has yet to formally claim the area, so any other government has equal right to declare it for themselves. There have been no treaties, no trade agreements, no declarations of protection. No Hamalin ship has ever been detected this far from the treaty zone. Likewise, even at maximum speed, we are more than five weeks from the edge of Burin-Jai space; even if the planet should be discovered to have an unlimited amount of natural wealth, the distances involved would make it very unlikely the Burin-Jai would attempt to claim it. If there is an alien culture involved, I would best guess it is a race we are currently unaware of.

"As far as type of weapon, the research stations insist no ship has orbited the planet in four months. In such a primitive culture, it is possible that the radiation may have been accidental, an unknown side effect of an explosion caused by normal technological development."

"That's something to keep in mind. Thank you, Lieutenant. Mr. Ti'onam, are there any natural phenomena that could account for radioactive explosions?"

"As a natural phenomenon, it is rare but not impossible," the Navaran said. "There are several naturally occurring elements that are radioactive, including rare isotopes of more inert elements. However, most are in stable forms that would not react under normal Class-M atmospheric conditions."

Ti'onam elaborated on the natural chemical properties of radioactive compounds for several minutes, and Jack found his attention slipping. He could hear the bed in his cabin two decks below calling to him with a stubborn persistence as Ti'onam droned on.

"So the odds are in favor of some sort of outside catalyst," Sullivan said when Ti'onam finished. "Allied Space Fleet has authorized the *Triumph* to be of assistance to the research facilities, up to a period of three months, to rule out cultural contamination violations and alien colonization that could place the survey teams in jeopardy."

"Three months!" Commander Raines interjected. "It's hard to keep a crew on their toes when they're spinning in place for three months. The cadets will get dizzy."

Sullivan almost smiled. "I have faith in you, Raines. You'll be in charge of the ship. Ever since the Alliance/Burin-Jai escalation on Bolivar VII, the Alliance has been extremely meticulous about enforcing the Law of Independent Destiny. Since Sigma Tau Ceti falls directly under that protection, you will be just as responsible as I in enforcing that. No technological weapons are to be put planetside; no exceptions. Questions?"

"Well, outside of nothing more exciting to do than maintain standard orbit and engage in personnel exchanges in the name of shore leave, I'm not sure I'm fond of the idea of a landing party being that unreachable for such an extended period of time," Raines said. "For security purposes, the planet has been shielded to molecular transport except for areas directly within the research compounds. The allotted windows are less than two square kilometers. If there's a sudden emergency, we have no way to retrieve you quickly – if we can reach you at all. We can communicate with the research base, but I'd doubt they'll allow direct communications ship to party. You could be in the middle of a town barbecue when the handicom started squawking. That would look damned peculiar in ancient Rome."

"There's subdermal tracking chips," Granger suggested. "We used those several times on the *Covenant*."

Engineer Ferrine Cash's thin nose flared in disgust. "Sure, we can find you with them, but hit a functioning energy shield with a loaded moley-beam, and you couldn't pay me to scoop up what we'd get back. Instant annihilation. Once that landing party's down there, if you're out of bounds, you're on your own."

"Concerns noted, Ms. Cash," Sullivan said. "As always, Mr. Raines, your first priority is the safety and operation of this ship. Kyle, the Chessorak Compound has been without a full-time physician for more than twelve months. They've requested medical assistance, both routine and a couple of delayed procedures. I'm going to have you accompany me, but you may want additional help. Ti'onam, your knowledge of chemistry and physics exceeds mine. Mr. Andreiev, you're a weapons expert. Are you up to field research for the next several weeks?"

"Aye, sir!" the lieutenant replied. "It would be a nice change of pace."

"Good. The party will meet here at …," Sullivan glanced at the chronometer, "15:30, at which time we should be approaching orbit at Sigma Tau Ceti IV. Mr. Raines, you have the bridge until 1200. Dismissed."

Jack gave a nod to his crew and moved briskly toward the door while he was still awake enough to do it. Captains didn't have to explain themselves.

Два ~ *Two* ~ *Shiva*

The investigation crew moley-beamed into the commander's small office at 16:35. The bright, naturalized lighting and large naturescapes covering the walls helped make them forget they were ten meters underground. A lean, silver-haired man stepped forward, hand out.

"Captain Sullivan? Commander Marc Guillaume, head of the Chessorak research compound. Thank you so much for your speedy assistance."

"Thank the Allied Fleet," Jack replied as he gave the hand a squeeze. "We go where we're needed."

"Of course, of course. This is my second-in-command, Lieutenant-Commander Jantzen Dickerson."

"Jan." A younger, handsomer man in brown leaned forward.

"Mr. Dickerson." The captain grasped the hand briefly, then introduced his crew.

"Pleased to meet you," Guillaume said. "Visitors here are a rare treat, so please bear with us if my crew asks too many questions. We have a close-knit group, but sometimes you get excited to see a new face, or hear some news about the real world out there. May I suggest we cross the hall to our briefing area, gentlemen? I think we might be more comfortable in there." He led the group to the larger, more functional room, where everyone could sit.

"Can I offer anyone refreshments? We grow almost everything we eat ourselves. I guarantee you won't find anything fresher unless you eat it still clinging to the vine. We finished first harvest two months ago; we're a month into the second growing period."

Sullivan returned the man's hospitable smile. "Thank you, that sounds most inviting. Perhaps after we've run through some of the details of your request. Twelve weeks is a long time to tie up an explorer. I sincerely hope you aren't overstating your difficulties."

"I'm well aware of the importance of a star explorer, Captain Sullivan," Guillaume said. "Ten years ago, I served as part of the xenoanthropology team on the *Odyssey*. The explorers have the best mobile science facilities of any class of ship out there. We aren't exactly on the beaten path.

"I'm also aware that for the last six years I've been running a research outpost without a major hitch – until now. I have nine seasoned field operatives spread over a 150-kilometer radius. I'd hate to have to call them back on a far-fetched possibility that one of them might be breaking their vow of non-interference."

"If you could describe the exact nature of the problem, we could better understand your difficulties," Ti'onam prompted.

"Mr. Dickerson?"

The lieutenant-commander picked up a small remote from the briefing table and stepped over to the wall. A screen glowed to life.

"This is a map of Pelonishala, one of eighteen regional divisions of the continent. This is the territory our long-range operatives cover." He circled a finger over a smaller area. "Four function as actual rangers, scanning new territory and reporting back. They pass as solitary craftsmen or trappers, recording news and anecdotes in the process.

"Five others are settled in a particular location, paying more attention to society and culture than physical geography and wildlife. They're chameleons, blending in with the native population and reporting back here in person every three to six months, depending on their distance."

Dickerson waved the remote, and the map zeroed in. He touched the screen. A glowing green line followed his finger as he drew it across the map. "This is the area in question. Here is our compound, and the towns of Lozintal, Arvijicanti, Vandijoc, and Ezoshalak."

The screen changed again, and a narrow-view picture began to rotate, showing a devastated area of dark green forestland. Not a tree stood for a hundred meters. Charred wrecks radiated outward from a cratered epicenter. Some tipped dangerously backwards, as if knocked askew by some giant hand.

The men shifted in their chairs and listened more attentively as Dickerson laid out his puzzle. "Here, on a planet with no working knowledge of solar power or fossil fuels – let alone nuclear fission or fusion – we found evidence of two major radioactive explosions, as well as more than ninety minutes' worth of intermittent, low-power particle bursts. The bursts were similar in pattern and strength to those found in the spectral analysis of modern EPSAR weapons, but not close enough to identify. Several of the bands fluctuated to levels not present in Allied Fleet weapons."

"Do you have any such weapons?" Sullivan asked. "Is it possible someone could have stolen one?" EPSARs were a military weapon, not available for civilian use. Not within the UPA, at least.

"No!" Guillaume said. "I'm sure you're aware, Captain Sullivan, since the escalation incident on Bolivar the Allied Fleet has tightened the regulations regarding use of tech items in non-tech cultures. We have exactly five hand weapons, locked in my quarters. Only Mr. Dickerson and I have access to them, not even my wife. They are visually accounted for on a monthly basis by each of us, resulting in a check every two weeks. And you can't just walk out of here with one, either. Anything carrying an active-potential power charge like an EPSAR would set off an alarm. We ran drills and checks to make sure; everything is in working order. If there's a weapon out there, it didn't come from here."

"Then where would it come from?"

"We assume it may be a weapon we aren't familiar with," Dickerson said. "In any case, we're mighty worried. None of those conditions should exist at all."

"And you suspect interference from an outside party," Sullivan surmised. "Have you tried adjusting your regional scanners for alien lifeforms?"

"We did," Guillaume admitted, "but bear in mind our facilities are extremely limited. Ninety-six hours' work came back negative. The other question is how someone *could* be out there, undetected. There's been a team on this planet in one form or another for more than eight years. An orbiting ship is such a rarity every compound wants a piece of it, and sensors would detect it long before orbit. I don't see how anyone could possibly slip down here unnoticed."

"If external factors have been ruled out, then the only remaining answer is an internal one," Ti'onam said.

"I know, I know, but I know my operatives. I might possibly question the motives of one or two rangers, but the rest are good people. We search everyone who leaves the compound two, sometimes three or four times, to keep potentially prohibited materials from getting loose in the community. The intermittent particle bursts were within five kilometers of one of our outposts, but the big ones were twenty and thirteen kilometers distant – an awful long way to carry a dangerous weapon just to cover your tracks."

"*Did* you question them?" Sullivan didn't want to be detained on a goose chase simply because a commander didn't have the nerve to accuse his men himself. "Have you ever caught anyone trying to slip materials past the checks?"

Guillaume gave an amused chuckle, and Dickerson smiled. "We

have one chronic offender, I'm afraid, a young girl. After several years, it's become a game. I think she does it purposely to keep us on our toes. It's never anything that would destroy society – underclothing that doesn't pass regulation, a color photograph, a computer stylus she slipped behind the ribbon on her underskirt – hardly worth our efforts, but rules are rules."

"If discipline has been a problem, I fail to understand why you continue to allow her free access to the community," Ti'onam said. "An ongoing disregard of rules should warrant that action be taken, not excluding removal from post."

"Unfortunately, she happens to be one of the greatest scientific and linguistic assets to our entire project. She does as much work on her own as my crew does here as a team," Guillaume said with visible pride. "And as I said, it's a game to see who's more on their toes. She did get the computer stylus past us; she sent it back by local carrier, with a letter detailing the flaws in our security. She's bored, Captain Sullivan. It's boring out there in the wilderness. It's her way of livening things up. If anything, our security is better because of her efforts."

"That remains to be seen," Sullivan mumbled under his breath. "You investigated the blast area yourself?"

"I headed a three-man investigation team, based for a week at the Vandijoc settlement," Dickerson said. He switched the wall display back to the map that detailed the crisis area and pointed out the location of Vandijoc relative to the Compound and the two explosions.

"The first area of destruction was three weeks old when we arrived. Animal life was returning, and there were signs of reforestation. Approximately one and a half hectares had been leveled, and there were still high levels of Warshan's emissions, gamma rays, and a minor increase in X-type radiation.

"The second site was only three or four days old, still dangerously radioactive, with a very similar picture of devastation. However," Dickerson raised an emphatic finger, "one person survived the blast, a local boy. All he could tell us was that he and two friends were cutting wood when the forest went *Boom!* without warning. He'd been unconscious for hours when they found him. He thought one of the moons had fallen."

"You said the particle emissions were detected near one of your outposts," Sullivan pressed. "No one at the outpost was aware of them? I find that strange."

"I don't," Guillaume said. "First, they have no equipment for that sort of thing whatsoever. Not beyond a compass, perhaps. Second, you don't know the operatives at that location. They've been here several years, but they're still young, a brother and sister pair – my chronic game-player? I've never seen a greener pair of recruits in my life, but I'll eat my rank insignia if they didn't turn out to be two of the best damned civilian researchers I've ever seen, quick to learn and ready to prove themselves. The boy's very friendly, a real people-person, blended right into the community. He even applied to marry a local at one point, but I guess it fell apart. The girl's terribly shy at first, but a real sweetheart when you get to know her; very eager to please. She's a radical when it comes to languages. She came here already fluent in several. In three months, she not only doubled the size of our knowledge base, but corrected what we'd already written as fact. She's our resident expert in the local dialect at this point, surpassing our xenolinguist Dickerson here." The lieutenant-commander blushed, but nodded his concession. "They're a unique team."

"And you don't suspect them? You don't think that such advanced abilities might have come from previous training elsewhere, that they didn't have a secondary purpose for working here?"

Guillaume laughed with conviction. "No more than I suspect my wife! If you'll help us, Captain, I'd like to send you out to Vandijoc to meet them. I don't have the authority to send equipment beyond the gates that could feasibly violate Independent Destiny. On occasion we've used the little discretion recorders, but as far as more advanced or dispersed equipment, I'm not allowed to risk it. Our mission is long-term; the longer we're here, the greater the risk of contaminating the planet with our knowledge, our methods. Therefore, my orders are strict and my abilities limited to keep that risk to an absolute minimum, no matter what appears to be happening. I've done as much as I can. My hands are now tied."

"And the *Triumph* is here on a very temporary basis, allowing us greater flexibility with regulations." Sullivan nodded, understanding. "I've got the rank, the authority, and the ability to supersede your orders. Very well, Commander. You have yourself the services of an explorer. The Allied Fleet has authorized us for ninety days, but I warn you now: unless I find information pointing directly to interference from another culture, I plan to spend no more than thirty. It is your duty to run internal investigations and control your people. I will be in full command of the operation, and I expect complete cooperation from your crew. You will provide Mr. Andreiev with all available data – the region, records, histories, anything remotely pertinent to our mission."

"I can do that right now, if you'd like," Dickerson said.

Andreiev glanced at Sullivan for the okay. He followed the lieutenant-commander out.

"Mr. Ti'onam will be in charge of setting up a personnel and information exchange – if any of your personnel wish to utilize the *Triumph*'s facilities for shore leave purposes, they may do so, and within reason we shall do the same down here. If necessary, we can temporarily replace personnel with those from the *Triumph*. Your original request specified a need for medical services?"

"Yes! Please!" Guillaume said. "We've been without a permanent physician for some eighteen months now. Routine exams are long overdue, and several people are in need of more extensive diagnostics."

"Kyle?"

Granger had a working plan started in his head. "I can have a team of two or three nurses and a couple of techs run standard physicals. Anything unusual can be sent up to the ship. I'll have Bakari and NaDar stand by to cover anything more involved. I'll head out with the crew. You never know what you're going to run into, and I can't risk a ship's captain that far away from immediate medical care. I can have a field team ready to go in twenty minutes, if you want to start lining people up."

"We have a two-bed sickbay you can use," Guillaume offered.

"Perfect. With your permission, Captain, I'll get everything in motion."

"Go."

"Take a left out of here, and it's six doors down on your left," Guillaume pointed. "I'll send someone down to help you."

The crew spent much of the night and next morning outfitting, a task more complicated than it sounded. A proper investigation required the proper equipment, but most such equipment was forbidden.

Granger dug through a box of supplies that had belonged to the former Compound physician.

"Are you familiar with those instruments?" Guillaume asked. The box contained a variety of primitive medical devices, some of which looked more like instruments of torture, and most of which looked like they didn't have any business in medical treatment at all.

Kyle sighed, poking a finger at a glass syringe with a hollow metal stilette attached. "Some, if I remember my medical history correctly. Not that I have any particular desire to use them. Please tell me this isn't for sealing wounds." He raised a glass cup containing a red candle, still mostly unburned.

Guillaume laughed. "No, that's not what it's for. I know there are more detailed explanations of procedures in Dr. Herzog's notes. Before you treat your patient, you light the candle and ask the Moons to shine favor on the patient and their family, especially the red moon, Allash, since they believe that one's the giver and healer of life. Any little prayer will do. Mysterious is good, but some practitioners get rather flamboyant. These people rely on touch for diagnosis, so do a lot of touching and probing, even if it's not required. If you can remove anything in the process, whether it's a louse or earwax or an ingrown hair, you'll be remembered as a great healer. And lots of medications, and rules to take them," Guillaume remembered.

He touched an assortment of small jars that rattled under his hand. "These bottles contain a number of modern medications in tablet form, and also in standardized solutions for that needle hypodermic there. Use that on any natives; they'll expect it. Whether it's sugar pills or skin smoothing paste, they'll feel satisfied you've helped them."

"That's not medicine, that's something between quackery and voodoo," Granger objected. Ancient methods had been required in med school, but he'd practiced on cadavers and mannequins, not squirming, screaming people.

"Yes, it is, but to them it's cutting-edge science; it's what they expect. You'll catch on."

They stood in the meeting house for the final check.

"No offense, Captain Sullivan," Guillaume frowned, "but I am worried about Commander Ti'onam. This is a rather uniform race of people. Even once you get to your location, there will be natives about, perhaps daily. I'm not sure how they'll react to Navaran characteristics. We've seen no evidence of discriminatory practices, but, as I said, the people have fairly similar features. We'd rather not attract attention to our researchers."

Sullivan eyed his tall phy-sci officer. Ti'onam looked even stranger wearing local clothing. Dickerson had clad him in dark green pants, a loose yellow shirt, and a brown cloth jacket, which only seemed to accentuate the subdued jaundice of his skin. On his head he wore a wide-brimmed hat that hid the ruffly curves of his ears, and could be pulled low to hide the down-like tufts of hair. There was little to be done about the thickness of his eyebrows, so necessary for keeping sand out of eyes on

Navara. Ti'onam tipped his head at the Captain, awaiting instruction.

"Mr. Ti'onam's appearance is the least of my concerns on this mission, and it should be the least of yours," Sullivan replied. "We'll manage as necessary."

"Of course, Captain," Guillaume said with embarrassment. "I'm sending Jan with you, at least as far as Vandijoc. He's familiar with the area, and an excellent translator. I'll send him on to Pozaranati to get word to some of the more distant rangers to check in with you. Once you get to our base, the Kirushenko girl can translate for you. Electronic translators are strictly forbidden outside the gates."

Andreiev thought aloud as he struggled to adjust the straps to his pack. "*Kirushenko*. That sounds like a Russian name."

Guillaume nodded. "I believe they are. At least, I know they have family there."

"Someone you know, Mr. Andreiev?" No matter what ship Jack served on, what colony he visited, or whom he met among the top brass, the Russian officers always seemed to know the person you spoke of, or the event, and chances were they'd been to the event themselves, or had a relative who was, or knew someone that had done it better. As captain, Jack could appreciate such loyalty, but sometimes … Sometimes such die-hard patriotism was exasperating.

"Nothing is impossible, Captain," Andreiev said. "I knew a Kirushenko back in grade school, but of course, there is more than one Kirushenko in Russia."

"Let's keep that in mind. Mr. Dickerson, if we're ready…?"

Jan Dickerson shrugged into his shoulder pack, which held some of the extra equipment for the ship's crew. "We'll have to hustle to make it to Otaiga before nightfall, unless you want to camp outside. We're starting rather late."

Granger peered out the open window, eyeing the drizzly skies with dismay. "I can't believe you're making us *walk* sixty-five kilometers. Any chance of the weather letting up before we leave?"

Guillaume gave a soft chuckle. "Did I fail to mention this is the height of the rainy season?"

Тρи ~ *Three* ~ *Chednash*

Picturesque Otaiga, the half-way point, appeared prosperous, with gaily painted wooden buildings flanking busy streets. Flowering shrubs flourished by buildings and fenceposts, oblivious to the weather. Despite the rain, business was brisk among the many establishments, and people scurried down the muddy streets on raised wooden walkways. Friendly locals gathered under roofed porches before the shops to greet each other and talk. The town had been built on the shore of a twenty-three kilometer lake. If it had not been for the dripping rain, to see a stunning sunrise reflected over the water would have made the journey worthwhile in itself. It was exactly the sort of place Jack Sullivan would have picked for shore leave – a long hike through wilderness, dinner pulled fresh from the sparkling water, an open campfire, and a night spent staring up at a million stars in a pollutionless sky. It was hard to imagine anything more prehistoric, more relaxing.

Vandijoc, on the other hand, had no such geological asset to promote tourism. Enshrouded by tall, thick forest, the longest vista outside of a farm field ran down the center of the deeply rutted, thickly mudded main street. Here, too, covered porches on the buildings gave the townsfolk respite from the skies, and boardwalks kept them from sinking knee-deep in the mud. Dense trees blocked any hope of a sun bursting over the horizon, and to the west rose steep hills, shattering any dreams of a fiery sunset. The village smelled of smoke, mud, and the unmistakable stench of excrement.

"This is it," Dickerson said under the brim of his *urpinta*-leather rain hat. "Welcome to Vandijoc, a lovely place to be. At least in the dry season."

Granger shivered against the raw dampness that invaded the woven cloth of his jacket. He stuffed his hands into his pockets to warm them. "A little sunshine might help that first impression, just a bit. Where are we, the wild west?"

Their guide laughed. "Not quite. The only thing wild around here is the landscape. The people are pretty placid. It's a farming community, with farm-oriented industry – milling, smoked meats, things like that. There was a murder here two years ago, but everyone knew right away who did it – a long-standing family feud over a woman. It caused a bit of a fuss, since the guilty party was the local cart maker, and he had orders that weren't finished yet. Finally they agreed he could finish his work, but at night he had to return to the jail."

"No one worried he'd disappear?" Sullivan said.

"Not really. The suspect was eighty if he was a day. It would have taken him an hour just to walk through town."

"He must be miserable in this weather," Granger rubbed his arms, "because I certainly am." It was hard to judge the time of day through the overcast sky, but it seemed to be getting darker.

"You won't be for much longer. In fact, this is where I leave you." Jan pointed a hundred meters down the mucky street. "See where that road comes in from the left? Take that left fork. About ten minutes farther, the road will 'V' again. Bear to the left, and it will take you straight to our outpost. You can't miss it."

"I'm sure we won't," the captain agreed. "Will you be at the compound when we return?"

"Probably, but I can't guarantee it." Dickerson shrugged off his pack, and the men divided the equipment he carried. "I'll make it as far as Demorak tonight, and I'll finish heading out to Pozaranati in the morning. I'll return by the back route, and stop in to see how you're faring. Figure four, maybe five days, depending, and I can bring anything back to base that's heading there." He squinted at the sky. "You better get moving. There's less than an hour of light left. You don't want to be tripping through the forest in the dark."

Sullivan eyed the two-story cabin at the end of the pathway. "This must be it. Left fork, and it's the only thing around."

Fragrant woodsmoke wafted from a pipe running up the building. A smaller cabin structure stood closer to the path, but it huddled dark and closed in the murky twilight, and it had no chimney. The larger building looked pieced together slap-dash over several years, one side perpendicular to the other. Three shuttered windows broke up the wall on the lower floor and another three above; two of the lower ones glowed through gaps in the rough shutters that covered them.

Granger's breath fogged in the failing light. "Well, what are you waiting for? Even if it's the wrong place, where there's light, there's warmth, and where there's a roof, it's usually dry."

Jack raised a hand to knock, but stopped as a loud cry leaked through the shutters, a long, wordless half shriek, half growl. The pitch and tone were too high to be anything but female.

The officers strained to hear. A quiet voice seemed to answer, but the words weren't clear. The tone was steady, not necessarily threatening, but Sullivan wasn't about to take chances. He positioned himself at the door, Ti'onam behind, while Andreiev and Granger covered the other side – not that they had a ready weapon between them. The captain banged his knuckles against the door, three times.

Silence erupted; after a pause, frantic scrabbling sounded. Jack readied his hand for a second knock when the door gave a scrape and a click, and it opened a mere handwidth.

Light reflected off the wet yard, and a young man's harried face pressed the opening. *<farrash Ixa?>*

"I'm looking for a Dmitri Kirushenko," Sullivan replied in Standard Interstellar. "Commander Guillaume told us he could give us lodging."

The eyes in the youthful face grew round, and the mouth dropped open. "Just a minute!" The door shut, followed by the scraping.

"Were we ever told what to do if he said 'no'?" Granger asked.

The captain held a silent finger to his lips as a metallic jingling was audible inside. He pointed the finger at Andreiev, then at the window behind him. The lieutenant stepped back, trying to peer through the cracks of the crude shutters.

The man's voice spoke, insistent, stern, and low. Andreiev couldn't make out all the words, but he knew the words that repeated at the end of every unintelligible sentence:

Minyeh pohnimayesh? Pohnimayesh?

It was Russian, but Andreiev couldn't see who the voice was speaking to, or ascertain what that person was supposed to *understand.* Footsteps pounded rapid and hollow, as if up a staircase. The lieutenant left the window to report his findings, but the door scraped and reopened, this time all the way.

"Please, come in!" the young man offered cordially, as if there had been no pause at all. He waved them into the warm and drier room. "My apologies for making you wait on such a miserable evening. I… had to clear a few things out of the way. We don't get many visitors this time of night, especially in the rain. You came from the compound?"

"Jazak Sullivan, Captain of the Star Explorer *Triumph.*" Jack slid his pack to the wooden floor. The cabin was as plain on the inside as the outside. A staircase rose against the left wall, and behind it, at the bottom, sat a wide, dark alcove. The other half of the cabin was divided off by a half-wall of cabinets, with two shelves above it holding household goods. Beyond the divide was a kitchen.

"We were sent to investigate the recent explosions in your area. Commander Guillaume said we could set up a temporary base here."

"Sure! People stay here all the time. We've got two empty rooms. Cryin' out loud! An Explorer! Marc must really be worried to call in a ship like that." The young man had a handsome, eager round face. He stood eight or ten centimeters shorter than the captain, perhaps eighteen kilos lighter. He wrinkled his face in concentration. "*Sullivan*. I don't remember that name. I thought the captain of the *Triumph* was someone named... Carries? Kiss?"

"Karras!" Sullivan corrected, impressed. "I assumed command from Pete Karras four years ago. You're familiar with the *Triumph*?"

The boy shrugged. "Not really. It was one of the ships that aided Outpost 62 during the Burin-Jai massacre of 2266."

"Captain Karras' final mission. You were on the Outpost?" Ti'onam asked, intrigued. He'd been a lieutenant-commander on the *Triumph* at the time, leading a damage assessment crew. The boy didn't look more than nineteen or twenty at the most, and the incident had been several years ago.

The boy nodded somberly. "My brother was a weapons specialist there. We were visiting him at the time. He was the fifth of fifty-eight Allied casualties. The *Triumph* carried him back to Earth. We hitched a ride on the *Hoberman* instead." He fell silent for a moment, reflecting.

"I'm sorry, I don't think I caught your name," Sullivan prompted.

"I'm sorry." The young man blushed under his shaggy dark hair. "Dmitri Kirushenko, Alliance Cultural Observer. The title doesn't mean much, but it sounds impressive." He grinned rakishly, and glanced at the stairs. "My sister Sarah's upstairs somewhere. She's a bit shy, especially around people she doesn't know. Sarah!" he called to the rough ceiling. "We have guests. Come down, please!" When not a footstep was heard overhead, he shrugged. "She may be involved in one of her projects. She'll be down later."

"This is my crew," Sullivan introduced. "Physical Sciences officer, Firinar nal Ti'onam; Weapons Specialist Danil Andreiev; and my Chief Medical Officer, Kyle Granger."

Kirushenko turned a sickly white. "A doctor? Can we please keep that fact quiet?" he asked in a whisper, pressing the air with his palms as if pushing the news down. Once more he glanced at the stairs. "Sarah's... not very fond of the medical profession. She's had a few bad run-ins with temperamental doctors."

"That's going to be kind of difficult," Granger reasoned, "since part of the reason for my being here is to run physical exams. They're required by regulation. She must have had them before."

Dmitri hesitated. "She has, but she got used to Dr. Herzog, and since he left she hasn't been comfortable with the occasional substitute. Please! I'm only asking you to give it a few days. Let her get to know you before you spring that on her. It will make it much easier on both of you."

"I can try, but I have to insist on it before I leave."

"Thank you. That's fine." The boy noticed the packs lined up on the floor. "Where's my manners! You must be beat, walking in like that without being used to it. Come, I'll show you the rooms. Tell me they sent a guide with you at least part of the way – Marc didn't send you crawling out here all alone, did he? Who brought you out, Dale, Jan, or Hule? That's who he usually sends with new people."

"Captain," Ti'onam hushed. He gestured toward the staircase with his eyes. Sullivan squinted, and sure enough, at the very top of the shadowy stairs, clothing could be seen between the spindles.

Dmitri saw the direction of their gaze. "You've been spotted, Sar. Why don't you come down and meet our guests? They're from the Allied Fleet – the Star Explorer *Triumph*. You remember the *Triumph*, back on the outpost? They're going to be staying here for a bit, so you might as well be introduced."

The hidden figure hesitated, then descended. The girl clung to the railing for a second or two, then darted across the room to hide behind her brother, face downward, observing through clandestine glances of peripheral vision. Tension drew her shoulders toward her ears, and she looked ready to flee. The boy pulled her out from behind, hands easing the raised shoulders downward.

"This is my sister, Sarah."

Guillaume said the pair had been young, but Sullivan hadn't expected mere children. There were plenty of bright and talented people in their early twenties – Andreiev himself had been such a person – but the girl before them could not have been older than her teens. Tall and muscular – as tall as her brother, despite bare feet – she wore a wrinkled skirt of dark blue and a sleeveless bodice over a white blouse. Her hair hung loose to her waist in a tangled sheet of blonde so pale it was almost white, and the darting little glimpses showed large, beautiful eyes of such a deep blue hue they appeared violet, though they were ringed with dark circles. She was strikingly pretty, despite the look of terror on her face.

"Sarah, this is Captain Sullivan," her brother said. "He and his men are reinvestigating those explosions east of here."

The girl clasped her hands and held them tight against her waist. Her eyes locked onto Sullivan's for two brief seconds before returning their gaze to the floor. She gave a short curtsey.

"I'm sorry, I don't remember your ship," she said in a clear, soft voice. "That was a tragic time for us. It is a pleasure to meet you anyway, sir."

Jack flashed her his best welcoming smile. A pretty girl deserved a smile, no matter what her age, and this one certainly fell into that category. The blue, blue eyes flicked up again. "The pleasure's all mine, Miss Kirushenko. Commander Guillaume said you would be able to translate for us. He spoke highly of your abilities."

The head lifted until the eyes focused on his throat. "Thank you, sir. Most of my translation work has dealt with literature – the computers miss nuances – but I am quite fluent in the spoken language of this area as well."

"We look forward to working with you. These are my men – one of my science officers, Mr. Ti'onam," he gestured.

The blonde head snapped up at the name, and the skittish gaze held, as if she'd only just noticed the officer. The strained shoulders slid into place.

"Miss Kirushenko," the Navaran acknowledged. He removed his hat, allowing his curious features to show.

//Qol tulos, miimna K'atiliam.// The girl bowed before him. Her face lost its fear, and, except for her eyes, now looked as devoid of feeling as the Navaran's.

Ti'onam raised his thick brows, unprepared for the proper formal greeting in his native language. "Thank you," he replied in Standard. "I congratulate you, Miss Kirushenko. For a human, your accent is superb."

"You do me great honor, sir." The girl bowed again, not as deep.

"You speak Navaran?" Sullivan couldn't make heads or tails of it himself.

The gaze fell. "I currently read, write, or speak eight languages," she told the floor. "Navaran is my third or fourth most fluent language, about even with Tau Cetan. However, I fear I am out of practice."

"Would Russian be among them?" Andreiev asked.

"Konyechna, govoryu." Sarah replied with the discreet glance. "It is my birth language."

Jack finished his introductions. "My weapons specialist, Danil Andreiev, and … Kyle Granger, part of our … biological sciences department."

The girl nodded, but spoke before anyone else could say a word. "Dimi, it's cool outside and they are wet. You haven't heated water for tea?"

"I didn't get that far. Take care of it for me? I'll get them settled. If you'll follow me, gentlemen." Kirushenko headed for the alcove.

The dark alcove was a short hallway, with a room at each end. The narrow beds weren't much more than a thick cushion over planks, but they seemed clean. The ranks were uneven – a captain, two commanders, and a lieutenant.

Don't you dare, Granger mouthed silently when Sullivan caught his eye, but Jack shook his head. He didn't need two of his officers killing each other. Navarans were strictly pacifist, but they had elevated self-defense to an art. And sharing quarters with Ti'onam would allow Jack to debate technical information long after lights out.

A narrow lavatory separated the two rooms. The Kirushenko boy showed them how to work the primitive facilities. "We have the only indoor plumbing outside of Vandijoc itself. I mean, some towns have it, but virtually no one outside them. The bath is my own design." He patted the side of a metal tub with pride. A metal drum sat on a small wood furnace, with valves and hoses allowing the contents to drain into the tub.

"Use the hand pump here to refill the barrel when you're done, so it stays full. We fire up the heater twice a day, morning and night, so even in a pinch you can wash with warmer water. Just keep the bottom of the tub plugged, even when the water's out," he warned. "If you don't, this time of year every bug in the forest will come up to get out of the rain."

Andreiev managed a sickly smile. "How delightful."

In the privacy of the borrowed room, Ti'onam unpacked his omnicomp and began to work.

"Anything interesting?" Sullivan asked, tying the strings to the neck of a dry shirt. He pulled two sealed envelopes from his pack and dropped them onto a bed, one considerably thicker than the other.

"I am scanning for various types of radioactive particles," the Navaran explained, moving about and aiming the instrument in various directions. He squatted to examine the thin layer of dust on a lamp table between the beds. "If my readings are correct, I am detecting an increase in Warshan's particles relative to those readings taken at the Chessorak Compound."

Sullivan frowned. "How much higher?" Warshan's rays could make someone very ill, very fast, and recovery wasn't guaranteed.

"Approximately one percent. One hundredth of a dose above normal, which is well within safety guidelines."

"One hundredth ... Can you think of any reasons for the difference?"

"It is a reasonable assumption that the difference is due to our closer proximity to the center of the explosion in question," Ti'onam said. "Warshan's rays are quite dangerous, but their range is limited, and their half-life is but five days; irrelevant in geologic terms. It is unlikely we shall suffer any ill effects at this location."

"The blast site is several weeks old. Would this area have been safe after the explosion?"

"If Mr. Dickerson's data is correct as to the distances and wind direction, this should have constituted a safe zone."

"Good. Keep me posted." Jack picked up the envelopes and headed for the main room.

The girl poured steaming water into cups while the boy leaned against the wall, talking with Granger and Andreiev.

"... It took six of us less than a week to complete," Kirushenko said. "I drew up the original ideas and worked it out with the engineer back at the Compound. The plumbing I worked out on my own. We survived three months without bathing facilities. If they wanted us to stay, we needed some semblance of civilization. Now we're a tourist attraction for the other observers wandering the area. A hot bath's an incredible luxury around here."

"I certainly can't blame you on that," Granger said. "With all that rain, I suppose we should be thankful you're not a nomad with a tent."

The conversation paused as the captain joined the group. Jack held the thin envelope out to the boy. "Commander Guillaume sent this to you. It's a summary of our mission, and his orders regarding our stay."

Dmitri accepted it. "Thank you. He sends these out now and then to keep us filled in. I'll look it over later." He placed the orders on a shelf.

Sullivan turned to the girl. "Miss Kirushenko?"

It was fortunate the girl had replaced the water on the heating unit, for she spun around fast, braced as if to run.

"I'm sorry, I didn't mean to startle you. Lieutenant-Commander Dickerson said I should give this one to you." He held out the thick envelope.

Sarah eyed the object with hunger before stretching out a timid hand. "Thank you, sir." She read the strange writing on the envelope, and a happy smile broke out. She hugged it before beaming at her brother.

"It's from Mr. Ennis!" She sucked her bottom lip, pleading with her eyes.

Dmitri tried to look stern, but he couldn't, the corner of his mouth drawing up in a roguish half-smile. He tipped his head toward the stairs. "Go."

"Thank you!" seemed to reach their ears the same instant as her feet pounded up the stairs, two rooms away. In seconds, she had disappeared.

Granger raised a lecherous eyebrow. "*Mister* Ennis? Do I detect a young romance in bloom?"

Dmitri snorted. "Has the sun gone nova and Earth burned to a cinder yet?" He finished the girl's task of placing the hot drinks on the table. "Hargan Ennis is the communications specialist at the compound. Sarah's best friend is our brother Vladimir back home – they're less than a year apart in age. They won't even breathe unless they've okayed it with the other. She's more than a little lonely without him, and as you probably know, we're too far out for direct, real-time communications. They're reduced to streaming text letters to each other. However," Dmitri sat, and motioned for the men to do the same, "we only get to the base every three months. If someone's coming out this way, Ennis will check to see what's waiting, print everything out, and send it with whoever's coming. There's at least four week's worth of letters in that envelope. We'll be lucky to see her again by midnight."

"I thought for sure it would have been a love letter, the way she jumped at it," Granger reflected as he sniffed his 'tea.' The hot liquid smelled like fresh-cut hay. "I would think an attractive young girl like that would have dozens."

"Not that one." The boy scooped spoonfuls of a thick, syrupy sweetener from a jar into his steaming cup. A drizzle caught the rim; the sticky sweetener melted with the heat and ran the length of the cup. He added a creamy substance from a pitcher on the table, stirred it, and took a satisfied sip.

"Sarah's been a die-hard tomboy since she first made a fist and poked someone in the eye with it. She's used to running *with* the boys, not making eyes at them. In her defense, it's not easy for her, here in the middle of nowhere. She doesn't attend the local school, and anyone not in school is busy on a farm. She doesn't have many opportunities to make friends. I think this might be our last year on Sigma Tau, because she really needs to be somewhere she can make those kinds of connections."

Sullivan reached for the pitcher of cream. Small fatty globules floated in the center. It was a milk of sorts, but raw and unprocessed. He tipped a bit in, doing his discreet best to keep the blobs out of his cup. "How old is she, if I may ask?"

"Sixteen, last month."

"It'll be easy to keep track of her." Granger grinned as he picked up his creamless cup. "Just follow the trail of broken hearts."

"Sixteen, and she speaks eight languages?" Andreiev said in awe. "From memory?"

Dmitri nodded as if the idea were quite natural. "I'm fluent in three myself, and can mangle my way around one or two more. We grew up bilingual. Our parents were bilingual, and Mother knew at least one more on top of that. Father could read some ancient ones. We also moved around a lot – I don't think we ever spent more than four years in one place. The rest of it is just Sarah, though. It's more than just a *talent* for her," he mused. "It's a … *gift*, I guess. She was always in an advanced academic program. If things hadn't gotten unsettled at home, she would have tried for her Basic Education diploma before she turned ten. Now she more or less teaches herself."

"Graduation by the age of ten? I'd call that a little more than gifted," Sullivan said. "More like exceptionally brilliant. There are dozens of institutions that would like to get hold of someone like that, the Allied Fleet included. It's a shame she's hiding out here in the wilderness. I can give you the names of some people she should contact, if she's interested."

"Thank you, sir, but she's not quite ready for that. Her time here hasn't been wasted. Curiosity kills cats, and Sarah's already on her seventh or eighth life. It takes a little while, but she reaches a point where her desire to know something overtakes the shyness factor, and that's when you have to keep a hand on her or she'll walk right into fire. You'll see! Give her time to get used to you and you won't be able to keep her out from under your feet. By the time you leave, you'll be grateful to escape."

Dmitri was fixing a late meal when Sarah crept down the stairs, hugging the outside walls of the cabin. She stopped next to him and waited for him to speak.

"How's everything on the homefront?" He threw the last handful of garnish into the stew and gave it a good stir.

"Good! Gal got promoted – she's now in charge of satellite programming for the European and Northern Asiatic quarter. She's getting married in February. Her fiancé works in communications, too."

"Good for her. Is Vlad for or against it?" Dmitri said strangely, almost hostile.

The girl's smile faded and her face tipped back to her feet, as if she were guilty of something. "He says the man's very nice, and Galina's very happy about it. He and Sergei are happy for her."

The brother muttered something that sounded like *imagine that.*

Sarah eyed the pot on the stove. "Dimi!" She whispered in Tau Cetan, <*Navarat to taranav Aji porshi! Cho ili shormesha!*>

Dmitri frowned. "I forgot about that. Take care of it for me? You know more rules about it than I do." Not only couldn't the vegetarian Navaran eat the stew, but anything cooked in the gravy would be forbidden as well. The girl set about rummaging through cabinets.

"Come, eat!" Kirushenko called at last, setting dishes on the wide table. "I can't cook like my mother, but I've never made anyone sick yet. Our neighbor cooks for us three nights a week, and she's better. "

"It smells wonderful," Sullivan said truthfully. "I'm sure we won't let it go to waste."

As host, Dmitri took the outside of the other bench, leaving the center seat next to the Russian lieutenant open for the girl. His sister placed a bowl of shredded-vegetable salad on the table, and stood waiting. When she failed to be noticed, she tapped a bare foot on the floor. Her brother tipped his head to the open seat. The worried look returned to the girl's face. She shook her head. With an exasperated sigh, Dmitri slid over, and she sat on the outside edge. When Ti'onam had served himself from the salad, she took a small portion as well.

"This is delicious," Granger said, taking a second bite.

Andreiev leaned around Dmitri to ask, "Do you also cook, Miss Kirushenko?"

The girl didn't appear to hear. Her eyes were closed, lips moving, fingers tented together before her.

Her brother elbowed her in the side. "Stop showing off. Someone's talking to you."

Sarah's eyes flew open and she blushed. "I'm sorry."

Andreiev hadn't meant to interrupt what looked like a prayer. "I'm sorry. I didn't mean to interrupt you. I only asked if you cook as well."

The girl flushed darker. "Sometimes."

"Sarah can bake a perfect loaf of bread when she wants," Dmitri bragged. "We used to buy our bread in town, two or three at a time, but it usually went stale before we finished it. I left her alone one afternoon, and she decided to figure bread out for herself. When I came back, you couldn't imagine the mess. She used up three months' worth of supplies, and there weren't less than fifteen loaves of bread stacked up." He laughed, remembering. "But Sarah didn't just bake too much bread! No, she can't do anything simple like that! She made notes on each batch – ingredients, time, temperature, size, each loaf slightly different than the one before. Only Sarah can turn a simple household task into a science project."

The head remained bent, but the eyes glared sideways, hurt. "You are a horrible, evil person for telling that story."

Sullivan smiled in sympathy, but she wouldn't look his way. "I suppose if you're going to learn to do something, you might as well learn to do it right at the very start. If it weren't for trial and error, we would never learn to walk, would we?" The bowed head gave a small nod.

"My dear, is there something your brother's not telling us about his cooking, or do you just prefer your food cold?" Granger said lightly. "You're not having any of the stew?" he clarified when the remark was met by a questioning frown. "It may not seem special to you, but it's been far too long since I've had a home-cooked meal. Replicated proteins will keep you going, but they can get pretty darned tiresome."

"I do not eat meat." Sarah poked her pile of salad with her fork, stirred it, then took a quick, tiny bite.

"Too many years on Navara," Dmitri explained for her. He speared a chunk of meat and waved it under her nose. "Too much brainwashing."

"I was not brainwashed by anybody! I have seen how meat is obtained on this planet and I refuse to participate in the barbarism. Bleeding to death is a very horrible way to die!" the girl snapped, lifting her head all the way this time.

"Enough, Sar. People are eating." To the table, Dmitri explained, "A few years ago, we were invited to help our neighbors with what we were told was an all-day job. When we got there, we found out the task was butchering a young animal Sarah had grown fond of. Needless to say, it didn't go over very well. She took off like they were coming after her next."

The introverted girl gave a sudden, short giggle, grinning to herself. Jack was having trouble keeping up with the changes in mood – fearful, withdrawn, angry, shy, amused – she never held a trait long enough to be judged by it. Guillaume had warned it would take a while to get to know her, but he hadn't said just how long.

"It wasn't just me," Sarah blurted to her dinner. "I heard what happened. Dimi got sick and passed out cold. It took two people to walk him home. And he didn't eat meat for a month, either."

Light laughter passed around the table – except for the Navaran, whose cool gray eyes held a quiet empathy.

Dmitri jabbed her with an elbow. *"Snitch."*

"You've been to Navara?" Sullivan inquired. One of six founding members of the United Planetary Alliance, Navara was infamous for its blistering, hostile deserts. Combined with the less-than-welcoming natives, it rarely made anyone's vacation itinerary. "I take it that's why you're able to speak the language. Were you there as tourists?" He'd meant to engage the girl, but her head was down, watching her fork stir her food.

Dmitri answered. "We were there four years while Father taught classes at the Fleet Academy branch out there. We lived thirteen kilometers outside Kar Kuomi."

"Four *years?*" Granger exclaimed. "I barely lasted six months! How did you survive four years on that fireball without going absolutely insane?"

Their host swallowed wrong and coughed on what he was chewing. He reached for his waterglass and drank half before speaking. The girl's chin dropped all the way to her chest, as if penitent.

"You don't. Those four years were the worst of our entire lives. It destroyed our family forever. No offense, sir," Dmitri said to Ti'onam. "It was not a fault of the Navaran people."

"None taken," Ti'onam replied. "The inability of other species to adapt to Navara's extreme climate is but one reason Navara discourages alien settlement, including those unable to accept short periods of discomfort in the name of education." The gray eyes slipped sideways in Granger's direction, but the doctor was intent on his meal.

"A little of it was good," Sarah told her plate, "but mostly it was bad."

Sullivan peered between the open shelves of the room divider, to the odd timepiece on the shelf in the sitting room. An open gold frame circled characters he took to be numbers.

"I take it that's telling local time. How would you convert that to standard?"

Dmitri looked over. "Add four extra minutes for every hour. Sarah broke the cover glass a while ago, but it still works. Standard, it's about a quarter to midnight."

Jack stood. "If you'll excuse me, I need to check in with my ship."

"How can you do that?" The girl's purple-blue eyes shot up to bore into Sullivan's, and she spoke to him directly. "You got a communication device past the security checks? *How?* If Commander Guillaume knew about that, he'd stop your investigation cold."

"Commander Guillaume not only knows, he gave his approval," Sullivan explained, trying his best friendly smile now that he had her attention. His reply met with deeper confusion.

"He didn't have much of a choice," Jack said. "Captain outranks Commander. I can't be out of contact with my ship for thirty days."

"That's not fair!" Sarah protested. "We're not allowed anything beyond – *smokesignals!*"

"No, but certain concessions had to be met before I agreed to this mission. Communication with my ship was one of them. If I don't see you before morning, Miss Kirushenko, I have enjoyed your company, and I bid you a pleasant 'good night'."

Jack met with his crew in private before retiring.

"Impressions, gentlemen? Our accommodations are primitive, but I've suffered worse. We're warm, dry, and I haven't seen any evidence of four- or six-legged tenants. The food is palatable. I'll take partial plumbing over a hole in the ground any day."

"It's a good thing these people have to walk everywhere," Granger said, "or they'd weigh a quarter ton apiece. Our host may be a decent cook, but that was unprocessed, unregulated animal fat in that meal. There were enough calories in what we ate for an entire day, and then some. The girl is smart for avoiding it. I want to make sure everyone gets some cholesterol inhibitors before breakfast, at least until I can run an analysis on the food."

"That's probably not a bad idea, Doc. Impressions of our hosts? Guillaume said they were young, but I didn't realize he meant children." No matter what the compound's commander said about their hosts' abilities, Jack had serious doubts about just how much help would be available. "Ti'onam?"

"As you mentioned, Captain, their age is unexpected. Commander Guillaume implied they have been here for some time. It is most unusual for a research facility to admit children. It is unlikely they were admitted for the sole purpose of translation. Computers would have done the original recording and analysis. We know that Lieutenant-Commander Dickerson is a fully qualified xenolinguist. A second for a research program this size would be superfluous."

47

"Obviously, we can't judge their knowledge of the local language," Sullivan said, "but the girl allegedly knows eight languages. That's a lot for anybody, let alone a teen who apparently hasn't had formal schooling for at least a year. She spoke Navaran to you, Ti'onam. How did you find her grasp of that language?"

"She used a standard formal greeting, but her intonation and accent are exceptional. She has had either extensive training in customs or an intensive, direct exposure to Navaran society. Her interrupted performance of a mealtime meditation ritual was nearly flawless."

"Could she have learned that in school, in a diplomacy class, perhaps?"

"Unlikely, but not impossible," Ti'onam conceded. "Kar Kuomi would best be described as a 'frontier' town. It is by far the largest city on Navara, tens of kilometers from any other. The land is leased to the Alliance so that offworlders who must reside on Navara have a place to live that does not disturb the Navaran cities. Kar Kuomi has a constantly shifting population of traders, businessmen, scientists, and others. The composition of the population varies, but has always managed to remain predominantly human in character. There are numerous public schools, all of which are required to teach a minimal exposure to mannerisms and survival phrases in the Navaran language, but none so far as I know that would delve that deeply into culture and tradition. Such things are not shared casually."

"Mr. Andreiev? She kept looking over at you. Your opinion?"

"She's a very beautiful girl," the young lieutenant said without hesitation.

"And ten years your junior," Sullivan reminded him just as fast.

"Yes, sir. She seems nice enough. I am interested to know if she is from Russia itself, or one of the colonies. She has attended Russian schools at some point."

"What makes you say that?"

Andreiev shrugged. "Her thoroughness of education. We already know she is highly intelligent and speaks Russian from birth. Where else would she receive such a strong educational base than Russia?"

"I can think of several places. Let's keep our eyes and ears open, gentlemen. Be friendly, find out what you can, but don't pry. This is their home, and we may be here for several weeks. We don't want to take over their lives any more than we need to. Let's try and get a look at those sites tomorrow."

Dmitri's lamp had been out for all of twenty seconds when he heard the tiptoeing whisper of bare feet and the hush of a blanket dragging on the wooden floor. He waited, but nothing followed. He opened his eyes to confront the shadow, darker than the dark of the room.

He sighed. "What, Sar? You know the answer is no."

"*Please*, Dimi! There's *four* of them! We don't know them at all! It's not like they're from the compound... You know my door doesn't shut. Yours shuts *and* locks. *Please?*"

"One of them's a Navaran, Sar. Since when did you stop trusting Navarans?"

"Three of them aren't!"

"Fine! But only tonight! Tomorrow they won't be strangers; you'll have to deal with it."

"*Thank you,*" she whispered with relief, shutting and locking his door by touch alone.

A knee pressed into his mattress, down by his feet. "Floor, Sar. You know the rules."

"Yes, Dim."

He waited until she was rolled up in her blanket, squashed against the side of his bed. With luck, he'd remember she was there and not step on her in the morning. Not that he expected her to sleep. It had been a while since she was afraid to stay in her room. He reached over the side of the bed, rummaged until he found her hand, and gave it a squeeze.

"You pulled yourself together pretty quick when they got here. That was good."

It was hard to tell if the replying choke was a laugh or cough. "You never know what fear will do."

"The orders from Guillaume are on my desk. Give them a look tomorrow. It says full cooperation, Sar. It's not just Marc's little research group, it's the actual Allied Space Fleet itself, real government-level stuff. We have to shine even harder, or it could make Marc look bad. We can't do that. He's been really good to us."

The sigh was laced with dread. "I can do it. I did try tonight, Dim. I really did."

"You did a great job tonight," he said. "It'll be okay. Trust me."

Четыре ~ *Four* ~ *Togant*

As often happened when she knew there were guests in the house, Sarah slept fitfully, hyperalert to every noise inside and out. She'd drift, then wake with a start, swearing she'd heard the creak of a stair. The bed rustled when Dmitri turned over, and a floorboard complained if she squirmed, but Sarah knew the difference. The stairs had been noisy when they'd first moved in; after two years Dmitri had had his fill of squeaks and groans, and he and his friend spent a rainy hour last year shoring up the steps with slivers of wood. No longer was there a reliable warning if someone came up the stairs. She could handle loneliness in the daylight, but the dark made it unbearable.

She dozed on the hard floor; insomnia was a faithful friend. An hour before dawn, she arose and crept down the stairs, a change of clothes balled under her arm. She hesitated at the bottom. The door to the bath lay not three meters from the stairs, but it was sandwiched between the doors of the guest rooms. The windowless hallway was dark as Navaran midnight. She could navigate the darkness blind, knew precisely where the door was, the lock, the hanging lamp in the back corner. She'd done it hundreds of times, but now there *could* be someone in the shadows, lying in wait for just such an opportunity. You were supposed to be able to trust Allied Space Fleet officers, but... .

Sarah chewed her upper lip, hating herself when she was this stupid and cowardly and indecisive. Hating herself twice as much, she dropped the clothes and ran upstairs to get the lamp from her room. All this cowardice for six steps of darkness!

Better safe than sorry, she'd learned the hard way.

She started a fire in the waterheater, waited, then washed and dressed, centimeters from the locked door, ears straining for someone lurking on the other side. Not that she had any weapon beyond a clumsy stick of firewood.

Silence.

Faint light filtered into the alcove by the time she left the room, carrying the extra lamp. To her surprise, the Navaran stood at the eastern window, shutters unlocked, pointing an instrument out the opening.

"Good morning, Miss Kirushenko."

Sarah blew out the lamp and placed it on the bottom stair.

//Aaristam,// she replied in Navaran. The device had her attention, and she approached. *//Kiso-ti, savven j'i opxann mn'ios gisoddat-ka mi'ock sto,//* she continued in his complicated language. *She did not anticipate he would rise so early.*

"As you may be aware," Ti'onam replied in Standard, "Navarans do not sleep as humans do. This was a quiet opportunity with which to begin my work."

The girl eased forward another step, watching the device's screens with fascination. It was the size of her old homework pad, but six or seven centimeters thick. *//My apologies for the disturbance.//* After a pause, she braved herself to inquire, "Have I caused offense?"

"Offense is not a Navaran attribute. I found nothing in your words to imply less than courtesy. Why do you ask?" He adjusted a setting, and the silver device in his hand gave a click and a chirp. The readout changed to a colorful fluctuating bar graph.

Navarans did not often recognize tact; in Sarah's experience, they were masters of bluntness, and they expected the same in return. "You do not answer me in Navaran. Is my speech that poor and out of practice?"

"Your speech is excellent, and I understood you quite well. It is considered impolite to converse in a language that excludes the participation of others in a group."

The girl's cheeks darkened. "Understood. We *are* alone right now, though. Perhaps – if you have time during your mission – you might choose to speak it with me? It is more than six years since I left Navara. I worked hard to learn the language well, and I do not wish to lose the ability. Or, if you could recommend any readings I might benefit from – literature, poetry, philosophy, anything – I'll have the Compound's computer print me a bound copy." An impolite level of eagerness crept into her voice.

"I am confident that can be arranged." Ti'onam made yet another adjustment. He probed a question from the night before. "I was unaware Kar Kuomi taught such intensive language courses."

"They don't. I don't think Dmitri ever got further than 'My name is' and 'Please assist me, I am lost.' I went to school in Shir P'an."

Ti'onam studied her with new interest. "Truly? I was unaware there is a foreign school in Shir P'an."

"There isn't!" Sarah agreed with too much pride. She caught herself at the last second and didn't smile, lapsing into the cool, aristocratic Navaran attitude she'd perfected so many years ago. "My parents arranged the program by special permission. I was too far ahead of the children in Kar Kuomi. It was considered inappropriate to put a five-year old in a classroom of eleven-year olds, and it was just as inappropriate to isolate me all day with a tutor. The Navarans resisted, but agreed to a thirty-day trial as an 'exchange' student. I stayed there three and a half years. I learned many things from my Navaran peers I never would have learned in Kuomi."

"A most impressive accomplishment," Ti'onam said with respect. "It is a credit to your parents to have seized such an opportunity."

"I suppose I must allow them that much. Father was strict about schooling. At some point he realized he had taken too many educational opportunities for granted, and he insisted none of us would make the same mistake. May I ask you a question?"

"You may."

"What *is* that you're holding? What does it do? Why were you allowed to bring it out here? What are you doing with it?"

"I believe that is four questions." Ti'onam turned the instrument so she could have a better view. "Regardless, this is a portable omnicomp. It records and processes various data, performs a vast array of computations and interpretations, transfers and receives data from the ship's computers, analyzes samples, as well as a wide variety of other scientific functions. Currently, I am analyzing and recording atmospheric gradients – barometric pressure, temperature, humidity, wind speed, chemical composition, background radiation, and pollen analysis, among others."

"An entire science lab in that little box!" Sarah knew better than to reach out and touch, though she ached to hold it and explore the functions herself. Her fingers wrapped tight in her skirt to make sure. Grabbing was impolite enough among Humans; to the Navarans, it was an obscene lack of self-restraint, on par with assault.

"It stopped raining at 03:20 this morning, local time," Sarah volunteered. "What's its power source? Is it self-charging, or does it require a power-cell replacement? Does it have a range limit? What's its memory capacity? Does it stay recording all the time? How hard is it to operate? Can your ship track you through that?"

"Chatter, chatter, chatter." Dmitri dragged himself down the stairs, clean shirt thrown over a bare shoulder. "It's too early to be thinking that much. I should have known who you'd be terrorizing first. If she's disturbing you or interfering with your work, Mr. Ti'onam, please tell me and I'll rein her in. Sarah has a habit of being a pest."

"I haven't been a pest in years!"

"We were having an informative conversation comparing educational systems," Ti'onam replied.

Her brother eyed her with distrust. "Why don't you get the heater going while I wash? You can play Navaran later. We have a lot of breakfast to make."

Sarah's eyes betrayed the annoyance she would not allow her face to show. She bowed her head to Ti'onam, as reserved as he was. "Please excuse me."

Breakfast was a repeat of dinner, with the Kirushenko girl pulled into herself, all traces of morning curiosity disappearing with the rising of the Earthmen. Shoulders up, head down, never looking at anyone, Sarah perched on the bench next to her brother. She spoke when spoken to, sometimes only after prodding. Just as her moods had changed so rapidly the night before, so did they in the daylight.

As they finished breakfast, a distant voice shouted outside, accompanied by a rhythmic thumping growing closer with each yell.

<*Hohai! Hohai! Hai! Hai! hai, vovorash Porshu!*>

The girl exploded to life. "Charlie!" She jumped up so fast her spoon flew off the table and slid under the heater as she ran for the door. "He's got the porshie!"

Dmitri's head shot up. "If – if you'll excuse me for just a minute." He, too, headed outside.

"Whoever Charlie is, he's obviously more interesting than we are. Shall we see for ourselves?" Jack followed.

<*Jenacha firat, Ahn! sorrat via Ahn Ixi!*> the girl chattered with delight. A shining grin ran ear to ear as she gushed Tau Cetan to a laughing boy who didn't look a day older than herself, sitting high atop a strange animal. She bounced on her bare toes and clapped her hands with excitement. "You did it! You rode him!"

Five meters nose to tail tip, the creature looked as if an apatosaurus had mated with a yak. A long brown neck supported a snake-like head with bulging eyes and a wide, toothy mouth that bawled an ungodly noise like metal scraping on stone. A heavy coat of rusty hair covered much of the elephantine body. The hair hung to bulky bare knees, and stopped at the base of a thick, lizard-like tail.

Granger stared at the beast. "What in the name of Darwin is that? Don't tell me they kept their dinosaurs alive by knitting them sweaters?"

The boy slid off the animal as the girl shifted personalities again and heartfully giggled.

Sarah petted a flank. "It's a porshie, Tau Ceti's answer to the all-purpose work animal. And it's not a dinosaur. Believe it or not, it's more of a mammal."

Dmitri seized a loop hanging from the harness. "We helped geld it almost a year ago. Charlie's been trying to break it. Geldings are the only ones you can ever hope to ride. The rest are too vicious and obstinate."

"You won't butcher them, but you'll geld them," Sullivan said. "That's more humane?"

"It's not killing it, for one thing," Sarah explained, the fear from inside the house seeming never to have existed at all. "A good rider is an invaluable animal, worth a small fortune. And I didn't have to see it up close. I only kept the tension on the head ropes. You wouldn't believe the nasty bite it could give."

"I would, too, if you did that to me!" Andreiev said.

<Dimi-tri, joladi lxi regavish chudaka?> The new youth stood as tall as the Kirushenko girl, with dark hair to his shoulders and a pleasant face.

"He wishes to know if you are also old friends of ours," Sarah translated instantly. "That's what we term our occasional house guests."

Dmitri waved a hand at the boy. "This is Charshfenaki Aletneshfaja, our neighbor and friend. We call him Charlie for short. His mother is our housekeeper. *Ixo*, Sullivan, Granger, Andreiev, and ..." Dmitri located the Navaran standing apart in the doorway of the cabin, the wide-brimmed rain hat he'd worn the previous day once more pulled low over his head. "... Ti'onam."

The boy was twice as enthusiastic as Dmitri, bowing before them. "Charshfenaki, yes! Please is I am you meet!" he recited in Standard. He shook hands all around, nearly cranking Jack's arm from its socket.

Sarah tugged a tree sprout from the wet ground and offered it to the animal. The great head gave a loud *whoosh* and ripped it from her hand. She jumped back with a screech, arms raised to fend off teeth. The boy laughed.

<gelatna, Niu ta bishnet porshi, lepivash Sarrah?>

Sarah stared up at the thick head, eighty centimeters above her, then looked to her brother with more horror than fear. Dmitri burst into laughter.

"Go on! You're the one who loves a challenge. I dare you!"

Sarah hesitated, eyeing the snorting head. *<torach lx?>* Of course she knew it wasn't safe – this was the first time *he'd* managed to ride it.

'Charlie' nodded. He flexed a muscular arm, patting his bicep her approval. Sarah turned away with a scowl. Charlie glanced at Dmitri, and they both smirked.

"You're not actually thinking of riding that, are you?" Granger asked. "If it's anything like an unbroken Montana mustang, you're taking your life in your hands, and I don't remember passing a hospital on the march in."

The girl noticed all the faces watching, waiting for her to pass, to chicken out, to demurely shake her head and admit the idea was a little too wild for her tastes.

"To hell with it!" she announced. "*Axa*. I'll do it! I've taken bigger lumps than I'll get falling off a porshie."

The animal's bulging, red-rimmed eyes rolled nervously as she approached. Charlie took the leads from Dmitri, wrapped the straps around his hands, and chattered directions. Sarah reached up, grabbed two handfuls of thick hair, and let her brother boost her.

Immediately, the creature tried to rear its head, squalling. The boy strained for control, fighting the mighty neck as it twisted to snap at the rider. The girl's face was white as snow but she hung on, and in a moment the beast calmed.

Charlie pulled the harness and gave soft orders, leading the animal around the wet yard, showing off his patient work. As they circled around the edge of the trees, it gave a sharp turn and headed for the forest.

Charlie ran to keep up, shouted, then swore, but found himself more or less dragged through the brush, the five admiring bystanders in pursuit. Sarah ducked, dodging branches that normally would have been far overhead. She leaned down to help Charlie after he was ground between the porshie and a tree, and saw the branch too late. Porshie hair wrapped around her fingers, Sarah toppled backwards over the trotting flank.

She hit the ground on her back, wincing as the undergrowth gouged her shoulder. Freed of its rider, the creature stopped as suddenly as it had started, and grazed on a leafy bush. Sarah reached Charlie as he stood up. He unwrapped his aching hands from the harness straps and swore a foul streak, losing his cheer and kicking the animal in a thick leg. The beast rolled a condescending eye, chewing.

Sarah touched his side. <*You are hurt?*>

Charlie rubbed his hands. The straps had left deep lines all around. <*Jah. Ahnax?*> he asked as the others swarmed them.

<*Unharmed. I think porshie need to train more, before you ride again.*>

Sullivan reached the girl the same time as Dmitri. He lay his hands

55

on her shoulders. "Are you all right? That was a rather acrobatic fall."

The girl shoved him away with a squeal. She darted behind her brother and stared at Sullivan with fear and defensiveness that promised violence if he tried more.

"Don't touch me! Please," she remembered to add.

"Calm down," her brother ordered. "For future reference, she doesn't like to be touched. She's one hell of a fighter, and you're likely to get hurt if you try it again."

"I'm sorry. I merely meant to express my concern over her safety… "

Dmitri cut him off with a raised hand. "I know. It's not your fault. She's just testy that way."

"A star captain should know you never touch another person without their permission!" Sarah scolded over Dmitri's shoulder. "What if I were an empath? You could have blown a neural conduit or something!"

"Point taken," Sullivan said. "I won't forget."

"Knock it off!" Dmitri grabbed his sister by the hand and dragged her to where Granger examined Charlie's hands. He picked up the hanging leads from the animal's harness before it could wander off.

"I don't think anything's broken," Granger said, "but he should have these abrasions treated."

"I have some antibiotic stuff in the cabin," Dmitri offered. He translated the proposition for Charlie, who nodded.

"Have him take off his shirt – he hit that tree kind of hard," Charlie shook his head, but Dmitri's manner suggested he agreed with Granger.

"Charlie!" Sarah exclaimed, seeing the raw scrape down the boy's shoulder and back.

<It nothing!>

Dmitri waved Charlie toward the cabin. *<Come! If you ask nice, maybe Sarah will rub on healing cream!>* Both he and Charlie laughed, though Charlie's face reddened.

"I'll do no such thing, ever!" Sarah declared, hands on her hips as Dmitri repeated his idea to the other men. "You were horrible to even suggest that, Dmitri Kirushenko! You know perfectly well I won't!"

"Nothing heals a man quite like a woman's touch," Granger said.

"Then you should have brought one with your crew!"

Dmitri clucked to the porshie and tugged the straps. It came willingly, having gotten what it was after. Charlie grabbed the opposite strap, and together they escorted it back to the yard and secured it to a tree before entering the cabin.

"Anyway," Sarah told her brother smugly, "I believe I have won that dare. *Your* turn."

"Hmph!" Dmitri handed their friend a jar, labeled in Tau Cetan, that contained an antibiotic gel never dreamed of by any native. "You know I can't get that close to porshie hair. I'm not sneezing myself silly."

"Poor excuse."

Charlie winced at the cold gel Dmitri helped him dab on his side. *<If you have old friends, then you not work today.>*

<What you have in mind?> Dmitri asked. Sarah stood out of the way, echoing their words in English for the ship's crew like a seasoned professional. The pause between spoken words and translation was a matter of seconds.

Charlie rubbed his hands with a fingers' worth of goo, sniffing at it. *<It good chance to start spreading fields during break in rain. Next wave, everything wash in.>*

Sarah wrinkled her nose, and her shoulders dropped.

"What did he suggest?" Andreiev asked.

"He wants to spread fertilizer on the fields. We've helped with that before. It's unprocessed, unsanitary, and it stinks. Horrible!"

<I needed here today,> Dmitri said, *<but Sarah can help.>*

"*What?!*" Revulsion turned to disbelief. "I'm not shoveling that... that... *stuff*!"

"Charlie needs the help, and I'm unavailable. You've done it before."

"*Dimi!* You know I don't do the farm work without you."

"You are today." He returned the ointment to a shelf in the kitchen.

Sarah dropped her voice to a whisper, following him room to room. "Dimi, I am not going out into a field with him!"

Dmitri switched to Russian for privacy. "*I'm not playing the games today! You will not make a scene! You know Charlie, you know the fields, you know the work, and you can work every bit as hard as me. You will go!*"

"*You promised! Clause three!*" The wide-eyed look flooded back, draining the color from her face.

The elder Kirushenko had been almost excessively friendly, tripping himself with enthusiasm. Now his face darkened into an icy sternness that bored into the girl. He held the stare, unblinking, as her forehead creased with dread. She seemed to shrink smaller under the harsh gaze.

Nyet! her lips begged. Her discomfort met with the thump of a bootheel slamming the floor. The retort made her jump.

"*Is that a disagreement or a disobedience? Do you need reminding?*"

"*Nyet.*"

"Then go upstairs and get my old boots," he told her in a manner more like himself, switching back to Standard. "You won't want your shoes in that muck." After a pause, the girl tore up the stairs.

Charlie pulled his shirt on. *<Dimi-tri, do not scare her like that. Please. I understand if she not want to work with me. I can start alone.>*

<She work, Charlie,> Dmitri assured his friend. *<I want her out from under feet.>*

The girl banged back down, boots in hand, as fast she could run. She spun back at the doorway, looking wounded and on the verge of tears.

Sarah pointed a finger at her brother. "Only until lunchtime!" She turned to Charlie, stabbing herself in the chest with her thumb. *<And I get pitchfork!>* she declared before sprinting out the door.

* * *

Dmitri cleared away the breakfast and unrolled a stack of meter-square papers across the table. "These are maps of the area."

"Commander Guillaume gave us maps," Sullivan said. "Everything's been fed into the omnicomps. We can navigate by them with pin-point accuracy."

"Unless his team has finished evaluating these and declared them fact, I'd doubt you have maps like these." Kirushenko tapped the pages proudly. "These are Sarah's own making, and I'd stake my lunch they're more accurate than what you've got."

What could a testy young girl possibly know about mapping that a planetary sensor array would overlook? Nothing, as far as Jack knew. He examined the top paper. "You place a lot of faith in your sister's abilities."

"When it comes to things like that, I do. She knows her references book, page, and paragraph."

Andreiev inspected a different page. "She enjoys making maps?"

"Not particularly. It was just something to do. She makes up projects to keep herself busy. These took her about a year to complete. Ultimately, the information is useful to the Compound, but she's bored stiff out here. Last visit there she managed to delay our return three days. Marc offered to let her stay a month, work in some of the labs, but she won't stay without me, and I'm happier out here."

"What about just a week, then?" Sullivan asked.

"She won't stay at *all* unless I'm there. Won't happen. Outside of

58

one, maybe two days when my brother watched her, and for a week or so after a bad fight, she and I have been together every day for the last six and a half years," Kirushenko said. "She won't stay with *anyone* unless they're family, and that means genetic relations."

"That must put a heavy strain on you," Granger said. "Even best friends need time away now and then. Eventually you're bound to get on one another's nerves."

"You most certainly do. We do okay, though. As long as she knows where I am, she's happy enough to go off on her own. She'll spend an afternoon with Charlie's mother, or work with some of the compound crew, and I can get a few hours without her."

Sullivan held out a map. "What do you think, Ti'onam? Are these any better than what we've got?"

"They do appear to be more detailed." Ti'onam accessed his omnicomp to compare the stored data to the paper. "I am curious, however, as to this alphanumeric code. According to the data Mr. Guillaume gave us, it does not correspond with elevation or positioning locators." Hundreds of tiny circles and numbers dotted each page.

Dmitri craned his neck to see. "Those? Those are trees. The numbers are the trunk circumference, and the letter refers to the type of tree. She has a key written down on one of these pages – try the last one, I think." He riffled through the stack. "She has the original data in a notebook somewhere. She didn't know the names of the trees, so she kept a leaf from each one and a rubbing of the bark, and then worked with the botanist at the compound to identify the types."

"Forest sampling." Ti'onam gave a label to the project. "An invaluable aid to categorizing climate types as well as recording the natural history of an area. I've never known such a large sampling, however. Due to the labor-intensive nature of the task only a small area of land is measured, and the data then extrapolated to an average. If the distances are correct, this data covers several hectares."

"You mean to say she measured every tree in the forest? By hand?" Granger stared at the number of notations on the sheet. The pile sat seven or eight sheets thick. "Isn't that a little obsessive?"

Dmitri shrugged the idea away. "If you're stuck in the middle of a forest and there's fourteen or so hours of daylight, what would you do? It kept her busy."

The Compound's charts had been made by scanning orbital mappers, a machine recording data on a single pass from several miles up. The girl lived right there; she knew the land face to face, tree by tree.

"We'll give her way a try," Sullivan decided, handing the first page to Andreiev and folding the remainder. "I'd like to get a look at the destruction zones."

Dmitri hesitated. "It's kind of late to start out for that. That's a good half-day's travel by foot, and Charlie's porshie still looks a bit risky. If the break in the weather holds, we can get a jump-start on that trip tomorrow. Is there anything closer you could do?"

"The intermittent energy pulses were located only four kilometers east-northeast of our present location," Ti'onam offered. "Perhaps we could begin our investigation at that site."

Пять ~ *Five* ~ *Chichiva*

With their guide in the lead, the four officers set off down a worn path that began where the yard ended and the forest took over. The land stayed flat for a short distance, then sloped gently downwards to a rocky stream rushing with the recent rains. Jack crossed rock to rock as nimbly as their host.

Ti'onam checked their present coordinates. "Three kilometers further east."

He, Granger, and Andreiev wore their omnicomps concealed in leather carrybags. A simple flap covered the front panel of the instrument, allowing covert access to the displays, a design Guillaume's men had worked out long ago. The skies above the trees remained gray, but the rain held off.

"So, your sister's not fond of the medical profession." Granger broached the subject to Dmitri as they walked. This was as good a time as any to bring it up. The girl wasn't around, and he wanted to know what he might be up against. He could do a basic exam without physical contact, but it would require a hefty amount of cooperation on the part of the patient, and after the morning's outburst, that didn't seem likely.

The boy choked back a sarcastic laugh. "She even avoids the study of it, if that says anything to you. She reached a working truce with Dr. Herzog at the compound, but the time before that, the doctor gave up, and two of us carried her away in hysterics. She wouldn't cooperate with the last two visiting doctors. She said it wasn't worth the effort, since she'd never see them again."

"Total phobia," the doctor surmised. "How long has she been like that? Do you know how it started? Does that extend to nurses as well? How about female physicians?"

"It's not really a phobia. If she was sick enough, she'd see a doctor. If she's not the patient, she's more than willing to go with you. She's had a decent relationship with one or two doctors, but that's it. When Sarah was born, she wasn't expected to live. She was born very early, and her lungs weren't developed – that's how she and Vladimir are only nine months apart. I remember it being a really big deal, my parents being all excited because the doctors had drained her lungs and she was breathing air. She was a couple of weeks old by then."

Granger understood. "Liquigen. They must have had her on Liquigen. It's a highly oxygenated fluid that keeps weakened lung tissue from collapsing. It's most often used in respiratory burns and premature infants."

"I guess." Dmitri paused with the rest of the crew to catch his breath. "Anyway, her lungs stayed weak, and she got pneumonia before she left the hospital. Constantly. They'd immunize her against one form, she'd get another. She'd swallow wrong, *bang!* she was sick. Someone brought home a germ? *Bang!* Sarah had pneumonia. Climate change? Pneumonia. Bath water up her nose? Pneumonia. At least two, three times a year she would wind up in a hospital, until she was six or seven. Navara was an awful place to live, but it did help her lungs."

"Due to the lack of moisture and thinner atmosphere, Navaran air contains considerably fewer air-borne pathogens than many other planetary environments," Ti'onam said.

"That type of sterility never surprised me," Granger muttered.

"That must have been very upsetting for a young child," Sullivan said. He started walking again, and the Kirushenko boy followed like a well-trained pup.

"Mother tried to keep her out of the hospitals, but Sarah'd turn blue around the edges, and Mother'd get scared and ship her out. Sarah *hated* the hospitals. She fought like hell, and got a bad reputation. Nobody listens to a five year old, even a literate one. If she wouldn't cooperate, they'd tie her down or drug her and do what they wanted anyway."

"Unfortunately, I can see both sides," Granger admitted. "Sometimes you have to do what's necessary despite the patient's objections. Pediatrics is different, though. It's a specialty for a reason. Just the fact she'd been on Liquigen should have led to a system of routine followups. She should have been on preventative therapies, been followed at least quarterly with well-visits to prevent exactly that type of fear from developing. Even a five-year old can be allowed to make enough decisions to feel as if they have some control over a chronic illness."

"We would have had to stay in one place for that to happen," the boy reminded him. "Father was an archaeologist. If we weren't following him to some dig somewhere, we were off to a new teaching position. That's how we wound up on Navara."

"How's she doing now, health-wise?"

"Excellent, as far as I know. Only two definite, maybe three, mild cases of pneumonia in the last six years. Dr. Herzog pumped her with immune boosters and vaccines every quarter, and he trusted us to keep a supply of medication in case she felt it coming on. We sent for him once, but we had everything under control by the time he got here, three days later. I think Sarah willed herself well on that one. I don't think she was about to give him the satisfaction of having to treat her like a patient."

Granger thought ahead to the scans and blood tests he would want to run. "When do you think I'll be able to check her over? I'd like to get the exams out of the way so we can forget about them. She seems a bit moody, even without knowing my official title."

"You noticed," the brother said acidly. "Dr. Herzog's official diagnosis to my complaint was, if I remember his quote, 'Teenage girls are notoriously moody; it will disappear sometime around the time they start their first serious relationship, and become permanent the moment they get married.'"

Granger broke into hard laughter. "I remember those days! That's just about the point when my first two marriages started to sour. I spent eight years sorting that out before I gave up."

"Guillaume mentioned you considered marriage once," Sullivan said to Dmitri.

The politeness in the boy's voice sounded forced. "I don't discuss my marriage, Captain Sullivan. It did not end voluntarily for either party. In five months, I did not know my wife to be disagreeable even once. I will not compare her to my sister in *any* way, unless I am forced to acknowledge the fact they were both somehow of the same gender."

"I'm sorry. I didn't mean to pry into old wounds."

"It's not your fault. You had nothing to do with it. But it's a private affair, and a closed subject. Shouldn't we be close to the area you're looking for?"

Ti'onam read the omnicomp. "Approximately one hundred more meters. Then we must turn left for three-quarters of a kilometer."

Andreiev folded a section of map. "No path that way. We'll have to go by coordinates alone." He gazed at the leafy canopy overhead, hearing dozens of unseen creatures barking and chirping back and forth. "Perhaps we should mark the trees, so we can find our way back."

"Worried, Mr. Andreiev?" Sullivan asked.

"I'm Moscow born and bred, Captain," he explained. "Unless they are labeled, such as in a park, all trees look alike to me."

"Anybody with two eyes and half a brain could follow our tracks back," the Kirushenko boy declared. "I'd never set foot in a forest like this either, until I came here. Follow me."

* * *

"I'll be damned!" Dmitri whistled. He crashed through the underbrush to where Commander Ti'onam and the captain examined a circular black mark on the side of a tree. Granger and Andreiev joined them. "What is it?"

Sullivan knelt down and scraped a fingernail over the damp blotch. He rubbed the resulting sludge between his thumb and finger, sniffing. "Soot. It's a burn mark."

"How could someone burn a tree like that? You'd need a torch or something."

"Why would you do it to start with?" Granger countered.

"Exactly the point. Let me see your knife," Sullivan asked their host.

Dmitri unsheathed it. It was a serious weapon, the mirrored blade longer than his hand, double-sided at the tip and some five centimeters wide across the base. Work on the farm had scratched the laser-sharpened edge, but he'd paid for a lifetime warranty, and so far it had lived up to the promise.

Sullivan hacked downwards at the scorch mark, chipping the bark. "It goes down several millimeters." He handed a piece to Ti'onam and stood up. "There's another one." He pointed to a splotch seven meters up another tree. "Over there, too."

Dmitri frowned. "Who would climb a tree just to mark it like that? I don't see how you even could."

"You don't. Whatever made those marks made them from the ground."

"Captain?" Andreiev called. "Here!"

The lieutenant flicked leaves from a spot on the ground, his omnicomp uncovered next to him. "The remains of a fire, sir. It doesn't seem very big. Just some half-burned twigs, no significant amount of fuel or ashes. It probably didn't get hot enough to melt lead."

Sullivan stirred the evidence with a finger. "Whoever it was cleared the leaves first, and covered everything over carefully with dirt. They knew enough to make sure the whole forest didn't catch fire. Here's a couple of stones underneath." He pulled out three rocks, each no bigger than a fist. "Someone set it up on purpose. Mr. Kirushenko, is there any kind of local religion or cult that might account for something like this? Secret rituals, initiation rites, mischief making?"

"Please, I'm not used all that formal stuff. Just 'Dmitri' is fine." He thought, then shook his head. "None that I've heard of. The religion is more or less monotheistic, a generally benevolent creator of life that oversees the people. The Sun and Moons are the tools the Creator uses to watch over his people – I don't get all of how – and the rainy season is supposed to be a time of rest, a reminder to take a break from farming and pay attention to other tasks that need doing. It's all tied to the growing seasons. But there's no sacrificial offerings, if that's what you mean. You might say a prayer of thanks with the first handful of harvest, or offer up the first blood from an animal you're butchering, but that's about it. Nothing evil. They don't seem to have any type of evil-thing at all; the Moons just turn their back on somebody, refusing to bless them. If there was any kind of mischief-making for fun, Charlie would have let me in on it long ago."

"Captain," Ti'onam called out, twenty meters away. The group moved to where the Navaran stood before a snapped tree, its trunk four hands wide.

"Captain, this tree did not fall naturally." He pointed to the evidence with a twig, as if teaching a lesson. "Note the line of separation: it is perfectly smooth. There are no axemarks, sawmarks, not even dust which would accompany frictional cutting methods. Nor were the roots disturbed or the trunk itself splintered, as might happen with brute force. Again, the exposed edges are blackened, as if burned."

"Cauterized," Granger understood. "Like slicing through a growth with a laser scalpel."

"An unusual but potentially accurate analogy."

"And not a leaf out of place anywhere else," Sullivan mused. "Ti'onam, how high a temperature would be necessary to do something like that?"

"Not less than 270 degrees Celsius, held in a steady line for several minutes, to cut through a trunk of that diameter. However, that is not taking into account the unknown density of the specific wood."

"Two hundred seventy degrees in a line no wider than a pencil, angled to ensure a fall in a specific direction. Any idea what might account for such an occurrence?"

Ti'onam paused, pondering the theoretical impossibility of his conclusion. "In this culture, with the exception of lightning, nothing of which I am aware. However, it is most improbable that lightning would strike the exact location so many times and cause precisely the same superficial damage. Nor would lightning sever a tree so cleanly. Elsewhere, I could conclude a narrow-beam energy source of some sort. A low EPSAR setting can cause this type of damage, as can a Burin-Jai disrupter, an Eridani energy blaster, an industrial laserwelder, and at least a dozen other forms of sustained thermal-emission particle beams."

"There's another one." Sullivan pointed as a diffuse mark caught his eye. "Ti'onam, if I had an EPSAR set on low, where would I have to stand to make that mark?"

Ti'onam aimed the omnicomp, stepped backwards a dozen paces and two to the right, and put his back directly against a wide trunk. "Approximately here, sir."

"And if you compute the theoretic angle of trajectory, how high would that EPSAR have been held?" Angle and distance would yield the approximate height of the perpetrator, narrowing the field of possible suspects.

"Approximately seventy-eight and one quarter centimeters from the ground."

Jack sighed with annoyance. "So we're either dealing with forest gnomes, or they were sitting against the tree. So much for that idea." He rubbed his chin, stymied.

"And the frequency-emission pattern Guillaume recorded did not match any known make of weapon. What if someone changed the identification frequency to cover their tracks, disguise the wave pattern? Mr. Andreiev?"

"In theory, it is possible, sir," Andreiev agreed, "but it's not easy. One would need a significant knowledge of crystalline-powered engineering, be able to read schematics, have the appropriate tools and know the frequency-modulation codes for the model they were working with. It would require a certain amount of training, or the power arrays could become unbalanced and result in an overload. The resulting explosion would level everything for at least seven meters."

Guillaume's words came flying back. *A chronic game player. A game to see who's more on their toes. She's bored, Captain. She did get the computer stylus past us.* Perhaps a stylus wasn't the only thing smuggled.

"Schematics – a *map* of internal workings – and hours of study," Sullivan said.

A dead silence befell the group. It didn't take a Campbell Davies or a Mendeleyev to connect the Captain's words. Dmitri's head snapped up. "Now wait a damned minute! My sister may be a pain in the ass, but you better not even *think* she did this! You've got a hell of a lot of nerve, accusing her!"

"I haven't accused her of anything, but she certainly seems to have

66

the intelligence, time, and the ability to diagram," Sullivan said. "She's obviously been in this area before. Are you saying she couldn't have done something like this?"

"Yes, that's what I'm saying! I think I know my sister! Where the hell would she get that kind of a weapon, anyway? Guillaume checks her over with a goddamned body scanner before she leaves! We have no tools like that stuff would require! Sarah's a lot of things, but she's no engineer. She doesn't know anything about the insides of electrical stuff. Go through her textbooks if you don't believe me! Art, music, science, maths, history, languages, philosophy, alien cultures, literature – *those* are the kinds of things she studies," Dmitri counted off on his fingers, "not – *mechanical engineering*. How in the hell would she learn what the identification codes on a weapon would be? I didn't even know they *had* them!"

"Perhaps not, but someone does. You said she made detailed notes on breadmaking. Does she keep notes on all her projects?"

"Yeah. So?"

"I'd like to see them. If she's not hiding anything, she shouldn't mind someone taking a look."

"You can't just walk up and demand to see her personal papers. Sarah's a very private person. Spook her like that and she'll pack everything up and hide them somewhere."

"I'll give you until tomorrow morning to convince her, then I will take them by force, if necessary," Sullivan said. "I don't take kindly to having my ship diverted because a child slipped into delinquency from boredom."

"Sarah's not a delinquent! Far from it! And you don't have that kind of authority out here."

"In fact, he does," Andreiev explained quietly. "In areas where no local Planetary Alliance government exists, the commander of an Allied Fleet vessel has final jurisdiction over legal…"

Dmitri threw his hands into the air. *"Fine!* I'll get them. And when you realize you're wrong, I expect a full apology! If you're smart, you'll never let her know about it, either. Neither one of us needs that kind of trouble." He turned and headed back in the direction of the main path.

That kind of trouble. What kind of trouble was the boy worried about? The question gnawed at Sullivan all the way back.

The Kirushenko's housekeeping neighbor and cook fawned over the visitors even more than her son. A short, fat woman with laughing brown eyes and rosy round cheeks, she refused to sit with the men, standing by to serve whatever was needed.

"She says it's easier this way; the kitchen isn't big enough for everyone to walk around," Sarah translated. "She insists she ate while waiting for everyone to return."

"Please give her our compliments." Sullivan smiled and bowed his head at the woman, who blushed hard and bowed back several times. "Now I know why you prefer to have her cook. This is exquisite." Lunch was a feast of baked *joubash* fowl and gravy, slices of orange vegetable, and a sweet, fluffy grain dish reminiscent of cashews. It sat much lighter on the stomach than their host's meal.

Jack claimed the diagonal seat from Sarah, close enough to watch without being obvious. The girl passed on the meat, but ate a reasonable amount of the alternate dishes. She sat in her end seat next to her brother, conversing across the table with the young Charlie fellow, laughing and happy as any young girl.

Dmitri broke a pause in the conversation. "Sar, I was talking with Mr. Ti'onam today, and I told him about your experiment with Mrs. Al's flowers. I thought maybe after lunch you could show him your research." Dmitri was too young to feel comfortable calling his best friend's mother by her first name, and 'Mrs. Al' was easier on the tongue than Aletneshfaja.

The girl froze, turned white, and lowered her fork. In an instant, she fell into what Sullivan started calling a red alert: the violet-blue eyes went wide, the head went down, the shoulders up. "Why did you do that, Dim?" she said, the carefree liveliness of the previous moments vaporized. "You had no right to talk about that stuff."

Dmitri passed his plate over her head for a refill. "Why not? You worked hard on that, and you got really good results. You were proud of all that work."

Sarah writhed in her seat. "It's not written up in any formal style. It's a primitive little Mendelian study in botanical genetics, nothing spectacular. I worked it mostly from my textbook. It's not up to modern scientific standards."

"Nothing spectacular!" Dmitri bragged, placing his refilled plate on the table. "At thirteen years old, she tracks and cross-pollinates a popular strain of flower through six generations, discovers which traits are recessive, and then crosses and recrosses them to wind up with a color and style that no one around here had ever seen before."

"I'd call that impressive," Granger said.

"Mother like Sarrah flower, much very," Charlie added. He spoke to his mother, who smiled and patted Sarah on the head. Mrs. Al said something in reply, and Charlie stumbled, "Mother say Sarrah know goodst flowers in … Pelonishala." He swung an arm to include the land from horizon to horizon.

"They're making it sound like more than it was," Sarah insisted.

"Nonetheless, I would be most interested to review your data," Ti'onam said, curious.

The girl looked trapped. "All right. But please, do not expect much."

* * *

Sarah didn't like anyone in the safe haven of her room; if it were anyone but the Navaran, she wouldn't have allowed it. Her room was her escape, her retreat from the world, containing all the comforts she could want – a soft bed; a workbench cluttered by a disarray of glass jars, fruit peels, dead insects and loose papers; as well as an appropriately primitive reflecting-light microscope built for her by the engineers at the Compound. A bookcase held her myriad textbooks and dictionaries and local stories, and her doorless closet contained a packing trunk in which she kept all her Compound-approved memories of years of travel. Order had never been high on her or Dmitri's list of concerns – her unmade bed resembled a pile of rags. The previous day's clothing lay in small piles on the floor, while a larger pile awaiting wash day festered in a corner. For the first time, Sarah was ashamed of her untidiness. Such disorder was most unforgivable to a Navaran, but it was too late to do something about it now.

"As I explained, it's not up to any standards." She apologized again as Ti'onam scanned through her third book of notes and charts. The data was written neatly in ink, with graphs and comments penciled in the margins. Under the shaggy brows, the Navaran officer's face gave no hint as to his thoughts; it was a small comfort to know he wouldn't laugh out loud at her fumbling concepts. "I stuck to things as best as I could remember. I wanted to try gene splicing, but Guillaume vetoed that."

"On the contrary, I find this to be impressive work," Ti'onam said, turning pages. "Your notes need to be reorganized, but the data is thorough and your conclusions sound. Have you considered publication of your findings?"

"Publication?!" Sarah's Navaran manners slipped. "You mean, as in an article in a scientific journal?"

"Correct. This is a new planet being researched. The work you performed is original, valid, and ended with unique results on a botanical specimen not previously examined. The publication of the results could yield insights into the botanical history of the planet, and would further the general knowledge database. Performing your research without the use of computer-generated genetic models does not invalidate it."

"No, I had never considered it," Sarah admitted, shocked at her simple game gone right. "I wouldn't know what to do – What journals to petition, what format they require... Father had articles published, but, I don't even have a diploma! Why would they look at my work?"

"Most of the greatest discoveries in science, Miss Kirushenko, were done by persons without formal training or doctoral degrees. Good science is evaluated by method and results, not by the number of degrees after the scientist's name."

"In theory, yes, but it doesn't hurt."

"If you wish, I will outline the formula most often followed for written articles, and suggest several journals that may be interested in your research. You have experiments in these other notebooks as well?" Ti'onam eyed the dozen or so remaining bound journals on the shelf above the workbench, the ruffles of his ears rippling with curiosity.

"Not as formal as that one. These two are my language notes. You probably don't care to see those." Sarah pulled the first pair from the shelf, hoping he couldn't hear how her heart drumming with excitement. She had never dreamed of the kind of reception he had just given her work – praise from a *Navaran*, no less!

"These here," she took another group from the shelf; several dried leaves fell from them, "are my tree notes. For a while, Dimi and I weren't on amicable terms, so I spent a lot of time wandering around the forest. I also have an insect collection," she offered, hand on yet another notebook. "That's written up in this one. Do you want to see that?"

"If I may," Ti'onam encouraged, skimming the pages of a language journal. "I am most intrigued."

* * *

Granger cornered Dmitri. "If you think Sarah's going to stay busy for a while, why don't we get your physical out of the way? It won't take long, I promise."

Dmitri gazed up the quiet stairs as if waiting for something. "Yeah, all right." He accompanied the doctor to one of the downstairs bedrooms.

"If you could take off your shirt and have a seat, I'll get my things." Granger closed the door. He retrieved a pack from the corner and pulled out equipment. "Any health concerns?"

"I need IG6 and IG7 boosters for a rotten allergy to porshies, that's about it," the boy said, sitting on one of the bunks and pulling off the loose shirt. "I can't remember the last time I was really sick. Just allergies."

"Good. That's simple enough to treat." Granger moved his scanner over the boy's slim form. "Lungs and heart are good. How old are you?"

"Twenty-four."

"Do you know your height?"

"A hundred and seventy five centimeters, without boots."

Granger started at the top of his standard list as he scanned the boy's head. "Any problems with your eyes? Blurriness? Pain? Spots?"

"They water a lot if my boosters are low, but that's it. And I get double vision if I drink too much," Dmitri added.

Granger chuckled. "Had that symptom myself. Comes and goes, mostly during social occasions and political functions?"

"Exactly."

"Do you drink often?"

"No. Once in a while Charlie and I will have a night on the town, and I'll let myself go. I don't drink much at home."

"You're better off that way. Lean forward a little, let me take a look at your spine. Any back pain?"

"Only after swinging an axe for two or three hours."

"I guess I'll allow that. What's this scar on your shoulder?" Kyle traced a centimeter-wide mark with his finger. It was as long as his entire hand. "If you'd had that treated, it wouldn't be visible. You have a couple smaller ones here, too. Old battle wounds?"

"You could call it that. Are we done?"

"Just about. I need a small blood sample. You shouldn't even feel it." Granger adjusted a setting on his hypo and pressed it against the young man's inner arm. A fine needle shot out and withdrew a minute specimen. He unclipped the tiny vial from the hypo and slid it into an analysis compartment in his omnicomp. "I'll have the results in just a minute. Your sister's quite an individual. How did you wind up in charge of her?"

Dmitri turned sour. "You think she's guilty, too, don't you."

"I didn't say that. That's up for the captain to decide. My business here is strictly medical," Granger insisted. "I merely meant I think she's a complicated person."

Dmitri settled his attitude for the moment. "She *is* complicated. Our mother died when Sarah was eight. Our family split up when she was nine. I volunteered to keep her."

"You couldn't have been more than … eighteen," Kyle counted back. "That's a pretty big responsibility for someone that young. How did you manage?"

"I *wasn't* eighteen yet," Dmitri admitted, twisting his shirt in his hands. "Not for a month or two. It was hard at first, until we settled into some routines. We've been around a bit, had a lot of hard knocks, but we've made it through. We've done okay by ourselves. We make rules for each other, a sort of contract, and we stick to that. If it stops working, we renegotiate."

Granger picked up the beeping omnicomp and examined the readout. "That was an interesting reaction she had this morning before she left with your neighbor. You seemed rather strict with her. If you don't mind my asking, what did you say to her? Go ahead, you can put your shirt back on."

"Sometimes you have to be." Dmitri shrugged his arms into the shirt gladly and pulled it on. The back bedrooms drew warmth from the heaters in the bathroom and kitchen, hence they grew chilly when the doors were closed.

"I told you, she doesn't like going *anywhere* without me. If I let her run rampant with every ridiculous obsession, she'd spend her life screaming in fright every time she heard a noise. I didn't say anything bad – I didn't swear or threaten her or anything. I merely reminded her of our current contract, which says she has to try to handle social situations on her own," he explained. "She wasn't happy, but she understood. She's very honorable when it comes to things like that. She just needs a push now and then."

"Well, your blood levels are fine, except for a high level of triglycerides and cholesterol," Granger informed him. "It's all that untreated meat and oils you're eating. I can help that with medication."

Dmitri stood up. "Unless I'm in imminent danger of coronary crisis, I'll pass, thank you. Dr. Herzog put me through that once. The middle of a two-day walk is no place to wind up with a greasy stomach. I think I left a trail from Otaiga to home."

Granger grinned. "I can't argue with that, but believe me, it's much worse in a space suit. I'll mark down your refusal, but I do recommend you receive treatment at your first opportunity. Hold still and I'll get you those immune boosters."

"That's fine, thank you." Dmitri watched the doctor press the injection against his arm and pull the trigger, hearing the soft hiss. They didn't keep livestock of their own, but he was around the neighbor's animals enough to make the allergies bothersome.

"Any idea when I might be able to collar your sister?" Granger asked hopefully. "Phobias are about the easiest troublesome behavior to treat. There's no reason for her to go on year after year in fear of medical care. That kind of fear is a health risk in itself."

"I asked you to trust me on this. If you give her time to adjust to you as a person, to realize you are not a threat bent on harming her, it will all go over a lot easier. Let me break it to her when I think the time is right. Just be ready to jump, because you might not get a second chance."

"I'll accept that for the moment, but if Captain Sullivan insists, I have to comply."

Dmitri sighed. "We'll cross that asteroid field if we have to. Just warn me first."

Шесть ~ *Six* ~ *Elmenan*

Sarah wandered out to the yard, in a vortex over Mr. Ti'onam's words. Dmitri had always encouraged her quests for learning, daring her, even insulting her to make her work that much harder, but Dmitri was... just Dmitri. He never cared a micron about schooling, had quit – quit! – with a year and a half left. Dimi couldn't proof anything she came up with, point out flaws in her calculations or logic, couldn't explain concepts that confused her. She'd done the plant experiments on one of his insults, flaunting not only how incredibly brilliant she was, but surpassing herself to breed a different variation on one of Mrs. Al's favorite flowers. It had taken a year and a half of painstaking work, but she'd bathed in the glory for weeks, and every year when the new plants bloomed in ever-increasing numbers, Mrs. Al would sing her praises all over again.

She stopped in the workshed and found the axe. On drier days, they caught up on outdoor work, like splitting wood for the heater. The axe was one of the few tools Sarah was allowed to use, as long as she was in sight of the cabin. To her great annoyance, Dimi didn't trust her with sharp things. Like anyone would deliberately hurt themself with an axe! She walked over to the chopping block on the side of the workshed, and worked while she thought.

Mrs. Al was nice enough. Smothering, too affectionate and touchy for Sarah's tastes, but underneath it, she knew Mrs. Al meant well. But her approval meant less to Sarah than her brother's. Mrs. Al was the willing product of a repressive, ignorant society, who was so illiterate when they met she couldn't spell her own name. Sodium bicarb and vinegar impressed the hell out of Mrs. Al.

But Mr. Ti'onam – *Light of the Moons!* She wouldn't have dreamed such a thing in a hundred years! He was a *real* scientist, a *Navaran*, a scholarly person with a whole *alphabet* of letters after his name. He was a science officer on a *Star Explorer* – the Top Resource, the Head of the Department, the Expert. And he felt her work was *impressive!* Her method was *logical!* Her conclusions were *sound!* And it was worthy of *pub-li-ca-tion!*

Oh! She couldn't wait to write all that to Vladimir! She would write it tonight, if not sooner, mark it urgent, to be sent immediately, and with a little luck Dmitri would go with her into Vandijoc tomorrow and she could post it right away to Mr. Ennis. Vlad would hear about it within ten days, less if she was lucky. Her mind was so full of awe she never saw the figure approach from the side.

"Hahtitye, ya vam pomoch?" Andreiev asked in Russian.

Sarah shrieked, startled. She spun, nearly hitting the intruder with the axe. The blue-violet eyes locked on his as her blood pounded through her arteries. She reverted to the little glances, but her knees were weak, and her heart wouldn't slow. She clutched the axe to her chest.

"It's not polite to sneak up like that!" she scolded in her native tongue. *"You should better announce yourself, sir! If my axe slipped, I could have been hurt!"*

"I didn't mean to frighten you. I thought you might like help."

The fair cheeks blushed, the glances grew longer, but the axe stayed at the ready. *"I warn you, sir, I am well-versed in two forms of self-defense. My axe is quite sharp, and I have many hours of practice using it. If you attempt to touch me, you will lose your hand. And I am most capable of splitting wood by myself."* To prove her point, Sarah swung the axe high and brought it down violently into a started split, shattering the piece into three parts and burying the axehead so deep in the chopping block it took several tries and most of her weight to wrench it free.

"I believe you!" Andreiev backed up a step anyway. *"I thought more along the lines of placing the logs for you. You lose your rhythm, stopping all the time."*

"I can do this with my eyes closed. I don't need help," Sarah insisted, but in the back of her head she heard Dmitri's voice nagging that she was being rude and needed to accept help when it was offered. Forcing herself to be social was part of her contract, no matter how much she hated it. She usually set up for Dimi, and when he grew tired, he'd set them up for her.

"But it does break my rhythm," she granted with less hostility, blinking sideways at the man's soft brown eyes. *"You may help, but watch yourself carefully, sir; I will not be held responsible for any injuries incurred if you are in my way."*

"I will," Danil promised. *"I thought perhaps, too, we might talk of Russia. There are eight hundred people on the* Triumph, *but I am the only one born in the Motherland. It's nice to hear my language."* He pulled away the remains of the shattered log and stood a new length in its place.

Sarah nodded, swung, and cleaved the brittle wood easily in two. Andreiev moved a half out of the way and centered the remaining piece. *"I feel that way, at times."* One, two swings and the half was done. *"At*

75

least Dmitri speaks it, too."

"I'm Moscovite," Andreiev claimed, putting a new log on the block. *"Your family is from where, originally?"*

Sarah adjusted the log so it sat better. *"We were born all over the Russias."* Swing, crack, swing, crack. Pause, new piece, swing, grunt, swing, crack. *"Three of us were born in Tbilisi, four in Moscow, four in Kiev. I'm one of the Kievs. Dmitri's one of the odd ones. He was born in Israel. And Marina was born on Navara."*

Danil appeared perplexed. *"How many of you were there?"* He threw the split wood to the side and reached for another log.

"Trinadzat," Sarah replied proudly, swinging. *"I have seven brothers and five sisters. Had. There's only eleven of us now. Two died."*

"I'm sorry to hear that. I can't imagine what that was like," Andreiev marveled. *"Your house must have been enormous!"*

"In Kiev, it was big." She leaned the edge of the axe against the block, resting. *"On Navara, it was too small. They don't have big families, you know. We slept two or three to a bed, four or five in a room. How many family did you have?"*

"Just me. I am an only child."

It was Sarah's turn to be confused. *"Ni brati ili sestri?"* The idea was as foreign to her as an eye in the back of her head. She was near the end of the crowd; to grow up alone was unimaginable. To have a room to yourself – or even a bed – was a rare and not always welcome luxury.

Sarah tapped the axehead into the chopping block and took a step back to reinforce the distance between them.

"How horrible!" She looked Andreiev in the face. *"Who did you play with? Whose hand did you hold? What did you do when you were afraid? Who looked after you? Weren't you* lonely?"

"My parents cared for me," Danil answered, just as unable to comprehend her situation. *"There were plenty of other children in our housing unit, but if I wanted time to myself, all I had to do was go home. How did you ever manage to study with so many other people around?"*

"It was a wonderful *way to grow up!"* Sarah said, indignant. *"You never felt unloved, because there were so many people to love and be loved by. And everyone had different talents, so no matter what your problem or what you needed done, there was someone who could help. You needed a hitman and could afford the price, you went to Alexei. Homework? Katya. A dance partner? Viktor. Negotiate a deal? Dmitri. Stuck on an abstract analogy? Sergei. A playmate? Vladimir. Bored? David taught us more ways to get into trouble than we had a right to*

know." A smile softened her face.

"That must have been very nice." Andreiev smiled back. He leaned against the workshed, arms crossed. *"What was your talent – besides languages and botany?"*

Sarah gave a short laugh. *"I had my share of blackmail. 'I'll pay you a credit if you do my homework for me.' 'If you don't want to see Vlad cry, you'll finish this for me.' I don't know. I was a good Scout,"* she decided. *"I'd hide for hours, listening to what people were saying or doing, and then report back to my commander – in that case, my brother David. Or I'd be the problem solver. He'd come up with the schemes, and it was my job to either carry them out or figure out how someone else could."*

"You miss your family?"

The blue, blue eyes darted away, as if the subject were improper to speak of in public.

"I miss Russia." Sarah avoided the question with a touch of sadness. *"I miss snow, and the little park over on Banorak Street. They had the best playground there. Mother made Katya take us there every Sunday afternoon. I guess I'm a little big to play there now, but I'd like to see it again."*

"What about Moscow? Have you ever been to the museums at the Kremlin?" Andreiev asked. *"It's a very famous fortress. It took more than fifty years to restore it after World War Three."*

"I've heard of it. It's more than a thousand years old, isn't it? I was in Moscow once," she remembered. *"Father gave some big lecture at the University. I wasn't very old, but we were all supposed to sit quietly and look perfect and help Father be impressive. I remember him pointing out a big church in the square, and there was a long luncheon afterwards, boring as sand, and Vladimir threw up on David on the flight home – he gets flight-sick on almost any trip longer than a half-hour – and I remember David having a screaming fit and Father spanking him for punching Vlad so hard."*

Danil chuckled. *"It's funny, what's memorable for us as children. If you ever get back, you must go to the ..."*

"What the hell is he saying to her?" Dmitri stood at the window of the cabin in amazement, gazing toward the workshed. "She not only stopped working, she let go of the axe! I don't know if I've *ever* seen her talk to someone that long. Not even Mrs. Al."

"Lieutenant Andreiev must be quite the charmer." Granger winked as he looked for himself.

"Anyone that can charm that wildcat deserves a medal in my book."

"Mr. Kirushenko." Sullivan approached from the hall. "Mr. Ti'onam has gone over your sister's notes. I checked with Commander Guillaume; he apparently has copies of all her papers as well."

"You didn't find anything, did you?" Dmitri interrupted.

"Her work is simple in design, but extremely thorough," Ti'onam said. "With little further training, she will make a reputable scientist. I urge her to pursue publication of her botanical research. Her diagramming style is primitive, but reasonably precise. I reviewed nine volumes of both organized and random investigations, examined the textbooks in her possession, and consulted the Compound as to the computer files she accesses most often when she is there. I found no evidence of electronics research, investigations, or schematics."

"I am sorry if I accused your sister of wrongdoing," Captain Sullivan said, "but please realize, there remains some strong, if circumstantial, evidence that could still point to her. She may not be a prime focus, but I would be foolish if I didn't keep her within the pool of suspicion."

"Why not put me there as well?" Dmitri snapped. "Hell, better put Charlie there, too! He's over here all the time. Maybe you should interrogate his mother! While you're at it, why not investigate Guillaume himself? He's the one in charge! No one ever suspects the leader to be the one causing problems. What better position to be in, how better to cover up your tracks, than be the one in command?"

"No one in the employ of the research facility is above suspicion," Sullivan said brusquely. "Can you back up your accusation against Guillaume?"

"Not at all. So that theory holds about as much water as yours, doesn't it?"

* * *

In the evening, Dmitri caught up on his paperwork for Guillaume, including documenting the morning's excursion. He wanted the real facts to stand up against whatever the captain put in his report. He worked upstairs at the desk in his room, Sarah on his bed. He wrote what he'd seen and some of the theories passed around, but he left out the porshie-crap accusations.

Sarah lay sideways across his bed, belly-up, feet on the wall, head and shoulders hanging over the edge. Her white-blonde hair poured over the side in a waterfall to pool on the dusty floor below. She'd finished her letter to Vladimir; it lay sealed and waiting on her workbench for its journey to the Compound. She liked the quiet moments like this, when Dimi had time to listen. It was a peaceful and comforting time when she could really talk to him, a time when he was less like her boss and more like a friend.

"… He really did! Can you believe that?" she said.

"I told you it was a worthy project," Dmitri said, writing. "And you didn't want to show it to him. Navarans don't lie. At least, that's what we were always told. He seems pretty straight to me."

"Yeah. He's not as cold as the Navarans back on Navara. He doesn't look at you like you're some lower form of life that's biting him in the ankle. He talks to you like you're a person. I mean, he's still stiff and formal and Navarany and all, but… Maybe it's because he's on a ship with so many other humans. I suppose he's had to learn to deal with them on their level, just as we had to learn to deal with the Navarans when we lived with them."

"Could be. I saw you talking to that lieutenant this afternoon." Dmitri turned around in his chair. "Whatever could you have been talking about?"

Sarah stuck her upside-down tongue at him. "Don't waste my time! I told him right out, if he took even one step toward me, I'd cut his toes off with the axe. I gave a couple of good swings, and I think he got the point."

Her brother chuckled, returning to his notes. "If we ever get back to Earth, I'm taking you to Iceland."

Sarah rolled over, vines of hair cascading down her face. She clawed them aside. "Iceland? Why?"

"Because the only man you might ever impress that way would have to be a Burin-Jai or a Viking, and even I wouldn't sell you out to the Burin-Jai."

Sarah wrinkled her nose. "That's such a comfort. The Vikings came to Russia, too, you know. Maybe we're descended from one."

"Father, maybe, but there was nothing remotely Viking about Mother. Except maybe her hair."

"Perhaps, but I'm not *trying* to impress anyone. I *want* them to leave me alone. He only wanted to speak Russian with me, because no one else can. Did you know he's from Moscow? He's even heard of David's school there. He says it's a very good school. He didn't manage to get in, but both David *and* Sergei did. That's pretty impressive, two from one

79

family. He's an only child. Can you imagine that, Dim? Growing up with nobody else but you?"

"Imagine? No. Fantasize? Yes. Frequently."

"Go play in an asteroid field! You know what I mean. I haven't had much chance to watch that old biologist, but so far I haven't seen him do even one thing in the way of studying any biology. You'd think he'd have jumped at my entomological study. Maybe he has a subspecialty they brought him along for. I'll tell you, though." She wriggled backwards on the bed and rested on her elbows. "I *don't* like that Captain-guy. Did you see him this morning? How presumptuous of him to walk up and grab me like that! Who the hell does he think he is? Just because he's in charge of a big space ship, he can walk around doing whatever he likes? I don't care if he's the president of the Alliance itself; it doesn't give him the right to violate people's personal space."

"I don't think he meant anything by it." Dmitri closed the notebook, placing it in a drawer of the desk. "I'm not particularly impressed with him, either. He – nah, I probably shouldn't tell you."

"What?" Sarah sat up on her heels, intrigued. "Tell me!"

"I don't want you going overboard. All that stuff we found today? He actually had the nerve to think you could have done it."

Sarah blinked her eyes, aghast. "Me?! How could – ? You're kidding! Dimi – How in hell could I do something like that? I can't even smuggle a pair of real *underwear* past Dickerson!"

"I know. He said you were the only one smart enough around here to figure out a weapon like that. I told him it was the craziest thing I'd ever heard. Right to his face, too. I made him apologize."

"Good for you! He should thank his space engines *I* wasn't there to hear it! I would have floored him quick, whatever his rank is. *Pow!*" She punched two alternating fists through the air. "If I were going to do something like that, I'd make a hyperspace link, or some kind of radio interface so I could access the Compound's computers from here. I wouldn't even know where to begin. And no, not even on a challenge."

"I didn't suggest it. At least not right now, with all these officers poking around. Game of cards before you sleep in your *own* room?"

Sarah slid over to make room for him. "I guess so. The cards, at least. I'll think about the other."

* * *

"Observations?" Jack Sullivan asked his men. "We've pretty much agreed on the fact that at some point recently, an energy weapon has been used on this planet. Our host is apparently more opinionated than he first appeared, especially when crossed. It's the girl I have questions about. Her behavior is erratic, at best. No matter what her brother's reservations, she had to have been out to those trees at least once to map them; that's a fact he can't deny."

"If she was out there, it was probably before those marks were made," Andreiev said.

"Reasoning?"

"If I were an overeager cadet mapping trees with the intent to impress my commander, and I found scorch marks like that, I would make note of them," the Russian said. "I would mark down anything unusual, such as damage by fire, that might prove significant later on."

"Good point, Mr. Andreiev," Sullivan said. "Guillaume thought highly of her work. Ti'onam, you looked through her studies. Impressions?"

"I agree with the lieutenant. I scrutinized the maps; while she made note of such incidental details as animal warrens and insect hives, there was no indication she had witnessed any blackened trees. She possesses a formidable intellect, Captain. She is well-educated, detail oriented, highly self-motivated, and a skilled observer. She is, however, both young and inexperienced. All of her recent education she has taught herself from university texts; none that I examined covers any type of engineering practices, mostly hard science and literature in various languages. She does present as lacking confidence and self-direction, looking to her brother for confirmation of simple daily routines. Even though she is aware of a task in need of completion, she will wait until she receives permission to act."

"The word that came to my mind was 'spoiled'," Jack admitted. "What Sarah demands, Sarah seems to get. She sits where she wants, even if someone else is already there. She makes her own rules over what she'll eat, what chores she'll do, who can touch her, and her failure to act may be just as much avoidance as indecision. Her brother is hardly old enough to be in charge of himself; he may not have the skills necessary to parent a stubborn teen."

"I believe perhaps in this case, 'eccentric' may be a more appropriate term," Ti'onam suggested. "High intellect among humans is often accompanied by behaviors that are perceived as idiosyncratic. Nor does she seem to have had the benefit of a traditional family structure. She has been living in an alien culture that we ourselves are unfamiliar with. One cannot be faulted for a lack of etiquette if there has never been a common model to follow."

"That's entirely possible as well. Kyle? What do you think?"

"Well, he may not be a qualified human psychologist, but Ti'onam's hit on some valid points. I haven't been able to get close enough to do anything but observe," Granger said with regret. "I talked to her brother, but as you saw yourself, he's rather defensive of her. He's been taking care of her since he was seventeen. No doubt that could be a factor in any lack of propriety. But spoiled? I don't know. He seems to have a handle on her. In fact, I suspect his grip is stronger than we think. Did you see her reaction when she gave him trouble, and he turned strict?"

Jack thought back. "She quieted down and did what he requested."

"More than that. She looked ready to drop and kiss his feet, as if she would have done anything to disobey but didn't dare. *That* bothers me more than anything else. According to Dmitri, they sign a contract between them, specifying what rules they expect the other to follow. I can't help but wonder what happens if she doesn't comply. When she's not riled up, she seems a bit nervous, but then again, four strange men invaded her home without warning. It's very possible she feels threatened. I want to put pressure on the brother for that exam. I'm interested to see what this alleged medical phobia consists of. Is it real, or is she hiding something she doesn't want anyone to know about?"

Sullivan knew Granger well enough to know the doctor didn't speculate unless he had an inkling in the first place. "Ideas, Doc? Have you checked the Compound's records? They must have some sort of files on her."

"Nothing I'm willing to discuss at this point. I was holding off on reading charts until I completed her physical. I'd rather not have my observations tainted by someone else's ideas. It's easy enough to compare notes afterward to answer any questions."

Sullivan nodded. "Mr. Andreiev, you managed to talk with her today. How did she strike you?"

"I tried very hard *not* to get struck by her, Captain," Andreiev said in jest. "The tool she was using was very sharp, and she has excellent aim. At first she was upset, warned me very explicitly I was not to approach her, but after a while she did relax. She may be lonely, Captain. She's from an exceptionally large family – twelve or thirteen children, and she seemed rather sad when she spoke of them. She misses Russia. The rest of her family lives there with an uncle, and she does her best to stay in contact. She didn't mention any friends, just her family. She grew up with a lot of brothers, besides Dmitri. That could account for her being less than ladylike."

Sullivan's eyebrows rose. *"Thirteen?"* That seemed a bit excessive for one family, but it could have been the accumulation of several marriages or adoptions. "Rebellion, perhaps? She misses home, wants to go back, but the brother wants to stay. What better way to make it happen than to get him kicked off the research team."

"We have no proof of anything, Jack," Granger reminded him. "You could be right, but if you're not, you could start unnecessary problems between her and her brother. It could still boil down to the fact she's completely innocent. It's not at all unusual for sixteen year old girls to be emotionally volatile and moody as a caged lion. Brain development is progressing at a rate second only to infancy, adult hormones are surging in waves... They're trying to figure out who they are, and meanwhile they're already becoming someone else. It's simply the stage of life they're at."

Sullivan noticed his Phy-Sci Officer staring into space. "Ti'onam? You're either falling asleep, or thinking of something."

"Apologies, Captain. I was pondering an alternative scenario."

"Specify."

Ti'onam clasped his hands and raised them to his chin, a Navaran custom that was acceptable among humans. "I was attempting a deeper analysis of the conversations from this morning, before we discredit the information. Mr. Kirushenko claimed his sister was body-scanned for prohibited objects whenever she left the research facility. He did not claim he was."

Andreiev nodded. "A decoy, and he is the one actually carrying the items."

"That's an interesting proposition," Jack said. "And while Miss Kirushenko doesn't claim an interest in engineering studies, her brother can create plumbing to suit his needs. Perhaps we're looking at teamwork."

"Or perhaps he just didn't mention the fact that he gets scanned, too, and we're grasping at straws," Granger reminded the group.

Sullivan relented. "Okay. The scanning fact is easy enough to prove with a page on the handicom. We'll put all suspicions on hold until we come up with concrete data. Let's continue exactly as we've been doing. Ti'onam, see if you can stay connected with Miss Kirushenko on an intellectual level. Andreiev, play the homefront. If she'll talk to you about Russia, then talk about Russia until you've exhausted every last city and province, and see what else might slip. Kyle, keep an eye on her. Keep probing the brother for information, even if it's only on a medical level. If he's raised her that long, he must have a pretty good understanding of her. I have a feeling I cut myself out of a level of confidence this morning, but I'll play things by ear. Tomorrow I want to get a look at that explosion site, rain or shine. Let's see if we can't convince Mr. Kirushenko to bring his sister along, too."

Семь ~ Seven ~ Jombass

Ti'onam lay awake long into the night, running various scenarios in his head and analyzing them, undistracted by the occasional snores of his captain. Navarans had spent millennia studying the brain and learning to control its functions. By puberty, the Navaran child was expected to be skilled in a number of mental techniques; sleeping and thinking at the same time was one of them.

He lay on his back, the soft pillow rolled under his neck where it did not rub against his sensitive ears. The pillow was filled with the feathers of slaughtered fowl. The concept weighed heavily against his upbringing, yet he admired the resourcefulness of the maker in not wasting the smallest portion of life. Like he did every day in dealing with the strange cultures he met in his work in the Allied Fleet, he accepted the reality of the moment and allowed his personal feelings to fall away in the name of experience and education. He relaxed his body until it used only the minimum energy necessary to support autonomic functions, then split his mind in two through higher meditation. While most of his mind slept, even dreamed, one small lobe on the right continued to think. His thoughts drifted.

The nights on Sigma Tau Ceti were exceptionally quiet, not unlike those on Navara. There were no distractions, no intercoms to squeal an unexpected emergency during peaceful meditation, no junior-grade lieutenants on their first assignment who wanted to check every fact with him before proceeding on a task.

Navara ...

Blistering red cloudless sky tinting ten thousand kilometers of desert stirred by scorching winds, and the lethal heat day after day after day. Navara was a harsh planet. Navaran schools were harsher. Only a steadfast race could survive such conditions; crying wasted precious fluids and was unproductive in the face of survival. Indeed, passionate outbursts were among the worst sins; the child who cried on his first day of school was expelled until the following year, the stigma bringing unyielding shame to his family for generations. 'Bully' had no equivalent on Navara, but there were those students who felt it their duty to weed out weaker children through subtle torment, waiting for a smile, a tear, a raised fist. A human child in a Navaran school would not have the strength of mind or cultural

85

background required. Yet the Kirushenko girl claimed to have survived three years.

Three years.

Based on her language, manners, and education, Ti'onam could accept the girl's success as potential fact, but he was unable to ascertain *how*. She was unpredictably emotional in a variety of settings. Just one smile, one scowl, one exasperated sigh, and she would have been expelled.

Hypothesis one: she was lying to impress the crew, and her knowledge of Navaran language and customs came from tireless research. Two: despite his reservations, she spoke the truth, which meant, Three: she possessed a greater mental capability than even he had believed.

Ti'onam never worried, but the ideas evoked enough concern that he kept it on his mental list of Things To Investigate More Closely.

Speculate: Given that necessity generates innovation, and given that there are no remarkable records of personal crime in the Vandijoc area, why would an isolated rural teen require a highly technical, highly forbidden energy weapon capable of mass destruction?

Unable to form a viable hypothesis at this time.

The high-pitched creak of a floorboard broke into his thoughts, out of place in the stillness. His consciousness faded, blended, became one, and he pulled his mind awake. Yellow light glowed under the door. The light disappeared as the door to the adjacent lavatory closed and locked. The heater door opened, was loaded with fuel, and a fire started. Water splashed into the tub, and someone bathed. Not long after, the door unlocked and reopened. The glow reappeared and faded, but the stairs gave no sound. Instead, someone kindled the fire in the kitchen heater.

Ti'onam sat up, located his omnicomp in the dark, and checked the luminous chronometer reading. Some two hours remained before sunrise.

He rose and opened the door without a sound. From the dark shadows of the alcove, he had an unimpeded view across the main room to the kitchen, where a single lamp burned. The Kirushenko girl, dressed for the day, mixed something in a large bowl. Ti'onam watched unseen for several minutes, then retreated to his room, closed the door, and returned to bed, filing the information in his head for future reference.

Восемь ~ *Eight* ~ *Shenava*

"**A**nybody seen Sarah?" Dmitri asked as he hunted for a cleaner pan to make breakfast. "She's been up for a while; she made bread. She hasn't done that in a long time." Two perfect round loaves sat on the table. They were her fanciest recipe, her local interpretation of the dark Russian bread Father had liked. The ingredients weren't the same, but it came pretty close, in their memory.

Sullivan glanced around the cabin. "No, actually, I haven't. Is she outside?" The door bar was off its holders. He peered outside. The cloud cover seemed thinner, the day brighter, but his breath steamed in the chilly air.

Dmitri loaded the heater with wood and put water over for tea. He stepped past the captain and walked outside. "Sarah! Breakfast!"

Birds were the only response. He returned to the cabin, unhappy.

"Does she often run off first thing in the morning?" Granger inquired.

"Sometimes, if she's upset." Dmitri took one of the warm loaves and began to slice it. "But she wasn't upset when she went to bed, so I don't know. If she's up that early, it means she didn't sleep well. I doubt she went ahead without us, and I can't imagine her staying behind."

"She left the building approximately one hour and three minutes ago," Ti'onam said, "but I could not ascertain as to which direction she went."

"She could have gone to the Al's to ask about eggs or something. She should be back soon, then."

Andreiev approached. "Captain, may I speak with you for a moment? I – think I have a little problem."

"Of course, Mr. Andreiev." Jack stepped away from the kitchen to gain some privacy. "What's on your mind?"

"Captain, I feel very foolish, sir, but – I – can't find my omnicomp, sir."

"What do mean, you can't find it? Lieutenant, you were only assigned four pieces of equipment. How can you be missing twenty-five percent of your complement?"

"I-I-I don't know, sir!" Andreiev stuttered, perplexed. "I accounted for everything last night, as per regulation, and I know I returned them all to the pack. When I went to get them this morning, the omnicomp was not there."

"Did anyone see you with it? Did you see anyone near the room?"

"No, sir. I packed everything up before the briefing last night. Dr. Granger and I went to sleep after that, sir. Our door was closed. We would have heard someone enter the room."

Keep the suspicions on hold, he'd told everyone, but Jack felt as if he'd walked in a circle. Four other people besides his crew had been in the cabin the day before, and just one of them was currently present.

"Mr. Andreiev, I don't think I need to remind you this is a technology-prohibited planet, and I have full responsibility for any mishaps. If that omnicomp falls into local hands, we're going to be in a shipload of trouble. Find it!"

"Aye, sir," the Russian replied, and went to search yet again.

"Andreiev can't find his omni," Sullivan said to Granger as he returned to the kitchen. "How can you misplace something like that?"

Granger frowned. "He had it last night. I know he did. He was complaining about trying to calibrate it in the lamp light."

Dmitri stopped pouring tea. "That's that computer you were using yesterday, isn't it?"

Sullivan noticed the apprehensive change. "Yes. Have you seen it?"

"No. No," Dmitri said, turning back to the heater. "I haven't. When Sarah gets back, I'll ask her about it."

A wild possibility in the woods was one thing; this was too convenient for coincidence. Still, by his own rule, Jack had no hard evidence. "You may have known about the *Triumph* under Pete Karras, but you may not be familiar with it under my command. I have the finest crew in the Allied Fleet, and I run a tight ship. I don't take lightly to theft, especially of classified field equipment I am personally responsible for."

"Are you accusing Sarah again? I thought we straightened that out yesterday? She doesn't do those things! If she did, she would have to have a life-or-death reason. My sister is not a thief!"

"You don't find the fact that I'm missing equipment, and the fact your sister is nowhere to be found, isn't highly coincidental?" Sullivan demanded. "I will not have a mission jeopardized by a rebellious child. I want that omnicomp accounted for!"

Dmitri whirled to face his guest. "Sarah is *not* rebellious! She takes walks when she needs to think. It's nothing unusual; she does it all the time! She'll be back any minute. You may be in charge of your mission, *sir,* but *I* am in charge of my sister. She's trying her best to be social in a houseful of strangers. I don't need you scaring her into hiding by accusing her of things she's innocent of!"

"And your idea of handling her is to allow her to run off before daybreak without leaving you so much as a note? At best, it demonstrates irresponsibility on both your parts."

Dmitri opened his mouth to respond, but Granger interceded. "Why don't we give it until after breakfast? Maybe by then Andreiev will have found his omnicomp, and we can all get on with the day."

"You're right, Doc," Jack said. "We don't seem to have much of a choice at the moment, do we?"

Dmitri merely burned in silence and banged a stack of plates on the table.

The door latch lifted at the end of breakfast, opening just enough for the girl to slide through. She saw the table and stopped, half-in, half-out.

"I guess I'm late, huh?" Sarah slipped inside, closing the door behind her. She wore a light jacket of her brother's against the raw air, and today the bare feet were covered by hard leather shoes. Both of her hands were visible, and they were both empty.

"Where'd you go, Sar?" Dmitri asked. "I was getting worried."

"I couldn't sleep." She took off his jacket and hung it on a peg next to the door. "I went for a walk after it got light – that rise out past the Al's east clearing? I didn't think I'd be gone that long. I counted eight *galishnixan* out foraging. I got within two meters of one! If there's anything left to eat, I just need to wash my hands... ."

"Sar... ." Dmitri began, but Sullivan cut in.

Jack rose from the bench. "Miss Kirushenko?"

"Mr. Sullivan!" Dmitri objected, but he was outranked, outregulated, and ignored.

The girl shrank against the door as he approached. "Please don't touch me!" she reminded him nervously.

Sullivan gave her one of his best charming smiles, the easy-going, boyish grin he used to pick up women, the one that told them not only was he listening, but he could be counted on to understand as well.

"No, no." He reassured her with a wave of his hand. "No touching. I remember. I just wanted to ask you something, as a matter of course. You're the only one in the room I haven't had a chance to ask yet. One of my men has misplaced a piece of miniaturized equipment. It's a case about this big." He motioned with his hands. "It has a viewscreen and controls and a number of indicators on it. I didn't know if you might have seen it somewhere. It's very important that we find it," he emphasized, resisting the impulse to reach out and touch her arm, to humanize the contact, establish himself as a trustable friend. "We need it for today's exploration."

The girl shrank farther into the door, a move Jack hadn't thought possible. "E-everyone was still asleep when I left. I didn't see anyone with something like that. I misplace things, too, sometimes. Eventually they turn up, usually right where I thought I left them. If I see it, I'll be sure to bring it to you."

Jack broadened the warm grin. "Thank you. Remember, it's very important we find it. Soon."

"Yes, sir."

"Hurry up, Sar." Dmitri gave her permission to escape. "We've got to get moving, or we'll never get back before dark."

The girl headed for the washroom, with its waiting warm water. Her gait seemed off, as if a leg were sore or stiff. Her difficulty increased with each step. By the time she reached the stairs, she stopped. Her weight shifted from one leg to the other, she scratched a calf with the opposite foot, pressed her knees together. In desperation, she sprinted the last few meters to the hall, but disaster hit on her second step. With a clatter, the missing omnicomp fell to the floor, along with a band of cloth knotted in a circle.

Sarah froze. Slowly, slowly, she looked over her shoulder, eyes shining darker as her face paled. One glance told her five other pairs of eyes had seen it, too. Caught, just four walking steps from safety.

"Sarah!" Dmitri whispered.

Jack Sullivan's eyes narrowed. He'd had enough lies for one mission. One more, and he would order Guillaume to send a team to remove the pair to the compound, hold them, and see just how fast the whole thing would resolve itself.

Sullivan overemphasized his words. "Mr. Ti'onam, correct me if I'm mistaken, but I swore I heard someone say, 'My sister doesn't do those things, she's not a thief' and, 'I haven't seen anything like that'."

"That was the implied meaning," Ti'onam said.

Jack stalked toward the girl. Sarah spun to face him, on the verge of panic. She stepped backward, but her heel came down on the omnicomp housing. She eased up in mid-step, and had to hop to keep her balance. The extra seconds ate up her window of escape. As Sullivan reached her, Dmitri right behind, she collapsed on her knees with a choked shriek, arms crossed over her head.

Sullivan wasn't buying the fear act anymore. Anyone that afraid of punishment didn't steal to begin with. He bent down and picked up the omnicomp. "Mr. Andreiev! Do you recognize this?"

"Yes, sir. It is mine." He flushed, retrieving the instrument.

"I'll assume you aren't in the habit of storing scientific instruments under girl's skirts. You didn't perhaps loan it out and forget about it, did you?"

"No sir! I did not."

"Is it damaged?"

The lieutenant gave it a fast check. "I don't think so, sir. The power is reduced, but acceptable. Everything else appears to be functioning."

"Can it be recharged?"

"Aye, sir," Andreiev nodded, "but it takes time. With conservation, it will last the day."

"Miss Kirushenko!" Sullivan barked.

The girl shuddered and gave a soft cry.

"Stop it!" Dmitri growled. He knelt and rubbed her back. "You're scaring her worse!"

"Another word, Mr. Kirushenko, and you'll be confined to your room," the captain ordered. "Stand up, both of you."

"Stand up, Sar." Dmitri whispered Russian to her ear. *"Own up to it. I'm right here. I won't let him hurt you."*

She allowed herself to be guided to the bottom stair. Sarah sat hunched, head bent to her knees. Dmitri pulled her long hair out of her face and flipped it down her back, smoothing it straight with his fingers.

"I want to know where you've been for the past two hours," Sullivan demanded. "Who did you have contact with? Who did you just show that omnicomp to?"

The girl stared at him with confusion.

"Yevo otvechai," her brother prompted, poking her with an elbow.

Sullivan whipped his head around to Andreiev. "What did he say?" The last thing he needed was coded messages. It was slower than a translator cube, but Jack would have to have Ti'onam program an omnicomp for recording and translating Russian, and any other language the girl knew. Unfortunately, the current availability of programs to translate Tau Cetan languages amounted to ten sentences meant to demonstrate the sound and rhythm of the particular dialect, not convey useful skills. In that area, Sullivan was at their mercy.

Dmitri glared. "I told her to answer you."

"Aye, sir. That is what he said," Andreiev agreed.

"I think we've established the fact that everyone in this room is fluent in Interstellar English," Sullivan said. "Things will go a lot smoother if we stay with the confines of one language and not waste time translating every sentence. Where did you go?"

Sarah snuggled against her brother. "Exactly where I said I did! The big rise east of the Aletneshfaja's. There's a hill that drops thirty or forty meters before the stream. You can see over the trees. If the sun is going to rise, that's the only place you'll see it around here, without walking back to Otaiga."

"Who did you meet there? That boy Charlie?"

"No one! Honest! I met no one, and no one saw me. The Al's are busy with their livestock at that hour. It's too hard for Mrs. Al to climb such a hill, and I would not meet Charlie alone in such a place."

"Why not?"

Sarah shook her head just a little, as if violating propriety was a worse crime than theft. "It's not right."

"Your honesty has proven itself grossly unreliable," Sullivan growled. "Why should I believe you?"

"Because it's the *truth*! I never lied! You never asked me if I had it; I never denied that! I said if I *saw* it, I would return it. I was – I was going to leave it in the other room, as if it had been forgotten," she confessed.

"If memory serves, Captain, she is correct," the Navaran agreed. "She denied seeing anyone *with* the omnicomp, but she never denied taking the omnicomp herself."

Sullivan's jaw clenched, but he held his tongue. "Unfortunately, I do trust your honesty, Mr. Ti'onam. Split hairs aside, Miss Kirushenko, I hope you've had enough upbringing to understand that snooping through other people's property and helping yourself to whatever suits your fancy is morally objectionable. Most people consider that theft, and theft is punishable by law."

"I didn't snoop! I never *dreamed* of taking it! It was just *there*! I came out of the bathroom last night and the door was open, and it was just sitting there on the bed. No one was there to ask, and it sounded like you were discussing something important in the other room, so I didn't want to disturb you. I only meant to look it over and put it back, but when I touched that button there, it opened." Sarah pointed a finger at the omnicomp as if it had bewitched her, and the machine was entirely to blame.

"And then the display came on and started flashing a reading of some sort, so I walked around the room to see if the numbers changed – and they did! I guess I got carried away, because the next thing I knew I was upstairs. By then it was very late, and I figured everyone was asleep. I never *meant* to take it! It kept me awake all night, figuring out the different functions.

"I snuck out early, figuring I could get some readings on the indigenous life forms and get back before anyone was awake. I reasoned if I left it in the bathroom, maybe you would think you'd left it there by accident. I got caught up in watching the *galishnixan* and lost track of time. Nobody saw me with it, I made sure of that. I'm not stupid; I know the rules about technology. I'm *sorry!*"

Sullivan wasn't moved. "Mr. Andreiev, replay the last thirty minutes of recordings, please."

"Aye, sir." Andreiev thumbed the controls, and the girl's voice could be heard squealing.

"Oh my goodness! Look at them! Come here! Come on! Don't run. I won't hurt you. Come here! I wish Vlad could see you. I wonder if this thing prints photographs?" On the tiny viewscreen, three fat, tailless squirrels – *galishnixan* – stretched up on their hind legs, sniffing the air in her direction. The visual jiggled and jumped as she knelt, calling to them.

Sarah closed her eyes, face crimson at her voice booming through the cabin. "I didn't know it recorded audio, too."

"Mr. Andreiev, maintain every minute of her recordings in the memory," Captain Sullivan ordered. "When we return from today's investigation, I want them analyzed as to time factors, content, and contacts. I want to know every single thing that omnicomp was used for."

"Aye, sir," Andreiev agreed, though the task would add hours to his own work.

"Miss Kirushenko! For the record: I view the unauthorized borrowing and/or use of my crew's equipment to fall under the category of theft," Sullivan said sternly. "If you should happen to wander off with our belongings again, I will in no uncertain terms file charges under the category of theft of Allied Fleet property, and enforce the penalties incurred therein. Do I make myself clear?"

"Yes, sir."

"Repeat it back to me."

The girl flashed a scowl but repeated, "If I touch any of your things again without express permission, you will charge me, wrong or right, with felonious acquisition."

"Correct. Now see to it you remember. And Mr. Kirushenko: I suggest you keep a tighter rein on your ward, or I will take into consideration charges of neglect. You had no knowledge of her whereabouts for a minimum of two hours, and you weren't the least bit concerned. I find that highly irresponsible of a guardian," Sullivan cautioned. "Gentlemen, we've wasted enough time. Gather your things. We'll rendezvous outside in five minutes."

Девять ~ *Nine* ~ *Dossan*

They made their way by means of Guillaume's coordinates and the omnicomps for much of the journey; Sarah's maps didn't extend so far. As they closed in, they encountered a downed tree, its leaves withered yellow, then a second, then the light in the forest brightened. The whole forest seemed to disappear, and before them lay a grisly scene of botanical carnage, as if the trees themselves had gone to battle and been massacred. Sarah pushed through the group to stand tight with Dmitri. She grabbed the waist of her brother's pants, but he reached behind and took her hand in his, squeezing it.

"Unbelievable," Jack Sullivan murmured, surveying the destruction. "The video doesn't do it justice."

A hectare and a half of trees lay flattened like so much kindling. In the middle of the holocaust, the ground lay churned and cratered, washed smoother again by the recent rains. Moving outward, trunks lay shattered and splintered on the ground, blown clear off their stumps, pointing away from the center like the spokes of some gigantic wheel. In the next ring of destruction, the trees had been uprooted as they fell over. Thick roots stretched four meters into the air, paying homage to the center emptiness. Beyond that, where the travelers stood, less sturdy trees leaned as if knocked askew by an unseen elbow.

Vandijoc's trees stood hardy and tall, sixty meters or more, nurtured by alternating seasons of moisture and sun. A good tree was semi-permanent, outliving a Tau Cetan and several generations of descendants. To see so many of them lying tortured and flat was... eerily unnatural, like the nose-cone of a flyer sticking out of sand, or a house flipped upside down.

"Now I know how an ant feels after you step on grass," Sarah said.

"Radiation?" Sullivan asked quietly, as if disturbing the peace would cause the culprit to reappear.

"Elevated, but not severely," Granger replied. "Deltas, gammas, and theta particles all within acceptable limits for single limited exposure. Warshan's rays are reading only a trace. I'd say we've got about two hours before we'll be at maximum safe exposure level. Of course, that's not saying we'll be better off if we don't stay that long. It's not like we're catching a moley beam out of the area. It will take time to put some distance between us and the source."

Sarah dared resorting to her little glances. "I understand the deltas, gammas, and thetas, but what's different with the – Warsham's? – rays? I don't think I've ever heard of them."

"Warshan's. They're a by-product caused by the breakdown of a half-dozen or so radioactive compounds," Granger explained, "named, of course, for Warshan, who identified them. They don't last particularly long, but they're rather nasty. They cause soft-tissue damage – a heavy enough exposure, and in a matter of hours your skin starts to bubble and peel. If you're still alive by the time you get treatment, your muscles and organs blister next. The survival rate for a high dose is less than ten percent."

Dmitri swallowed hard. "I didn't need to hear that."

Sarah gripped his hand even tighter. "Are you absolutely sure we're safe right now?"

"If it wasn't, my dear, you can bet your money I wouldn't be standing here," Granger said, and followed the captain's lead into the destruction.

The epicenter of the blast was a crater seven meters wide, sloping down to a narrow pit. Jack stepped over the rim and half-ran, half slid the short drop, followed by Ti'onam. Dmitri stayed at the top, holding Sarah's hand. She gave a tug toward the crater, but he pulled her back.

"This looks like the origin," Sullivan said, surveying the depressed area in the center. "Readings, Ti'onam?"

"There is an elevation in radiation," Ti'onam confirmed, kneeling by the central core. "Gamma particles, twenty percent above norm, beta particles, eleven percent, Warshan's rays, eight percent above normal. I am detecting an unusually high concentration of aliothite."

The captain tried to remember his chemistry. "Aliothite? Isn't that rare?"

"It's only known to exist in five star systems," a distinctly female voice answered behind him.

Sullivan turned.

Freed of her brother's restraint, Sarah radiated an eager enthusiasm. She turned to Ti'onam. "Discovered in the Epsilon Ursa Major system, also known as Alioth, and subsequently on New Asia, Algedi, Izar II, and Beta Leoni. Correct?"

"Quite correct."

"You've been to those places?" Sullivan asked.

"Goodness no! Moscow State University course guide, Chemistry 101, 102, 231, 232, 335 and 374," Sarah explained with pride. "Of course, that's just the texts. I can't get the supplies or equipment to do most of the lab work. I do as much as I can when I visit the compound, but Commander Guillaume claims he doesn't have the staff to have someone babysit me in the labs around the clock, so at most I work through two or three short projects."

"She's not allowed anywhere but communications without an escort." Dmitri came up behind her, brushing dirt off his leg where he'd slipped coming down. "She got caught trying to program the main replicators without permission. Marc's threatened to ban her from the complex if she messes with anything again."

"He overreacted," Sarah insisted. "I was trying to remember the code for chocolate pudding. I've never touched them since."

Sullivan turned back to his work; there was enough to do without siblings squabbling over past incidents. He estimated the measure of the center of the pit with his hands. "It's about ten centimeters wide here in the middle. Can you tell how deep it goes, Ti'onam?"

"The center narrows, but appears to continue downward more than one hundred meters."

Sarah's eyes widened in amazement, and she moved so fast she cracked heads with Sullivan, trying to peer into the hole. "Supra cosmic! As in, if I dropped a stone down that hole, it would fall a hundred meters without stopping? Does that qualify as a bottomless pit?" Her eyes scanned the ground for a suitable pebble.

"If the stone were small enough and did not catch on subterranean materials, in theory, yes," Ti'onam said. "However, it is beyond improbable that the chamber does not come to an end beyond the range of my scan. Therefore, it should not be classified as bottomless."

"A hundred meters qualifies as bottomless in my book. Don't even think you're playing near it, either." Dmitri pulled on her sleeve. "You have no idea if it's a soft edge or not. You could collapse it wider and kill us all. Get back up top."

Soft edge – the term Father gave to the edges of an archaeological dig that couldn't support weight. One bad step and down you'd go, however deep the excavation went. The idea hit home. Sarah sat back, eyeing the hole with respect.

"You know, that's probably a very good idea," Sullivan said. She may have meant well, but every time the Kirushenko girl interrupted, they lost precious minutes.

Or was that her purpose? After the morning, he'd reinstated all his suspicions, conceivable or not. He laid a hand on Dmitri's shoulder and turned him toward the slope.

"We *don't* know how safe it is down here. The less stress we put on it, the better it's bound to be. There's no point in risking more lives than necessary. Get back up top. If we have trouble, we'll need you in position to help."

"Will do," Dmitri agreed. He pulled his sister by the hand; she followed reluctantly.

Sullivan got back on track. "Where were we? Judging by the blast pattern, I would say this was an explosion, not an impact crater. Guesses, Ti'onam, at what could cause such an explosion?"

"I have no workable hypothesis at this moment." Ti'onam readjusted the omnicomp to scan for a new set of data. "I concur the damage was caused by an explosion, but I am currently unable to ascertain exactly what the causative agent was. I detect a high iron content in the soil surrounding the center crater, along with traces of aliothite, jovium, nickel, sulfur, silica, and carbon."

"Could this explosion have been caused by an artificial device containing those compounds?"

"Unknown. I am unaware of any instances of jovium being used in a weapon of mass destruction. Nor is it volatile enough to explode in its natural state. It must have a heavy industrial processing to be of any value – impossible in this society. I am interested in the central core of the crater, however. The atmosphere directly around the opening reads traces of radioactive gasses. If the area was known for volcanic activity, I would accept that the shaft was similar to a volcanic vent, but I detect no significant change of thermal radiation, no deposits of magma, ash, or volcanic stones. There is evidence of charring of nearby trees from the explosion, but not to the degree expected from a volcanic disturbance."

"And no evidence of little burned spots," Sullivan said, glancing around. "Unfortunately, you can't track planetary-wide volcanic activity with an omnicomp, but I know who can." He dug his handicom from his carry pack. "Mr. Raines?"

"Cash here, Captain," a female voice answered.

"Mr. Cash?" Ferrine Cash was a seasoned member of the bridge crew and could more than adequately handle the ship in a routine orbit, but he couldn't help asking, "Where's Mr. Raines?"

"Off duty until 1900, Captain. Shall I transfer you to his quarters?"

"No, no need to bother him," Sullivan said. "You can answer my questions just as well. Mr. Cash, lock my signal and scan this area for volcanic activity. Anything within a thousand-kilometer radius."

"Presently, sir?"

"Ideally."

"Currently, we're orbiting out of range, Captain. I can give you the information from our last orbit, approximately two hours ago."

"That would be fine."

There was a short pause as the information was recalled from the ship's vast computers. "Captain? Sensors read no active volcanic activity anywhere near the coordinates you listed. The nearest signs of surface-level volcanic turbulence are approximately 2500 kilometers north-east of your current position."

"Thank you, Ferrine. That's good to know. Sullivan out." He closed the transmitter to the handicom and returned it to its hiding place with a sigh.

"So much for that theory. Next?"

* * *

Dmitri dragged Sarah far from the crater. The other two officers were at opposite ends of the destruction zone, busy with their individual tasks. The Russian officer was closer, examining one of the downed trees.

"You owe him an apology for this morning," Dmitri reminded her. "Now's as good a time as any."

"I can't do that!" If she spoke to the officer, he might speak back.

"You can, and you will," Dmitri decided. "You stole his equipment, made him look bad in front of his commanding officer. They're not from Guillaume's isolated happy family grouping, Sar. They're trained military men. They have protocols and penalties. At some point, he *will* get in trouble for you taking his recorder. The least you can do is tell him you're sorry, and that he's allowed to break your fingers if you ever do something like that again."

Sarah's fingers curled inward for safety. "I will not tell him any such thing! I didn't steal it! I just … borrowed it for a little while."

"Fine. I'll tell him the finger part, but get going." Dmitri gave her a no-nonsense push in Andreiev's direction. Sarah turned to plead, but it was met with a hard look that dared her to disobey.

Damn her unceasing need to know things! Her leaden feet shuffled forward.

Dmitri hiked himself onto a fallen trunk. "I'll be right here. You're okay."

Heart pounding in a chest that felt constricted smaller than a heater pipe, Sarah tiptoed within three meters of Andreiev's back, waiting silently to be noticed. Nerves on edge, if he'd turned and said a single sharp word, she would have collapsed in tears. At last she was forced to speak up.

"That's a *shaparika* tree," Sarah offered louder than she meant. "You can tell by the purple streaks on the bark. The leaves have radially symmetric veins, and they put out large but inedible dicot seed pods. The wood is softer and more prone to insect damage than others, but they grow faster than harder woods."

The young man turned to look at her. He had dark eyes, like most of her brothers, but his hair was a lighter brown. His face was boyishly round, like Dmitri's, pleasantly inviting. He smiled at her. "*Spasiba.* That's a help, I guess. I'm not much of a botanist."

"*I'm most sorry to take your equipment without permission,*" Sarah said rapidly in Russian while she still had the nerve. "*It will not happen again. I apologize if I have caused you trouble with your commander. I take full responsibility, and I am prepared to accept punishment for you. It was my error of judgment, not yours. I assure you, I in no way violated the rules regarding technology.*"

Andreiev's face radiated forgiveness. "*Apology accepted. However, I don't think you can take my reprimand for me. It was my equipment, I left it out, the responsibility was still mine. Thank you for the offer. I would have been happy to show it to you, if you'd asked.*"

Sarah nodded, and turned to flee.

"Don't run away so fast. I could use your help with this. You must know more about these trees?"

"I can't interfere with your work. A-ask the biologist! I-I have to get back to Dmitri." Before he could say another word, she was gone.

Close. Almost! Not that time, either. Sarah retreated from the officers and scrounged the forest for small stones among the rocky outcroppings of the area. With careful hunting she found a few of use, along with many more *shaparika* seeds in various stages of sprouting. While the officers clustered with Dmitri to discuss their findings, she sneaked back to the crater to sink a stone in the irresistible center pit. Trying to hit a ten-centimeter hole three meters away and three meters up was next to impossible, but it was still fun to try. *Weight plus force equaled speed, minus wind resistance, accounting for gravity...* She could do the math, but she couldn't make her arm understand exactly what it needed to do.

Nope. So close! Damn!

"Yes!" Sarah squealed as one stone *ping'd* on something hard and actually appeared to go down the hole. "I did it!"

She raised her arms high in victory, only to gasp as her hand was grabbed from behind and held while the remaining stones and seeds were swept from her fingers. She wrenched away, and lost her footing on the edge of the crater.

Sullivan didn't let her fall, maintaining his hold until she regained her balance. She held the assaulted hand close, cringing.

"I would thank you not to throw stones down there, Miss Kirushenko," the captain said. "We've left some rather sophisticated recording devices buried around the hole, and they don't need to be disturbed or broken in the name of target practice."

The wary face nodded. She spun to flee, only to trample her brother as he ran up behind her.

"You okay?" Dmitri asked as she tackled him in a strong embrace. "We're starting back. Get over there with the group." He gave her a swat on the rump as she bounded for the spot where they'd first entered the area.

Dmitri glared at the captain. "You couldn't have simply asked her to stop? I'll say it again: please refrain from touching her. She doesn't like it."

"And I don't like my data recorders being pelted with rocks in the name of entertainment," Sullivan said, not the least bit intimidated. "If she damaged one, I'm four days away from a replacement. That's too long for me to take a chance on being misinterpreted. I believe my point was made without any undue injury to your sister. I'm afraid my mission takes precedence over personal comfort."

"That may be a valid fact, but I will ask you once again: let me handle my sister. If you have a problem, need something from her, want her cooperation, need her out of the way, please ask me. I can get her to agree with a lot less stress than if you confront her directly. She'll never get used to you if you keep attacking her like that. *Please*."

"I was unaware that removing stones from a hand constituted an attack." Sullivan pursed his lips, then gave a nod. "All right. Unless I feel the situation requires immediate intervention, I will not approach her directly, though I fail to see how she can function as a translator that way. In the meantime, I expect you to keep her under tighter control."

"Translating's not a problem," Dmitri insisted. "She knows that's her job. She can handle that. A helpful hint: if you grant her a little respect where it's deserved, you'll find she'll live up to that respect. Guillaume caught on to that fast. He treats her as a full-fledged member of his crew, expects as much out of her as he does them, and she hasn't failed him yet. You might do well to try it."

"Respect is generally something that has to be earned," Sullivan said. "And as far as I'm concerned, she has a long way to go."

Sarah stayed close to her brother on the return hike, sometimes falling back near the Navaran, but never-never near that bossy captain. She spoke quietly when spoken to, but felt, after all the screw-ups today, it just might be better if she didn't draw any more bad attention to herself.

How was she supposed to know they'd left sensors down there, when they'd chased her away in the first place?

They rested briefly at the half-way point. Sarah sat on the damp ground and leaned against a tree behind her brother. She closed her eyes, listening to the conversations. Miserable with embarrassment, smothered by shame, she turned her thoughts inward, pretending there was nothing wrong in the world and the Allied Space Fleet hadn't invaded their undiscovered corner of the universe. No thanks for getting hours' worth of new data, just a hissy-fit over not telling anyone first. *Grown-ups.* She didn't miss them for anything! When she went back home and grew up, she'd never treat someone that way, ever.

Dmitri's sudden "Look!" snapped Sarah from her swim in self-pity. A black-furred animal the size of a large rabbit bounded over Andreiev and through their circle, giving them no heed. It sprinted several meters past, changed direction sharply and sped off elsewhere.

Andreiev straightened his legs out. "I didn't know this was the middle of the highway."

"Are all the animals that indifferent to people?" Jack asked. He checked behind to make sure there weren't more.

"Hey! Easy there!" Granger protested as his hand almost twisted from his arm. "Where's the fire?"

"Come *on!*" Sarah tried desperately to pull him to his feet. She watched the animal disappear into the undergrowth. "It's getting away! How could you sit there with all that equipment and let it get away? What kind of a biologist *are* you? We'll never have a chance like this again! It's not *fair!*"

Granger hauled himself up, avoiding her attempt to yank him down the path. "Slow down a minute, Missy! Just what was that, to start with?"

"You don't care!" Sarah realized. "You're not from around here, so you don't care! This is just some specific agenda to you, and you couldn't care less about the greater need for information! It's a *chirfana,* and I've only seen one other in all the time I've been here, and that one was dead. They're quite rare and their fur is highly prized, but we'll never know anything else about them because we didn't go after it!"

Dmitri whistled. "You sure, Sar? Man! Wouldn't Charlie like to get a hold of that!"

Jack stood up. "Is it dangerous?"

"They're herbivores. They'll fight if cornered." Sarah grabbed for Granger's omnicomp, flipped the flap out of the way, and aimed it in the animal's direction. She reached for the activation switch, but the controls on this one were – *different? How could that be?*

Granger pulled the omni back before she could explore it further, activating it himself. Ti'onam, too, realized the fast-fading opportunity, and scanned the area belatedly.

"I wonder where it was going so fast?" Dmitri said. "It's a little late for mating season."

"Maybe it's just a straggler. I wish Charlie were here to see it," Sarah said. "He'll never believe us."

"Charlie would have tracked it until he killed it," Dmitri reminded her. "You know the price he could get for a *chirfana* skin?"

"Hmph! Leave it to you to think about killing something rare." Sarah seized Granger's omni again, shame forgotten in the name of discovery. "Is it still around? Did you get any readings? There's only some still-photos in the computer files on them. I don't think anybody's ever gotten video footage. Guillaume would have gone supernova if we'd gotten that! How come your omni's different from the other two? Is it an older model, or does it do different things?"

"I thought you promised not to touch the equipment?" Once more Granger wrestled his machine from curious hands. "It's considered polite to ask first."

The girl's hands pulled back and folded themselves against her middle; the head bent. "I promised I wouldn't walk off with it," she said meekly. "I can't do that, it's still attached to you."

"And it's going to stay that way. This is a m– " Granger stopped as Dmitri gave a hacking cough. He caught the boy's shake of his head. "– more advanced biological version. It's extremely sensitive, and the less you play with it, the better off you'll be. I've got a few readings on birds, and a rodent or two on the ground, but I'll analyze them later. If you'd like, I can give you the data when I finish."

"Too Moonstruck for words!" Sarah breathed, mixing Terran and Tau Cetan metaphors. "I would be most grateful if you would do that! Did you hear that, Dim? He got readings on the birds!" But Dmitri had already shouldered his pack to walk; the others followed his lead. She hurried to catch up.

"Are you always so full of questions, Miss Kirushenko?" Sullivan asked.

Sarah dared to validate herself. "When there's something I wish to know or don't understand. If Commander Guillaume would just *trust* me with a little piece of wizardry like that, I'd be able to ask less, explain more, and the whole database for the planet would be that much further ahead that much faster. It's not fair! He let *you* take things out here! Marc can be very narrow-minded when it comes to research."

Sullivan suppressed a smile. "He didn't let me take anything. I told him what I was taking."

The girl stopped dead in the middle of the group; Granger narrowly avoided crashing into her. She opened her mouth to protest, but no words would come out. Heaving a strangled cry, she flounced off the path to lean against a tree, waiting for the impotent anger to fade.

Dmitri grinned. "Oh, you've made her mad now! Marc's going to get an earful next time she sees him. She's been trying to get something more advanced out of there for years. He said even if he wasn't bound by the interference reg's, he couldn't let her have a piece of field equipment until she was legally old enough to be responsible for it."

"I don't see what difference a year makes!" Sarah called from her sulking spot. "I should be on my third university degree by now! You'd think that would count for *something!*" Tearing herself from the tree, she jogged to catch up.

"Knowledge isn't everything, Miss Kirushenko," Jack pointed out. "Experience is almost as important. What good is information without application? You can read a dozen texts on piloting a ship, but until you've actually done it at least once, the knowledge is meaningless."

"I know, I know, I know," Sarah griped sourly. "But that's only true in *some* cases." She pushed past her brother and walked backward in front of the captain. "It *is* true in languages," she agreed. "You can have an excellent vocabulary and perfect grammar and written skills, but unless you *hear* the language spoken, you'll never know intonation, rhythm, pitch, accent, phonetics, and all that stuff. Then, if you're *really* looking for fluency, you have to throw in colloquialisms, slang, and dialect.

That stuff's rarely in language texts.

"But all that *isn't* true in math or history or art. I can look at a photo of a fifth-century Pre-Sil'anak weather mural, study the form, style, content of subject, content of materials, and nuclear dating all in a text, and when presented with an actual artifact, compare the present data with the learned data and come to the proper conclusion based on prior learning. True, a hologram can misrepresent color and depth, and doesn't always accurately replicate texture or give you odor or taste, but the knowledge base is sound."

"That may be, but what about wisdom?"

"Wisdom?" Sarah wrinkled her nose in distaste. "Wisdom's just a philosophical state of being. A word ascribed to cranky old scholars who think they know the answer to every question."

"Yes," Jack conceded, "but people seek out those scholars precisely *because* they are learned people who tend to know right from wrong more often than not. Wisdom should be a by-product of knowledge."

"That's exactly my *point*, though! I *know* the rules regarding use of restricted equipment beyond the compound gates! I can write them out from memory! Test me on them if you don't believe me! All I need is the chance to *prove* myself!"

"What do the regulations say about misappropriation?"

Sarah stopped walking again, hurt plain on her face. "You walked me into that trap on purpose. It's not nice to take advantage of people's trust like that."

"I think you walked into that on your own," Sullivan said with amusement. "It merely underscores my point that wisdom comes with age and experience." He stepped around her and continued on the path.

"Grown-ups are all alike!" she said bitterly. "The older I get, the more I understand why we've stayed away from Earth. It doesn't matter if you're six or sixteen, you get treated the same, as long as there's somebody who thinks they're better than you."

Sarah ran up and tagged her brother on the arm. "Race you!" she challenged, knowing full well he couldn't when grown-ups were around. She sprinted ahead as fast as she could.

* * *

Sarah's hiking bag sat in her chair, confirming the fact she did arrive home at some point. Mrs. Aletneshfaja had made and left a meal waiting. She'd taken Sarah's letter with her, to bring to the mail drop in the village. The darkening skies began to drizzle as the temperatures fell with the setting of the hidden sun; the men walked the last three minutes in a steady, cold rain. The girl didn't appear for dinner, despite her brother's call.

Dmitri sought her out before he went to bed. Using a baking pan as a tray, he assembled a light snack and carried it to her room. He placed it on her workbench, found her lamp, and lit it. Overhead, a downpour thundered with symphonic fury.

"You in here?"

"Yeah," came a breath from the direction of her closet.

"Coming out? I brought tea for us."

"Not yet."

"Always got to make it difficult." Dmitri carried the lamp to the doorless space in one hand and the makeshift tray in the other, placed them on the floor, and sat down. Sarah sprawled belly-down on top of her storage trunk, knees bent, toes against the wall. Her arms crossed under her chin as she stared into what had been darkness. She didn't turn, but he could see the shining tear-marks on her cheek in the lamplight.

"You okay?"

It was a deeper question than it sounded. If too upset, Sarah had been known to cry for days on end, and the following melancholia would last for weeks, sometimes months.

"Yeah." She coughed, sniffed, and knew she was. At least for now.

"Then sit up," Dmitri instructed, and poured a cup of tea from a covered pitcher.

She pulled her knees under her and pushed until she sat, balanced cross-legged on the curved lid of the trunk. She ran the back of her sleeve under her nose all the way to her elbow before accepting the cup. Dmitri poured himself a cup, then offered her a plate of bread bits spread with one of Mrs. Al's soft cheeses and shreds of raw vegetable – a known weakness of hers. Sarah stared vacantly at the plate before taking one of the treats.

"He got you good this afternoon," Dmitri remarked with a sense of admiration. He stuffed an entire bread bit in his mouth at once and tried to chew. "It was rather funny, actually. You were so busy waving your own flag, you forgot to watch where the parade was going."

"Thank you so much for reminding me." Sarah took a morose sip of tea. It was hot but not blistering, and gruesomely sweet. Extra-sweet tea was one of the few things they shared in common. The drink was the only comforting thing in a horrible damned day that should have been so

106

damned fascinating. She picked the green sliver off her bread bit, ate it, licked away the cheese, then nibbled the bread.

Dmitri turned serious, taking another snack and biting only half this time. "You have no stinking idea how mad I am. I mean, what the hell were you *thinking* this morning?"

"I don't know!" Sarah wailed. "I never meant to get caught."

"Caught or not, Sar, you know what kind of an *idiot* I looked like? Swearing up and down you couldn't have taken that thing, that you aren't in the habit of stealing things –"

"I've never stolen *anything*!"

"– and you walk in with empty hands, and I'm really proud to prove my point after Sullivan's crazy idea yesterday, figuring now maybe he'll really believe me, and son of a bitch, it drops out of your dress because you *did* steal it! You not only made yourself look like a lying thief – and a lousy one at that – but you made *me* out to be a liar as well! Now how the hell can I ever defend you? He'll never believe a word I say."

"Don't you think I know that?" Sarah cried anew. "I never meant to take it. That Navaran – Ti'onam – was using one. He showed it to me when I asked, and I knew better than even to point at it! But when I saw that other one just lying there, with no one around, I didn't think it would hurt for just a minute. I never meant for anyone to find out! I got that Mr. Andreiev in trouble, so now he'll be mad at me, too, and to top it off I had to spend the day next to those people. Danil asked me to identify some of the trees for him, but I couldn't. I couldn't face him after that!" She sniffed hard, no longer fighting the tears.

"You can't kick my *zhopa* any harder than I am already, but even a hundred apologies aren't going to make anybody forget today. The whole rest of the time they're here, no matter what I do right, they're only going to remember I took an omnicomp without permission. And that Captain Sullivan is rotten enough to rat about it to Marc, and I'll *never* be trusted, *ever*! Red Moon rising, I hate that captain!" Sigma Tau Ceti's red moon, Allash, was the biggest of the three, and folklore held it was the most powerful. Sarah knew better than to invoke the wrath of Allash, but Mrs. Al wasn't around to lecture her.

Dmitri took a final treat from the plate. "It's not his fault. He runs a big ship. He's used to giving orders, and expects them to be followed exactly. You don't get to be a captain without being the best at your job. How many times did Viktor get passed up for promotion, not because he was bad, but because his heart wasn't in it? You have to be on top of everything. Someone takes Sullivan's things, of course he's going to jump all over that person. You jeopardized his mission. Cryin' out loud, Sar! You know better than that! I know damned well you weren't raised that way. Not even David would have been that stupid, even on a dare. Like it or not, we're accountable to Guillaume, and right now Guillaume is accountable to the captain. My strong advice is to stay out of Sullivan's way, and not do anything remotely like that again."

"No kidding! And how am I supposed to do that when he's living here? No matter how good I am, I'm bound to screw up at some point. At least Mr. Ti'onam understands I have potential. It's only his captain that sees me as some dumb kid."

"Because that's what you acted like.

"I've got an idea, though," Dmitri said more thoughtfully. He rolled it around in his head before smiling. "How'd you like to get even with him?"

Sarah frowned. Dmitri loved a good joke, but the bigger his ideas, the more disastrous they always turned out. She shook her head. "No, Dim. It's not worth it. We're in enough trouble."

"Nothing bad! You're nothing but some dumb kid to him, right? What do you say we give him the ol' Kirushenko One-Two? Like we used to do with the card games at Toban's when I worked there?"

Sarah smiled through the tears at the memory. They'd made out like bandits, a well-practiced team of cardsharks swindling people out of pennies. It had worked well because she was so young no one suspected anything. She'd lost the youth advantage, but she hadn't forgotten the routine. Dimi was right. If it worked, it was a harmless way to put the captain in his place. If it didn't, they'd still have a good game of cards.

"If you think it would work," she agreed, feeling better than she had all day.

Dmitri's ideas flowed faster. "Trust me! We'll do it up right – a dinner party and everything! First thing tomorrow, run over to Mrs. Al's and tell her I'll need to talk to her right off – you can tell her why – and I'll arrange it with Captain Sullivan. Now come out of there and get to bed," he ordered, returning the empty dishes to the tray. "Tomorrow will be a late night, and you need to get *some* sleep this week."

Десять ~ *Ten* ~ *Xvala*

The rain pounded hard and steady in the morning, and the temperature dropped to a miserable three degrees above freezing. After breakfast, Sarah pulled on Dmitri's jacket, then swathed herself in a mustard-brown cloth. The center draped her shoulders; she folded the upper half over her head with a practiced hand, pinched up the middle folds and clasped them with a spring-clip, covering her head to almost dress-hem against the wet weather. Once more she wore shoes on her feet.

"You're not thinking of going out to play in this?" Granger asked. "You'll catch a chill that will leave you open to every virus from here to the *Triumph*."

"I must run a message to the Al's. I will return within an hour, I hope. If I hurry, it's less than a ten-minute walk. Rainy season lasts three, sometimes even four months; you can't be afraid of it. And I've had all my anti-virals," she assured him as she slipped out the door.

"It doesn't look too promising, does it?" Jack sighed, peering out the shutters. "I was hoping to get a look at that second site today. I guess we'll stay put and work on the data we've already gathered. Kyle, you had wanted to interview the surviving victim. Perhaps today's a good day for that."

"We're not exactly dressed for this kind of weather," Granger hinted. "I'm beginning to think that all that planet shielding nonsense may be a little excessive. You sure you can't convince the compound to drop the energy field just long enough to move us wherever we need to go? My legs are willing to trade half a week's pay to sweeten the deal."

"Nice try, Doc, but I don't think so."

Granger turned to their host. "How far a walk are we talking?"

"I don't know for sure," Dmitri said. "I'm not sure where the family lives. Somewhere out towards Demorak. Five to seven kilometers, I'd guess. I'll have to ask in town. I can't leave until Sarah gets back."

"I'm in no rush." Granger glanced at the window and rubbed knuckles that were aching in the cold. "Take your time. Maybe things will ease up by then."

* * *

109

"Mr. Sullivan? Captain," Dmitri corrected himself.

"Yes, Mr. Kirushenko?"

"I realize our relationship hasn't gotten off to the best of starts. Things are often ... *unpredictable* when Sarah's involved. I swear to you, I had no more knowledge about what she did yesterday than you did, and I was just as shocked. She's really never done anything like that before, and the way she cried about her mistake last night, I'm sure she won't repeat it.

"Either way," he continued, "I think it might help things if we spent an evening just socializing. I probably should have made the offer the first night you arrived, but you got here a little late, and yesterday's trip took up all the available time. We'd like to throw you and your men a proper welcome, a dinner party of sorts, where work is not the primary topic of concern, try to make up a little for our screw-ups, and show you we don't hold anything against you. We don't have an extraordinary amount of entertainment at our disposal, but Sarah's made herself a makeshift chess board, and we play cards. There are a number of local games we'd be happy to show you as well. I'm sure, coming off a star explorer, the culture-shock is worse for you than it was for us."

Sullivan hoped the boy was as sincere as he looked. He, too, had felt the animosity building between himself and their host. Maybe that's all the problem was, a growing misunderstanding borne of unfamiliarity. The girl was so odd; withdrawn one minute, defensive and argumentative or hyperactively inquisitive the next, it was difficult to know the best way to approach her. Jack hadn't decided if the boy did have some control over her or just knew precisely how to dance around an outburst. Maybe some casual getting-acquainted would bring about a relaxation of hostilities.

"Thank you, Dmitri," Sullivan said. "That sounds like a wonderful idea. I'm not used to having my crew's abilities limited by political regulations, or having to be separated from my ship so long. I think taking an evening off to sit back and adjust to our surroundings might be a good thing."

"I'm glad you agree. We'll aim to have dinner at the six and a half mark, then."

* * *

Sarah returned in half an hour, Charlie right behind.

"Hell-lo! Good days!" He bowed to Sullivan, having been coached

110

by Sarah on the way. "Glad I see you more one time," he said, holding up a *one* finger. He hung his rain hat and jacket over Sarah's on the peg by the door, and flapped the water off the ends of his shaggy hair.

Sullivan bowed his head. "It's nice to see you again, too."

To Dmitri, Charlie said, <*Mother come soon. You have good fun in mind?*>

Dmitri paused. He'd forgotten about Charlie. It was beyond rudeness to throw a party, ask your best friend's mother to cater it, and then not invite your best friend, but how could Charlie enjoy himself when he wouldn't understand more than a dozen words every few minutes? How could he and Sarah enjoy themselves if they had to translate every sentence spoken? *Screw it.* Friends were friends. They'd find a way.

<*Yeah, Charlie. We have big party tonight. You will come later?*>

Charlie glanced at Sullivan and his men. Outside of the friend Dikkersson, who lived near enough to visit two or three times a year and spoke the language, Charlie'd never socialized with the friends-from-far-lands before. <*Yeah, 1 come back.*>

"Good!" Dmitri clapped him on the shoulder. Thinking further, he asked , <*Hey, Charlie, you know where family lives, that boy who live through explosion near Demorak?*>

Charlie looked pensive. < *1 think so. He younger boy, work with father, transport goods from Demorak to Vandijoc every week. Why?*>

<*My friends – they interested in forest explosions. They wish to talk with him.*>

Charlie made a regretful face. <*Last 1 hear, he bad sick, but 1 can take you there.*>

<*Need not bother!*> Dmitri said quickly. <*You have much work. 1 will find, if you tell.*>

<*No problem!*> Charlie insisted. <*Not far, if you know short way. We go!*>

Dmitri looked helpless. All along, Sarah had translated the conversation for the crew almost as fast as it was spoken. Her eyes held the same worry.

"Tell him it's better if he doesn't," Granger hesitated. "Tell him … it could be contagious or something."

An exchange followed, but didn't seem to help. "Charlie says if it's important to Dmitri's friends, it's important to him, too. If Dmitri's willing to risk it, then he is, too," Sarah repeated.

Dmitri shrugged. *What could he do?* "Let's go."

The dismal rain eased half way to their destination, but it didn't relieve the chill. The dampness slid under jacket collars, crept up pant legs, made the walk seem endless. Charlie led the way across the muddy Aletneshfaja fields until they came to the road to Demorak, shaving two kilometers off the journey.

<Best of days,> Dmitri greeted the child at the door. <Your mother is nearby?>

The little girl was no more than five or six. She disappeared inside the crude house, leaving the door open to the dampness. An irritating scent wafted out, as if last week's dinner had escaped being thrown to a porshie.

A woman appeared. Dull bronze eyes gazed at them with a sunken emptiness of exhaustion and grief. Her dark hair had not been combed and retied any time recently, and her green dress hung limp and spotted. <Mr. Tanishwahdani away at town. I can help?>

<My name Dmitri Kirushenko, from Vandijoc. My friend, Charshfenaki Aletneshfaja. I speak for this doctor, Kylegranger. He important doctor from beyond Rizoshanti. He hear about son in accident. He help others sick like son. He come to help you.>

<Alikinashta cannot be disturbed. He too sick for visitors.> She closed the door, Dmitri translating as fast as he could.

Granger stuck his foot out to prevent the door from closing all the way. "Tell her I know that. Tell her I can at least help his pain. My help comes at no cost to her."

Dmitri pleaded with the woman, but her resolution didn't waver until he mentioned pain. She opened the door and invited them in. <Only five intervals!>

Charlie grabbed Dmitri's shoulder. His buoyant face appeared unsettled, perhaps even green. <Dimi-tri, I not go in. Look in circle. They not prosperous farmers, make extra money selling firewood to towns. If boy long sick, they will have much work not done. I strong fast worker, I can help. Catch up on some of boy's work.>

Given a choice, Dmitri'd rather help outside, too. <That nice idea, Charlie.>

Dank, stuffy air filled the little house. Dmitri'd gotten accustomed to barn-stink, and the ghastly stink of outdoor sanitaries, but not people-stink inside a house. Dirty dishes littered the kitchen workspace, a clutch of *joubash* nestlings chugged from a box in the corner, and laundry hung dreary from a rope by a heater that didn't seem to give enough warmth. The woman led them to the back room, a bedroom whose sole window remained shuttered and draped. A bedsheet divided the room into two tiny, semi-private spaces. The mother waved the little girl out and pushed the curtain-sheet back.

A young teen lay in a narrow bed, cradled on pillows, a blanket pulled to his chin. With his eyes closed, the boy didn't look real, and it was a lot better to think he wasn't.

The balding scalp, face, even the boy's lips bore dark, scabby crusts. Some had cracked; clear liquid oozed up, making the edges shiny. Stains marred the pillows and covers where the liquid had dried. The choking stink in this area was much worse.

Granger bowed before the woman and placed his sack of tricks on the bed. "How long has it been since he first fell ill?" he asked, waiting for Dmitri to translate.

The pause became a silence.

"Dmitri?"

Dmitri stared fixedly at the pillowed head, his insides as flaky as the boy's crumbling skin. Cold sweat greased his neck as the sickly-sweet stench of the room sucked away every molecule of breathable air. Outside, he could hear the steady *crack - split - clunk* of Charlie's woodcutting banging into his head like a drumbeat. He jumped at Granger's fingers on his shoulder.

"You okay?"

"Uh, yeah, I guess. What was that you said?" Granger repeated his words, and Dmitri dutifully translated, his back to the bed and its nightmare inhabitant.

"Fifteen days since the explosion, nine since he couldn't get out of bed anymore. She's hoping that when Allash, the red moon, is full two nights from now, the rays will start him healing. They'll move him outside so he can get the full power of the red light."

"Oh my." Granger realized just how primitive the local medicine was. "Tell me they didn't bleed him with leeches."

"That's not their style. Blood is strength – hence the red moon can make you stronger, because it's filled with blood. Letting blood out weakens the body and causes the soul to suffer. If anything, they've fed him the blood and meat of their strongest, healthiest animal."

"Well, there's worse things they could have done than that," Granger conceded. "Ask her if he's been able to eat."

An exchange went on for a number of minutes. Granger interrupted several times, but Dmitri held up a hand to silence him.

"She says she tries, but he doesn't eat enough. It hurts him to swallow, even though he's very thirsty. She feeds him meat broths and gelatins made from boiled bones and blood, and fruit juices with a lot of sweeteners."

Granger smiled, bowing. The woman bowed back, but her face was unsure. "Tell her she's doing a wonderful job. She couldn't have done better."

Dmitri relayed the news, and the woman's worry eased.

Granger asked, "I'd like to examine him a little; tell her I'll try my best not to hurt him. What do I have to do to look like I know what I'm doing, local-style?" He tried to remember the guidelines in the staff physician's notes.

"I don't know for sure. I only saw a local practitioner in action once. The big porshie stepped on Mrs. Al's foot, and she broke three toes. He lit a candle, stood over it and waved the smoke to his face. He breathed it in for a minute, then raised his hands to the Moons and asked a blessing that he could help the patient, asked the Moons to lend their great powers to heal the sick, or in her case, injured. That was about it."

Granger pulled things from his bag. "Okay. Here goes. Coach me if you think I need it."

The boy opened his eyes as Granger began his incantation. His mother dropped to her knees beside the bed, and Kyle abandoned the prayer.

<Kina! An important healer from far away, come to help you!> The boy's mother smiled, touching a gentle finger to the crusty cheek. *<He promise to stop pain.>*

The glassy eyes shone like aged porcelain, but were very much aware. The boy tipped his head off the pillow in greeting. His mother dabbed an ointment on the cracked lips, then dipped a cloth in water and squeezed it into the boy's mouth. He grimaced as he swallowed, causing a scab on his face to crack and ooze blood.

"If I can, I'd like to examine him," Kyle asked. "Tell him if it hurts too much, I'll stop. Dmitri? Hey!"

Dmitri was lost again, staring at the scab-creature. "Take a deep breath and let it out slow," Granger said. "Fix your face. This could be much worse than it is. Look cheerful, no matter what you feel."

"I'm *trying* not to think about what I feel." Dmitri gulped, paler by the second.

The last straw was Granger and the mother turning the boy on his side. A mass of scabs covered the boy's back, with palm-sized flakes of skin lying on the sheet under him and oozing sores where the crusts had been. The mother peeled padding from her son's rump and heels where the pressure of the mattress had left ugly wounds, now green with infection. The sore on one heel had a dull-white center that looked like bone.

The room reeled and faded, Dmitri's stomach pulsed. "I'm sorry! I – I can't do this! I can't – " With a lurch, he pushed the doctor aside and ran for the door.

"You've got three minutes!" Granger called after him. He turned back to the patient and forced an optimistic face.

Granger was mixing two compounds from bottles in his bag when Dmitri slunk in, shame-faced. Holding the new bottle up to the light, the doc corked and shook it, then gifted it to the mother with a little bow. He addressed Dmitri as if he'd never left.

"Tell her this is for his pain. One spoonful every few hours should help. He will sleep more, but that's good. Tell her sleep will help him feel better. Tell her to keep making him drink all the broth she can, even water. That's the best thing."

He reached into the bag again and withdrew the small box that, for him, held the most horrible part of the visit. As Dmitri translated, the doctor took out the parts of the primitive glass syringe and tried to assemble them as if he were used to it. Granger sucked up a measured amount of medication into the needle. Dmitri looked away.

In less than a minute, the boy relaxed. *<Is better!>* he whispered. *<Pain fades!>*

His agony manageable, the boy related some information about the day of the explosion, but too soon the medication made him sleepy, and he didn't have the strength to stave it off.

They walked home in silence for quite a while.

"Will he live?" Dmitri asked, unable to rid his mind of the images.

"No," Granger said softly. "I'd guess he's got less than a week left. His liver's been affected – you notice the yellowness of his eyes and face? He's losing fluid from his skin, and he can't swallow well enough to replace it because his esophagus is blistered. He's dehydrating, which only makes the skin condition worse. The more it cracks, the more fluid he loses, so the skin cracks more, and so on. If the liver doesn't kill him, and if his kidneys don't shut down first, the infection from that open heel will. He's too weak to fight it. That's Warshan's radiation at its worst. I put a hefty dose of painkillers in the concoction I gave his mother. It should keep him sedated and fairly pain-free for the time he's got left."

"Did you tell his mother? That he's dying, I mean?"

"She knows. Her eyes said it all. She's trying her best to care for him, but every little movement puts him in agony, and she can't bear to hurt him. That's why he's got the sores – she can't bring herself to move him every hour. The pain medication is as much for her benefit as his. He needs skin replacement, electrolyte monitoring and an anti-grav, zero-pressure surgical bed, not moonbeams."

<We can catch sickness like that?> Charlie worried. Dmitri didn't translate continuously as Sarah did, and Charlie was forced at times to guess at the gist of the conversation from the few words he did recognize.

"There's no chance we've been exposed to something like that, is there?" Dmitri asked.

"I doubt it. You'd be symptomatic by now as well." Granger pulled the collar of his jacket up higher around his neck, until the back touched the underside of the hat he wore.

It was raining again.

* * *

<Why he do that?> Mrs. Al whispered to Sarah behind the open broom closet door, stealing curious glances at Ti'onam through the crack. *<It not right for big grown man to wrap head like old woman. He very strange man!>*

Sarah was forbidden, on pain of death, to ever tell a lie. It was part of her penance for telling a doozy that got her in more trouble than she ever thought possible, but certain things about their true situation had to be shaded to fit with the current culture. As far as she could tell, this instance fit into that category. Even Navarans believed in shades of grey.

<It not his fault,> she whispered back. *<He catch fire as young boy, burn head and ears some terrible. Hair grow back but strange, and he not want anyone to see scarred-up ears.>*

<Ah!> Mrs. Al's chubby face nodded. *<Poor man! It terrible to wear scarf like old woman. No wonder such nice tall man like that not*

116

have wife.>

The captain and his officer sat in the two chairs in the living area, going over data. Andreiev remained in his room to analyze the details still in the omnicomp; he couldn't do that in the current company. A rain hat inside a house would have seemed odd, so Ti'onam kept a black cloth wrapped around his head like a scarf to discourage questions about his unusual appearance. Through the room-dividing shelves, they glanced now and then at the housekeeper and girl in the kitchen.

"Any guess what they're saying, Ti'onam?" Sullivan asked, curious. Tau Cetan Pelonishalak had a distinctive accent and rhythm all its own, unlike any Earth languages the captain knew. It was pretty, full of soft rising and falling sounds that were pleasant on the ear.

"None, sir," Ti'onam replied. "If you are referring to the possibility they may be discussing our presence, I do not believe so. Names are particular to language and culture; on Earth, you will find Ians, Juans, Johanns, Jeans, Seans, Ivans, and Johns, all different language forms of the same name from the same planet. However, the name will not translate away from Earth. Should John theoretically travel to Navara, he will still be John, as will John on Capricorn, John on Orion, and John on Sigma Tau Ceti. I have not heard any terms that might be mistaken for the names of the investigation party. Both women use the name 'Charshfe' to refer to the boy our hosts call 'Charlie,' and there is a different accent on the name 'Dmitri,' but it is still recognizable. They also do not glance over here, which is often a sign of interest. That is all I have been able to deduce, being completely unfamiliar with the local language."

The older woman listened to the girl's descriptions, and together they made a list. They disappeared into the town for an hour and returned carrying armloads of new groceries. The rest of the morning was spent busily, the girl chopping and slicing and fetching ingredients and fuel for the stove, the woman mixing and stirring and cooking. During a particularly chaotic surge of activity, with the cooks trying to mix, pour, watch the oven, feed the stove, and stir an over-boiling pot all at the same time, the captain felt obligated to offer his services.

"You're sure there's nothing we can do to help?" Jack offered a second time, embarrassed over the amount of time it was taking to prepare a meal on his behalf. "Cut something up for you, at least? I'm not exactly a gourmet, but I can stir a pot."

Sarah looked up from the pan in which she was spreading a thick brown paste, once again shriveling at his presence. Her hand clenched the spreading stick as if it were a weapon. "No, thank you, sir. Unless you have something specific you wish to request for dinner. We'll imitate it as best we can."

"I'll trust your judgment. I haven't been disappointed yet." The girl didn't relax, waiting for him to make the next move. Jack decided to confront the problem head on.

"How do you manage to do that?" He caught a small drip on the outside of the pan with his finger and tasted it. The mixture was too sweet to be anything but a dessert.

"Do what?"

Jack pointed the finger. "That, right there. You shrink yourself up whenever someone talks to you. Your brother said you were shy of strangers, but I get the feeling it may be more than that. Do I somehow frighten you, Miss Kirushenko?"

"No, sir?" Sarah whispered without conviction. "I was unaware I was acting abnormally. If I am, I apologize. In the future, I will be more alert to my position when speaking."

"No offense taken. You seemed uncomfortable, and if I was doing something to contribute to that, I wanted to stop. Please don't be afraid to tell me. That's very good." He peered into the pan, hoping to find another drip. "What do you call that?"

"*Kannishad.* It's a sweet cake with chopped fruit," Sarah replied, giving the batter a final poke. "Or at least it will be. I am aware of the fact that you are in command of the current investigation, as well as still responsible for your ship in orbit. I have been sufficiently warned to leave you alone and not interfere with the work done by your men. I am to cooperate if you need my assistance, but I must wait for you to ask, lest I interfere. I am strictly forbidden to harass you with questions. I am merely following *my* orders. Sir," she remembered to add.

"That seems a little Draconian, considering we all have to live together under one roof. You're a well-educated young woman who has a lot to contribute. I'm sure if we try, we can come to some sort of middle ground on … " His progress was interrupted by a loud knock.

Sarah looked at the door, startled, then at the neighbor woman. She opened it a small crack, blocking it with her foot, until she recognized the traveler and opened the door wide. "Lieutenant-Commander Dickerson! Please, come in!"

<*Sarrah! tozhto Ahnax ti kappera!*> Dickerson grinned, entering the cabin and removing his wet hat.

<*esa mangato, Ahnax,*> she bowed in reply.

<Mrs. Aletneshtaja.> Dickerson bowed to the cook, who smiled and bowed in return. "Captain Sullivan. You look like you're adjusting well. How goes the investigation?"

"Too slow, thanks to this lovely weather you have," Sullivan said as Sarah took Jan's hat and jacket. "We've eliminated several theories, but no solid conclusions yet."

"Some progress is better than no progress." Dickerson accepted a cup of tea from Mrs. Al. He dropped an arm over Sarah's shoulders; she stiffened but didn't cringe or scream out as when Sullivan came near. "Has our best translator proved helpful to you? The commander's impatient for her to reach seventeen so he can get her working for us full time. Right now, he can't ask her to do more than keep a journal of observations. All the wonderful things she brings us have been her own ideas."

"She has a very inquisitive nature," Sullivan acknowledged. "And her language abilities are impressive, to say the least."

"I knew she'd be a help. Is Dmitri around, Sarah?"

"No, he and Charlie went with one of the other men toward Demorak," she replied, quiet and subdued but not shrunken. "I expect him to return after lunch."

"Do you think it would be a problem if I joined the crowd tonight?" Jan asked. "I promised the captain I would stop by on my return trip. I want to go over his information, see if there's anything our team missed."

"I'm sure that would be fine. We're – having a kind of dinner party tonight, in honor of our guests. I'm sure Dmitri would be more than happy for you to join us."

"Only Dmitri? Not you?"

The fair cheeks blushed crimson, and this time she did seem to shrink, just a little.

"I would be most glad if you stayed," she told the floor. "Dimi invited Charlie to join us, and if you stay, I won't be stuck with all the translating."

Dickerson laughed. "I guess I'll have to work for my dinner. Well, that explains the food all over you." He pointed to her dress, which was covered with no fewer than a half-dozen ingredients. "I've worked harder for less. Don't let me keep you from Mrs. Al. Whatever you're making, it smells great! Why don't you let me talk to the captain for a while, and when Dmitri gets back, I'll talk with the two of you."

"Absolutely," Sarah murmured, and returned to the kitchen.

Dmitri returned more or less on time, more than glad to see Dickerson. Finally, someone familiar who wouldn't go crazy with accusations! He, Jan, and Sarah sat in his room, trading gossip, comparing findings, discussing the landing party. Sarah and Jan listened in horror to Dimi's descriptions of his morning.

"You have to relax," Jan explained. "Sullivan's a captain on a star explorer, a big shebang. He's like an expert surgeon, called in for a consult. He's used to walking in, telling people what they should do, and he expects to see them jump. Guillaume runs a looser ship because he can afford to. A lot of his support staff are civilian – yourselves, for example. I can tell you, Marc's not happy being overruled, either. By the time the *Triumph* leaves orbit, he'll have torn out what's left of his hair."

Dmitri tried to be optimistic. "I guess I can see that. I'm used to being in charge here in the cabin. It's just hard to have to put up with that 'expert' attitude when he doesn't know his food from a pile of porshie shit. I think we know a little more about living out here than he does."

"I know, but that doesn't matter in the fleet. Don't question, just do," Jan reminded him. "They'll be out of your hair in a few weeks. I think the party idea's good, though. Drop all that other crap, get to know the person behind the title, let him know you guys are really up to speed, and I'm sure everything will work itself out."

* * *

At the equivalent of five in the afternoon, Dmitri banned everyone from the main rooms until third-quarter-plus-half. He and Charlie, with the help of Jan and Sarah, dragged the heavy kitchen table around the divider to the main sitting area, allowing plenty of elbow room.

Dmitri sent Sarah to wash while he and Charlie brought in fuel for the heaters, and he helped Mrs. Al hunt for enough dishes for eight people. When the table was set, Dimi, too, disappeared upstairs, while Charlie ran home to fetch more serving bowls and set his livestock for the night.

Sarah sat at her workbench, thumbing her plant notebooks, thinking. After a while Dmitri's door opened and he flew down the stairs; he wore his best clothes. Sarah had changed into a clean dress and brushed her hair smooth, but that was all. If he was dressing up, he'd probably want her to as well. Just because they were stuck at the edge of explored space and lived in the Dark Ages didn't mean they hadn't once traveled the galaxy, too, eating the finest of foods and staying in the fanciest of places. The Allied Fleet wasn't the only place to learn a thing or two about the universe.

She poked through her clothes until she remembered something, and dug it out of her trunk. It was a blue outfit Mrs. Al had made for her with her own hands, a gift of thanks for the one-of-a-kind breed of flowers Sarah had grown for her. Sarah'd never worn it, never had a reason for such finery. The fabric was soft and finely woven, a terrible expense for someone like Mrs. Al, whose sole income came from the land itself. The border of the skirt, blouse, and bodice piece were hand-embroidered with expensive threads, a process which no doubt had taken an entire rainy season, perhaps more, to complete.

Somewhere, somewhere ... Sarah uncovered her best shoes, flattened under stacks of papers at the bottom of her packing trunk, brushing them with her hands until they regained their shape. She looked herself over in the small reflecting glass. Too tall, too square, strong as a Cossack with a lumpy-dumpy nose and a thick bone structure courtesy of Father, made worse by the layers of odd clothing and undergarments that left her even more lumpy. Her oldest sisters were tall and lanky, her favorite sister slender and beautiful. Her younger sister had had tireless curls that hung to her waist and their mother's tiny frame. *Not me,* Sarah sighed hopelessly.

Her hair. She'd always liked her hair, so blonde it was almost colorless. It hung loose and thick, all the way to her *zhopa*, but a fancy dress called for fancy hair. She brushed it once more and tried to twist the whole thing up like Dimi did for her on special occasions.

Eight tries later, she gave up and tried something simpler. She was just finishing the final tuck when Dmitri came in; she turned proudly to show him

"Sar, do you think that... " He stopped, speechless.

She smoothed the front of the wrinkled skirt with her fingers. "What do you think?"

"I'm – stunned." He walked around her to inspect the whole effect. "You did your hair like Mother. What have you got in it?"

Sarah bent her head, touching it lightly with her fingers. She'd woven her hair into two heavy braids and wrapped them around her head, like their mother often did with her own hair. "I didn't have any hair pins, so I used some bits of wire. Does it look okay?"

"I might as well go downstairs naked now, because no one will ever notice, not with you dressed like that."

Sarah frowned warily. "What do you mean?"

"I mean you look absolutely beautiful, Sar. No matter what you may think. Every eye in that room is going to be on you. I hope you're not doing it to tease Charlie."

"You know I don't do that, ever!!"

"I'm warning you, anyway. Don't you dare be rude to Charlie, dressed like that. He has my permission to kiss you, if he wants. You *are* beautiful, Sar. You can't deny it, no matter how much you try."

Butterflies began their familiar wing-flapping dance in the rafters of her stomach, adding nausea to her nerves. "Maybe I should change. I'm not ready for that. I – I just saw you all dressed up, and I figured you'd want me to look special, too. I didn't think about.... "

Dmitri held her hands. "No! Don't change a hair. Tonight is one of those nights we're going to shine, Kid, and you couldn't shine any brighter if you tried."

"I don't want all those men looking at me like that! I forgot about those kinds of things. Maybe it's not such a good idea, with them staying here. I don't want them to get any ideas. And I don't care what you say, Charlie's not touching me."

"You'll be fine."

"You won't leave me alone? Not even for a second?"

"I will be *right there*. No one's going to touch you. Come on, it's time." He headed for the stairs.

"Dimi?"

He stopped at the doorway. Sarah smiled, just a little. "You look really nice, too."

Одиннадцать
Eleven
Obench

The men stood near the table, waiting for their hosts. It wasn't flower season, so leafy braids of colored ivies formed a decorative centerpiece. Mrs. Al marched back and forth, puffed with pride, loading the big table with mounded platters. In a moment or two, Dmitri came down the stairs, in black pants and his best white shirt. Over the shirt he wore a black vest, embroidered across the front in red and yellow threads, and he didn't wear his every-day boots, but polished black shoes. He'd wet his hair down and touched it lightly with boot grease until it got the idea it was supposed to stay in place.

Charlie gave a teasing whistle. *<If I know this dress party, I would bring shoes! You invite girls to party, too, all dressed like that?>*

Dmitri blushed and shook his head, knowing what kind of girls his friend had in mind. "No, Charlie. Not today. Just one. *olashana, kirich, to uma Imarak nagosti gis privashak. Imarak, nagosti, lajafashto!>* he announced. "Gentlemen, tonight we are forbidden from discussing work. Tonight, we party!"

"I'll drink to that!" Granger declared over Charlie's animal-shriek of approval. "After today, I could stand a little shoreleave."

"I'll second that," Andreiev agreed heartily.

"Is Sarah joining us this evening?" Sullivan asked. "She worked all morning with your cook. I'd hate to see her miss out on all her efforts."

"She is most definitely joining us," Dmitri beamed, looking like the cat that ate the Casseiopeian canary. "Sarah?"

He extended his arm to the stairs. As if awaiting her cue, Sarah descended with hesitant steps, clenching the proffered hand when she reached the bottom. The only sound in the room was the hiss of the fire in the heater, as all eyes focused on her.

Sarah held her chin up, but her eyes stayed on her brother. She flashed him a faint, brave smile. Her eyes began their flicking glances; the four Earth men pulled themselves taller and sucked in their stomachs. From the kitchen, Mrs. Al sighed with approval.

"Gentlemen, I believe we are in the presence of a lady." Granger's

Western gentility reared itself, and he stared too long in admiration.

Dressed in the unflattering native costume, her long hair helter-skelter, bare feet dirty and scratched from plowing through underbrush, the girl had managed to radiate an untamed natural beauty. Standing before them now, cleaned, combed, and civilized, her beauty was commanding, despite the mask of stark terror that had taken hold. Longer than Sarah's regular dresses, the full skirt matched her eyes, emphasizing their deep purple-blue. The bottom eight centimeters of skirt were embroidered in a pattern resembling spraying waves in shining gold and silver threads, offset by darker blue. She, too, wore a white blouse, an impractical thing with wide sleeves and tight bands at her wrists, the cuffs embroidered in a narrow geometric pattern in blue thread. A strapless band of cornflower fabric fit tightly around her upper half, revealing a pleasantly trim waist. Her braided hair circled her head like a halo, adding age and sophistication to her youthful features, her height emphasizing her majesty. She clung to Dmitri's hand as if her life depended on it.

Dickerson bowed. "Miss Kirushenko, if I wasn't *almost* old enough to be your father, I'm afraid I would monopolize your company all evening. Unless the captain wishes to pull rank, may I be the first to ask if I may have the pleasure of dining next to a ravishingly beautiful young hostess."

Sarah collapsed into her routine, until she seemed only half as wide as she was the second before. She pulled back toward the stairs.

"M-maybe this is too much... "

Her brother dragged her a step farther into the room. "Come on. It's only a question. Answer him."

Sarah stole a nervous glance, hunting for words. In the process, she caught sight of Charlie alone at the back of the group, his face achingly sad. A shudder seemed to pass through her, and she glanced away.

Sarah turned to Dickerson with a face that mirrored Charlie's, then shook her head. *<I most sorry,>* she declined in Tau Cetan. *<I will sit next to brother. I not care about rank; I must favor seniority. Charshfe is oldest friend; I must give first choice of seat to him. He must have frequent translation. I think it only fair.>*

Dickerson bowed again. "You are perfectly right. Well, Charshfenaki? *Honor open to you."*

Charlie didn't move, staring at the girl with a heartsick expression. After a strained pause, he walked forward and bowed so low before Sarah his hair touched the floor.

<I understand if you not wish to,> Sarah whispered.

124

Her air of sadness was tainted by an overwhelming sense of – was it guilt? Jack Sullivan wasn't sure, but there seemed to be more tension between the pair than anyone was talking about.

Charlie broke into a broad smile. *<Why 1 not share Mother's good dinner with good friends?>* He held out his hand. Sarah gave a fast, painful smile in return and allowed herself to be escorted to her seat.

Charlie rubbed his straining stomach, coaxing it to make room for something else. *<After meal like that, know what perfect? Zappirash. Just little taste, chase after dinner. If 1 think sooner, 1 go to town this morning and get some.>*

Dmitri's face lit up. He held up a single finger as he got to his feet. "One minute!" He climbed off the bench and headed upstairs. "I be right back!"

<1 glad you say that,> he said, returning with an armload of bottles. "I've been saving some of these for the right occasion, and this sure seems like a good time to me." He arranged them on the table and scurried to help Mrs. Al find clean glasses.

"Dimi-tri!" Charlie held up a globe with a wax *Zappirash* label. *<You not tell me you hide this!>*

"Drink up, my friend!" Dmitri urged, passing out glassware. He pried the stopper off a started bottle with a grunt.

"This is my local favorite. Sweet like brandy, but a bite more on line with vodka." He poured a small amount all around, stopping abruptly when he recognized the sleeve holding out a glass among the crowd.

"What?" Sarah demanded. "I'm old enough!"

"But you don't drink! You won't even use rubbing alcohol, because you might absorb it through your skin."

"Normally, yes, but this is a party, isn't it? If you care to recall, I've drank it before. I was even drunk once."

"When was *that*?"

"Back on Navara, on a dare from David, before he broke his ribs," she prompted, tapping her finger on the rim of her waiting glass.

It took a moment, but Dimi recalled the fallout. Sarah wasn't mentioning the fact she was only five or six at the time, and her resulting deep slumber had so frightened her siblings they took turns sitting with her all night.

And, instantly, Dmitri understood the unusual request. The Tomboy was out to prove herself one of the crowd once again. It didn't matter if she was dressed like a princess, or as beauteous as a queen. It wouldn't have mattered if she was under or over the minimum legal age for private use of alcohol – if there'd been such a law on the planet. Sarah didn't notice things like that, never gave them a thought. As she did long ago at home, growing up arm in arm with seven brothers, she considered herself no less than one of the boys. What was good for the men was good enough for her, and she wasn't about to be left out if she had to beat up every man in the room to prove it. And Dmitri knew that, if necessary, she'd do it.

"If that's what you want," he shrugged. He poured her two finger's worth of the amber liquid before pouring some for himself.

"To foreign *countries*, big and small," Dmitri held his glass high, catching himself before he could say *planets*, "and to good friends, far and near."

Granger raised his glass. "Hear, hear!"

"To exploration and diplomacy," Sullivan offered in return.

"To family far away," Sarah beamed.

"To Mother countries," Andreiev added faithfully, catching Sarah's eye before she smiled and looked away.

"And adopted ones." Dickerson raised his glass to Sigma Tau Ceti.

<*For best of friends from strangest of places,*> Charlie ended, pausing for Sarah's translation.

Sullivan took a small taste of the drink, feeling it out. As he lowered his glass he did a double-take, catching sight of the girl.

The Kirushenko girl waited until they'd had an appreciative taste, then tipped her head back and poured her drink down her throat all at once. She turned the thick glass upside down on the table.

"Sarah!" Dmitri hissed in disbelief. She held her head high with a self-satisfied smirk, but she couldn't stop her eyes from watering. Once again, all eyes were on her.

Charlie grinned, slamming a hand on Sarah's back several times in admiration. <*Dimi-tri, when you teach her to drink like that? She better than you!*>

"Sarah, that's not how you drink this."

"That's how Father did it," she reminded him, face flushing fiery hot. "That's how David taught me."

"David's not here. I am in charge." Dmitri leaned across the table and whispered in Russian, *"Do it again and you'll spend the evening upstairs.* Pohnimaiesh? *This will sneak up on you!"*

"Pohnimayu," Sarah grumbled. She turned her glass right side up,

but her brother was in no hurry to issue a refill.

Dmitri restarted the friendlier conversation. "Captain Sullivan, with all those fancy forms of entertainment on your ship, do you ever stoop to playing cards?"

Jack swallowed the mouthful he'd been savoring, breathing in against the fire. "I've enjoyed a game or two. Anything particular in mind?"

"I know at least twenty different games, but I have a certain fatal attraction toward poker."

Sullivan looked at his men. They were split evenly, four *Triumph* crew against four Tau Cetan planeteers. "Do you know poker, Ti'onam?"

"I would think all that numerical analysis and card counting would be right up your alley, Commander," Granger said over the rim of his glass. "But then, they don't play games on Navara, do they?"

"The term 'game' may have a different meaning than the one you speak of, but Navaran children do play games," Ti'onam said. "Of course, they are not performed in the interest of self-entertainment, but to gain proficiency in skills and strength."

"Like *Na Rau*," Sarah added. "It's an exercise similar to our Hangman, but done with shapes of objects instead of words. It teaches precision in hand-eye-brain coordination, as well as gestalt closure and estimation."

"Precisely. I am familiar with the principles of poker, but, if given a choice, I would prefer to observe," Ti'onam said.

"I'm in, then, Jack. That gives us … seven," Granger counted. "Seven's a little much for poker."

"Don't count me." Sarah slumped morosely on an elbow, finger tapping a hint next to her empty glass. Dmitri ignored her. "I can deal Twenty-one, and Ninesquare, but 'Poker's no good with only two,' " she mimicked her brother. "I'm used to just watching."

"Charlie plays." Dmitri retrieved a deck of cards.

"Pokker? Yes I can!" Charlie replied without translation.

Dmitri pulled the extra sets of face cards from the alien-disguised deck. "Sarah, go find the markers."

* * *

Jack Sullivan fanned his cards, using them as a blind from which to observe the other players. He studied the playing of the game more than the game itself. Games of chance and skill could often be a silent means

127

to uncover the character of the people you played with; he couldn't let such an opportunity be wasted.

Charlie kept his liquor glass encircled in his arms, deep concentration on his face. He was sharper than he looked, following with only minimal need for translation, but every so often he would not-so-discreetly lean to peer at Dmitri's cards.

The Kirushenko boy was much more carefree, joking and laughing as he glanced at his cards and covered them up again. When his cards were bad, he made impulsive plays, betting wild and trying to bluff his way to a win. He was a skilled player, but overall Jack felt he was trying too hard to make a good impression.

Jantzen Dickerson was more reserved. He never lost his quiet dignity, even in the face of a bad loss – a worthy skill for a second-in-command. He seemed quite familiar with the Kirushenkos, and they both seemed quite at ease with him. In speaking with him that afternoon, Jack had pointed out the numerous coincidences they'd come across, without making them into direct accusations, but Dickerson didn't see them as significant. He'd laughed at the story of the missing omnicomp.

"She tied it to her leg!" Dickerson roared, shaking his head in admiration. "I'll be damned! Wait 'til I tell Marc. *Galishnixan*, nonetheless! She'll tame one of those gophers yet. I'm not surprised, Captain. She's been crying for analysis equipment for years. You dropped a whole shipment of it right on her table and wouldn't let her touch. If it were up to me, I'd team her up with one of your men and let her do all the boring detail work with it. She'll kill herself trying to prove she can."

Dickerson's casual dismissal of the problem wasn't enough to erase the doubts in Sullivan's mind. He observed the Kirushenko girl more than anyone. The girl watched the opening hands with interest; by the third deal she fought her brother to toss the appropriate wooden counters into the center for him. She'd try to look at his cards and follow the play, but Dmitri would close the hand, slapping her fingers if she tried to peek. He allowed her a second fill on her glass, and she sipped it between bids. By the eighth deal she was openly fed up, slouching sideways with her head propped on a fist, translating anything Charlie said with all the enthusiasm of a spectator at a snail race.

Jack patted the table next to him. "Why don't you sit down here, Miss Kirushenko? Poker's a lot more interesting when you know what you're watching. I'm sure between Kyle and myself we can teach you the rules of the game."

Sarah began to shrink, shoulders sucking in, then suddenly gave a jump. "Ow!" She glared at her brother, then explained, "Hit my knee on the table." Taking her glass, she sat between the two men.

"It is acceptable and appropriate to address me as Miss Sarah," she announced stiffly. "That is the equivalent of what the Tau Cetan's use." She held her breath and emptied her glass as Sullivan explained the rules.

Granger picked up a brown bottle from the table. "What's this like?"

"Very good but very aromatic," Dmitri said. "Two or three shots and you'll be sweating orange mint until tomorrow."

"It's worth trying once," Kyle surmised, pulling the stopper and taking a sniff. He poured himself a taste of the green liquid, then tipped some into the girl's glass as it appeared waiting next to his.

After several hands, the girl seemed to have a reasonable grasp of the game, pointing to which cards she thought Sullivan should play, and questioning him as to why he might disagree. Disaster almost struck when Granger let her play his hand. He leaned close to point out a card on the far side of the spread, his arm snaking across her shoulders.

Sarah twisted violently and leapt to her feet before catching herself. She gave a sick smile before sitting down.

"I'm sorry. I was not expecting you to touch me." She reached for a bottle on her own, poured herself a sizeable amount, and choked down a gulp.

"My fault," Kyle apologized in turn. "I certainly didn't mean anything by it."

"If you think you know what you're doing, Sar, come take over for me," Dmitri invited, stretching. "You can't do much worse. I've got bad luck tonight." He'd lost almost everything he'd started with.

Sarah took her glass and moved to her brother's seat.

Mrs. Al had been listening from the kitchen while she sewed. Dmitri came over to help with the desserts.

Sarah watched him leave from the corner of her eye, then downed the bit of liquid he'd left in his glass. She opened the hand dealt her, frowned, and shuffled cards around. She hesitated before making her moves, confused and uncertain, but gave a happy smile when she won the hand and raked in the wooden tokens. She won the next hand, too.

"Beginner's luck!" Dickerson said.

"I had very good teachers," Sarah replied demurely. She won the third hand on a heavy bluff.

* * *

"How are we doing?" Dmitri claimed his seat more than a half-hour later. Not only were his starting tokens back, but a whole lot more.

Sarah laid down her cards, unable to stop her giggle from dissolving into gleeful laughter. She clapped her hands. "Full house, kings over eights!"

"Damn!" Andreiev swore, the last holdout for the hand. "Jacks over tens! I thought I had it!"

"That's my girl!" Dmitri raked in the large pile from the center of the table.

Granger eyed the Kirushenkos. "Jack, do you smell a rat? I've heard of beginner's luck, but six out of nine hands?"

"As in, I'd bet my last chips that we've been cleaned out by a team of professionals?" Sullivan nodded, knowing he'd been beat. "You already knew how to play poker, didn't you, Miss Kirushenko?"

Sarah tried ineffectively to look innocent. "I said poker with two isn't any fun. I never said I didn't know how to play. My brothers taught me before I started school. *They* were the best of teachers!" She held her breath as she drained the last of the horrid green stuff from her glass.

<saffa to alle minatori 1x, ekwari, sofrawi...> Jan Dickerson sang in Tau Cetan; Charlie recognized the song and joined him. Dmitri laughed as he listened, but Sarah merely looked annoyed and turned away.

"What's it about?" Sullivan inquired as the duet finished.

"It's a folk song, warning young men not to marry a girl who thinks she's smarter than they are." Dickerson winked at Sarah.

"Hmph!" Sarah snorted. "Obviously no one ever takes the advice seriously, or no marriages would ever take place. 'And she took the poor fool/ Under her wing/ Lest he die of stupidity,/ So lost was he/ Without some kind-hearted Maternity.' Antigious Kaspar, *Queen of Paradise*, verse fourteen."

Sullivan nodded. "The feminist poet of Aldebaran V."

"You're familiar with the poem?"

"Not that one in particular, but I'm familiar with some of her anthropological essays. I was unaware you were sympathetic to her female-centric viewpoint."

"I'm afraid I know only the one poem," Sarah confessed, pouring a splash of something into her glass and sniffing at it. "I do not consider myself an ardent feminist. If I lived in a repressive society such as this one all my life, I might be, but having grown up on modern worlds with a houseful of siblings, half of them brothers, we never saw a difference. I knew that, biological differences aside, there was nothing my brothers could do that I couldn't. I never gave it a thought until I lived here."

"There is the other side of the coin as well," Andreiev spoke up. "Dmitri, perhaps you know this one?" He sang the few first few lines of a widely known Russian song.

Dmitri perked up. "Of course!" Together they finished the ballad.

Charlie looked to Sarah for translation, but she had resumed her annoyed expression, rolling her eyes and drumming her fingers on the table, waiting for the harassment to finish. She flushed terribly warm under all the layers of clothing. Mrs. Al must really have been packing fuel into the heater. Sarah hated teasing – she knew the ballad of a young girl's unending love for the cold-hearted soldier she'd fallen for was meant to pull at her leg – but she wasn't mad this time. She actually thought it a good comeback, but she had to keep up appearances. She wasn't used to being – *peaceful*, but that was the best word for how she felt. She was – *happy* inside, like when she'd been home, watching her family tease each other.

The Fleet officers were nice men. They could see she was just one of the guys, too, not some brainless little doll to be pushed aside, like the love-blind girl in the song. These guys were all right. Like that Lieutenant Danil. He could be very down-to-business when performing his duties, but when he wasn't, he could be very pleasant, too... She jumped when her glass was yanked away.

"Hey! Lay off this stuff, will you?" Dmitri chided her. "You're going to make yourself sick. Your face is all red."

"I am not going to get sick! Rings over Jupiter! *You* never do! I'm fine!"

"Then come on!"

"Come where?"

"Didn't you hear me? Danil knows that dance Mother taught us. Come out here with us."

Sarah made a derogatory face. "You know I don't dance! Not for anything."

<*Please, Miss Sarrah? You see me dance, and that not pretty sight,*> Charlie begged, hearing Dickerson translate.

The table erupted in encouragement, and for a moment Sarah truly hated her brother. She had an overwhelming urge to slide under the table, crawl down the length and exit near the stairs, the faster to run to her room without all those eyes and expectations upon her. The worst of all was that polite Mr. Andreiev coming over and offering his hand.

"Pozhal'sta?" he said brightly. "I promise not to step on your feet."

Sarah looked up at his warm, inviting eyes, feeling smaller and smaller with every passing millisecond. His face had that eager, ever-hopeful spark to it that Dmitri's got whenever he talked to a girl. She swallowed hard, unable to breathe from nerves. Her chest cramped so tight she didn't see how her heart could possibly continue to pound so strong. It stole the oxygen from her brain, leaving her dizzy.

His hand was waiting. The longer she hesitated, the more impolite she became. She gasped such fast little breaths against the strangulation in her chest, she could barely find the air to speak. Even if she said yes, she felt so weak and shivery she wasn't sure her legs would hold her up.

"That was a long time ago. I – I have forgotten the steps."

"So what. Come on." Dmitri dragged her to the open floor.

To pull away now would not only be rude to Mr. Andreiev, but look bad to everyone else, and Dimi would be mad. She tried to stop shaking, but it was hard to get a deep breath, standing this close to the Russian man, touching his hand. It happened every time she came near him.

Allergies.

With a start, Sarah realized she must have an allergy to something on him. That was the only logical explanation. She would have to ask about allergies next time they went to the Compound. This was unbearable, and she felt ridiculous. At least she wasn't sneezing and dripping like Dimi did near porshies, thank the Moons. She clung to her brother's hand and left her other hand limp. She kept her eyes on the floor, clumsily copying the moving feet on either side of her, the clapping of the other men crashing through her head like thunder. The second they stopped, she retreated to the table, held her breath and gulped whatever was in Dimi's glass before working on her own. Anything that might calm her down. Someone spoke to her. Sarah faked a smile and answered, feeling her face flush in the overheated room.

Allergies could do that.

* * *

<*...to, migaris dosh chynopradesh lxo satti!*> Sarah finished translating Mr. Sullivan's humorous story seconds after he finished telling it.

Charlie laughed only a breath later than everyone else. He gazed at his translator with transparent adoration, but she looked at the table, hands clenched around her glass, which was nearly empty again.

"How do you do that, Miss Sarah?" Kyle asked. "How can you

translate so fast? You barely hear what's being said. You're as fast as a computer."

(Dmitri's eyes widened at the forbidden word, but Dickerson substituted *as fast as the wind.*)

Sarah snapped out of her trance and took another swig of her glass. "I'm embarrassed to tell you."

"Cerebral implant?"

(*Head surgery?* Dickerson said carefully.)

"No." Sarah shook her head, unable to erase her self-satisfied grin. "The ability's mine, naturally. I spoke my first word at seven months. I taught myself to decode Russian print at two, and English at three. My parents were amazed. Mother was somewhat fluent in Terran French, having relatives in France that she visited when she was young. She taught it to me as a game, a parlor trick she and my father could use to impress company. The more she taught me, the faster I learned. By the time I turned four, I would stand in the middle of the table and recite whole speeches from Saint Exupéry, or perhaps Pushkin. I could be asked to translate what people said, be quizzed on math or geography or history, and guests would leave thinking my parents were these incredible people. *That* was the biggest joke of all."

Sullivan watched the girl with amusement. When filled with alcohol, she was pleasant. Her shoulders were down where shoulders belonged, and the wary formal speech and split hairs relaxed into social chatter. She didn't growl or cringe when Charlie leaned his head on her shoulder while laughing, but laid a hand on his back.

Jack made note to discuss the behavior with Dr. Granger. If her anxieties were that simple to overcome, then Kyle would have medications that could help her. In the mean time, he wasn't going to waste the opportunity to make a friend.

"A born show-off," he said with understanding.

"*Insufferably*. But I liked it," the girl conceded. She sloshed the remaining liquid around her glass, watching it swirl and spiral.

"I liked that attention. Mother made learning a game, and to me, it *was* a game. I tried to do things faster, or better, always challenging myself. You see, the honest truth is," Sarah confided, "I'm *proud* of that ability. I know it's wrong, I *try* not to be that way, but deep down inside, I *am*! I'm better than everyone else, and I sure-as-damned-well-shit know it. I should be punished for that much pride. But translating what people say gets dull, so I race myself, see just how fast I can go without losing accuracy, or translate backwards in my head or something. Anything to

133

put an extra shine on my gift."

"Were all your subjects that easy for you, Miss Kirushenko?" Sullivan asked.

Sarah swung her head in overemphasized arcs. "Definitely *not!* Not once I got to Navara. I'd never had to learn other subjects in a foreign language. Navaran isn't an easy language to read, worse yet to speak, and they made no allowances for me beyond a tutor. No translators. I had to memorize at least a hundred new vocabulary words a day."

"That is not possible," the tall and serene Navaran Master said.

"You have the ability to **make** *it possible," the taller but unusually serene Alexander Kirushenko insisted. His precocious daughter had been suffering the last three months in a special program at the local school. The arrangement proved poor from the start; it dissolved to the point where she disappeared somewhere between disembarking the school transport and her classroom. For two days she caught the transport back home with her brothers; the third day she fell asleep in her hiding place and slept through dismissal. When she didn't arrive home, the school had no record of her attendance. Somewhere, a five-year old child was lost in a city of 200,000. It did not take long to locate her, alone and scared inside the empty airlock to the school. She'd had enough sense not to go outside in the 55-degree heat. Sasha Kirushenko exploded his fury on the school. The school kissed his feet and more, but they had nothing else to offer.*

"The lack of self-discipline in human offspring is known throughout the galaxy," the Master said with distaste. "Such a child would disturb classes, disrupt the learning process our students are taught to respect. A child that young cannot physically keep up with Navaran peers, and would find herself outcast when she continued to act in a manner her classmates would find abhorrent. The confusion created between the encouragement for such behavior at home and the intolerance for such behavior in the educational setting would lead to further outbursts in a child who is, by Human nature, unable to adjust. We cannot allow the education of our students to suffer for the purposes of a social experiment."

"If you would just meet her!" Maryana Kirushenko

remembered not to smile a fraction of a second after she did. A stunning woman by human standards, she radiated a cheerful friendliness that melted all but the coldest of hearts, the type of human personality that grated against everything a Navaran believed. "She's a very exceptional child, very obedient, very capable. Please, sir, if you would just speak to her before making your final decision, you'll see for yourself."

The Master gave his permission. His expression did not change, but his assumptions soon did.

Sarah entered the office with trepidation. Mother said this would be her most important performance ever. She had to be perfect. She couldn't forget a thing. If she wanted out of the Kar Kuomi school, she had to be perfect. Without Fail. *Father had coached her on how to stand, how to look, how to show profound respect. Manners counted double for Navarans. She'd studied the grammar files until her head hurt, listened to the language programs until she could barely remember how to speak anything else. Ten-year old David, the most rambunctious and obnoxious of them all, took it upon himself to be her personal trainer in Navaran customs. He invented his own lessons in torment, pushing, hitting, pinching, and pulling her hair when she least expected it, only to yell, "Nyah, nyah! You lose! Gotta keep a straight face!" when she turned to retaliate. She had to admit, his efforts helped a great deal, but in her heart she still wanted to fill his mouth with sand and pound him with a rock every time.*

It was a performance, that was all. She had only to impress her parents, that was all. That was what counted, not the funny, wrinkly-eared old man behind the table. He was just part of the game. She greeted the man in his own language, flawlessly. She answered his questions without hesitation. She was impeccable. She was impassive. She was five years, eight months, twenty-three days, and seventeen and a half hours old, and in two days she would begin commuting alone forty-five minutes each way, to an alien school, in an alien city, on a blistering alien planet, a hundred and twenty kilometers from home.

Sarah shook a reprimanding finger. "See, I was supposed to fail. Those arrogant bastards expected me to fall on my face, cry for my parents to come and get me, so they could say I didn't belong there. Once

I figured that out, I refused to give them a chance. I had a month to prove myself, and I did. After eight months, no one thought twice. By the end, I needed a tutor for only three subjects – Russian language, Earth history, and some of the science that the Navaran students had learned in earlier courses, but I hadn't. I was never, *ever* bored there."

"I'm sure you did much for improving Navaran-Human relations," Sullivan said. "Are there many exchange students like that in Navaran schools, Ti'onam?"

"None of which I am aware," Ti'onam replied. "There are schools on Navara for off-world children, but this is the first occasion of which I have heard of a human child attending a Navaran school. I can attest from experience, it would have been most difficult."

Dmitri leaned past Sullivan to clear two empty bottles off the table. "*Never* underestimate my sister. She'll outstubborn a black hole."

Twelve

Shtvash

Dmitri clapped a sleepy Charlie on the back and gave his mother a long embrace, thanking her once again. He watched them disappear into the darkness of the damp night, then shut and barred the door. He hadn't forgotten the days of seven people sharing a single lavatory, and headed for the hall while he had a chance.

At the table, Dickerson finished the punchline on a truly horrible pun. He managed a chuckle from the captain, and outright laughter from the lieutenant and Mr. Granger, but the girl found it the most humorous of all. Consumed by laughter, she slid off the bench with a thump, gasping.

Sullivan watched her roll on the floor with growing distaste. Drinking socially to relax was one thing, but Jack saw little humor in a teen-aged girl outdrinking a roomful of men. She was a show-off all right, and a bragging one at that.

And a braggart loves to talk about themselves, Jack realized. He bent down next to her.

"Are you hurt?" he asked Sarah, sticky-sweet. "I don't think you were expecting that. Let me help you up." He offered a hand, but didn't touch.

The girl stared past him to the ceiling, watching the flickering shadows from the oil lamps dance across the beams with autistic fascination. "I fell. Down. Here lies Sarah K. / It was gravity / That made her that way!" She choked with laughter until tears ran. "I made a physics rhyme!

"Yes, you did. That was very clever! You're a very clever girl."

"Yes, I am."

"Clever enough to tell me how you set those explosions."

"*Something* big went *boom!* out there," Sarah replied with grave seriousness. "I could graph you the damage. X-plosions, y-plosions, and z-plosions!" she howled. "That's a math joke!"

Sullivan gave up. She was past the point of coherent conversation, and she wasn't even funny. He stood as he heard the bathroom door open.

"You were right, Dmitri," the captain said as the boy returned. "This was a most welcome diversion from the task at hand. A pleasant evening, all around. Tomorrow, however, I'm afraid it's back to the job. I might be inclined to overlook a late morning, though," he told his crew. "Maybe an hour or two?"

"I'll second that order," Granger said, slow and sleepy.

"Good night, then," Dmitri replied, capping the last bottle with enough worth saving in it.

"Good night, Miss Sarah." Andreiev spoke to her, but the girl lay on the floor, eyes closed.

"*'Noch,*" she mumbled. *'Night.*

It was quiet when the room emptied. Dmitri finished clearing the table.

Sarah stared upwards with a dazed expression. Dmitri was right. Liquor *did* give you strength to do things you couldn't otherwise bear to do, and she didn't feel the least bit violent. Maybe only vodka did that.

"Dimi, I don't feel so good."

"So what do you want me to do about it?" He pinched up four dirty glasses between the fingers of each hand and carried them to the kitchen. "You're the fool who should most definitely know better."

The room spun one way, then it tipped up and doooown, then it came back uuuup and spun the other way. Sarah didn't like anti-grav simulators to start with, and the floor had no handholds. "I mean it, Dim!"

"Then go to bed." He blew out two of the lamps.

Dickerson emerged from the hallway. "Where should I sleep, Dmitri?"

Dmitri bounced a palm off the top of his head. "Aw hell! I'm sorry, Jan. I forgot about you. Know what?" He sighed, watching his sister rolling on the floor in her best clothing and giggling to herself. "Take my bed. I have a bad feeling I'm not going to see much of it tonight."

"No, no. I couldn't do that. I can bunk down in front of the stove just fine."

"I insist. Please! I've slept on her floor before. She's got a cozy little nest built into her closet, if you don't stretch your legs."

"Thank you, then. I haven't slept in a real bed in almost a week. My body won't know what happened." He disappeared up the stairs.

Dimi poked Sarah with a toe. "Come on. Upstairs." He hauled her to her feet.

Sarah swayed, and he grabbed her with both hands. She collapsed against him.

"How the hell much did you *drink*?"

"Just a little. A little bit of this, a little bit of that, a little bit of all of them?" She burst into a wave of giggles. "Now I know what tipsy means, 'cause I'm tipsying all over!"

"Cryin' out loud, Sar! Come on! Stand up! I have to carry the light." He let go of her to reach for the remaining lamp. Sarah stood for a moment, backstepped, then sat hard on the floor, instigating another burst of laughter. She crawled to her feet and let him prod her up the stairs.

* * *

Granger had just exited the lavatory when the cry caught his attention. He paused. Light tumbled down the stairs.

"No!" a girl's tearful voice wailed.

"Dammit, Sarah! Stop fighting me!" said an angry male. "Take it off!"

"Don't!"

Something in the tone made Granger uneasy, but he hesitated. His job wasn't to get involved in family disputes. But... Something about the pair bothered him. He wasn't sure yet, didn't want to put his finger on it, but the uncertainty remained. He climbed the stairs.

The elder Kirushenko sat cross-legged on the floor, clothing loosened, weary head propped on his hand. The younger knelt beside him, arms folded across a metal pail. Her head rested on her arms, hair hanging to the floor loose and wavy from the unraveled braids, and she wept pitifully. She sat in a soiled white underskirt, the embroidered blue skirt balled up on the floor.

Granger tapped on the doorframe. "I don't mean to bother you. Is everything okay? From downstairs it sounded like you might need help."

The Kirushenko boy rubbed his eyes. "No. My fault she got like this, I'll deal with it. Some lessons have to be learned the hard way. Like playing with the wrong chemicals can make the lab explode if you don't know what you're doing, *right, Sar?*" He leaned close to the girl and shouted the last words. Sarah flinched and cried harder.

"Actually, if you'll stay with her a minute, I'll go get ... "

Sarah grabbed at her brother. "No! No! Don't! Don't leave me, Dimi! Don't leave me!"

The boy wrenched the hands away with disgust. "All right! Get off me! Your hands are filthy!" To Granger he asked, "Do you think you could bring me up half a pail of water and a clean glass? There's still a few on the shelf."

"Sure. I've got some anti-nausea tablets in my pack; I'll get them

139

while I'm down there."

"No, thank you. I want her to suffer every minute of this, so she doesn't forget."

"Your choice."

By the time Kyle returned, the girl retched miserably into the pail, her brother holding back the great mane of hair. Granger placed the bucket of water nearby and handed over the glass.

Dmitri dipped a glass of water and set it aside, then dipped a clean corner of the blue skirt into the pail and proceeded to wipe his sister's hands and face.

Sarah squirmed at the cold water, too sleepy to fight.

"I'm sorry, Dim," she mumbled. "I'm sorry I made trouble. You're too good to me. I didn't mean to get sick. I really, really didn't. I love you, Dim. You take such good care of me, and all I do is get in trouble on you. I don't mean to! I don't!"

"Shut up, Sarah," Dmitri growled, sponging vomit from her hair. "You're one damned drunk I *don't* have to listen to." He held out the glass of water. "Drink, and then you can sleep it off."

"I don't want it." She twisted her head, but the glass followed. "It'll just come back. I *hate* getting sick! No!"

"No, it won't, and you'll be happier in the morning if you drink it now. Drink it, or I'll sit on you and pour it down your throat." The girl complied with a sob. Handing back the glass, she slouched against him.

"Come on, get up," Dmitri said after a minute. "I'm beat. Get yourself to bed." Sarah lay heavy on his leg. He pushed her, but she didn't stir.

"Aw, hell. Hey," he said to Granger, "wanna give me a hand?"

"Sure." Kyle knelt down and checked the pulse in the girl's neck, lifted one eyelid, then the other. "She looks okay. Does she do this often?" He took the feet, Dmitri lifted the shoulders, and together they hefted the girl onto the bed.

"Never. That's the joke, I guess. And if she has any sense at all, she never will again."

"Keep her on her side or belly," Granger suggested. "That way if she gets sick again, she won't choke."

"*I* – . I know." Dmitri stopped himself. He looked down at his sleeping sister. Souring splotches marked the sleeves of the blouse and underskirt.

"Can you grab me her nightwear from the bottom drawer there?" He rolled Sarah onto her stomach and unfastened the bodice band.

Granger handed him a soft white nightdress. "Let me help you," he offered, pulling a limp arm from a sleeve.

"No!" the boy said too forcefully, waving him away. "I can do it. I've done it before when she's been sick. She's very private about things like this." He wrestled the floppy head through the opening of the nightwear, pulled the fabric over her as far as it would go, reached underneath and took the other arm from its blouse sleeve. Reaching inside the neck of the nightdress, he pulled the blouse up and out, tugging it over her head.

"I *am* a doctor," Granger reminded him. "I'm licensed to help."

Dmitri flashed a grateful half-smile. "You've *been* a help, but I can handle this. Get some sleep while you can." He reached under the nightdress to struggle blindly with the complicated fasteners to her under-blouse. A hard tug at a tiny hook caused his arm to raise the fabric of the nightwear, exposing several centimeters of skin on the girl's back.

What the...? Granger's eyes were drawn to the sight.

Couldn't be. Not like that. No qualified physician would leave a mess like that. An untreated burn? He grasped the nightdress, lifting it further.

Dmitri grabbed the invading hand. One glance, and he saw it was too late. He released the doctor's wrist and finished the last fastener. Lifting the girl under her belly, he slid the garment free, pulling the nightdress down beneath her.

"Don't look at me like that. I didn't do it." Dmitri took a step back, allowing the inevitable.

Granger slid the nightwear up to expose the girl's back.

"Good Lord!" As a Fleet doctor, he was experienced with trauma, from battle wounds to energy burns, but his stomach tightened at the destruction before him. Stripes of scar tissue crossed the young flesh, some wide, some narrow, some white, some pink, some thick, some smooth and barely noticeable, from the waist of the underskirt up to the shoulders, scar upon scar upon scar.

He traced one with his fingers. An accident wouldn't leave such an even mark, an even distribution. This was something deliberate. This was brutality. Only one small mark still seemed to be healing; none of the others seemed that recent. Granger glanced up.

Dmitri held his head high. "Look if you have to. That fresh mark's from falling off the porshie the other day. I told you, I'm not responsible. Father fed a bad temper with a liter of vodka a day. One day it was Sarah who pissed him off. That was the result. They're in her medical files. She was six. You see her flinch when someone's mad at her, it's not from me.

That's an old, old behavior."

Granger nodded, speechless. Things like this weren't supposed to happen to children anymore, not on Alliance worlds. There were laws to prevent that. But then, not all worlds belonged to the Alliance. *Like this one.* "They were never treated?"

"No."

"Those scars on your shoulder," the doctor realized, "they're from the same cause, aren't they? Is that why you're so far out in space? Escape?"

The boy hesitated. "I've had my share. Indirectly, I suppose it might have had something to do with our leaving." He pointed to the thickest marks. "This one here, and this one, hurt if clothing rubs them, or if something hits them, like a branch or a door latch or something. She was told they could be removed when she was older. Do you think – Is she old enough yet?"

"Sixteen? Sure, that's old enough," Granger agreed, prodding the scarred skin gently with a finger. The boy was right; none of the scars was recent, and the smaller ones were fading away on their own. The big ones, though … Some were longer than Granger's hand. "All this can't be fixed at once. It will take several surgeries, maybe even some grafting, but with patience I don't see why every one of these can't be removed. It will take time, maybe even a year to get them all. I don't see why not."

"Thank you. That's good to know." Dmitri tugged and smoothed the nightdress all the way down. Reaching under the hem, he pulled off the underskirt. If the fastener hadn't given him a hassle, he would have had her clothing changed without ever exposing bare skin.

"Whatever you do, don't mention you've seen them," he warned, tossing the underskirt onto the pile of dirty clothes. "She's very self-conscious about it, and she doesn't like anyone to know. You've stumbled onto one of her worst secrets; I ask you in the name of patient privacy, don't share the discovery."

Granger nodded. "Unless I read it in her files or she tells me herself, I won't mention it." Together they wrestled the unconscious form under the blankets.

"That's why you know what to do, because of your father?"

The boy's jaw clenched, and his mouth pressed into a hard, unhappy line. It seemed a long time before he dropped his stance. "Yeah. Mother dealt with it most of the time, and then my brother, and when I got older I helped him. It was a long time ago, though. I'm sorry if I seemed angry. Her doing this just brought it all back, I guess."

"How old was older?"

Dmitri gave a slight shrug. "I dunno. Ten? Eleven? Definitely by twelve. It wasn't as bad as you're thinking." Stretching, he gave a yawn, rubbing a hand over his eyes. "I've got to get some sleep. Thanks for your help."

Granger knew a cue when he heard one. "Goodnight, then. Don't be afraid to wake me, if need be. I'm used to being on call."

"We'll be fine."

Тринадцать
Thirteen
Chednashak

reakfast had been cleared and the floor swept clear of the night's party by the time Sarah slunk down the stairs, cocooned in a blanket, uncombed, barefoot, but wearing a clean shirt and unfastened jumper.

Having the big table in the main room allowed not only more space at meal times, but provided enough seating, so Dimi left the sitting chairs in the kitchen and didn't bother to put the table back. Sarah slid onto a bench.

"Now there's a face for an abstinence poster," Granger said. The glare he received from the depths of the blanket promised murder. The girl pulled the top corner over her face, shutting out the world.

Dmitri watched without a shred of sympathy. He took fruit from a cabinet, sliced some into a glass, then filled it with water and sweetener and placed it in front of her.

"WHAT'S THE MATTER, SAR? YOU DON'T LOOK SO GOOD!" he shouted.

The blanket gave a whimper and a fist shot out, brushing him in the side of the head as he ducked. "Leave me alone!" came a tearful whine. "Stop being mean to me!"

"Drink every bit of that, and go back to sleep. I'm going into town with everyone. Jan's going back to the Compound, if you want to send anything. Mr. Ti'onam is going to stay here and work, so keep out of his way and don't be a pest. We should be back sometime this afternoon."

The blanket nodded. After a pause, she retrieved paper, pen, and ink. In the sloppiest penmanship she'd ever used, she scrawled a quick note.

Dear Vlad,

> *I tasted a local drink. If I ever THINK of doing it again, you must swear you will glue my lips shut and beat me over the head until my eyes fall out. I am sick all the way to my bones. Ugh!*
> *I MISS YOU.*

Sarah blew on it to hurry the drying process, folded it, and handed it to Dickerson. "Please give that to Mr. Ennis. He knows where to send it. It's nothing secret. Thank you."

She took the glass, wrapped herself up, and trudged upstairs to suffer in the silence of her closet.

Several hours passed before Sarah crept down again, minus her cocoon. Ti'onam didn't look up until the feet had been waiting silently next to him for a number of minutes.

"Is there something you desire?"

Sarah startled at his sudden inquiry, and took an uncertain step back. She bowed in greeting, hugging something to her chest.

//Forgiveness for the interruption. If you would prefer, I can speak to you at a more convenient time.//

//We are currently alone. If you desire private conversation, now would be the most opportune moment. You wish to converse in Navaran?// He had promised he would speak his language with her.

//May I sit?//

He waved his permission to the opposite bench. She sat and placed the object on the table before her. It was a large, thick booklet. She crossed her arms over it protectively. //If you will pardon my errors, I would appreciate the opportunity to practice my Navaran. It has been many years, and I anticipate much inaccuracies due to lack of recent practices.//

//As you wish.//

//I was led to believe you hold the rank of Alliance Commander.// she said, hesitating only a fraction of a second to remember the correct declensions.

//That is correct.//

Sarah hesitated again, this time from dread. She'd been through this same conversation so many times with so many people, hoping so hard, only to have things crash each time. Why should now be any different? Still, being a high-ranking science officer, there was a chance, and she forced herself to ask.

//If I may inquiring, are you qualified to proctor the Basic Education Exam?//

//'Inquire', not 'inquiring.' I am.//

Sarah couldn't stop her eyes from widening, and she forgot about her error. //You are?!// She pushed the booklet across the table.

United Planetary Alliance
Basic Education Exit Exam
Level II, Form 13-C, Type NC
Issued to: Kirushenko, Sarah I.
Sigma Tau Ceti IV
Subspecialty code FLN, HS3
Do not accept if seal is broken.

read the cover.

//I have been in possession of this for several years. As you may know, it can be proctored by an Alliance officer of commander rank or higher, if they have been qualified to do so. Commander Guillaume has rank, but no teaching credits, and remains unqualified. Jan Dickerson has credentials, but does not have the required rank. So far, no visiting ship had an officer who met the criteria. If you have the time, sir, would you be willing to proctor the exam to me? I would do it at your convenience – early morning, late night – middle of the night, if necessary.// Sarah tried not to pester, tried not to beg, showing more emotion than she knew was polite. Desperation hung over her like a cloud. //I have studied the guidebooks for seven years. If I am not ready, I deserve to fail.//

Ti'onam examined the booklet. It was sealed on all four sides. The cover was worn, streaked by oils from constant fingering, but the seals were intact. It was a special bound version, meant for students whose present circumstances prevented the use of computers or other technical means to read and record responses. Answers would be recorded by hand on a special form within, and the form then fed through a computer when processed by the proctor, who was responsible for processing, recording, and ultimately conferring or refusing a Basic Diploma on the applicant. It was a long test, four hours, covering communications, mathematics, sciences, and political history. In addition, the applicant had to choose two of twenty specialty areas for additional examination.

//I shall speak to Captain Sullivan upon his return.// Ti'onam said, returning the booklet. //I am reasonably certain he will allow me the time necessary to administer it. You are aware that I cannot score it until I return to the *Triumph*, and therefore it will be necessary to send you the results via the Chessorak Compound?//

//Yes, sir. I have tiny doubt I can pass the exam. I merely wish to have the

146

official paper to state it.//

//I believe you mean 'little,' not 'tiny.' You have chosen an unusual pairing for electives. Frequently, electives are seen as complementary: technical and computer science, planetary history with a language of the planet. You have chosen Navaran language and Earth history.//

Sarah knew better than to allow the discourtesy of a smile. That was probably the first lesson they'd gotten from the tourist bureau when they moved to Navara. //My apologies for the error; it is an honor for you to correct me. Those specific subjects are the easiest concentrations for me. To claim English or Russian as a second language would be false. I do not consider either of them to be foreign, and Tau Cetan is not an option. Earth's history has been taught to me from an early age. Father had some program chips with fascinating stories, and some reconstruction videos that made everything seem real to me.//

Ti'onam nodded, understanding. //I am curious as to which school you attended in Shir P'an.//

//Shir-Tal Nin, on K'Layam Street, in the east quarter.//

//I am unfamiliar with that particular school.//

//I was told it was typical for a Navaran school. I simply accepted it. It presented a unique opportunity to learn, and was far better than decaying in Kuomi.//

//Your father was a Professor at the Allied Fleet branch at Kar Kuomi?//

Sarah nodded. //Associate Professor of Archaeology and Ancient Cultures. He considered it a demotion. He was the co-chair of his department when we were in Kiev, but he thought teaching for the Fleet would be an even greater honor. You may have read about him. He discovered the Gamma Europa IV dragon back in '58.// Sarah's eyes shone with pride. Father gave little reason for his children to be proud of him, but it was the one event of his life where he did deserve honor, and at the time, the galaxy had thought so, too. //I was very young then, but I do remember some of it. Seeing the digs, seeing the processes involved and the excitement of the results was what started my interest in the sciences.//

147

//Indeed// Ti'onam said. //I believe I may have read something about that discovery. Does he currently teach for the Allied Fleet?//

Sarah fell back into Standard. Navaran was Navaran, and that was fine, but it was constraining when emotional content was involved, and the word *father* dredged up an awful lot of emotional content. .

She fixed her eyes on the table. "N-no. I know he doesn't. I – don't know where he is right now. I haven't had contact with him in a number of years."

"There was a murder in Kar Kuomi approximately the same time your family would have been there," Ti'onam probed.

The hair on Sarah's neck prickled up. *Factual statement/ non-accusatory. General information,* she categorized his words. "Yes, there was. I was unaware it was of sufficient importance to make galactic headlines."

"Murder on a planet with an uncompromising position of non-violence is a newsworthy item," Ti'onam said. "I recall it because of a correspondence from my stepmother. As the wife of an Alliance Legislator, she believed it important in the name of interplanetary relations to attend the trial. The accused was a human professor at the Allied Fleet branch, whose family testified to his unusually violent nature. My stepmother recounted her impressions of the children, who were frightened but willing to testify. She was especially impressed by a young girl who allegedly attended classes at a school in Shir P'an. I was curious if this child attended your school as well."

Sarah didn't dare raise her eyes from the table, concentrating instead on a small knothole at the edge of one of the boards. The knot had fallen out, leaving an empty crescent that went clear through the thick tabletop. She didn't need a mirror to know her cheeks were red. *Why couldn't the past ever stay in the past where it belonged!*

"Sir, you do me a dishonor if you believe I don't know what you are truly asking," Sarah said, wishing she could shrink small enough to escape through the innocuous little knothole. "The child of whom you speak did attend my school, because you have surmised correctly that I am she." She lifted her face, as cold and composed as any Navaran's.

//I am not proud of my testimony. What I related was the concern of no one in that courtroom but the juries, and I objected to saying some of what I did. I did what I felt I had to, to protect someone whose welfare I was concerned about, nothing more. If that one factor were not pertinent, I would never have testified at all. And I would prefer to converse about another subject.//

//Understood. Forgive my discourtesy.//

Outside, a downpour let loose, splattering the soggy ground.

Sarah glanced at the window. "Dimi won't be happy with that. If you'll excuse me, I shall stir the heater. Everyone will be soaked when they return." She rose and walked to the kitchen.

"I am uncertain as to how long Captain Sullivan will be detained. It is possible there will be sufficient time for you to complete the exam. If my work would not disturb you, I am able to both proctor and work at the same time," Ti'onam offered. "Would this time be convenient?"

Sarah froze. She'd waited seven endless years for this very moment; to have it really about to happen was overwhelming. She remembered just in time not to shout for joy.

"Five minutes!" she pleaded, trying not to jump in place. "Give me five minutes to build the fire and grab my supplies!"

"Shut up, Dimi! I'm taking my exam!" Sarah announced the moment the door opened. "I just started the last part! Give me a half hour!" She hadn't needed the full time allotment on any section, but Mr. Ti'onam made her suffer just the same.

"I am required to follow protocol lest you disagree with your score. The accuracy of a standardized exam is invalidated if the conditions are altered," he insisted.

Damned Navarans!

Dmitri was happy for her, happy he wouldn't have to listen to her mope about missed opportunities ever again. He collapsed into his chair, tired from a productive day. They had walked at least thirteen kilometers, too much of it in the rain. Most of the morning was wasted in town, hanging out in the places the local men gathered to socialize, listening to gossip and inquiring about what people had heard about the explosions. They'd uncovered a few more clues, but it had been a tortuous process, translating back and forth. He wasn't Sarah; translating all day like that was a pain in the… brain. They'd visited some of the families, found out where the people had been, where they liked to cut wood, why they were in that particular spot that day, seen some much milder symptoms of radiation poisoning, but nothing to shine a spotlight on an answer.

Sarah finished the exam with a flourish, skimmed over her work, and turned in the answer sheets. Finished! She wasn't going to sit and twiddle her thumbs this time! She thanked Mr. Ti'onam in a dignified manner, but gave a squeal of joy as she jumped on her brother's lap and gave him a neck-wrenching hug.

"I did it! I did it! I finally took it!"

"Good for you. Now get down before you kill me." Dmitri pushed her off. "You can tell me all about it later, so I'll know what I missed."

Sarah stood up, but she couldn't calm herself. Her spirits flew beyond the ionosphere, held aloft by pure joy. She paced restlessly, wanting to run and shout and kick her feet from happiness, but she couldn't do that with all the adults around.

"Most people are terrified by their educational exams," Granger said. "I don't think you could look happier if you tried."

"I don't think I could be!" Sarah beamed, hugging herself. "How often do you get the chance to do something you've been looking forward to all your life?"

She opened the shutters on a front window. "The rain's stopped. Dim? I'm going for a run before it starts again. I've been sitting forever, and I'm all wound up. It's not that cold."

"Wear a wrap," Dmitri warned as she shut the window. He lounged sideways in his chair, one leg over the arm. His eyes were closed, and he didn't bother to open them. "No chills! I'll be starting dinner soon."

Sarah dug under his jacket by the door and pulled out a length of wide grey cloth. She wrapped it around her back and shoulders, crossed it over her chest, behind her back, and brought the ends around her waist to tie in front. It was wide enough that the part that covered her shoulders came up to make a high collar, protecting her neck. She paused to pull her hair out from under it.

"I'll probably just head out toward the fields. I won't be long."

"May I accompany you?" Andreiev asked. "I haven't seen that area yet."

Sarah turned away. Imaginary cold fingers scraped her spine, weakened her knees, stole her breath. "I'm – just going to get some exercise, run up and down the path a few times. Nothing exciting. There's nothing planted in the fields right now; it's not very interesting. I'm sure you'd rather rest, just coming back from town."

"I don't mind. You can tell me about the fields."

A fast glance at Dmitri brought no relief; he hiked a thumb at the door.

"I guess." To change her mind now and hide in her room would be unacceptably rude. Away from Dimi - with a stranger? How fast could he run after walking all day? How long would her knees hold out?

They started down the path behind the workshed, Sarah leading but not leading, refusing to allow the lieutenant to walk behind her. They walked in heavy silence until she reminded him, "Don't touch me."

"I remember," Andreiev said with a tinge of annoyance. He was at least a meter away.

"Just – making sure."

Silence descended for another long pause.

"I can run fast," Sarah announced to the air. "Very fast."

It was difficult to tell if she intended it as a boast, a warning, or an odd comment meant to start a conversation, but Andreiev nodded. "I can run fast, too."

Sarah glanced at him several times as they walked, face riddled with indecision. Without warning, she spun and shoved him hard in the chest with both hands. "You're It!" she yelled, and ran down the path for all she was worth.

Andreiev stumbled backwards. It took a confused second to realize what she meant. He took off after her.

He had caught up within ten meters when Sarah stopped, gasping. She gave a breathless shriek as he closed in, and held her arm up to stop him.

"I concede! Don't touch me!"

"Win accepted." Danil bowed his head as he neared. He bent over with his hands on his knees, breathing hard. Within shouting distance across the fields stood a small white cottage, and beyond it, a workshed four times as large. It looked peaceful and story-book perfect, right down to the smoke rising from the chimney.

"That is your neighbor's house?"

"Yes. That is the Aletneshfaja's."

"You wish to visit with them?"

"No. Their house is simply at the other end of the path. I told you, I only wanted to go for a run."

Danil looked around. Both sides of the path were surrounded by wide fields covered with brown stubble from the previous season's crops and the present season's low, dense layer of green. Now and then a large tree still stood; across the fields, the forest took over again.

"These are the fields you help work?" He scooped a handful of wet soil to examine. "Tell me about them."

Sarah shrugged, walking for home. "What's there to tell? It's

151

boring."

He brushed the soil from his hands and walked along side her. "So's the ship, unless you're engaged in battle or an asteroid field, but you always want me to talk about that. I've never farmed, so to me it's not boring. It's fascinating, actually. Eating food that you grow yourself. It's so... natural."

"You rough up the dirt, throw the seeds in, and wait for them to grow. They do it on their own. It's not like you have to come out here and give them a pep talk." Sarah giggled. She could just imagine the round and very opinionated Mrs. Al scolding a field of vegetables that wasn't growing fast enough.

Andreiev smiled back. "Do that again."

"Do what?"

"Smile like that. You look much happier when you do."

Sarah snorted. "Hmph! Perhaps when I find more to be happy about, I will smile more."

"You aren't happy, here?"

"I'm sure I could be happier elsewhere."

"Could you smile for me anyway?"

"Why?" Sarah's defenses flew up. She took two steps backward. The Al's house was a closer haven than home. If necessary, she'd stake Charlie's porshie-wrestling brute strength against this city-bred, space-weakened yacht-jockey any day, especially where she was concerned.

"Potamu shto," Danil replied. "Because ... I ... think you have a very nice smile, and I like happy people. Because ... If you don't, I will feel that my being here is the reason for your unhappiness. Because ... I think this is a very beautiful planet; if my hosts walk around sad all the time, I will think it's a terrible place to live. I will dread my time here, and leave with bad memories of it."

Sarah allowed a fragile smile to etch her face. She tipped her head to look at him with more than just a sideways glance, violet-blue eyes sparkling with cautious humor. She dared to catch his eye for a millisecond before looking back at the ground, cheeks pinking.

"I think I can accept that reasoning," she decided, and began walking once more.

They walked back slower, stopping for Sarah to explain a particular crop, or a harvest method, or a tree that grew near the path, and she grilled him on astrophysics and space travel. Danil was pleasant, she decided. He'd been alone with her several times now, this time with no

152

one else remotely near, and he had been nothing but polite and considerate, always respecting her wishes to keep some distance, not even threatening to touch her as a joke.

Charlie was gullible like her brother Vladimir, easy-going and playful like Dmitri, and occasionally let loose a hell-raising streak that reminded her of David, a DM-V-DA cross. He was fun to be around, a fearless defender, but not a source for intellectual stimulation.

Danil was different, with Viktor's gentle patience, Sergei's educated interest in things around him, and Dmitri's rakish looks, a VI-SE-DM cross. That made him interesting, predictable, dependable, and a willing cohort for almost any activity. It was a very respectable combination, worthy of trust. Sarah made a conscious effort at looking more cheerful and less nervous for him, despite the intensity of the trembling she felt inside. The pressure in her chest made her breathe fast until she felt light-headed again, but without the burning pain of pneumonia.

"Do you know anything about allergies?" she dared to inquire.

"Not much," Danil answered. "I have reactions to three kinds of plant oils and two medications, but I don't know much about the process. Why? Do you have one?"

"I'm not sure. Dimi does, but I've never had one before." She paused, frowning. She'd looked like a fool enough already; she didn't want to make things worse. She was tired of being treated like some dumb kid when interesting work was afoot, and she'd never get any respect if she kept looking stupid. But if she didn't ask, she'd never know.

"May I ask you a personal question?"

"If you'd like."

"Are you… . Do you wear some sort of personal scent? A cologne of some sort, or perhaps a scented cleanser?"

"Why? Do I smell like I need one?" Danil teased, then regretted it when she stopped walking and folded inward.

"That's not what I meant." She twisted a lock of hair around her finger and gave it several hard tugs.

"It was a joke," he said, but Sarah remained upset. "Yes, sometimes I do. Why? Do you like it?"

"I don't know," Sarah said vaguely. Ten more paces on the path and they'd round the final bend, and the cabin would be in sight. "I only asked because – every time you come near me, my chest hurts, and I feel like I'm having trouble breathing. I know allergies can affect the respiratory system in strange ways, so I merely wanted to know if there was something specific I could be allergic to."

"I'm sorry, I didn't know that," Danil said, concerned. "I can stop if it bothers you."

"It's not that bad! Maybe it will lessen the more I'm exposed to it." Sarah remembered to smile.

* * *

She sat in her evening position, cross-legged on Dmitri's bed.

"Are you feeling all right?" he asked.

Sarah frowned. "Why?"

"You must be dying of some God forsaken ailment, to go off with that lieutenant like that. You won't even walk to town with Charlie."

Sarah made a face and gave her brother a less-than-polite Russian hand gesture. "*Fig!* You know why I won't walk with Charlie. Danil doesn't think like that. He has a much more advanced and educated mind. We walked toward the Al's and I showed him the fields, explained how we work them. It's so mortally *boring* compared to what he does every day. I was embarrassed to tell him about it. We must be two of the dullest people in the universe, living this way.

"Anyway, he explained some of the logarithms involved in trajectory calculations – how they plot courses? – and the algorithms involved in achieving a stable planetary orbit. You don't think of it, but do you realize planets aren't perfectly round? All those fluctuations of mass and gravity have to be taken into account, especially when weapons programming, along with speed and angle of motion, and ship's mass and stuff. It's nowhere near as easy as we think. He's a weaponry officer, and he has a deep-space pilot's license, too; he has to know things like that.

"He's really interesting to talk to." Sarah sighed. "He *is* an Academy graduate, after all. He's a Class-One Weapons Specialist. Viktor was only a three. And it's just the biggest coincidence he's also from Russia. Don't you think that's the most awesome thing, all the way out here? And he really does keep his distance, just like I asked. He's never tried to touch me, even once. But you're sort of right. I do get a little sick every time he comes near me. I've narrowed it down to an allergy to the cologne he wears, or his soap or something."

"Allergy? What makes you say that?"

"Because." Sarah flipped her hair behind and stood up to stretch. "Every time he's close enough for me to smell him, I get lightheaded and my heart starts pounding really hard. Sometimes it gets hard to breathe, and I feel really shaky. I keep going over it in my head, but that's the only reason I can come up with."

"Sarah-Irina Kirushenko!" Dmitri stared, dumbfounded. An incredulous look spread across his face, as if he'd stumbled on something astounding. "So you *are* Human, after all."

"What do you mean?" Dmitri looked as if he could see through her clothing. Sarah folded her arms protectively over her chest.

"You're coo-ey over Danil, aren't you!" Dmitri crowed. "Aren't you!"

"I am no such thing, ever! Don't you *dare* spread a false rumor like that!"

"Ohhh, yes you are!" Dmitri grinned maliciously, delighted to be on the giving end at last. "It makes perfect sense! You don't talk that long to anyone but me, ever! Since when do you get up in the middle of the night to cook something? You don't even want *Charlie* walking out to the fields with you alone! You can't wait for him to notice you so he'll talk to you, can you. Is that why you took his recorder? You're not allergic to anything he wears! For the first time in your life you're having an honest-to-goodness normal human feeling, and you can't even recognize it, can you. Welcome to the Human race, Sarah! You might even reach adulthood some day!"

"I most certainly am not!" Sarah cried, unable to blush any harder. "I don't like him that way at all! I-I was simply trying to be nice! You're always nagging me to be more social, and that's all I was doing! He's from Russia, he speaks Russian, he tells me about Moscow and St. Petersburg, and places like that. He can explain questions I have on mathematics and astrophysics and things you can't! That's all!"

No! No! That *couldn't* be it!

Could it?

She wasn't acting *anything* like that!

Was she?

Did Danil like her that way? Is that why he wanted to walk with her?

"Sar-ah wants a boy-friend! Sar-ah wants a boy-friend!" Dmitri taunted, dancing about.

"I talk to Mr. Ti'onam, too! I speak to him in Navaran about Navara! And I try to approximate Navaran-style foods for his benefit, too! You wouldn't think of saying that about him!"

"No, but he's not the one that's got your heart in your throat, either! Now you know what poor Charlie's suffered all these years." He leaned around to meet her avoidant eyes, puckered his lips and made kissing noises. "I know some-thing Da-nil does-n't!"

A tight fist swung hard in his direction, but missed. *"Stop it!"* Sarah cried, tears breaking through. *"Stop it!* If you spread such a lie, Dimi, I swear on Viktor's grave! I will run away forever and you will not find me! If it takes me a year, I will walk barefoot to another compound and wait for the next ship to take me home. If you say anything remotely like that to a single person downstairs, I will be gone long before you even know it!" She turned away and hugged herself.

Dmitri shook his head sadly. "Come here." He turned her around.

"Hey." He lifted her chin, but she crossed her arms and turned sideways. He moved in front of her again; Sarah turned stubbornly back to where they'd started. Undaunted, Dmitri rubbed her shoulders.

"Who knows every embarrassing secret that's ever happened to you, hmmm? Even the ones you'd rather die than let someone know actually happened?"

"You do."

"And who knows every embarrassing thing that's happened to *me* in the last seven years?"

"I do."

"And we don't talk about those things, do we? Just Our Little Secrets. Like that time at the Compound last year… ?"

Sarah couldn't help a faint smile at the memory. "I think Nora was more embarrassed than you were," she sniffed. "Almost as much as that girl. At least you didn't have to face Nora every day."

"Yeah, well." Dmitri reddened. He got her to turn and face him. "That was the *only* good thing about it, I guess. I wish I'd known she was Nora's niece. The point is, I don't want you going off the deep end. Your secret's safe with me, just like all the others. I won't tell."

"There's nothing to *be* made secret, because there is nothing *to* be secret about," Sarah persisted. "I'm *not* that type of girl! I don't want you spreading false ideas that create wrongful impressions of me and put me in situations that I am not prepared to deal with!"

"If you insist. I wish you'd relax and run with it, though. He's nice enough, but I'm still your big brother and I'm not about to let anyone mess with my little sister, but I'm glad to see you finally feeling something for someone else. I'd rather have to follow you around picking up pieces of broken heart than have you freeze everyone out of your life."

Sarah's face set like stone. "The only thing I might *'feel'* is kinship for a fellow compatriot, that's *all*. And in my experience – and yours as well, I am very aware – broken hearts cannot be healed; they bleed forever. I cannot bear to inflict any more of that type of pain on myself. I carry enough of that already."

Dmitri gave her a firm hug that she squirmed against. "No, I don't think they bleed forever. They're just very slow to heal."

* * *

"Mr. Andreiev, may I speak with you, please?" Jack Sullivan said that night when their hosts had retired.

"Of course, Captain." The younger officer followed him alone to the higher-ranking bedroom.

"Mr. Andreiev, for better or worse, you seem to have established a working rapport with Miss Kirushenko, far better than I have," he admitted. "She acts as if she expects me to bite her, but she allowed you to accompany her on a walk. If I may ask, what do you talk to her about?"

Andreiev shrugged. "Nothing in particular, sir. Mostly we speak of Russia. Sometimes she speaks of her family, or some of the places she has visited, and she asks about the places I have been."

"I see. Does she ever ask you technical information? Other cultures, governments, weapon systems, ship's capabilities, politics, anything like that?"

Andreiev frowned. "Not exactly. She has been aboard an Explorer-class ship before, so she is somewhat familiar with its capabilities. She asks many questions about astrophysics, Davies Warp theory, and astronomy in general. Some of them were specific questions on areas she was having difficulty with in her studies, like clarifying Wilm's Theory of Particle Expansion in warp-field generation. Others appeared to be more for the benefit of conversation, such as asking about my duties as a weapons officer. I don't think any of her questions bordered on classified information, sir, if that's what you mean."

"Good. Does she ever speak of her life here?"

Andreiev shook his head. "Not much, sir. She claims this planet is very boring and I would not be interested in hearing how to tell if a vegetable is ripe."

"A farm can be a dull place to live if it's not your choice to be there," Sullivan agreed, having fled the wheatfields outside Alberta the first chance he got. "Andreiev, try and push her to speak of her life here anyway. Who are her friends? What towns do they visit? Has she taken a vacation? Does she keep up a correspondence with anyone but her family? Any information whatsoever. I don't care if it's last year's rainfall totals or the iron workers' strike three towns over. Try and get a picture of her life here – who or what she considers interesting, where she goes to find excitement. Try and find out any unusual contacts she might make during the year – traveling salesmen, perhaps. I want to know if she might be unwittingly in contact with some sort of double-agent, perhaps a member of another alien race doing the same thing she herself is doing, posing as a native to gain information and report back somewhere else."

"I can try, sir. However, she claims to have no need for friends beyond the neighbors we have met. She says the natives here are 'boring as dry sand,' and she has no desire to associate with them at all."

"Do your best. Mr. Andreiev, what's your opinion of her?" Sullivan thought further.

"As a person, sir?"

"As a person."

He hesitated. "She's – interesting to talk with. She's highly intelligent, widely traveled, and she is very knowledgeable about many things. But ..."

"But?"

"She... has many odd rules I must follow before I can speak with her," Danil frowned.

The captain looked puzzled. "Rules? What kind of rules?"

"I must keep so many meters from her, I must never attempt to touch her, I must always walk in front of her, never behind, and she prefers to stay within sight of the cabin," the lieutenant recited. "She seems very... restless at times, like she's unsure what she's supposed to do. It's as if she *wants* to build a friendship, but she doesn't know *how*. In many ways, she seems very much like a young child."

Sullivan nodded. "I've noticed that myself. But she's not a child, Lieutenant. I shouldn't have to remind you that teenage girls can be – *impressionable*. They're emotionally vulnerable, and can misinterpret simple gestures between friends. She's a very attractive young girl, far from home, with limited human contacts and no doubt starved for contemporary human companionship. I'm glad you've been able to win her confidence, but keep in mind, it could be very easy to abuse such a position, should the opportunity present itself."

"Captain! I assure you, I – "

Sullivan held up a hand. "I believe your intentions are nothing but honorable, Danil. I'm warning you for your own sake. Be her friend, find out what you can, but if you feel the situation becoming uncomfortable or uncertain, back off," he ordered. "If necessary, I can have Mr. Ti'onam assign you simple work that will give you an excuse to be alone. Her brother seems to have his hands full as it is. We don't want to leave any broken hearts behind."

"Aye, sir." Andreiev shifted feet. The girl's ability to discuss complicated technical matters made her seem far older and more experienced than she was. Danil knew she was young. He was aware of that. He reminded himself consciously of it, every time he caught those big, beautiful eyes watching him.

Though the problem remained in the back of his mind, Danil didn't have long to worry. In the morning Sarah was nowhere to be found. The first thing Sullivan had everyone do was check their equipment; to Dmitri's snide satisfaction, everything was present. The morning wore on, with no sign.

Dmitri shrugged off her absence. "Honestly, I have no idea. Sometimes she needs to be alone. She'll be back by dark."

"We're wasting time," Sullivan tried to impress on him. "We need to explore the other site, and it's dry at the moment. Every time it rains, we may be losing critical information that could put this whole thing to rest."

"I told you, *I can't leave the cabin* until Sarah returns," Dmitri insisted as he cleaned the breakfast dishes. "You're free to go on your own, but I can't go that far without her knowing where I am."

"You have to be accounted for, but she doesn't? Where's the logic in that? Leave her a note, then."

"It's not the same! Trust me," Dmitri said irritably. "You think I like sitting here scratching my ass any more than you? She was a little upset last night. It's better I wait here."

"Upset about what?" Granger inquired.

"Nothing important," was all Dmitri would admit. "I merely pointed out something personal she'd overlooked."

It didn't make sense to Jack Sullivan why someone prone to illness would disappear into damp, cold wilderness all day, when she could avoid people by moving to another room.

"I don't understand this," he said to his officers in the privacy of the back room. "Eight hours is a damned long time to be wandering around thinking."

"A lot can be accomplished in eight hours," Kyle pointed out. "That's a nice chunk of time to finish something you're working on."

"Or move it to another location," Andreiev said.

"Or destroy it," Ti'onam added.

"She could be more than a third of the way back to the compound,"

160

Sullivan said with frustration. "She could be off trading information with an accomplice. She could go all the way back to the explosion site, tamper with evidence, destroy the data collectors. And her brother claims to not have a clue as to where she is."

"Does he or doesn't he?" Granger said. "He's a pretty smooth talker. If she's the brains, maybe his job is covering up. They're all alone out here. Outside of Dickerson stopping by the other day, what supervision do they have? They visit the compound every so often, but who checks on them here? What if we walked in on something in progress, and our being here is interfering with its completion?"

"As much as I am loathe to agree with Dr. Granger," Ti'onam said, "I think his idea bears further investigation. When we arrived, Mr. Kirushenko delayed our entry so that he could, quote, 'clear away some things,' unquote."

Memory curled into concern on Sullivan's brow. "I want answers, and I want them now. That girl gets up early again, I want her tailed. If they're going to delay us, intentionally or not, we're going to detain them in exactly the same manner. It's time to start prying."

"Where does she like to go?" Sullivan inquired at lunch. "Does she have a favorite place where she hides? A sheltered area? An abandoned shack, perhaps?"

"I have no idea," Dmitri said with perfect innocence. "I've never followed her. She takes off when she needs to think. She says she just walks around a lot. She likes to lay out bait on the paths, watching the animals that come to feed. She's dragged me along once or twice, but I think it's boring. She'll be back by dark," he repeated with certainty. "She always is."

Andreiev made his daily rounds, visiting the twelve air-and-rain sample collectors spread around the yard, feeding the samples into his omnicomp and analyzing the results. Over time, they should show a picture of lessening atmospheric contamination. If they didn't, the source of radiation could be continuous. After these, another dozen awaited him on the paths radiating from the cabin. He must have been concentrating very hard on his readings, for he never heard so much as a leaf rustle, but the next time he looked up she stood only a few meters away.

He smiled welcomingly. "Sarah, I'm glad you're here. You're just in time to help. If you'd like, I'll show you how to run a sample analysis with the omnicomp."

Sarah stayed where she was, dress damp and dirty, leaves caught in her wild hair, impassive as a Navaran. The pink-rimmed eyes were puffy to anyone who cared to look, but they gazed at the world with arrogant detachment. She spoke to him, cool and distant.

"It was brought to my attention that, unbeknownst to me, I was behaving in a foolish manner that might possibly have been misinterpreted to mean something that it did not. I assure you, it was not my intention to mislead you through conversation. If I have given you a false impression of myself, sir, I apologize, and I shall endeavor to make absolutely certain I do not create such an ambiguous situation again. While I find your offer to broaden my educational aspirations most intriguing, I – have other matters that require my attention at this time. I have found your presence to be acceptable and non-threatening, and I would welcome the opportunity to accept instruction at a later date. I thank you most kindly for your offer."

She spun on her heel and disappeared into the forest at a run, leaving Danil confused and not a little hurt.

* * *

"Kyle, how sensitive is your omnicomp?" Jack asked his medical officer.

"Depends on how you define sensitive," Granger replied. "I can pick out a flying canary a kilometer away, but I can't read its heartbeat from that distance."

"I'm not looking for heartbeats. I'm looking for a girl."

"I take it you mean one specific missing one, not a temporary romantic conquest."

Jack shot his friend a look of annoyance. "What can you pick up from a footprint?"

"Well, if it's fresh, it'll show up on infra-red. If it's deep enough, I'll catch it on depth scan, but if you mean can it track someone through a forest, unless she's barefoot and leaving a trail of bio-detectable materials, it would be tedious and slow. You planning on tracking her?"

"I think it's time we played a little hide and seek ourselves," the captain thought aloud. "Let me get Ti'onam and Andreiev to keep the brother occupied. You and I are going to take a stroll through the forest, and if we just happen to come across Little Red Riding Hood, so be it."

"Closing in on a hundred meters, Captain. I suggest we move

162

cautiously."

"She still in the same place?"

"Assuming it is her, yes," Granger said, watching his readout. They'd followed the far bank of the roaring stream the entire way. "There's movement, but it stays within a few meters. Whoever it is, they're caged, or they like to pace."

A minute later, Jack touched the doc on the arm. "That's her," he whispered. "By that bend." He pulled Granger behind a wide trunk. They crept forward, gaining some fifteen meters before stopping to observe again, the crashing water covering their noise.

The Kirushenko girl sat on a flat slab of stone that protruded halfway across the water, knees pulled up under her skirts. A cloth was spread nearby, out of reach of the churning spray. Several items sat on it, arranged with geometric precision. Sarah held something in her hand; it appeared to be a small book, but she wasn't reading it. She hugged herself, rocked a little, then wiped her face with a striped cloth. Jack realized she was crying.

Several minutes' observation revealed little else. Twice she glanced in the book, appeared to speak, then went back to rocking.

Sullivan decided to make himself known. "Come on." He and Kyle walked to the water's edge.

"Miss Kirushenko." Jack announced their presence from a distance of six meters. She was flighty enough; he didn't want to intrude too closely. "Fancy meeting you here. I don't suppose you're checking for contamination as well?"

Sarah gave a screech and leapt onto the bank. The book fell, but the cloth stayed balled in her hand. "Get back! Don't touch me!"

"I remember," Sullivan assured her. "I only meant 'Hello'."

"Don't touch me!"

"This is a pretty little spot," Jack said, looking around. "Very peaceful. Is this where you come to be alone?"

"Don't touch me!" Sarah pleaded, trembling.

"Take it easy, there, Miss," Granger said. "No one wants to touch you. You'll make more friends if you just say 'Hello' back. I'm sorry if we frightened you."

"I have a badge in Navaran So-Tau-Kam, and I have a blue belt in karate! I can very well defend myself!" Sarah's empty hand slid into a skirt pocket. When she pulled it out, it gripped a small paring knife. She held it close, pointed at herself for the moment but ready to strike if necessary.

163

The blade was too small to do much harm, but Jack took the move seriously. "Put that away. Neither Mr. Granger nor I have done anything to warrant violence."

Sarah whirled and tossed the cloth as far as she could. Before it could land, she charged across the flat rock and leaped from the end. She missed the opposite bank by half a meter, landing up to her knees in the cold water. She sprang up the other bank, speeding through the trees as fast as her legs could carry her.

"Let her go," Kyle said, watching her disappear. "I think we may have done more harm than good."

Jack frowned. "What is it with her and touching? Not even a paranoid, 'How did you find me here?' or 'Why are you following me?,' just an automatic 'Don't touch!' What's she afraid of?" He picked up the book, brushing damp soil from it.

Ni'iloran's Comprehensive Lexicon of Navaran Gantaan, Customs, and Idioms, read the translated subtitle on the cover. "Of course. A text reader would be forbidden; anything she wanted to read would have to be in a bound copy."

"Why in God's Great Name would anyone need a Navaran phrase book on Sigma Tau Ceti?" Granger snorted.

"She likes languages." Jack ruffled the pages, unable to decipher the alien paragraphs. "She's got photos stuffed in here. This must be her." He kept her place with his finger and held up the colorless picture. It showed a close-up of a small boy and a tow-headed girl, both grinning wildly over a huge cake with seven candles. Whose birthday was involved wasn't clear. It was imprinted with a date almost exactly ten years previous.

"Here's another one. It looks like a graduation picture, but not Dmitri. *Bukmop,* 2261," Jack read off the back. "I take it that's Russian for something. There's a couple more here."

Kyle retrieved the tossed cloth. "This is a shirt," he said with confusion. "It can't belong to either of them; it wouldn't fit anyone but a small child."

"A book to study, an old shirt, family photos, fruit and some bread, a jackknife... That's hardly the making of a bomb expert." Sullivan sighed, eyeing the arrangement. "It looks like you might have been right all along, Kyle."

"You said she was emotionally upset before you disturbed her?" Ti'onam clarified, examining the Navaran text.

Jack leaned against the bedroom door, listening for encroaching footsteps. "She was crying while we observed her. Does that make a difference?"

"The page on which you found that particular picture is an appeal to the deceased for strength and understanding in a time of great difficulty," the Navaran explained.

"Like a prayer?" Granger snickered. He stood by the window, watching for eavesdroppers. "I would think praying's too passionate and purposeless an activity for a Navaran. Wouldn't that be the same as admitting defeat? What do they pray to? Oh Holy Father of Pythagoras, show me the numbers?"

"Kyle!" Sullivan barked, but Ti'onam ignored the insults.

"Not exactly. There is no deity involved. On Navara, death is seen as an end to physical existence only. The consciousness, composed of energy, continues to exist. In times of dire circumstances - mortal illness, for example, or perhaps losing one's way in the desert, it is not unusual for one to seek out the circulating energies of one's ancestors, admitting to failures in correcting the condition and asking to tap into any memories of deceased relations that could be of assistance."

"That makes sense." Andreiev waved the graduation photo that had held the placemark at the prayer. "Viktor was the brother who died at Outpost 62. She could be praying to him."

"Ti'onam, is it possible she could have learned to tap into this 'collective consciousness,' so to speak?" Jack said. "Putting Navaran theology aside for the moment and assuming what you say is fact, could she feasibly receive information on subjects she has no knowledge of, simply by contacting the spirits of people who once did?"

The Navaran's shaggy brows rose surprisingly high as he contemplated the idea. "It is a concept I had not considered. In theory, I would have to say it is possible, though I cannot envision it being accomplished. In practice, I would estimate the chances to be close to zero."

"Why?"

"Even if she were raised her entire life in Navaran custom," Ti'onam postulated, "intelligence aside, she remains genetically human. She would not have the mental disciplines necessary to achieve such power, nor would her brother have the knowledge to receive such contact. Many years of intensive study are required to learn to communicate with ancestral identities – five standard years on average. Even then, it is not a clear means of communication, involving more intuitive content than actual conversation. We know for a fact she spent no more than four years on Navara. Even a native would not gain such skills before they were thirty years of age, possibly. However, it is a moot point. In most likelihood, I am the first Navaran to set foot on this world. There are no energies here to contact."

"Point taken."

"I don't think that would stop her from trying," Andreiev surmised. "We already know she will go to great lengths to learn something."

"Ignoring the Navaran mumbo-jumbo, it makes sense," Kyle said. "She felt upset for whatever reason, and prayed to a dead relative for guidance and strength. There's nothing unusual about that; people do it all the time. Whether it works or not has never been proven, but many religious practices encourage it. She brought her lunch, a couple of mementos that give her comfort, and she retreated to a private place to collect her thoughts. Perfectly normal, especially for a teen."

"So what does the shirt have to do with it?" Jack asked.

Granger shrugged. "Could be hers from when she was little, a favorite shirt worn for something special, something that brings back good memories. A secret security item, like a teddy bear. It's possible we surprised her in the middle of hugging her blankie, so to speak. Maybe her upset was caused by embarrassment – a big, highly intelligent girl confronted by someone catching her in a very private, childish moment. Again, perfectly normal."

Sullivan at last gave a nod. "She's immature enough for me to believe that. In any case, gentlemen, it certainly doesn't point toward anything illegal. I should have brought cards with apologies printed on them. It would have saved me a lot of time."

A wail through the quiet cabin announced the return of Trouble. Jack heard the tears and rapid-fire Russian as soon as he opened the door. He retrieved the parcel of items and swallowed his pride.

The girl clung to her brother, face buried in his neck. His arms circled her, comforting. Dmitri glanced over as Jack appeared.

"Can you *please* tell me what the hell you did out there?" he demanded. "What the hell is she talking about?"

"Kyle and I came upon her while walking along the river. We'd barely said hello when she threatened us with a knife and ran. We never meant to frighten her. And no, we didn't attempt to touch her."

Dmitri's features shifted from hapless victim to angry parent. He pushed the girl off and held her chin so she would look at him. "What knife? What's he talking about?"

Sarah shrank small. "I-it was just the little kitchen knife, to slice my *jichinas.*"

"Give it here!"

The tears evaporated, replaced by disbelief. She hung her head as she reached into her pocket and handed him the item.

"You know the rules about knives!"

"Yes, Dim, I know. It was only for the fruit. I swear! You can check!" She held her arms out, as if waiting to be frisked.

"Upstairs! And think about how stupid you were in the meantime." Dmitri swatted her backside once as she turned.

Sullivan stood by the stairs. Sarah stopped a safe distance away, and he held out the bundle wrapped in the ground-cloth.

"You forgot these. I didn't think you meant to leave them there with such a high chance for rain."

The eyes flicked at him. She reached for the cloth. "Thank you," she squeaked, and fled to her room.

Ti'onam approached Sullivan after dinner. "Captain? If I may have a moment of your time, I have found something I believe you may find interesting,"

"Of course, Commander." Sullivan waved his head toward their room. He shut the door behind them, then checked out the window to make sure no one was outside. Nightfall or no, the girl unnerved him with her ability to move silently from place to place, appearing out of nowhere. It made him jumpy. It wasn't that the investigation was a secret; it was the idea of privacy in general.

"What is it?"

"I spoke with Miss Kirushenko yesterday during your absence. We discussed her time on Navara, and the fact that her father was an archaeologist. When I inquired as to his current status, she became evasive and began to discuss one of his more important studies. It was then that I began to connect the name and occupation with an event that occurred some seven years ago on Navara."

Ti'onam activated his omnicomp, called up a file, then handed it to the captain. "Miss Kirushenko confirmed my suspicions, though she did not wish to discuss the subject further."

Academy Professor Guilty of Homicide read a headline from a galactic news article. Sullivan adjusted the magnification on the small screen to skim the print.

"I requested Lieutenant Reese to check the ship's computers for me, cross-referencing the name Kirushenko and Allied Space Fleet. She discovered this article, among others, and transmitted them to me. I first heard of the incident through media sources, but I did not pay more than passing attention to it until my stepmother mentioned it in a correspondence," Ti'onam explained. "She attended the trial of a widowered Allied Fleet professor accused of inadvertently killing his six-year-old daughter in an alcohol-induced rage. Seven of the surviving siblings testified against the father at the trial. The professor was one Alexander *Kirushenko*, an archeologist formerly of the Kiev Scientific Institute, and the youngest witness called, a child just nine years old, was a *Sarah* Kirushenko."

"I don't suppose that could be a coincidence? I guess I can understand why she might be reluctant to speak about her father. Witness to murder at nine years old. That would explain some things," the captain mused with regret. "The cringing near authority figures. The way she flinches when a voice is raised. When I confronted her about the omnicomp, she curled into a ball. I thought it was an act, a gesture meant to extort sympathy out of me. If she'd lived with that kind of violence before, she probably expected a violent response from me as well. I was aggravated over the incident, over what seemed like a deliberate lie directed at me. No wonder she won't come near me."

"Understandable, but there is more, sir," Ti'onam continued, looking serious even for a Navaran. "There was ample evidence and testimony that the Sarah of the trial was also severely mistreated as a child. At the age of eight years old, she was indeed hospitalized – not for pneumonia, but for emotional collapse and suicidal behavior."

"And you're suggesting that, if this is the very same Sarah Kirushenko, we may be dealing with a mind that is mentally unstable."

"It is a possibility we have not considered," Ti'onam conceded. "While she may seem more or less rational to us, it may be that she experiences episodes of less cohesive behavior, and that during these episodes she is creating the disturbances which have brought us here. Perhaps it is during these episodes she disappears. Her brother could be unaware of her difficulties."

"Is she, or isn't she? I haven't been able to catch her for certain either way. I can see where there could be a possibility, but we've got to have *evidence*, Ti'onam." Jack tapped a fist in the air with a sigh. "We have absolutely no evidence. Could she be doing something on one hand, and not remember it on the other? We need Dr. Granger's input, but how can we find out when we're not supposed to mention the fact he *is* a doctor?

Or *is* that the reason why?" He walked to the door and called Kyle in.

Granger blanched, reading the article in the omnicomp. "Good God! That fits, Jack! That takes care of several missing pieces to the puzzle that's been bugging me."

"What do you mean?"

Granger held the omnicomp up and shook it. "The information here. I told you I helped Dmitri get her to bed when the girl was incapacitated the other night. What I'm not supposed to mention is what I saw. I accidentally got a view of the girl's back. She's covered with scars, Captain. I can't begin to tell you how many, but at some point, someone beat that child within a centimeter of her life. There's some mean ones on her back, but there are much fainter ones on her arms and face. The brother insisted it wasn't him, that the father liked to drink and had a bad temper. At first I didn't believe it – all he has to do is look at her and she obeys him, but the more I thought about it, the more sense it made, based on the fact that the boy also has a few scars, and the fact he seemed rather used to dealing with someone who was less than sober. This article confirms his story."

"So Ti'onam's theory seems reasonable to you?"

"Well, I certainly know better than to disagree with a Navaran," Kyle said dryly, "but medically, it bears further investigation. There's a bigger worry in my mind, though, Jack."

"Mental illness that's been neglected for seven years?"

"Not quite." Granger rolled the idea around in his head, thinking. "More likely the possibility of an undiagnosed one."

"How do you mean? A new illness superimposed on an old one?"

"No, I mean the brother. Severe abuse leaves scars, Jack. Not just physical ones, but mental and emotional ones. We know for a fact she's had problems: a history of physical illness resulting in a medical phobia, and now treatment for a severe emotional crisis. My concern right now is the brother: they lived in the same house, suffered similar abuse, at the very least witnessed the death of a sibling at the hands of a parent. She collapsed from the stress and received help, but *he didn't*. He admitted he took care of his father when his father'd had a few too many, starting as young as ten years old. Do you know what that does to emotional development? The kind of example that sets? If Sarah lived with that for nine years, that means her brother lived with it until he was seventeen. That's an entire childhood lost in a grossly dysfunctional environment."

Sullivan nodded, absorbing the truth. "That's not much of a

childhood, parenting a parent. You think he may be more affected by it than he appears?"

"I'm just saying it's not outside the realm of possibility. You've seen how she jumps when he gets mad at her. His model for discipline was physical violence. Who's to say he's not as strict a disciplinarian as his father? And whose to say there isn't more than that article is telling."

"Like what, Kyle?"

Granger's brow furrowed with indecision. "I have no proof of any wrongdoing, Jack. I don't like to mention things without facts."

"Do it anyway."

"I told you, the girl was feeling some pretty bad aftereffects of the party, and I helped get her to bed. I woke up several hours later, and a light was still burning upstairs. I went up to make sure things were still okay."

"And were they?"

"Yeah, everything was quiet," Granger said, playing with the omnicomp. "They were both asleep. Dmitri in his sister's bed, and Sarah curled up tight in his arms."

Jack Sullivan's eyes widened, and he stared at his chief medical officer. "Two emotionally unstable teens, out in a wilderness, kilometers from anywhere, all alone with each other, day after day...."

"We don't know anything for a fact, Jack," Granger said quickly. "Yeah, it seemed a little inappropriate, but he'd also been sitting up with her while she was sick. He may have simply decided to sleep there to keep a closer eye on her."

"Kyle, I want you to get that physical," Sullivan ordered. "Get her alone, see what she'll tell you. We were told she has a problem with doctors, but we've only the brother's word, and we've tripped him out of several half-truths already. What if he's lying, doesn't want her to be examined lest she reveal some mistreatment? Or she may be afraid for someone to find out, afraid it would make a bad situation worse. This is your department, Doctor. I want an answer by this time tomorrow."

"Aye, Captain," Kyle said grimly, not looking forward to the task at all.

Prologue, revisited

It was all she'd thought about for nine days. Nine blasted long days and nights, until Dmitri left her alone again. As soon as she felt the coast was clear, she made a beeline for the safe. She reached deep and drew out the EPSAR – *Electron Particle Stimulation and Amplification Ray*. Long ago she'd been promised a chance to fire it, but the Burin-Jai invaded and Viktor died before she got her turn. The shape fit her palm, the weight distribution and curves ergonomically correct for a humanoid hand. A thrill shivered her spine. A forbidden weapon she was forbidden to touch, from a place she was forbidden access. Ooooh, she was being bad, and she knew it!

She checked the setting on the dial and aimed it out the window. Vrrrrt! she hummed in her mind, pretending to press the trigger. Vrrrrt! at the little rug on the floor. Vrrrrt! at the bottle of cologne on Dmitri's chest of drawers. If only she could really shoot at something! She didn't dare, though.

Did she?

She was all alone. No one would ever know. She knew the settings; Viktor had explained them. She turned the dial all the way up, then all the way back, hearing the faint clicking.

She'd keep it on the lowest setting, she **swore** she would! Dimi'd kill her if he found out. She was already indebted to him up past her head for causing trouble. As she turned it over in her hands, her finger **accidentally** brushed the safety and turned it off. Fate must have meant for it to happen. All she had to do then was push that little button there...

She chose the metal pail Dmitri threw refuse in. If it got too hot, it shouldn't burn. Not with a short low-level blast. Checking the setting once, twice, she aimed, squinted, sight-measured, braced herself, took a deep breath, and pressed the trigger, having no idea what to expect.

Nothing happened.

Disappointed, she tried again. Still nothing. A beam of blue-white light should have come out of the front and heated the pail. She put the safety on and examined it. Everything seemed right.

Like she would know if it wasn't!

She tried again. Nothing, not even a dying hum. She turned it over, locating the nearly invisible seams. Ruining the metal nib of an ink

171

pen, she pried the cover plate off.

No wonder! Son of a – ! The power pack was missing. Damn Dimi and his overly cautious paranoia around her! She hadn't hurt herself in years, but he still didn't trust her! Dammit all. All this excitement for nothing. Now what?

Two weeks passed before she found it, wrapped in a cloth in the very back corner of his bottom drawer, among a whole mess of personal things she had no business knowing about. It took a minute to figure out the connections, but at last she snapped the powerpack in place, replaced the cover, undid the safety, aimed, pressed the switch, and ...

Nothing happened.

*She jammed her finger on the trigger several times, squealing with frustration. She shook it, slapped it against her palm, with no effect. What **now**? She bent her head close while firing toward the window. It gave the faintest whine, as if it wanted to fire, but was just too tired.*

Of course. Four years had passed since its last charge. The power cells were dead. Wasn't that just her luck! She disassembled everything and returned the pieces to their exact places yet again.

All that hope for nothing! And no way to fix it, either.

Was there?

Sarah sprawled sulking on the floor of her room, watching her fingers tap the boards. For every problem, there is a solution, *her Navaran schoolmaster used to claim, but this was a puzzle that would take some pondering.*

She was forced to wait until the next visit to the compound. She downloaded her mail files herself; she had to, they were privacy-encrypted. Bless dear, sweet Vladimir! She printed out the three pages of engineering text, stuffing them in the middle of the fifty-two pages of regular mail she had printed from her brothers, three months' worth. Then she dumped the file, erasing the contents from the mail cache, purging it from the main memory banks.

Once home, she read through them, memorizing the text line by line. How to do it, though? With no micro adjusters, display monitors, computer-aided feedback safety mechanisms, insulated wiring, and no master quantum-particle energy supply?

For every problem there is a solution.

She could try, but how? **How?**

172

How to build something that was still hundreds of years of development away on this planet? She scribbled ideas on random bits of paper, and began to collect her materials.

The tension in the silent room crushed any desire to speak. It wasn't fair to say that the opening of the door was a relief; for some the sound brought a flood of panic, trapped with no escape from bad memories. Sasha Kirushenko entered with trepidation, followed by his Family Reintegration Counselor, a sharply dressed man by the name of Najar Shahir.

"And Satan walked in …, " David muttered, a photo-copy image of his father, thirty-something years younger.

"Father!" Valeria greeted him with a hug and kiss, followed immediately by her twin sister Galina. "Welcome back! It's so good to see you. How was your trip here? We've missed you."

"It - It was - adequate," Sasha stumbled. "Thank you."

"This is Nikky!" Valeria smiled too forcefully as she pushed the boy forward. "He's ten now. Do you remember your father, Nik?"

Nikky looked up, up and up at his towering father, filled with brutal stories from David. "Not really," he decided as he shook the big hand. "It's a pleasure to meet you, sir. You look like your pictures in the book at home."

Polite conversation had never been one of Sasha's strengths. "That's … nice to know, Nikolai. Thank you."

Katerina came forward next, stretching on her toes as he leaned down to receive her kiss. Her hands trembled, but her face was ever cheerful. "Hello, Father! Welcome back. May I introduce my husband, Doctor John Carver." She took the baby from her spouse.

"Mr. Kirushenko, sir." John took his turn shaking the giant sweaty hand. "It's nice to meet you."

"And this," Katerina beamed, showing off the baby, "is your very first grandson! Roman Alexander Ivanovitch Carver. He just had his first birthday."

"He's very beautiful," Sasha said. Soft blue eyes gazed at him in innocent wonder; chubby fingers reached up to comb the scratchy beard.

"Touch gentle, Roman," Kat urged, but the grandfather merely smiled.

Sergei held out his hand as if nothing had ever been wrong. "Good

174

morning, Father. It's nice to see you looking well."

"Thank you, Sergei." Six favorable responses. Sasha began to relax.

"Good morning, Father," Vladimir mumbled from the far corner of the table. His ashen face glanced upward for no more than a second, and his eyes didn't try to make contact.

"Vladimir," Sasha remembered. "You've grown." Vlad tried to get more words out, but the best he could do was nod.

"Perhaps if we take a seat at the table," Shahir directed, "we can all talk at length. Now, your father here…"

"Is … Is that her?" Sasha asked Valeria. He pointed to the smallest girl in the room. Honey-brown hair swung about her shoulders and her sable eyes sparked with excitement, impatient for her turn to be introduced. Another mongrel, Sasha realized, not showing a predominance of either parent's distinctive genes but a random sampling of the two. Her mother's cheeks and chin, her father's darker coloring, a medium skeletal structure with average height. In a way he felt disappointed; all the girls should have looked liked their mother, this one perhaps more than any other.

Valeria nodded. "Yes, Father. This is Marina. Say hello to your father, Marina."

Sasha sat, the better to greet the child. "Marina," he whispered, needles of guilt spearing him in the heart. His youngest child, whose conception was unplanned, unwanted, and whose disastrous birth stole her mother's life. The heartache of Maryana's absence surged up and nearly brought tears to the dark eyes.

The little girl hugged him fearlessly. "Hello, sir! Valeria-Mom says you're my real Papa. Is that true?"

"Da. Pravda."

Marina grabbed him around the neck with a squeal. "I knew it! I knew it! I'm so glad! Tanya Padachevsky's always teasing me because I'm the only girl in class that doesn't have a father. Now I can tell her I really do, and mine's bigger than hers! Can you come to my school so I can show her? I'm in third form at Leonov Academy."

"No, Marina," Valeria said swiftly. "Father's just returned. Perhaps at a later date."

"I want to sit with you, then." Marina climbed onto Sasha's lap.

Nikky grabbed his father's hand. "*I* wanted to sit next to him! I said it first, yesterday! I want to tell him about my skiing."

Sasha, a twenty-three-year, thirteen-time veteran of the parent brigade, whose older children would never have dreamed of fighting in front of him, sat speechless. The best he'd hoped for was a drawn-out, painful, fumbling faux-pas. After everything said at his trial, he never expected such a blameless welcome.

"Hush!" Galina said. "Down, Marina. You'll hurt Father's knee. Sit in the chair, here. Nik, sit next to Marina. You're still close."

The group took seats around the table, though Vladimir hid behind Sergei at the furthest corner, and David stayed standing.

"Please, sit," Shahir invited. "There's a chair over here."

"I'm not here by choice." David's words fogged with cold. He dug in a pocket for an expensive Centauran black-stem cigarette and stuffed it between his lips. "The *only* reason I'm here is out of a favor to someone I respect too much to refuse. If it were up to me, I'd rather be branded than sit here and smell the stench of the filth you brought in."

Valeria closed her eyes and squeezed her forehead with her fingers.

"David!" Galina exclaimed. "Apologize!"

Sasha took a steadying breath. "He is entitled to an opinion. It is better to have open honesty than walk in the shadow of a falsehood. Thank you, David, for your honesty."

"Fuck you, too."

"There's no smoking allowed in public buildings, sir," Shahir reminded the tall youth. "You'll have to put that out."

"Yeah? Well, maybe I'll just go wait outside, then."

"Don't do it, David," John Carver said. His tone never suggested anything less than pleasant, but some sort of threat hung between the words. The younger man rolled his eyes and swore under his breath. He took a final drag of tobacco before snuffing it on the sole of his shoe. He stuffed the cigarette back into his pocket and slouched in his corner with an angry huff.

"Fine!" David pulled a tin of candies from another pocket and stuffed two in his mouth.

The counselor began before the hostility could escalate. "Very well. The purpose of today's meeting is to reintroduce everyone, and perhaps catch up on the time that has passed. This is not easy for anyone involved, but I ask everyone, please remain civil. We are not here to settle old scores. Some of you have shown a desire to re-establish ties with your father. Our meeting here is a chance to get things off on the right foot. Feel free to ask any questions you may have. If you feel uncomfortable saying something, there are scribe pads around the table that will send directly to my screen here, and I can answer them anonymously for you."

"Aw fucking Christ!" David spat from his corner. "Here we go! You bring diapers for him, too, Kat? Serg, do something with him!"

Sasha was confused until he realized the comment wasn't directed at him. At the corner of the table, Vladimir wiped away tears.

"Tough it up, man," Sergei said. "It's not that bad."

Vlad scrubbed at an eye. "It's not that. I just keep thinking about Sarah. I don't know how to break this to her. She's not gonna like it. I don't want her to think I went traitor by coming here. I'm not!"

Sergei shrugged with ease. "Then don't tell her right away. Wait and see how it goes first."

Sasha scanned the crowded room and realized there were children missing. He knew about the two that died, but... "Who is missing?" He counted around, trying to remember the order. "Dmitri and ... Sarah could not be here? Will they be here later?"

"Gee, Val! Why don't *you* tell him why they're not here?" David stabbed, eyes narrowed. "Why don't you tell him why Vlad's bawling like a motherless pup the last six years? You haven't told him what you did to them? Coward!"

Valeria looked ill. "David, please don't do this! Not now! Why do you have to ruin this?"

Sergei scowled at David. "Why do you have to go digging that up now? You really want him to start puking?" He meant Vlad.

"They couldn't get here in time," Galina said. "They're doing research on a distant planet. Vlad knows which one, don't you, Vlad?"

"No!" Vladimir stared at her with disbelief. He sniffed his tears and lied to his father for the first time in his life. "She never told me. It's – way out in the Epsilon quadrant somewheres."

Shahir directed the conversation through the awkward moment. "That's very interesting. What kind of research are they involved in?"

Valeria regained her voice. "I don't really know the details. She doesn't write me."

"They do culture studies and language research on a newly explored planet," Sergei said. "They've been there a while now, but the distance makes communication difficult."

"It's nice to know she's using her abilities," Sasha said, unnaturally humble.

Shahir jotted down notes. "Marina, I think you brought a booklet of photos to show your father. Perhaps you'd like to tell him about them?"

The girl nodded. She handed her father a small book and opened it to the first page. "That's me!..."

177

Пятнадзать

Fifteen

Chichvash

Granger spoke to Dmitri about the exam the following morning.

"Please!" Dmitri begged. "One more day! You upset her too much yesterday for me to say anything. I'll break it to her tonight. I promise!"

"I have my orders, and today's the day," Granger insisted.

"Tomorrow! First thing! You can't rush her on these things. I'll – I'll send her out for the day," Dmitri threatened. "I don't have the energy to fight with her today."

Sarah entered the cabin, arms loaded with firewood. She dropped it near the heater with a clatter and brushed the wood chips from her dress. "Fight over what, Dim?"

Sullivan broke the rule. "Your brother is trying to prevent Doctor Granger … "

"Doctor?!" Sarah took a step backwards. "Who's a doctor? You said he was a biologist!" Her eyes locked on Granger. "Is that an academic title, or a medical title?"

"Sar…," Dmitri tried.

"… Prevent Doctor Granger from carrying out your required physical exam," Sullivan repeated, watching her reaction with acute interest.

Kyle ended the deception. "I'm the … Chief of Medical Services aboard the *Triumph*."

Not a sound was heard in the cabin, not a breath, not a floorboard; even the birds outside seemed to stop and listen.

The girl sprang for the still-open door.

Sarah was fast as lightning and determined to escape, but Dmitri had been expecting the reaction for six days, and was amazingly faster. His arm flew out and caught her around the waist, pulling her back just before her fingers could grab the doorframe.

"NO! You knew it all the time, didn't you! You lied to me! *Every one of you lied!* Navarans aren't supposed to lie!"

"I provided no false information," Ti'onam insisted, duplicating Sarah's hair-splitting semantic precision. "You never questioned me as to

Dr. Granger's status aboard the ship."

Sullivan watched with morbid curiosity. Obviously the brother had told the truth this time. He felt he should have been stepping in to help, but the girl had made it quite clear he shouldn't touch her. And sometimes observing was more educational than intervention.

"Sarah, stop!" Dmitri commanded. He locked his arms around her waist, but she pushed at them, trying to drop her weight down and slide out from under the straining grip, until his arms were more around her chest than her middle. Dimi waited for a jump, then leaned back and tightened his grip, pulling her off the ground against his hip.

"*Stop it! Enough!* Just *listen* to me!" he ordered. "You know the rules as well as I do. Field research personnel have to have a physical once a year if there is no regular medical service available. You've managed to extend that to a year and a half. Time's up."

"NO!" Sarah shrieked, stabbing him with her elbows. "I won't! He's not touching me! I won't let him! Dimi, you know that! Let go!"

Ti'onam looked down his nose at Granger. "It would seem your reputation has preceded you."

Kyle didn't have time to do more than shoot the commander a fiery glare. There was certainly a problem, but was it a real phobia, or just another rebellious 'rule' the girl had created, perhaps to insulate herself against further hospitalizations? Perhaps years of abuse had left her skin sensitive to touch. Perhaps she was afraid he'd discover the scars.

"Give me ten minutes," he said. "If you cooperate, I won't have to touch you at all."

"You can't do it!" Sarah screeched, kicking. "I know my rights! There's no other female present! I can legally refuse!"

Dmitri's grip weakened. "Should I send for Mrs. Al?"

"I can't use my equipment if she's in the room. If that's the problem, we can do it right here in the open."

"*Pervert!*" Sarah wriggled her feet back to the floor. She fought to lean her weight forward, pulling her brother onto her back so she could run.

Dmitri looked as trapped as the girl. With an aggravated sigh, he let go. The abrupt release of tension made Sarah stumble, and in the single instant it took her to reorient herself, he slid his arm up and locked it around her throat, pulling her head tight against his shoulder.

"*Listen to me!*" he hissed in her ear. "*You will go upstairs right now and get this over with! You are not dealing with Guillaume! These people don't play! I won't leave you alone. Don't make me have to get the*

Navaran to hold you!"

The feet stopped kicking; the struggling ceased. "You wouldn't!"

"I will if I have to. It's not like I have a choice in this, either." Dmitri relaxed his arm, allowing her to straighten up. Sarah didn't bolt but faced him, pleading.

No! she breathed.

Dmitri nodded.

What about...!

He motioned toward the stairs with his head, face filled with sorrow. Sarah looked over her shoulder at Granger, eyes wide with terror and already brimming with tears.

In seconds, she broke away and pounded up the stairs, Dmitri no more than a heartbeat behind.

"You've got about ten seconds to get up here," he warned Granger on the run, "and about five minutes to finish."

Kyle sprinted for his pack.

"Yell if you need reinforcements," Sullivan called after him.

The girl crouched in the farthest corner of the room, boxed in by walls and bookshelves, and though the bed was more than a meter away, it still limited access. She held her knees to her chest. Tears shone wet on her cheeks, but the cold eyes radiated distrust and fear. Dmitri blocked the doorway. He stepped aside to let the doc enter.

Granger hesitated, watching. This was what he'd been waiting for, wasn't it?

Yes, but was he risking his life to do it?

Concealing his caution, Kyle walked to the girl's clothes drawers, opened his pack, took out his omnicomp and field kit, and laid everything out across the top.

"Well, we're both in the same room. That's a start. I think I understand some of your reluctance, but if you can meet me half way, I promise not to touch you if I can at all avoid it."

The head turned away, fingers plugged the ears. Kyle waited, and sure enough, as the seconds passed, the eyes spun back just enough to observe him peripherally.

"Maybe we should talk first. Ask me some questions, if you'd like. Give yourself time to relax. If you'd prefer, I can give you a light tranquilizer."

The girl jumped to her feet, uncorking her ears. "NO DRUGS! No drugs, no tricks, no games, no lies! And DON'T TOUCH ME!"

Granger accepted the rules calmly, staying by the dresser. "Okay. As I said, I will try my very best to abide by that. I promise, this will be completely painless, and I'll be as fast as I can Overall, how have you been feeling?"

Sarah eyed him with contempt. "I won't answer psychological. questions."

"It's a basic health question," Granger said, though the answer set a warning flag waving in his mind. "Aches, pains, stiffness. What makes you think I meant it psychologically?"

He could see the gears turning in the girl's head. She'd been caught off guard, jumping the gun on defensiveness.

"How I am feeling. Feeling implies emotion, emotion impacts behavior, behavior equals psychology."

"That's logical, I guess. Let me be more precise. From a medical standpoint, how has your health been?"

"None of your business." The eyes shifted to Dmitri.

"Healthy," Dmitri answered from the doorway. "She eats a modified vegetarian diet – unfertilized eggs, cheeses, milk. She'll eat vegetables that have been cooked with meat, and she'll strain the meat out of soups, so she's still getting some protein from the broth. And she dips into gravies now and then."

"I do not!"

"I've seen you. She hasn't been ill for about, oh, nineteen months?" Dmitri counted back. "She's had splinters in her hands, and cut her feet a couple times. Nipped by porshies now and then, nothing serious. Nothing we haven't been able to treat ourselves."

Granger nodded. He'd rather have had the girl answer, but the information was useful, anyhow. "Any problems with your eyes? Visual disturbances? Eye strain?"

"You're the doctor, you tell me." Sarah crossed her eyes as far as she could. "Actually, I do," she said, suddenly sincere. "My vision fades every evening until I can't see a thing. I can't see to read or write for hours."

"How long have you had that?" Migraines could do that. Pressure on the optic nerves. Tumors growing into the visual centers of the brain.

"Knock it off, Sar," Dmitri said from the doorway. "You're wasting time. She's talking about nightfall, Dr. Granger. Her vision returns just fine when she lights a lamp."

Granger realized he wasn't going to get a straight answer without his sensor readings. "I see. Why don't you sit on the bed for me, and we'll get this over with."

"It's bad enough you're in my room!" Sarah spat. "I will not allow you near my bed! Don't look at it. Don't think about it. If you so much as touch it, I will injure you."

Dmitri took Sarah's work stool and dragged it to the center of the room. "You're better off putting her here."

"That's fine." Granger opened the display of the omnicomp. The girl remained cornered. "Sarah?"

The nervous eyes waited. When he made no move, she mumbled something unintelligible.

"Sarah!" Dmitri barked, understanding. "She's not allowed to use that kind of language, Dr. Granger. I apologize for her."

"I can't take offense at something I can't understand. People often seem angry when they're really just afraid. I don't take it personally. I've been called all sorts of names in the line of duty, my dear, but it won't do you any good if I don't speak the language. You're going to have to try pretty hard to come up with something new."

"Necrophiliac! And I will never be your '*dear.*'"

Granger had the audacity to give her an upbeat smile. "That's certainly more creative."

"Coprophiliac!"

"Another big word, but only in the line of duty, I'm afraid. Try again – from the chair this time."

Clearly, it wasn't the reaction she was used to. Another worried glance at the brother.

"Dvigaisya!" Dmitri ordered in Russian. A final glare, and the girl ran up and over the head of the bed to the workstool, keeping the maximum possible distance from Granger. Real fear replaced the anger. Again the almost tearful, pleading look at Dmitri.

Granger weighed his choices. He understood how a visiting physician would give up in the face of such opposition. It wasn't worth the aggravation for a one-shot routine exam when there were sixty other people waiting. A general question or two answered by the brother, a notation on the form about the refusal, and the legal responsibility was fulfilled. Let the next physician deal with it. Even without the captain's orders, Granger had questions, and he wasn't about to take no for an answer. He had only one patient at the moment. If it took the rest of the day, he was prepared to work her through it.

How far, though? Easing phobias was a lengthy process. You didn't just walk into a room and throw snakes at someone and call it therapy.

182

That kind of shock could work, but it took hours, even weeks of preparation to get to that point, or the fear could worsen. Should he get the basics over with and let her go? Or, in the girl's interest, should he push further? She was a minor with an appointed guardian. Did she look to her brother for support, or out of fear? Was his presence to calm her, or make sure she didn't say something he didn't want said? Was he answering for her to simplify the process, or to keep her quiet? Or were they performing an oft-rehearsed act to avoid an exam, and she looked to him for the next cue?

"Dmitri, I'd like to talk to Sarah alone. Would you mind waiting outside for a minute or two?"

"NO!" Sarah flew halfway to the door before he finished the sentence. "He stays with me!"

"Five minutes," Granger promised. "Stay on the seat, and I won't touch you. I won't even come close. Just a few questions, then he can come back if you want."

"I know what you're going to ask! Not without Dimi!" Sarah looked about to panic again, but her brother guided her back to the stool.

"Cooperate," Dmitri said, pushing until she sat. "I'll be in my room if you need me. I warn you," he told Granger, "the door in here doesn't shut. The floor's warped. It takes five minutes of pounding to get it to close, and two people to push it open again. Yell if you need help."

"Dimi!" came the desperate cry, but Panic stayed rooted on the chair.

"I'm right next door. You're okay," he assured her, and stepped out.

The girl curled herself up on the seat, chin tucked to her chest, shoulders sucked in, hyperventilating. Granger watched the withdrawal with clinical interest. He gave her a moment to compose herself.

"If you come near me, I *will* hurt you."

"I think we've already established that fact. You stay in the chair, I'll stay here against the wall." Granger held the omnicomp aimlessly in one hand, letting it run without telling her it was on, as non-threatening as he could be. He wasn't sure how long she'd cooperate. He wanted the session recorded, so he could examine her reactions in more detail when he had time to think.

"What you tell me will be kept in strictest confidence, so please answer truthfully. Do you want your brother in here with you?"

"Yes! Right now! Call him back, please?"

"Are you comfortable with your brother being in charge of you? Does he ever do anything that makes you unhappy or uncomfortable with his authority?"

"Why? What are you implying? What are you going to do to him? What do you think you're going to do to me? I won't allow you to separate us. We're all we have left!"

"I just want to make sure you're happy with your current living arrangement. If you're in a situation that's making you uncomfortable, or you feel threatened, or if someone is hurting you, I want to stop whatever's upsetting you. If you'd rather not discuss it now, you can bring it up to me privately at any time."

"*YOU* are the only thing that's upsetting me!" Sarah growled, violet flames flaring in her eyes. "I will not allow you to insult Dmitri with your carefully shaded, open-ended, multi-interpretational accusations! If you want that question answered, I suggest you ask it to his face, because I will not lower myself to it! If he were to ask, I would give my life for him. Dmitri has put his life on the line for me, more than once, and what you insinuate sickens me to no end! No one in my entire life has taken care of me as well as he has! Your entire profession has no right to *ever* say those things to people when you don't know a damned thing about them!"

They were standard, everyday questions, required as a matter of course, 99.9 percent of the time answered in the negative. A violent reaction was a warning for further investigation, but somehow Granger didn't think he'd get much further. She was too smart, too used to medical protocol. "I don't think I've said anything specific, Sarah. What do you feel I'm insinuating?"

"Dimi!" Sarah called tearfully. "I want you in here! I won't allow myself to be treated this way!" He reappeared in seconds.

"Fine." Granger sighed. He'd made the attempt. He'd followed regulations. The offer to help had been extended, but he'd gained no new insight. Was she that loyal, or did she only say it because Dmitri was close enough to hear?

He picked out his integrated bioscanner from the spread of equipment. "We'll finish up, and you can go. Just a simple body scan," he said, holding up the pencil-like instrument. "I'm sure you've had those before. I don't have to touch you if you cooperate. Stand up for me, please."

Kyle stepped within arm's length and scanned near her head, checking the readouts on the omnicomp's display screen. No gross structural anomalies in the brain.

Amazingly enough, he couldn't help thinking.

Distrust oozed from the girl's pores. He passed the scanner in front of her face; she snapped her teeth at it.

Granger yanked his hand back. He raised an eyebrow, but held his tongue. He'd never had a patient bite a scanner before. The doctor, yes; the equipment, no. He tried again; again she snapped at it. The hate-filled eyes dared him to act. Her arms shielded her chest as the scanner moved downward. He changed the diagnostics and went through the motions anyway.

"Any shortness of breath? Chest pains? Breast tenderness?"

"No."

"Digestive problems? Back pains? Muscle aches? Joint pains?"

"No, no, no, no, no, no, no, no," Sarah recited even after he stopped, gazing out the window with pretend boredom.

"Menstrual irregularities?"

The eyes snapped back to glare with deadly intent. "That's none of your goddamn business. Wave that near me again, and I will throw it from the window." Again, the worried look to the brother.

"No, you won't, Sar," Dmitri warned from the doorway.

"As your doctor for the moment, I'm afraid it *is* my business," Granger replied, making mental note of the change in attitude. He tried a sideline. "Are you sexually active?"

That did it. A hand shot out faster than light and gripped his wrist. Sarah slid off the seat, twisting his hand until the slim scanner was bent painfully under his chin.

"THAT'S NONE OF YOUR GODDAMNED BUSINESS AND IT NEVER WILL BE! Is it written somewhere I'm supposed to be? Is there a law that says I have to be forced to die so young? Point that thing at me again and I will KILL you!"

"Sit down, Sar." Dmitri took several steps into the room, directing but not touching. "He's just doing his job. Shh. Sit."

With a shudder, Sarah released Granger's hand and balanced on the edge of the seat. She pressed her wrists hard against her temples and took a shaky breath, blinking back tears.

Kyle Granger had brawled in barfights on a dozen different planets, got his ass kicked once by an eight-foot-tall Cirelian, and had been thrown from more wild mustangs on the family ranch than he could count. He would not be intimidated by a half-grown devil of a filly. The strength of her reaction was wrong, very wrong. Her nonsensical statements, coming from someone who until now had always spoken rationally, worried him more. Such turmoil usually had a reason.

185

"It's just a basic question," he explained with authority. "Sometimes people your age are, sometimes they aren't. If you said yes, I'd run a screen for transmittable diseases, that's all. I wasn't suggesting or accusing." He placed the scanner on her dresser and made up his mind. Stepping close, he placed one hand on her back, the other on her belly, unsure what the heavy dress might be hiding.

Dmitri realized what he was doing three seconds too late. "NO!"

The power behind the fist was stronger than Kyle expected. No warning cry, no protest, just a slammer of an uppercut that caught him full strength under his jaw. His head snapped back, making him stumble. Crashing into the dresser, he flailed backwards, knocking his things from the top.

"YOU SON OF A BITCH!" She leapt for him, trying her damnedest to finish what she'd started, but Dmitri held her from behind in a wrestling lock. It was all he could do not to be carried forward by the force of her resolve.

"LIAR! You promised you wouldn't touch me! You can't be trusted, either! Not one of you! You're just like every other one of your unholy profession! I don't have to put up with that! Come on! Come near me again and see what you get! *Let go of me!"*

"Are you all right?" Dmitri asked him, struggling. "She warned you not to touch her. *Calm down*!" Tears of outrage fell as Sarah fought madly against the indignity of the touch, the indignity of the suspicions, the indignity of the hold.

"And I said I'd do my best to avoid it unless I had to." The doc climbed to his feet, holding his jaw. Nothing seemed to be broken, as far as he could tell. "Temper's a little short, but I can see there aren't any problems with coordination or muscle tone."

"Are you done?" the boy grunted. "I don't know how much longer I can hold her."

"One second." Granger snatched his scanner from the floor. He gave a quick pass down one side of the girl's middle and back up the other, dodging fingernails and feet.

"All right. Let her go."

Dmitri released her.

Granger braced for further assault, but the girl dove for the window instead, flinging herself through the opening. He watched with horror as she disappeared, head-first.

"She just ...!" He dashed to the opening, but the girl was nowhere to be seen, injured or not.

Dmitri shook his head, unperturbed. "She's fine. There's a ledge out there. She slides to the corner where the logs intersect and she scales it like a ladder. It's less than three meters. In a pinch, she swings from the edge. It took me a while to figure out how she kept turning up outside when I'd banish her to her room. I could never catch her sneaking down the stairs. She wasn't.

"Now do you believe me?"

Шестнадцать
Sixteen
Elmench

"How'd you do, Doc?" Sullivan asked from Granger's doorway. "We could hear the commotion all the way outside."

"If I'm talking funny tomorrow, it's due to muscle strain from having my jaw all but dislocated by a hell of a fist." Granger's mouth twisted into a mirthless line as he went over his readings. "The only person I treated up there was myself. She wasn't kidding when she said she'd hurt me. If she tells you not to touch her, I suggest you take her advice."

"Don't tell me you're losing your touch with the fairer sex?"

"It's not funny, Jack. There's something not right with that girl, and I'm more worried now than I was before."

Sullivan grew serious. "What do you mean?"

Granger motioned for the captain to shut the door. When it was closed, he continued, "I mean that at first she refused to be examined without her brother present. Strange for a girl her age, but if she had a real phobia, he might be a person she trusts in such a situation. I'd allow that. Half the time he answered for her, and she almost never opened her mouth without looking for approval first. It got stranger from there.

"I can accept smart-ass answers to my questions. Half your teen patients with a chip on their shoulder will make things difficult any given day. That's normal enough. The scanners will turn up any major problem that might need attention. If she's been abused in the past, her efforts to make me dislike her could very well be a survival mechanism: push me to the breaking point, and when I blow up she can prove to herself I'm not trustworthy. I'll accept that, too. However, it wasn't until I touched on anything regarding personal relations or reproduction that she turned violent."

"You think she may have had a bad relationship?" Sullivan asked. "Maybe something she was pushed into?"

"I didn't know what to think. Now I'm afraid to." Kyle handed the captain his omnicomp. "Take a look."

Sullivan studied the readout, a humanoid outline with a pinpoint spot flashing near the waist. "What is it?"

"Possibly a reason for her medical phobia. It's a long-term medical capsule, buried in the fatty tissue at the back of the hip. They're quite common, used for lengthy administration of a medication. Depending on the drug and the dosage, you insert so many capsules into the fat layer and they dissolve slowly over time, releasing a steady stream of medication without having to worry about patients forgetting to take it. No mess, no fuss, no one knows but you."

"Any idea what kind?"

"Ohhh, yes. I figured there was no way in hell she'd give me a blood sample, so I did the next best thing. I took a sample from her hairbrush – not that she appears to use it much – and ran that through the omnicomp. It's Norval Estrate, an older, less commonly used form of birthcontrol."

"Birthcontrol? It's not *that* uncommon in teens, is it? At least in my day."

"It is when you take into account the fact this one is most often given in five-year doses," Granger said. "Going by the scanners, she's got less than a year left in there. Subtract five from sixteen, and she's been on it since she was eleven or twelve. My original fear was that she might be trying to hide a pregnancy, maybe the neighbor boy's, or worse, the brother's. I'm glad she's not, but this scares me more."

"Eleven? Is there – some other medical reason she might be taking it?"

"Not at that age. Not Norval. It has its legitimate gynecological uses, but that specific compound is prohibited in women under eighteen because in rare instances it can cause severe endocrine issues, including permanent sterility. You'd need a board of review to approve it, and no board in its right mind would approve Norval at eleven years old," Granger swore firmly. "I'd stake my license on it."

Jack Sullivan clenched his jaw. "And her brother's been in charge of her since she was nine. Have you reviewed her medical records?"

"Not yet. She won't answer questions regarding her relationship with her brother, outside of defending him. I'd also like to get a look at the contract they made with each other. I wanted to give him the courtesy of a chance to answer my questions first, before I go around him. Then I'll review her records and compare them to what he tells me. I'll make my final recommendation after that."

Sullivan stood up, troubled. "Do what you feel is necessary, Doc. Until otherwise, you are legally her current physician, whether she wants you to be or not."

"I'm aware of that. And Captain?" Kyle stopped Jack before he could open the door. "I shouldn't have to remind you, I'm walking a thin line here. This is a confidential conversation. She's still a child, with a court-appointed guardian who has yet to be proven anything but a concerned caretaker. I'll update you as soon as I know more."

Sullivan met the doctor's gaze with an equal amount of gravity. "Understood."

* * *

Dmitri poked his head in the door. "Captain Sullivan said you wanted to see me?"

Granger sat at the small writing table in the room. "Yes, if you have a moment. Come in and close the door."

"I apologize again for this morning. I should have expected the fist sooner. I hope you're not hurt too bad. She's done serious damage to doctors before."

"Just my dignity," Kyle said without levity. "I guess I got off easy. Have a seat, Dmitri. I have a few questions I'm hoping you can clarify for me."

Dmitri sat on the closest bed. "I take it they're about this morning."

"The bioscanners showed the presence of a long-term medication capsule. Hair analysis identified the compound. Do you know what that compound was?"

The boy heaved a heavy sigh. "Yeah. And it's not what you're thinking, so stop staring at me like that." He lifted his head shamelessly. "You can dope me with any truth serum you want, but my answer won't change. I've never laid a hand on her. I've been with her day and night for the last seven years, and to the best of my knowledge, no one's ever laid a hand on her like that."

"Then why? That's a highly dangerous drug for someone her age. Why risk her health if there wasn't a need? Why would she get that upset over general questions if there wasn't a problem?"

"Her level of upset was caused by *you*! By doctors, because no matter where we ever traveled, we'd get the same attitude you're giving me right now! 'Why would a boy be in charge of a young girl if he wasn't up to something no good?' Combine it with Sarah's very real fear of doctors, and it was like escaping a black hole! Her fear this morning was that you *would* find out, and do exactly like you're doing. You want to know why I'm in charge of her? Because our bitch of an older sister abandoned us on Navara – packed everyone else up and headed back to Earth without us. No food, no transportation, nothing but burning sand.

What was I supposed to say to a nine-year old kid who was losing her orbit over that fact? 'Can I drop you in an orphanage somewhere?' "

"You didn't answer my question."

"You have to understand Sarah. We haven't had an easy time of things. She guards her privacy really close. She hates to be embarrassed, and body functions embarrass her. She'd rather spend hours in pain rather than admit she needs to use the sanitary. She won't wear the right underthings because she refuses to acknowledge she's grown – um – you know – a chest." Dmitri motioned awkwardly with his hands. "She'd rather beat the daylights out of you than to allow you to find out something you're going to grill her on and she doesn't want to discuss. *Won't* discuss. Not that I want to do it, either."

"I'd like to hear it anyway," Granger said. The boy talked a lot, but he never said anything.

Dmitri looked at the floor again, forearms on his knees. "Sarah was only eight when our mother died."

"You said that before."

"Yeah, but Sarah was the one that found her." Dmitri added the all-important detail. "She found Mother on the floor, hemorrhaging and about to give birth. There was blood everywhere. It got on her feet, her clothes, her hands, her hair… Sarah called for a medical team, and in the midst of it all she learned without any warning how babies are born. Mother died a few hours later. Sarah blamed herself. She had nightmares about it, couldn't even look at the color red because it made her think back to all the blood. It totally messed her up on the idea of reproduction and growing up."

"An avoidance reaction, triggered by a traumatically stressful event," Granger diagnosed.

The boy nodded. He knew all the terms. "Later, when she was like eleven or something, she got her – you know – The monthly thing?

"All she could do was think back to Mother. She became absolutely convinced she was about to give birth and die, and nothing I could do would change her mind. When I tell you it was all I could do to keep her from hurting herself, I *mean* it! If you're really convinced you're about to die and you can't do anything to stop it, anything you do to speed it up and get it over with is good.

"Even when *It* finally ended, she'd touch her legs two or three times a minute, checking to see if *It* was starting again. She couldn't sleep, because she had to stay alert in case *It* came back. She's a really smart kid, but you just couldn't talk rationally to her about it. I got her to

Outpost 62, where our brother was. Viktor arranged for the doctor there to give her something to stop the cycles, at least until she could get used to the idea, maybe get some counseling or something, but she freaked so bad at the preliminary exams, they refused. Finally he found someone who implanted the drug she's got now. The cycles stopped, the panic stopped, the suicide stopped. And outside of constant insinuations wherever we go, and a terror that someone's going to remove the drug, she's been *fine*!"

"Obsessive-compulsive behavior, anxiety disorder, traumatic stress reaction," Granger rattled off, seeing the scope of the difficulty. "Great galaxies! I can understand the problem, but Norval Estrate is *not* the solution! Who was the physician that administered it? I take it that it was all done very quietly, and I won't find that in her medical records?"

"Probably not. I don't remember the name," Dmitri said. "The raid on the outpost happened right after. He could have been one of the casualties."

"If she still had a substantial amount of the drug left, I'd insist on it being removed, but there's only a few months left. I couldn't detect any immediate worries – no tumors or growth problems, but that doesn't mean any won't develop." The more he thought about it, the angrier he became.

"I can't believe they allowed you to bring her to a planet with no direct medical supervision. What if she suddenly started hemorrhaging? She'd be dead before you made it to the town, let alone to medical help! What are you planning on doing when the medication runs out? She should be receiving some sort of cognitive therapy to get her off that as fast as possible, not running wild in the middle of a – a – medieval forest!"

"This place was *exactly* what we needed after that raid!" Dmitri bristled. "You watch your brother be gutted alive and see how much peace and quiet you need!" He stood up, discussion over.

"Look, I hate to bring you down out of your lofty little Explorer, but all you are is a temporary visiting physician who barely examined her for five minutes. You never met her before, and you'll never see her again. You don't know a damned thing about her. I've lived with her day after day after day. I've done everything I could to keep her healthy and in one piece. So far I've managed to do that, and I don't need crap out of one-shot do-gooders like you to tell me I'm doing it wrong!" He gave a last look of disgust and left, closing the door a bit too firmly behind him.

Granger didn't stop him. The boy might have been telling the truth. It was plausible, at least. If it was a lie, it was well-rehearsed. And untraceable. The only other person who might back the story up was the girl, and after the morning's fiasco, Granger felt he had a better chance of growing wings than getting an honest answer. He hunted through his bag for his handicom. Activating it, he called back to the compound. It was time to get some real information.

*　*　*

Kyle called the captain into a second conference several hours later. "We might have big problems, Jack."

"What kind of problems?" Sullivan demanded. "Were your suspicions correct?"

"No, for the moment the brother's off my list of problems. I believe his story at this point. I'm glad I went slow. I had the compound transmit me the girl's medical file, and at least half of what he told me was substantiated by the records."

"I would think that would be a relief. You look worse than before."

"I feel it," Granger said with a sigh. "I skimmed through the information on file. It's a full copy of her medical history, all the way to her birth. Sixteen to eighteen weeks premature, Liquigen ventilation, repeated cases of pneumonia with frequent hospitalization, just like her brother said."

"And?"

"And then there's the details neither of them have cared to mention. The five *hundred* pages of text covering a nervous breakdown when she was eight."

Jack frowned. "Breakdown? I thought Ti'onam's article mentioned a stress-related illness?"

"To the point of a full nervous breakdown," Kyle said grimly. "She did find her mother dying. She did just what her brother said – wallowed in guilt that she'd somehow screwed up and if she'd only known more, her mother wouldn't have died. A big worry for a little kid, more so for a very smart one. Several months later her younger sister was killed – right after Sarah fought with her – and she blamed herself. A few weeks later, she cracked. Three months in a psychiatric facility for suicidal behavior, psychotic depression, a whole list of diagnoses."

"*Psychotic* depression? Aren't those two separate categories?"

"Not in extreme cases," Kyle explained. "Get depressed enough and you start imagining there are coffins waiting for you in the next room, maybe even glimpse them now and then, or perhaps see corpses where there aren't any. With her it seemed to be voices tormenting her, her dead sister among them, reminding her how she'd let the mother die. The files mention the distrust of doctors. I got off easy with a clock to the jaw – she's broken faces, stolen scalpels, even used a stun-control weapon on a roomful of therapists, so the fear aspect is very real. She responded well to chemical treatment, they found a psychiatrist she was willing to work with, but she had trouble with the outpatient therapist and refused further treatment. Same as what I've seen – fear, distrust, refusal to cooperate, panic with accompanying aggression and self-destruction."

"Be extra careful, then, Doc," Jack said, uneasy. "Treat any threats of violence as real, and take precautions to avoid them. I need my m.o. in one piece. I'll tell Ti'onam and Andreiev the same. I want any verbal or physical threats reported to me immediately, and I don't think it would hurt to make sure we lock our doors at night. You think she may still be having problems? That she may still hear voices?"

"That's the problem, I don't know. Unless I can get her to trust me, talk to me, I have no way of finding out. I can scan brainwave patterns, but she'd have to hold still for that. I can't do it without her knowledge."

"Would that explain some of the fast personality changes we've seen? Is it possible she has some sort of – split personality? That she could actually be doing something illegal and have no memory of it?"

"Like two separate minds sharing one body?" Granger thought a moment. "Outside of alien influences, mental transfer machinery, symbionts, and other physical causes, as an organic syndrome in humans, it's not really proven. *Theoretically* it's possible, but theoretically's an awful big category. Theoretically, she could have an identical twin around here we don't know about, too. It *can* be an effect of severe emotional trauma, but if there were two personalities, you would notice gaps in memory where one personality stopped listening and another started – she wouldn't remember a conversation you'd had, wouldn't remember being introduced, have no idea why you're in her home. She wouldn't respond to her name, have an entirely separate identity that acted, spoke, thought, even dressed differently. That would be pretty difficult to maintain in this culture. Most identity issues are single-incidence, you flip into it once, maybe eventually flip out of it, but not back and forth. From what I've seen, she's far too dependent, self-absorbed and introverted, but she holds a conversation when spoken to, and unless she's frightened, she's generally rational. As far as I can tell, her memory recall is intact. I don't think that's her problem."

"Then what is?" Jack still wasn't sure they should rule out brat.

"It's impossible to say without a full workup. With a raw deal like that, I think the brother's done the best he can, but based on observation? Emotional disturbance, immaturity, arrested development, history of mental instability. Give her a year in a stable, caring environment with normal rules for behavior, a structured learning program geared toward her unique abilities, the opportunity for normal peer relations, psycho- , perhaps even neurochemical therapy, and I think you'd see a teen who could conquer the world."

Sullivan nodded. If the girl had had a normal homelife ... she'd have been swallowed up by a thinktank. Was that any better a life than she had now? Was that kind of pressure any better? Isolated with a bunch of cranky old men and women, doing nothing but scribbling out ideas that were supposed to revolutionize mankind? The girl belonged at a debutante ball, fending off the attentions of a dozen potential suitors, not working on quantum-warp equations in some windowless spacelab somewhere.

"Do what you can, Kyle," he said at last.

"I'm working on it, Jack."

* * *

The cloudy night hung black as starless void, and the rain thundered down during dinner. Dmitri got up from his seat for the third time in ten minutes. He stared out the kitchen window into the dense velvet. Sarah didn't care if it rained or not, but she avoided the darkness as if it were alive.

Sullivan watched him. "I thought you said she's always back by sunset?"

"There are some absolutes to Sarah," Dmitri said. "She *absolutely* refuses to eat pickled cabbage. She *absolutely* hates deep water. And she *absolutely* will not be caught outside alone in the dark. It scares her. It doesn't happen, ever. Not voluntarily." He picked up the lantern from its hook in the corner. "I'm going to check the workshed again."

"Perhaps she stayed at your neighbors?" Andreiev suggested.

"Charlie would have walked her home by now. She won't stay there overnight." Dmitri spent five full minutes combing their small shed, but she wasn't to be found. Not on his bed, not in her closet or his, not under her bed. As a last resort, he climbed out her window to the slippery wet ledge and gave a check of the roof.

Nothing.

Damn her! Perhaps she'd hidden in the Al's barn. To find out would mean a long walk in pouring black rain. He shook his head. No. Sarah sitting in the dark in the same building as two porshies? Not in *his* lifetime. Sarah feared porshies almost as much as the dark.

He paused as he descended the stairs, foot in mid-air. A smothered cough, somewhere in his room. Dmitri went limp with relief. The one place he didn't look. He fixed a plate of food and brought it upstairs. He placed it on the floor and pushed it wordlessly to the edge of the bed with his toe, then returned downstairs, leaving the room in darkness.

An hour later he returned to an empty plate. Dimi sat on the side of the bed, turning the dish in his hands. "The rats are getting awfully big this rainy season. I think I'm going to have to fumigate."

"I'm not coming out!" squeaked a spiteful voice under the bed. "Not until they've left."

"That's an awful long time to stay under a bed."

"You knew, and you didn't tell me. You knew all along!"

"It wasn't my choice. I'm sorry. I wanted to break it to you at a good time. The captain decided he'd waited long enough. I wanted to tell you; I just hadn't found the right moment yet."

"And now we're in trouble, huh?" *sniff* "I really messed that up, didn't I. He knows now, doesn't he."

"Yeah. I had to face the inquisition on that one, thank you so much. I think it's okay, though. He wasn't happy, but he seemed to understand. He's really pretty nice, if you give him a chance."

The voice quavered. "You mad at me?"

"I suppose, but I've been madder. I'm not ready to feed you to the Burin-Jai yet."

"I hit him! Isn't that a crime or something, hitting an officer? Make them leave! I don't want to translate anymore."

"It's only a crime if you're an officer, too. You warned him, he chose to ignore it. His problem. Why don't you go to bed? You'll feel better about it in the morning."

"I'm not coming out. Ever."

"Okay. Have it your way, but I'm not covering for you. Anybody asks, I'm telling them where you are." He left, only to return and drop her blankets and pillow by the bed. When he came back to his room to sleep himself, the items were gone, and the room was silent.

The little house slumbered quiet and dark, except for light rain on the roof and Dmitri's soft breathing, when the rat squeezed out from under the bed. The support ropes under the mattress sagged; with Dimi in the bed, there was hardly room to move. Ears alert, the rat crept onto the bottom of the bed, careful not to wake the occupant. She curled up in the small space between the wall and her brother, wrapped in her own blanket, and fell asleep at last.

* * *

Breakfast came and went, and the rain poured. Jack Sullivan paced the floor from room to room, helpless over time wasted by weather. No wonder Guillaume's men hadn't gotten anywhere.

Sarah remained hidden. Dmitri insisted she was upstairs, but he wouldn't let anyone venture up to confirm it. Knowing more of her history, the disappearance made Granger uneasy, but he could now make allowances for it. He wanted to speak to her, perhaps make a sort of peace agreement. She couldn't hide for the rest of their mission.

He spent the morning making notes to himself, ideas to confirm, questions to ask, information to document in his own log. The doctor hadn't heard a sound beyond his thoughts, so he startled when he looked up to see Sarah standing in the doorway. She hadn't been seen in almost twenty-six hours. Dark circles ringing her eyes made her face seem ghostly. She wore the previous day's clothes, and her long, long hair was more disheveled than usual.

"I'm sorry for punching you yesterday," she announced before he could speak. Her face was as hard and distant as any Navaran's, but the weary eyes brimmed with betrayal. "I did not wish to cause you harm, but, as was inevitable by your profession, you violated our agreement, and I had to follow through."

Granger didn't move a muscle, lest he spook her. "I guess I knew that when I did it. No real harm done. I'm sorry I touched you. If you'd given me straight answers, I wouldn't have needed to."

Apologies exchanged and accepted, Sarah turned to leave.

"Please wait." The figure halted at the doorway. "I'm genuinely concerned about you, Sarah. Please stay a moment to talk. I won't approach you, I won't touch you, I won't stop you if you leave. You might not believe me, but I'm asking anyway. Five minutes, that's all."

There was a pause. "Depending on the topic, you may speak."

"I feel more comfortable speaking to people's faces."

"Ears work from both directions," but she did turn around.

197

"We'll have more privacy if you close the door."

"I am aware of the privacy factor involved. The door remains as is." Sarah peeked into the hall anyway.

"Are you aware just how dangerous that medication is?"

"I am aware there are risks. I find the level of risk acceptable. I have no intention of ever reproducing."

Granger suppressed a shudder. There was just something ... *unnatural* about a young, pretty human girl who could sound and act so much like a goddamned Navaran. "Are you aware there's less than a year left to it?"

A flicker of fear crossed the granite face, no more than half a second long, but it was too late. The stone cracked. "How long do you estimate remains?"

"Six months on the outside."

"And I am to understand you will not replace it for me?"

"Absolutely not. You're damned lucky I didn't find any complications. You should never have been near that medication, Sarah. It was a very dangerous and foolhardy thing for someone to do. There are much safer ways to achieve the same results, if I understand the reasons correctly."

"*Why* I am on it is *none* of your concern." She moved to leave.

"I've seen your file, Sarah! I know your little secrets!" Granger called. "I read the write-up by Dr. Cronan at Outpost 62. That much is in there. He refused to treat the problem without a physical *and mental* exam. I would have done the same, given his descriptions and your medical history. And so far, I don't see any signs of improvement. Would you be willing to cooperate on those now? If you can do that, I am willing to discuss an alternative medication."

The bait had its effect. The stone fell away to reveal gut-twisting anxiety. Sarah's eyes roved toward the door, around the room, searched the floor, but her brother was not there to give her advice, to decide for her. She was Alone. She took a step into the room, then another, keeping two meters between them. Granger got the feeling he was seeing the real girl at last; fearful, but wanting to trust; hurting, and wanting to be helped; terrified, but trying to stand on her own.

Sarah tore at the nail on her little finger with her teeth. "I don't know. Maybe some of it... I know Dimi would want me to try. I know you think I'm on this drug for some diabolical reason, but I'm not." She looked Granger in the eye. "I swear to you, I have never been put in a position of ... *procreation*, by *anyone*, friend or foe. That is an absolute truth, by the Code of Sil'anak himself."

"Okay." He made a mental note to clarify Sil'anak of Navara's statements on absolute truths with Ti'onam. "As long as it's what *you* want, not your brother. Answer me this, as honest as you can: Are you comfortable with your brother as your legal guardian? Do you feel he makes the right decisions for you? Is there anything he does that you wish he *wouldn't* do? Any times you don't like him having that kind of control over you?"

"Never," Sarah said without hesitation. "Dimi always thinks of me. I would not want anyone else in the universe to be in charge of me. Ever."

"Okay. Just one more thing: What's your relationship with that neighbor boy, Charlie? I've seen you appear very comfortable with him, but I've also seen you almost afraid of him. How do you feel about him?"

"I find your constant questions about my personal life to be out of line. Surely a doctor has other things to think about besides gossip. Nonetheless. Charlie is our very best friend," Sarah explained. "Charlie has also been crying over me since I was twelve. He would marry me if he could, but I can not and will not marry him. I have made it clear to Charlie that, while I value him as a friend, that is *all* we are, and all we will ever be. His head accepts this, but his heart still wishes it were different. I simply try to avoid putting myself in positions that might make him feel I have changed my mind, such as walking with him alone, giving him gifts, or allowing physical contact that might be misconstrued. Either way, he is a good friend, and I do not wish to see him hurting more than he does."

"He's very lucky to have a friend like you. I can't tell you the number of girls I knew at his age who couldn't be that honest with a boy. If more women would be like that at the outset, a lot fewer hearts would be broken."

The stone face rebuilt itself. Sarah fell silent, then took several steps until she stood before him. She pushed her sleeve up and held her arm before him, exposing the inside. Kyle resisted the urge to examine it; the reports said he'd find numerous thin scars – this time, self-induced. He looked at her questioningly

"Dimi says you're pretty straight. You honored his wishes as long as you could, and that I should at least try to trust you. I can't promise full cooperation, and I may yet back out of the deal, depending on how I'm treated. Do not touch me, do not attempt to restrain me in any form, but it is my experience that all medical exams begin with bloodwork."

"Yes, they often do," Granger said with amazement. *Was this a peace offering? Was it because the brother wasn't around? Or did her desire to continue her medication outweigh the fear?* Ignoring the risk of further injury, he rose to retrieve his medikit.

Семьнадзать

Seventeen

Jombashak

Sarah reappeared to the household the following morning, drawn into herself. Her lips mimed *Good morning*, but no sound accompanied it. She sat at the table, head bent so low her bangs brushed her plate, never speaking a word. It was her turn to clear breakfast, and she clung to the task as a lifeline.

Seeing the girl occupied, Granger called the captain and the Kirushenko boy into a conference in the hallway alcove. From there they could see her, and if she came their way, change the subject.

"I think made a small breakthrough yesterday in the fear," Granger whispered to Dmitri, "but I think it's best to use you as a go-between. You can filter things, tell me what might be feasible, explain things to her in terms she might feel more comfortable with. I made some promises not to share the information I came across with anyone, and I think it would be in everyone's best interest if I kept that promise. The last thing she needs is another doctor double-crossing her. Dmitri, you already know the details, but Jack, you're going to have to trust me on this. Unless I feel the information to be relevant to the mission or a matter of life and death, I can't tell you a thing more. I assure you, I'm giving your concerns the utmost attention."

"I can't say I'm exactly happy with that, but I trust your judgment, Doc."

"Thank you, Captain. Now, my second reason needs cooperation on both your parts," Granger told them. "Guillaume said one of the reasons they don't have much information on the local inhabitants is the difficulty involved in getting high-quality scans in sufficient quantity to put together reliable data. The neighbors come around often enough, but to go and get the omnicomp, set it to their specifications and let it run where it can't be seen isn't always feasible. While I'm out here with the proper tools, I hate to waste the opportunity to help advance a branch of science.

"What I propose is to set a subroutine for that specific data, and leave the omni running when they're around. I'll have to keep an eye on the power, but it would make it easier to gather data without anyone knowing about it. I know how to set up the system after it's reconfigured, but it'll

201

take some tinkering to override the programming on the autoconservation mechanisms."

"That sounds reasonable enough," Jack said. "I'm sure Guillaume would appreciate anything you can give him. Ti'onam would probably know how to change the settings."

"I expected that. Problem is," Granger sighed, "to do that, he's going to have to open the casing and get at the internals. We've already had one instance of omnicomp investigation. We have two general omni's, but mine's the only medical one. Say a curious someone with an eye for memorization and a grudge against medicine decided to imitate something they saw, and managed to wipe out the workings of a medicomp in the process. We can detect radiation hazards with the other two, but mine's the only one with a biocomp that can run analyses on medical samples. We lose my omni, and we could all be in danger."

"She won't touch one of those again," Dmitri said. "I can promise you that for a fact."

Sullivan bore a distinct lack of confidence in the boy's promises. "Dr. Granger is right in pointing out that even to risk losing his omnicomp would be a major setback for this mission. Can you get her out of here for a few hours? Send her to help your neighbors, to borrow something, perhaps? Just until Ti'onam has a chance to work on the omnicomp. Three hours at most."

Dmitri shook his head. "I can't guarantee anything like that. I could send her there, but there's no saying that Mrs. Al won't tell her she doesn't need help today and send her back. Anything I can get her to do in the workshed won't take more than fifteen minutes."

Dickerson's words came back to the captain. "Does Commander Guillaume ever give her special work to do?"

"Sometimes. Mostly she writes up her own things, hands them in, and then he'll ask her to go back and focus deeper on some aspect of it."

"And she does it?"

"Sure. She likes to feel important."

"Perfect." Sullivan left the alcove and approached the girl, carefully sweeping the kitchen area.

Jack summoned up his charm. He announced himself from a small distance, hoping to ease the duck-and-cover reaction. "Miss Kirushenko? If you have a minute, I'd like to speak with you. Your brother said it was okay."

Sarah didn't duck, but the beautiful eyes dissected him, and she gripped the handle of the broom as if preparing for combat. "About

202

what?"

"About something I could use your help with. Please, sit down." He motioned to her rocking chair, now settled where the table used to be.

After a pause, the girl moved so the chair stood between them. Jack ignored the apprehension.

"As you are probably aware, there was a limit to how much equipment we could carry. We tried to prepare for every conceivable situation, but there were some things we either overlooked or were forced to leave behind for the sake of space. While we have sensors and collectors to measure ground and air contamination, we didn't realize there would be a stream so close by, and we didn't bring any equipment to study cumulative water data."

"So? You've been here more than a week. What does that have to do with me?"

"You're much more familiar with the local resources than we are," Jack pointed out. "You know what substitute equipment might be available far better than Mr. Ti'onam or I would. Your brother has already attested to your affinity for scientific work. I need you to think about what resources are available, and help us devise a method for collecting data on water contamination. It would have to be something that would remain suspended below water level to avoid contamination from sediment, yet be small enough to be removed for examination. It doesn't matter how simple the system is, as long as it fits those criteria. Is that something I can count on you to do for me?"

"So, in other words, I design your system, build it, and implement it, but your men will manage the collection and interpretation and take all the credit for it."

Jack hadn't thought about that factor. "I can't give you the equipment, but perhaps you can accompany my officers during collection, learn how the data is recorded, and if I can trust your reliability, I will allow you to be responsible for all data gathered from it," he conceded. "That includes, of course, being able to present a full statistical analysis upon request. Can you do that?"

Sarah stuck her chin out with a palpable air of offense. "Of course! I can do logarithms in my sleep."

"Then it shouldn't be a problem."

The defensive attitude relaxed ever so slightly. "When do you need it by?"

"As soon as possible. I'd prefer to have it in place by sundown at the latest. I hoped to send you into the town to locate materials immediately.

203

We've already missed a week's data, and the sooner we start, the more accurate our results will be."

The spark of interest faded as he spoke. "Dimi'll need to come with me."

"It would have to be your mission alone. I can't be left without a translator."

The indecision tripled.

"I don't go into town alone," Sarah said with disappointment.

"You've done it by yourself a couple of times," Dmitri encouraged. He walked around the divider to stand behind the captain. "This is your big chance, Sar! Walk over to the Al's first; Charlie will go with you. Tell him you're looking for a letter or something. If nothing else, it's a shorter walk from their house."

Sarah shot him a nasty look.

Sullivan gave one last artful push. "I'm asking you to be a part of my team. Commander Guillaume mentioned what an asset you'd been to his research, and that I would be able to count on your help. I wouldn't bother you with the project if I didn't think it was important."

Dmitri gave her shoulder a pat. "Here's your chance to redeem yourself. I thought you were still David's Number One Scout, running dangerous missions where no one else dared?"

The tension on the girl's face was so strong, for a moment Sullivan thought she would be sick.

Sarah buckled. "I can do it. I'll do it."

Jack smiled his very best. "Thank you, Miss Kirushenko. I knew I could count on you."

* * *

The omnicomp adjustment took an hour, but four hours passed before Sarah slipped into the house.

Dmitri greeted her with relief. "Where you been? I was getting worried. You were gone long enough to buy the whole town."

"Miss Kirushenko," Sullivan called out. "Were you able to find something suitable?" The girl's hands were distinctly empty.

"Yeah." She returned the remainder of the local currency he had given her. "That's what's left."

"What'd you get?" Dimi asked.

"It's outside. I ran in by myself, so I was back pretty quick, but everyone seemed to be involved in something really interesting and technical here at the table. I'm not stupid," she said, wounded. "The other day you tell me I'm not worthy because I have no experience, but today I'm a good ol' boy part of the team? I know when I'm not welcome. Therefore, I left you to finish what you were doing uninterrupted. I went to the Al's."

Jack Sullivan approached within a meter of her. No one had seen or heard her brief return, not even Ti'onam. She was as quick and silent as a breeze. The injured eyes met his with dignity, daring him to deny the accusation. "Every word I said this morning was meant with the utmost sincerity, Miss Kirushenko. I have an honest need for that data. I meant what I said about letting you manage it."

The gaze dropped. "I hoped that part was true. Charlie helped me. He likes helping me with things like that. I told him you wanted to know how much dirt might be washing into the stream. It's up and running."

"Indeed!" Ti'onam raised a thick eyebrow. "May I inquire as to the system you used?"

Sarah still looked hurt at her exclusion, but she headed grudgingly for the door. "I'll show you."

Ti'onam passed judgment from the streambank. "Simple, yet most effective."

"I think that wins the resourcefulness award," Sullivan agreed.

"Get out of the water, Sar! You're going to get sick!" her brother ordered.

Sarah stood knee-deep in the frigid water, skirts tucked into the waist of the matching-colored shorts she wore beneath. A thin rope stretched the width of the water, and from it hung five long-handled wooden dippers, their flat bottoms sawed off. Around the cup, she'd tied a piece of loosely woven cloth, and inside the bag of cloth, nestled in the shell of dipper, sat a small square of thicker, absorbent cloth.

She held a dipper up. "The rope should keep them at a constant depth. Charlie sawed the bottoms off and drilled the holes to string it. The outer cloth should filter anything larger than fine sand, and the heavy cloth should trap any kind of contaminants. You can read it as is, or take the inner pad out for closer study."

"Miss Kirushenko, you really shouldn't be in that water," Granger warned, motioning her to shore. "It's eight degrees Centigrade. It's not good for your circulation." He offered a hand, but she climbed out on her own.

"You expect us to wade in there every day?" Andreiev watched with trepidation as the swift water broke and boiled over rocks.

"I guess you don't have to if you don't want to," she conceded, as if wading in the ice-cold water was half the fun. "You could pull them to the side with a stick, or untie the rope and pull it over. I thought multiple sampling would give an increase to reliability. If the stream was consistently deep, I'm sure the accuracy would have benefited from multiple depth readings as well." She readily accepted the jacket her brother took off and draped around her shoulders. He helped her untuck the skirt, and rubbed her legs briskly through it.

"A most ingenious design," Sullivan said, quite pleased. "Thank you, for your swift and thoughtful attention to the matter." He held a hand out. "Welcome to the investigation team."

Sarah eyed him skeptically. She'd done his dirty work. Time would tell if he kept the other half of the bargain. She shook the hand with two dubious fingers.

"Yeah," she grunted, and headed to the cabin an uncommunicative distance ahead.

Восемьнадзать
Eighteen
Shenevash

Rain. Guillaume hadn't been kidding about the rainy season. For days, downpours trapped the *Triumph* officers inside. Omni's weren't meant for use in monsoons. Jack Sullivan stared out the open shutters at the pond-sized puddles in the dirt yard and sighed, unable to do a damned thing about the wasted time ticking by. The *Triumph*'s scanners showed a solid line of rain across half the continent, headed directly for them, but a large patch of empty sky after that. There was nothing to do but wait.

A shout jolted everyone from sleep on the fifth morning.

"Dimi!" yelled a joyful voice. "Dimi, get up! The sun's rising! There's a sunrise!" Footsteps slammed up the staircase. "Hurry! You'll miss it!"

Dmitri stumbled down the stairs the same time the officers appeared. He pulled on a shirt and headed outside to the cold muddy yard, yawning. A bright glow swelled behind the trees toward the east. Overhead, purple and white clouds boiled thickly over patches of periwinkle sky.

"Isn't it glorious!" Sarah yelled from above.

Jack located her sitting on the damp roofpeak, hugging her knees, scanning the heavens through squinting eyes, enraptured.

"It's certainly a welcome sight. I was beginning to wonder if you ever saw sunlight."

Dmitri shivered. "It's been a month. That's a long time, even for the rainy season. It should hold, though. If you wanted to check out that second site, I would say today's your day. It'll be colder without the cloud cover, but you won't get a better day than this. Get down from there, Sar," he called, heading in. "The roof is wet. You're going to slip."

"I haven't yet." She disappeared over the side, to meet the men in the main room before they finished entering the cabin.

"Is there a trap door or something you have hidden up there?" Jack asked. "You come and go rather quickly."

"Window, ledge, and three toeholds to the peak," Sarah explained. "It's easier if you don't wear shoes. You have to watch for splinters, though."

207

"I'll bet you've had your fair share," he said, thinking of how fast she seemed to appear out of nowhere.

"Some," she admitted, helping Dmitri get breakfast with a new-found vigor.

The forest paths were wet, the leaf litter squishing like a sponge. Moisture seeped into the men's boots along seam lines. Small animals skittered in the treetops, knocking showers of drops onto the hikers below. Fungi sprouted in rainbows of color; brilliant reds and oranges dotted rotting logs, screaming yellows bubbled over dark leaves like fluorescent butter. The air was crisp with a light western breeze, cool enough to make breath steam and cheeks redden and wet hands chill and chap, but no one cared. The day was too beautiful to be spoiled by trifles.

Maybe it was some pre-programmed, ancient biological drive. Maybe it was because there had been clouds for four solid weeks, and suns didn't rise on star explorers. Maybe it was because six people had been trapped in a small cabin for four days with very little to do, but the sunshine sparkling through the trees seemed the brightest, most pleasurable sunshine anyone could remember seeing. It didn't seem like three hours passed before they came upon the site of the second explosion, another place of flattened and singed trees, only half as large as the first.

The crater was smaller, too, a meter deep and six across, and the mighty trees had suffered less damage. What differed was the pattern of destruction.

"What do you make of it, Ti'onam?" the captain asked, shading his eyes against the glare of the brilliant *sun*. "It starts out circular here, but the trees are downed over there as well." He pointed to an area away from the crater. "The trees here are knocked over and charred, but over there they're … gone. How can trees just – disappear?"

"I have no feasible explanation, Captain," Ti'onam said. "Any single explosion follows a specific pattern, by the very nature of the action. Whether natural or artificial, the forces follow a predictable, three-dimensional spherical pattern of expansion. I cannot recall any reason why, in an open area such as this, an elliptical pattern should develop. Certainly not with more destruction occurring at the edges, rather than the epicenter."

"Readings, Doc?" Sullivan called to Granger.

Kyle turned in a circle. "The radiation levels here are significantly less, Captain. Atmospheric levels are within three percent of norm, no doubt due to the rain. However, soil samples are reading as much as twenty percent higher than expected; again, probably due to the rains washing contaminated particles off the trees. It's safe enough for now, but it might not be a bad idea to wade through that river with your boots on before we head back to the cabin. I'll scan us again before we set foot in the yard. No sense bringing contaminated soil where people run barefoot."

"Understood. Dmitri, – ? Where's … ?" Sullivan looked around for his field guides. "Where'd they go?"

The Kirushenkos, most of all, seemed heartened by the respite from rain. Dmitri had been full of chatter, explaining things he knew about the area, relating stories he'd heard and telling others he'd actually experienced. Sarah was pleasantly social, adding amusing comments, laughing with casual ease, and even offering small stories of her own. Just when Sullivan thought he finally understood her moods and rules and quirks, here came a whole new set. Her fears had evaporated with the clouds, even reaching out to offer him – *him!* – a steadying hand while they crossed the stream. Was it because of his assigning her a piece of the action, or was she really just sick of the rain?

Jack returned to where they'd entered the area. He waved to Andreiev, calling him back. It wouldn't be impossible for them to find their way back alone, but he would be anything but amused by it. "Mr. Andreiev, have you seen either of our guides since we arrived?"

Danil thought. "No, sir, I haven't."

A girl's voice giggled close by, becoming outright laughter as the men looked upwards. One tree away, Sarah's mustard-gold dress was bright among the leaves, seven or eight meters off the ground. A meter or so higher, Dmitri sat on another branch.

Dmitri waved. "Come on up! You get a great aerial view!"

Jack moved under the tree. "If I wanted an aerial map, I would have requested one from the *Triumph*. Would you mind coming down here, please? We *are* here for a purpose."

"Sure." Dmitri started down.

"Didn't anyone ever tell you it's not polite to look up a girl's skirt?" Sarah chastised Andreiev. She giggled when he turned his head and blushed. Ducking under a branch, she grasped the trunk, scampered down three branches, held another and swung herself down with a jump to land next to her brother, agile as a monkey.

"That was a joke," she told Danil.

"Enough joking," Sullivan said. "You were here before with

Guillaume's men. What did they make out of the area over there?" he asked, and led them back to Ti'onam.

"I don't remember it looking like this before," Dmitri frowned. "We didn't get a good look, because the radiation was still high, but I don't remember everything being bare like this. Could there have been another explosion over here?"

Sarah looked around, perplexed. "Dimi's right. There were trees lying all over, big ones. The stumps are here, but all the trees are gone." She wandered among the table-sized stumps, thinking.

"A second explosion seems unlikely," Ti'onam said. "Neither the damage nor the radiation levels would indicate a secondary blast. Also, if you examine the remains, you will note an even pattern of breakage, not a tearing or ripping as from force. It is likely the trees in this section were removed on purpose."

"Not by an energy beam, I hope," Jack said.

"Negative." Ti'onam brushed his long fingers over a stump. "There are irregularities that are consistent with bladed methods."

"I think I found the answer," Dmitri called with disgust, scraping his boot on a humped root. Stump to stump, Sarah hopped over to him as far as she could before having to walk on the ground.

"Right there." He pointed to a mound, smoothed by rain, with a boot's toeprint in it. "Porshie pile."

"Those big hairy animals?" Sullivan asked, holding a hand high to suggest a porshie's long neck. "They eat trees?"

"Not entirely, but they drag them." Dmitri examined the ground. The forest floor didn't hold footprints to start with, and the heavy rains would have erased anything left. But a dragged tree, on the other hand...

"Here it is." He pointed to a line where the leaf litter seemed rougher than the surrounding area. "The boy we talked to said they were out here cutting timber. If you're looking for big trees, ones resistant to rot, you won't find that many in civilized areas, they've already been cut. You have to come out to the wilderness. We found that out when we needed timber to add on to the cabin."

"Found it!" Sarah held up a broken branch at the edge of the destruction. "They went this way."

"But all the people from the explosion were killed," Andreiev reasoned. "By all data, the nearest settlement is two kilometers away. Who would risk their life to get trees? There are millions all around."

"Just because you can't see the town doesn't mean it's not there," Dmitri reminded him. "We're not terribly far from Pozaranati. Anybody could have come out and taken what they'd left behind. The hardest part had been done. They don't know a thing about radiation, so it wouldn't deter them."

Sarah pointed, zig-zagging around stumps to a dark circle in the clearing. "What's that spot? It looks burnt." She dropped to her hands and knees to peer closer, hair falling before her eyes. She hooked it behind her ears, the long ends trailing in the damp litter. "But why over here, this far from the crater?"

Sullivan pulled at Sarah's elbow. "Get up. Brush your hands off. The soil could be contaminated."

"What?!" Sarah jumped up, wiping her dirty hands on her dirtier skirt.

"Ti'onam?"

"Unknown." Ti'onam scanned the ground. More than two meters long and not quite as wide, the dark area mounded a few centimeters higher than the surrounding dirt. "I am attempting to analyze it now."

"Could their porshie have been caught in the blast?" Dmitri guessed. "Roasted, right where it stood?"

Sarah made a face. "That's really stupid, Dimi. Do you see any bones? If the fire was hot enough to incinerate bone, then the rest of the forest would be gone, rain or no rain. It was probably a tree that caught fire and burned flat."

"Dummy yourself! You see any roots or stumps?"

"How would you know? I thought *you're* the one that's always stumped!" She gave a shriek as Dmitri launched into a game of chase. They ran between the stumps, circling a large one in a stalemate, until Dmitri jumped over it and pulled her to the ground. They wrestled on the wet leaves amid Sarah's squeals and Dimi's laughing shouts.

Sullivan watched the play in disbelief, then stalked over.

"Children!" He dragged Dmitri to his feet, and Sarah followed on her own. "Recess is over! School is in session. Brush yourselves off! I just get through telling you the soil is contaminated, and here you are rolling in it."

"Yes, sir, you did," Dmitri said. "I'm sorry, sir. It's just the first really nice day in I can't remember how long. It's hard to have to be tied down to something like this."

"I don't care if we're on Perry's Pleasure Planet!" Sullivan spat. "When you're assigned to aid my investigation, I expect you to act like a functioning part of my crew. I will accept no less than I do from my officers, whether you're trained for it or not. I expect the same respect, the same effort, the same attention to detail that you provide for Commander Guillaume. I don't care if you can dance circles around everyone in his command; if you can't behave yourselves and act like adults, you might as well march yourselves back to the compound and have him send me two new personnel who can."

Dmitri stood at perfect attention. "That won't be necessary, sir. I'm sorry if we got carried away."

Sarah's eyes grew to the size of joubash eggs, watching the captain. A fingernail slipped into her mouth, but it took longer than usual to find a rough spot with her teeth. With the bedraggled hair and dirty clothes, she looked more like a preschooler sucking a finger.

"What part of *contamination* can't you get!" Jack yanked the hand out and held up the grubby fingers for her to see. "Dirty! Contaminated! *Ra-di-a-tion.* Very bad. No eat!"

Sarah wrenched her hand away and wrapped it in the folds of her skirt, folding herself inward. She clung to Dmitri as he followed the captain back to the group.

"It is not of animal origin," Ti'onam informed them. "Whatever burned was botanical. Below the top layer of ash, which has been smoothed and condensed due to the recent rains, one can find evidence of charred wood."

Dmitri returned to task. "If all you're after is the body of the tree, you'd cut the main branches off before you haul it back. It not only weighs less, it's easier to drag. It's possible they stacked the branches in one place to make it easier to move around. What if the pile caught fire in the blast? If they were all dead or unconscious, it could have burned to ashes. The trees and ground were already wet. Nothing else caught fire."

"That is a plausible theory."

"We'll add it to the file," Sullivan said as Granger rejoined the group. "Let's get the sensors in place, and we can get out of here." He pointed a disgusted thumb at his guides. "Kyle, check these two over. They came in contact with the dirt."

* * *

"Kyle, what do you make of them?" Jack asked that evening.

"How do you mean?"

"I mean their relationship." Creases formed around his mouth as Sullivan struggled to put his feelings into words. "I don't see how they're able to *survive* out here. I've seen kids not old enough to enter the space academy that you knew, just *knew*, were going to make admiral someday. You wanted to follow them into the 'fleet just so you could serve under their command, because you trusted them that much. Here we are in a moderately dangerous situation, and despite repeated warnings, they're playing tag and climbing trees. I just don't get it, Doc. Is there something I've failed to get across?"

"Not everyone is fleet material, Jack. You know that," Granger reminded him. "You can't judge maturity by age or intelligence. How many sixty-year old commanders are out there, crossing their fingers that just maybe they'll make captain before they retire? They've lived on their own a long time. They're not used to having a supervisor over their heads. They do their work when they're ready, and report back on schedule. They're used to flexibility."

"You mean, flexibility as opposed to discipline," Sullivan said sourly.

"That could be one interpretation. I think you're trying to make them into something they're not. If the rain made us a little edgy after four days, imagine what it must be like for them after a month or more. It was the first nice day in ages; they played a little hooky from today's work. You called them on it, they straightened up. I wouldn't overdo it too much, Jack. You need cooperation, not perfection. They're only civilians."

"At what point, Doc, does immaturity become abnormal?"

"You're thinking about the girl?"

"Either one."

Granger crossed his arms, sighing. "The textbook answer would be, when it interferes with daily functioning, or is a cause of distress to the person involved. I don't think that's what you're looking for."

"You don't think she's abnormal? You don't think her immaturity is interfering with her functioning potential?"

"Potential is a whole other solar system, Jack. Technically speaking, anyone with an IQ over 130 is severely abnormal. That covers half the Allied Space Fleet and the entire Navaran race."

"You're avoiding my question."

"Without a lot of diagnostics, I can't give you a solid answer. Yes, I see a number of things that could indicate a distorted level of functioning, but you have to look at the whole picture. She's happy in her little niche. She has a few close friends – her neighbors, maybe some people at the compound, that other brother she writes to. She may be slow to warm up to new people, but she does manage to do it – even to me. She's proven she has quite a few skills necessary for future work in the field of science or linguistics – or cartography, for that matter. I'd hardly call that dysfunctional," Granger said. "Everyone has their own personal quirks – always checking a lock twice, washing your left arm before your right, rubbing a charm for good luck. We're not here as social workers. They're happy, healthy, and productive. Unless it directly impacts our investigation, it's not our business how people choose to run their lives."

"We came very close to that line this morning," Jack said, "and it wasn't the first time. Let's just say, I hope we don't have a situation where our lives are depending on them."

* * *

Jupiter Raines jammed his finger on the communications switch as soon as the signal came through. "Captain Sullivan, right on schedule."

Jack caught the subtle hint of relief in the officer's voice. "What's going on, Commander?"

"It's something you may want to discuss with Doctor Granger. We've been taking on shoreleave personnel and medical patients from the three compounds as per arrangement, but Dr. Bakari's come upon an urgent medical case, and he'd like Dr. Granger's opinion."

"Hold on." Sullivan went to pass the handicom to the doctor.

"Granger here." There was a pause as the second doctor came on line.

"Kyle, I've got a progressive case of Durwood's Palsy on my hands, a woman from the Kinonah compound," Dr. Bakari informed him.

The chief medical officer frowned at the handicom as if the signal weren't clear enough. "That's an unusual diagnosis. Are you sure? Did you rule out autoimmune factors and run a metabolite uptake screen?"

"As soon as I realized it. I waited to contact you until I'd run out of alternatives. Ergold's factor came in at forty-nine each time. It's already up to stage three."

Granger glanced at the captain with a look of alarm. "You can try a spinal blockade as a temporary measure, or maybe a Galtrex-induced coma, but that's not going to help for long."

"I agree, we can't treat it here," Bakari knew, "but I did a little research. From here, at Davies seven, it's only three days to Starbase 79, and they're set up to handle that. If you're not likely to be returning soon, we could deliver the patient and be back here in six days."

"Stand by." Granger paused the transmission. "It's serious enough to warrant the speed, Jack. If you wait until stage four, the area of the brain that controls breathing is affected, and your chances of recovery drop from eighty-five percent to fifteen. Treatment requires immobilization in a whole-nerve scanning regeneration bed. That's a high-tech specialty; you won't find that kind of equipment in any mobile sickbay, not even ours. If you can spare the ship for five or six days, I recommend allowing them to start treatment as soon as possible. Waiting for us to finish up could be too late."

Sullivan took back the handicom. "Ship's status, Mr. Raines?"

"Running at one hundred percent efficiency, Captain. There are currently twenty-four crewmen spread through the various compounds, and seventeen compound staff currently aboard the *Triumph*. Nothing unusual to report. No planetary anomalies yet observed that would account for two large explosions. We're continuing progressive geologic scans. No other ships in orbit or within sensor range. Absolutely nothing out of the ordinary."

"You sound rather eager to take the ship out of here, Mr. Raines. Is perpetual orbit becoming tedious?"

"Why, no, sir," Raines stumbled. "It's rather nice, actually, not having to worry about anything sneaking up. Lieutenant-Commander Cash has been the slaver. She had engineering replace the Gadsen conduit on the field generator relay while everything was calm, and made them rebuild the seals on the secondary energy inversion chamber just for practice. I've been avoiding her request to take a short run to test them."

Sullivan tried not to laugh. "If I know Ferrine, the only wear on those parts was fingerprints. Very well. Have it your way, Commander. Check with Mr. Ti'onam to make sure he's finished his current need for the ship's computers. He'll have to make do with the computers at the compound in the meantime. Please return all ship's personnel and planetary crew to their respective locations, and deliver Dr. Bakari's patient to Starbase 79, maximum speed. I want you back here as fast as possible, Jupiter. Contact me at 25:00 local time upon your return."

"Aye, sir. Maximum speed to Starbase 79. We'll leave orbit in one standard hour. Raines out."

Девятнадцать
Nineteen
Dossanch

The odd pair solidified inside the open meeting house of the Chessorak Compound. The men looked about, amazed by the unexpected roughness of the structure. The shorter of the two sneezed several times as his feet stirred up unfamiliar dust.

Two other men in workworn clothing had been seated on a bench; they rose to greet the newcomers.

The older man extended a hand. "Marcel Guillaume, Commander of Chessorak. My second-in-command, Jantzen Dickerson."

"Najar Shahir," the newcomer said. "Family reintegration counselor for Versan Albat Interstellar Rehabilitation Center." He gestured to the towering man next to him. "My client, Alexander Kirushenko."

Guillaume offered an empty bench. "Please, sit down."

"As I tried to explain in our communication," Shahir said as he took a seat, "this is the last phase of Mr. Kirushenko's requirements for final parole. He is not here to remove his children; he cannot do that. He just wishes to meet with them, speak with them. It might take an hour, it might take five minutes. We would like to speak at least to Dmitri. Could you please notify him that we wish to see him?"

"And as I started to explain before you insisted on meeting in person, I can't do that," Guillaume said with a gesture of helplessness. "The Kirushenkos are field operatives; they live in the community among the natives, *as* natives. We have no rapid transportation, no videolinks, no wave communications systems. I cannot contact them and receive a reply in under fifty hours, and that's an absolute minimum. To walk there and back is a three or four day journey of itself. Even if you had the time to wait, I'm afraid they are currently involved in aiding an important investigation for the Allied Space Fleet. Short of aborting our program and evacuating the planet, I cannot call them back. I'm sorry."

"Like an anthropological study?" the elder Kirushenko pondered aloud, several sentences behind the conversation. "Observations, notetaking?"

"Yes, you could say that," Dickerson agreed.

"Our ship is a private charter; we have the time to wait," Shahir said.

216

"It could be a month or more," Guillaume insisted. "I don't think that's the best ... "

"Could we go out there?" Kirushenko suggested. "See them in action? I would like to see how they live, how they adapt, what they think of the culture."

Dickerson shook his head, and Guillaume responded, "Absolutely not. I can't let two people with no background training take off across the countryside. At this moment, I can't spare anyone to accompany you on a wilderness goosechase. There's no guarantee anyone is even at the outpost right now.

"No," the commander insisted. "It cannot be done. The risks are too great."

"What risks?" Kirushenko demanded gruffly. At times, he had exploited his size and thunderous voice to sway opinions. In his prime, no one dared cross him, not to his face. His rage against the world was gone, but not the lessons he'd learned from it. "Who is untrained? I have a doctorate in archaeology and a second in ancient civ. I worked for the Allied Fleet; I used to carry a Grade Seven interstellar pass. This planet ranks only Grade Four. I understand as much as you the risks of cultural contamination – I could write you a paper on it! In this case, the risk is minimal."

Dickerson and Guillaume exchanged glances. Qualified people never wandered this far out into space. Not without serious educational or financial incentives.

"They are my *children*," Kirushenko reiterated. "It took us three months just to locate them."

"This time of year, you're looking at a two-day walk in cold rain and ankle-deep mud," Dickerson said. "I was there the other week; it's not a pleasant trip. You won't speak the language, you can't have a translator, you'd have to wear native clothing, and even if we gave you a paper with your destination written on it, there's no guarantee you'll find someone who can read it. Can you follow a map?"

"Read one?" Kirushenko rumbled with building excitement. "I used to chart my own sites, make detailed maps of discovery areas, second-guess measurements by eye alone! If you'd like, I can map our route for you as we travel."

Guillaume and Dickerson both chuckled. "I guess that's where she gets it from," Dickerson said.

"There's no need for that, sir," he said to the visitor. "I'm afraid your daughter's already done part of that work. She's quite the map-maker herself, we've discovered, and she does it without scanners. If you'd like, I can show them to you."

The big man nodded, a fleeting shadow of smile flickering behind the greying beard. "I would like that."

"We're not really prepared for an extended stay in such – *non-standard* conditions," Shahir said politely. "We expected to meet them here. Our charter expects us to return within a number of hours."

"Nonsense!" Kirushenko interjected in a voice that rolled somewhere under the floor. "They are paid to wait. I've dealt with worse conditions. This is the last item left on my list of fulfillments. I have made it through everything else; I can do this."

Guillaume bit his lip. "No. I can't allow it. Perhaps another time, when I don't have an explorer's crew already out there. If you'd given advanced notice, we could have called them back, had them here, but I can't let you leave the Compound."

"I assure you, the risks are negligible!"

Guillaume hesitated. "I'm not comfortable saying this, and it's not meant to reflect on you personally, sir, but I am within my legal rights as head of this project. Facts are facts. The people of this area average five centimeters shorter than humans, and they have sparse body hair. The tallest local we've ever seen just brushed one-point-eight meters. If I may be presumptive, sir, you are a good deal taller than one-point-eight."

Kirushenko's big head dropped in defeat. He'd never had a fighting chance, having had a father who was two meters even, and a mother who was one-point-eight-three herself.

"Our mission here is to blend in with the natives as much as we can," Guillaume pointed out. "We don't want to attract attention. If I send an inexperienced foreigner out there who looks, speaks, and acts nothing like the general populace, it's going to start a circus parade. You'll lead them straight to two of my most dependable operatives, and that could destroy their cover. I cannot allow that to happen, especially now with the Fleet out there."

"Commander?" Dickerson spoke in Tau Cetan for privacy. *<What you think of short route? Little traffic, more direct, less time. If he does mean what he say, there not be as much risk.>*

Guillaume didn't want anyone else loose, under any circumstances. His program was running exceptionally well. It was bad enough Sullivan took a Navaran out there. A platinum blonde in a land of dark-haired people, a Navaran, *and* a giant? It would turn the Vandijoc outpost into a veritable zoo exhibit.

"I'd have to run your credentials first, before I'd even consider it. It means at least fifteen solid hours of walking in cold air, possibly rain, sleeping outdoors with no warmth but a sputtering campfire, no food but what you carry. You'll have to wear a tracking device, and if you're not back in five days I will, *without fail*, report you to the Allied Fleet and let them handle it from there. Is that clear?"

Shahir looked distraught. "We're not prepared for wilderness travel of that caliber. My client has had serious leg surgery. I'm not sure he can walk that far, and I certainly cannot carry him back if he can't. Perhaps we can send them a message, and we will wait aboard our ship for a response. Depending on the reply, we can change our plans accordingly."

Kirushenko looked Guillaume in the eye and let the slightest trace of a lop-sided smile curl one corner of his mouth. "I can do it," he rumbled with a determination that could wear away stone. "When do we start?"

* * *

"I'm surprised at you, Sasha," Shahir said an hour into their journey. "I don't think I've ever seen you so certain of something before. You were positively ill before meeting with your other children, and you weren't too healthy on the trip here. Why the big change?"

"I don't know." The big man shook his head, at a loss to understand it himself. "Because my wife would have insisted upon it? Because we traveled three weeks to get here, and I don't like being told something is impossible when it isn't. Because it seemed like fate was trying to do everything it could to discourage me, to make me give up and fail when I am so close to success. To come this far and not finish – you might as well take me back to prison. I like to win."

"Have you given thought to the idea that, after all this effort, they might not want to see you?"

Shame and uncertainty flashed across the oversized features. "I am – trying to stay positive. You were at the other meeting. Out of eight, four had open arms, and three were polite. Only one was openly hostile, and he's always been like that. What is the worst they will do? Say 'no, please leave, we don't want to talk to you'? I've gone over that in my head a thousand times. If I accept their rejection peacefully, they will be more inclined to believe my intentions are honest."

"Just making sure." Shahir rubbed his hands, shivering from the cold dampness that hung around them like fog. He slipped on the thick mud in the unfamiliar hard boots, waving his arms for balance. The sudden movement strained his back, but this time he didn't fall. Wilderness survival had never been a part of his job description. Water dripped down the back of his collar, pain speared his twisted ankle, his hiking bag hurt his back, and they hadn't gone seven kilometers yet. When he returned to the penitentiary, he would demand a hazardous-duty bonus.

"Did you see the maps?"

"No." Shahir adjusted the pack strap where it dug mercilessly into his shoulder. "I'm afraid I'm not much of a map person. I've never had need, beyond finding the blue stops on the guide at my shuttle stop."

"It's a shame you can't appreciate them, then. She did an admirable job, my daughter. Sarah had an eye for detail like that." Kirushenko paused for the counselor to catch up to his longer-legged pace. "I gave her her first lessons in map reading."

"She's the smart one?"

The father dared let a drop of pride show. "If you wish to minimize her abilities like that. She is smarter than you and I put together. She was jumped five years – five! on her second day of school. She could not learn fast enough, and she forgot nothing. We had to put her in a Navaran school to slow her down."

"Did it work?"

"I think so." Kirushenko swatted an insect hovering in his face. "School wasn't a joke any more. She wasn't used to working at it."

Shahir swiped much more savagely at the insect as it buzzed his ear. A larger fly with iridescent pink wings flew at him from the other side, and he ducked in fear of being bitten and coming down with some incurable plague. A reedy swampland bordered their right, and the brush crackled with unfamiliar chirps and whirrs of insects, and the shrieking creatures hunting them.

"What about the boy?"

"Dmitri? He was bright enough," Kirushenko thought back, "but he had The Eye. He knew every girl in his school by name. He was never without at least one girl by his side for any social function. He got that skill from his mother. Of course, he was a good-looking boy to start with."

"And he got that from his father, right?" Shahir looked over, expecting the inevitable wink and possibly crude reply that any of a hundred men would have given.

Kirushenko didn't look up. He shook his head, the half-smile nudging the corner of his mouth once more, as if lost in a pleasant memory. "*Nyet.* That one is all his mother. You'll see."

Dmitri was glad when Captain Sullivan called a formal meeting around the table. The captain still had eight and a half weeks left to work by the Allied Fleet's timetable, but only five days by his own. Dimi prayed to the Moons of Sigma Tau the five days would win. The responsibilities the captain had dropped on Sarah had worked as promised: for the past week she'd stopped hiding, stopped worrying, made a very adult effort to be seen and included. Her overeager brilliance began to shine through, just as it did for Guillaume. Each day Sullivan raised the bar a little higher, and each day Sarah cleared it with increasing agility. Dmitri couldn't help but be proud. Maybe, just maybe, everything would get back to normal.

"As expected, the samples taken around the cabin show more concentration of fallout in the open areas as opposed to those collected within the forest areas," Andreiev reported. "However, none of the samples from any of the twenty-five subsequent days showed a rise in contaminants. All traces of radioactive particles fade at a rate consistent with a single-occasion exposure. Whatever the cause was, it stopped within a short period of time." Without a computer display screen, he had been forced to copy eight different graphs from the omnicomp onto paper for group display.

"Wouldn't it have been easier to use a dual-axis Nylan analysis?" Sarah asked, kneeling on the bench and grabbing for a complicated page.

"Not in this instance." Andreiev pointed to several items on the page. "A Nylan analysis would lend a false correlation between the air and soil contamination levels because it doesn't take into account the foliage absorbed some contaminants, preventing the rain from washing it into the soil. It wouldn't account for correction of binding with molecular mineral concentrations in the soil, either."

"Oh," Sarah said, dismayed at being wrong. "But wouldn't the accumulation of radioactive dust from the initial explosions binding with soil minerals make everything toxic?"

"While that is true in some cases, it is not significant here," Ti'onam explained. "Due to the short half-life of the elements involved, it is improbable that there would be a lasting damage to the landscape itself. Before the temporary sensors we planted disintegrated, they, too, confirmed a steadily decreasing amount of radiation in the immediate area of the explosions. A slight but real possibility remains, however, that any flora or fauna that survived could have sustained mutations in DNA."

"They won't get it from the water," Sarah said, eager to mention her work again. Mr. Ti'onam had checked her data and pronounced it accurate. "Not from the stream, at least. It is possible that contaminants are collecting and concentrating wherever the stream ends, but if you plot the rate of decay and compare it against distance traveled and potential evaporation, taking into account an estimate of the sheer volume of rain we've had in the past two weeks and the speed of the water, even if the stream ended in a body of water the size of a puddle, the dilution rate would indicate that the water should be completely safe by now."

Granger watched the girl spout her jargon, both impressed and annoyed. "Now hold on just a minute, Miss. You're going to hurt yourself, running off sentences like that. I know you like to play scientist, but don't tell me you went beyond the data for decay ratios and worked out calculations for volume and dilution?"

"Yes?" she admitted uncertainly. "It's just formulas. I didn't want to overlook anything of significance. Mr. Andreiev let me use his omnicomp – under supervision, of course. I figured out the ratios for ten different sets of figures, took the average, and extrapolated that to … "

"Ho! Just … Stop there. Jack, you need to put a stop to this." Granger appeared quite serious. "She may have a head for numbers, but she's not a goddamn computer. I can't stand by and watch a Navaran warp a child like that, especially a human one."

Sarah shrank inward. She glanced at Dmitri, then at the men. "I've studied under several Navaran Masters. Mr. Ti'onam didn't actually teach me…"

Ti'onam tipped his head forward; his features remained unreadable, but the shadow created under his thick brows made the grey eyes seem cold and ominous. He clipped his words. "Current Alliance laws recommend educating all youth, both Human and Navaran, to the best of their capabilities. Although Miss Kirushenko is an apt pupil, I would base her expertise more on her superb education in Navaran schools and her own personal ambition than to any instruction of mine. Despite her youth and heritage, I have found her to be a far more compatible associate than those accredited professionals whose scope of learning has been narrowed by an approach based on unwarranted arrogance."

It took several seconds for Granger to decipher the speech. He glanced at Jack for confirmation. "Was that an insult? Did he just insult me? *Arrogance?* How the hell do you get off calling *me* arrogant when your entire civilization has looked down its nose at the rest of the galaxy since time immemorial? You want …"

"Kyle!" Sullivan warned. "Enough. No one ever said Navarans don't have opinions; they just don't voice them as often. If I were to keep count of the insults, I'd say Ti'onam still owes you several dozen."

Granger's eyes stabbed at the captain, but he couldn't stop one last barb. "It must be the height of narcissism for you, Commander, not being able to work with anyone who doesn't remind you of yourself."

Ti'onam raised the cold eyes to stare directly at the doctor. "I am not as familiar with human psychology, but I am aware that humans often insult others to whom they feel inferior."

"That's it!" Granger slammed to his feet. "Why don't you and me take a little walk outside, and we'll investigate the full meaning of inferior?"

Ti'onam rose. "If it will correct your grammar, I shall accompany you willingly. If you are suggesting physical violence, you will not succeed."

"Gentlemen!" Sullivan commanded. "One step, one more word, and I'll file a reprimand. Settle your personal disagreements on your own time. Don't waste mine."

Ti'onam bowed his head, then sat. "Apologies, Captain. I should not have allowed myself to be distracted."

"Sorry, Captain." Granger sat, his mouth pulled tight lest any unapproved words slip out.

"Kyle, what about the local population?" Sullivan asked. "Air currents didn't bring this area into danger, but certainly there must be people living downwind that received heavier doses? At the very least, the people that rescued the casualties must have had some exposure?"

The doctor gave a sour nod and refocused himself. "That's a concern, and one I don't have a lot of answers for. Part of the problem is the distance involved. We could have spent the entire month roving around asking people that very question, but they know nothing at all about radiation, and we can't teach them until they discover it for themselves first, however long that takes. Based on our information, there were two suspicious deaths among rescue persons from the first explosion that could have been Warshan's-related, and a couple of illnesses that might also fall into the category. The sparseness of population is a blessing, in

223

this case. The Tanishwahdani boy received a heavy dose, not necessarily from the initial explosion but from the fact he lay in the middle of it for at least an hour before someone hauled him to safety. It's possible to have genetic damage occur, but with such a low birthrate it could be many, many years before such damage becomes apparent, if ever. Neither the Kirushenkos nor their neighbors show any signs of contamination at all."

"Say that, for whatever reason, the events were natural occurrences," Jack pondered aloud. "Would that *explain* the low birthrate?"

"Not impossible, but I doubt it. From the reports of the other two research teams, their populations suffer more or less the same difficulties as this one, with no reported increases in radioactivity at all. Due to the frequency of contact with the Kirushenko's neighbors, I've been collecting minute samples of biological materials every time they visit – saliva from cups, shed hairs, items I left out that were coated with a sticky substance to pull skin cells from fingers. I can't do much with the data down here, but once we get back to the ship, or at least to the compound, we'll run it through the computers and get a detailed analysis on the DNA."

"If that were true, though, wouldn't it affect animal reproduction as well?" Dmitri said. "I mean, where there's people, there's usually porshies. They have a long gestation, but they seem to have no problem reproducing. If they did, the meat and leather industries would take a heavy loss. A lot of people would star... "

He stopped as a pounding bang at the door interrupted him. *Who the hell?* It was rather late for Charlie to call, but not unusual. It could be stragglers from the Compound, and you never knew when a ranger might show up, especially if there were something important to relay. He rose from the table and opened the door a crack. A strange man stood in the misty fog; another man hung back several meters.

<farrash lxa!>

The man at the door overenunciated, loud and deliberate. "IS THIS THE HOME OF DI MI TRI KIR U SHENK KO? I AM LOOK KING FOR DI MI TRI KIR U SHENK KO." He tapped a damp paper with

Dmitri Kirushenko,

Vandijoc

smeared in the local script.

Dimi was well able to recognize his own name. "That's me."

The stranger slouched with relief, and nodded at the person behind him.

"Come on in," Dmitri invited.

"Thank you, very much! Mr. – uh – Guillaume allowed us to try and find you." The man stumbled in his rush to get inside the shelter, away from the mist and mud and the god-awful plague of insects that had hunted him like vampires the entire way. He stopped short, noticing the roomful of people. "I'm sorry to disturb you. I see you have guests."

Dmitri shrugged. "Not really. They've been here a while now. We've gotten kind of used to them."

"My name is Najar Shahir." The man dug into a pocket and handed Dimi a damp paper version of his electronic ID card. "I represent the Family Reintegration Services at Versan Albat Penitentiary and Rehab Center. I – ."

Dmitri cut him off with a raised finger. He still held the door open, and all the warmth they'd coaxed out of the heater fled into the wet air outside.

"Come in!" he called to the figure hanging back near the forest. "No one stands in the rain if they can avoid it. *to ruxnu Ahnax Pelonishalan!*" Just because one man spoke Standard didn't mean the other did. Reluctantly, the second man came forward, head bowed.

He's no native, Dmitri thought to himself as the man neared. He was far too tall. *Man, he was big!* Like Dmitri's father had been, poor bastard! He must not have had any trouble handling porshies. The man had to duck just to fit through the door. *Damn!* His head, with its customary wide-brimmed rain hat, almost brushed the low ceiling of the cabin.

Dmitri shut the door. The smaller man removed his hat; drops of water fell to the floor with a soft patter. The other man hugged the door, massive shoulders hunched, hat pulled low over his downcast face, as if trying to disappear.

"I'm sorry. What were you saying?" Dmitri paid attention at last. "Guillaume sent you, you said? Are you from the *Triumph*?" He jerked a thumb at the officers.

"No! No. I'm with the Family Reintegration Service of Versan Albat Rehabilitation Center and Penitentiary. My client, … ."

Again the twitchy man didn't get a chance to explain, jumping off the floor as a scream shattered the calm, a heart-stopping shriek that paused just long enough for the screamer to gasp, then continued as long and loud and high as the original. Dmitri whirled around.

Sarah had backed away from the bench until she hit the wall, pushing up onto her toes. Her eyes fixed on the newcomers, face ghostly with terror, hands clamped over her mouth in a futile attempt to restrain the screams. The hands twisted until the fingers clenched her cheeks, the ragged nails tearing into flesh. The fingers scraped downwards, leaving gouges in the fair skin that quickly turned to red.

"Sarah?" Granger reached out, but the girl shoved past him and bolted up the stairs, two at a time. He hesitated only a moment before following her almost as fast.

Dmitri's head snapped back to the newcomers.

No.

No!

His jaw dropped as he realized what Sarah saw.

It couldn't be!

How? Son of a bitch! North polar, super solar shit!

The head had lifted, the face now visible under the hat. The dark, dark familiar eyes, like the wrong side of the moon, clear as glass this time, not glazed and shiny and vacant, looking abnormally shy and uncertain, not hateful and invincible and cold as space... The beard was gone from the broad jaw, the persistent shadow of stubble dark against his skin, not wet and sour with drunken drool from snoring with the mouth open, or drink that hadn't found its way in. The big nose in the big face with the thick black eyebrows, and the mysterious fine scar that ran eight centimeters from the bridge of the nose under the left eye and across the cheek. The body was thinner, but still as tall and wide as an ancient colossus...

Dmitri forgot about everyone else in the room, forgot the room itself. He backed up, insides shrinking until he bent over with the pull. He retreated until the bench hit him in the back of his knees and he sat down, hard. The edge of the table slammed his back just below his shoulderblades, leaving a mark that would become a thin, linear bruise, as if reminding and preparing him to resume what had stopped so many years ago. His mind accepted what his eyes insisted was real.

"*Father?!*"

"*Zdravst'vie, D'misha,*" Alexander Kirushenko said softly, hopefully.

"*Father?! How –* ? *Who –* ? *Ummm –*." Dmitri scrambled to his feet, standing at attention before the man having been ingrained decades ago. "Won't – won't you come in? Sit down. *Pozhal'sta,*" he said, performing the expected courtesies as if in a fog.

"*Spasiba. Vashi druzya – shto yazik, oni govoryat?*"

"*Po-angliski, sair.*"

"I speak that." Sasha crossed the room, a slight limp to his right leg. It took both of the huge hands to lift it up and over the bench to sit. His counselor followed him to the table.

Dmitri fought to breathe against the flopping-fish feeling of his heart. "Can – I – offer you a drink? We had a little party the other week. I'm afraid I don't have much left."

"Water would be fine. Thank you." Father's eyes stayed focused on the table, save occasional glances upward through his hair, a behavior eerily familiar. "I have undergone genetic therapy. I cannot consume alcohol in any form, or I risk violent illness."

"Oh. I – I guess that must be good – in a way?"

Dmitri took a fleeting glimpse at the stairs. It was far too quiet up there. He pushed Sarah out of his mind for the moment. He should check on her, but... . He didn't dare risk insulting Father by leaving the room. Sarah was most likely under her bed, watching through the cracks in the floor, or, even more probable, under his bed, with his door locked. Dr. Granger was gone, too. That couldn't be good, either, but at least she wasn't alone. It would have to do for the moment. Dmitri didn't know what he felt about the man who sat before him at his own table, in his own house. He had never done any soul-searching over it. He had plenty of reasons to hate him, but ... he *was* his father, and the concept of absolute obedience had been implanted beyond a doubt. As long as the man was civil, Dmitri would be courteous and hear him out.

What else could he do?

Sit, stand, run upstairs, get a glass of water, have a nervous breakdown – he stood in the center of the room, unable to choose.

Captain Sullivan rescued him.

"Sit," Jack ordered, placing a hand on the flustered boy's shoulder and steering him in the direction of the table. "Visit with your father. I think I can fill water glasses."

* * *

"Sarah! What's wrong? What's frightened you?" Granger squeezed through the narrowed opening as her door gave a grinding scrape and moved ten centimeters closer to shutting. "Who are those men?"

Sarah shrieked, raising an arm to ward off an attack.

Friend/ no immediate danger

She threw herself belly-down on the edge of her workbench and released a powerful, two-footed kick at the door. It moved another few centimeters, too far away now to use the workbench for leverage. She threw her shoulder to the door, nudging it. Half a meter more to go.

"What is it?" Granger repeated. He reached out, but she flung him away.

"My father!" Sarah gasped, throwing herself at the door. "He found me! He's come back to kill me! I said so many bad things about him at his trial! He watched me! He never forgets anything! I shamed him in public. Now he's come to make me pay!"

"Your father? I thought you didn't know where he was? I thought you didn't have contact with him?"

"I don't! I don't! He was in prison! He's escaped! He's loose and he's come back for me because he's downstairs *right now!*" she sobbed, shoving furiously at the unyielding door. "I know it! I know it! He killed my sister, and now he's after *me!*" The door stuck fast.

Sarah grabbed Granger with both hands, clawing at him with such force she tore a tie from his shirt. "You wanted to help me? Help me now! Help me now, because *he's going to kill me!*"

Granger gripped her arms. She was strong to start with, and her terror made her stronger. "Calm down, Sarah! Calm down. What you want me to do?"

"Go down there! I have to know what he wants. Tell me how mad he is. Tell me what he's doing to Dimi. Don't let him hurt Dimi!" she cried. "Please don't let him hurt Dimi! He doesn't deserve it! We have to protect Dimi!"

"Okay. I can do that," Kyle soothed. "Take a deep breath. There are five of us down there, and at least four of us are trained for combat. I think we can manage to protect you from one man."

"*No!* You *can't!* Not *that* one you can't! It takes a …"

Something clicked in the distant recesses of Sarah's mind, something she'd seen before on that dreadful night her sister died, something she'd fantasized about but had never had the opportunity. But the opportunity was *here.*

Now.

Something in the fabric of the universe had brought together the three things necessary, be it called *rok, timurshil.* kharma, *zar'i nar,* or Divine Intervention; she couldn't ignore that kind of coincidence. She had to do it. She would do it for her brother Viktor. She would do it for her sister Katya. She would do it for Dimi, and David and Sergei and Nikky. Vladimir would understand; she would do this for him, most of all. She would protect him, one final time. They could not go back to that life. She couldn't allow it. And she knew how to stop it, here and now.

Sarah tightened her knees to give them strength. She met Granger's eye, the faintest trace of a forced smile on her face.

"Okay." She breathed slow, patting his hand between hers. "Please do that for me? Listen to everything he says, tell me everything he does, tell me why he's here. I will wait for you in Dmitri's room. His door shuts and locks. Make sure Dimi doesn't buckle and agree to let him stay here. Tell him there is no room. Tell him we're radioactive. Make up a reason, if you must." She pushed the doctor out the narrowed doorway, squeezing after.

"Go!" Sarah ordered in a whisper. "Listen carefully for me. And Mr. Granger? Don't stand too close. You *are* a nice person, even if we cannot be friends through your choice of profession. I wouldn't want to see you hurt."

"I'll be careful," Granger assured her.

* * *

Dmitri remembered to introduce the other men before his tongue dried up. He'd spoken to his father plenty of times, sometimes by choice and sometimes not, but in all his life, they'd never had a single meaningful *conversation*. The last time Dmitri'd spoken to him, Father had been sprawled in his favorite chair, angry words slurring from his after-dinner binge. This man seemed a stranger, but he wasn't – but in many ways he *was* – but then again, he wasn't... Calm like this, sober like this, Father was just – *strange*.

Father broke the pause this time. He pointed to the stairs. "That was Sarah?" His hands had been folded over each other on the table; a prison tattoo shone through the hair of the bottom hand.

"Yeah."

"She's grown tall."

"Yeah."

"The commander at the base showed me her maps. They are very good."

"Yeah. She worked on them a long time."

"It shows in her details. Will she – be coming back down?"

"I – I – I don't think so." *What the hell should he say?* No matter how old he was, Dmitri couldn't bring himself to lie to the man, not even a white one. He'd done it once, and the welts still flamed in his memory, twenty years later. "I think she's a little surprised. We had no idea you had been released. No one is supposed to know where we are. How did you find us? Why are you here? I mean, what brings you all the way out here?"

"It was most difficult to locate you," Shahir interceded. "That was the problem. Your family said you were attached to a research team on a newly discovered planet. The Fleet is the only agency allowed to run that kind of study on inhabited worlds. Your names turned up on the personnel list for Sigma Tau. Then there was the issue of communication. We waited two months for a reply to an inquiry we sent through the research compound, but you never responded. We chartered a ship and came out here in person. The base commander didn't want us out here at all, but we couldn't wait two weeks for a reply to a hand-written letter. In fact, we have a very tight schedule. If we aren't back on time, we're in very big trouble with Mr. Guillaume."

"We only get back to the base every three months," Dmitri mumbled in a daze. "The investigation delayed us. It must still be waiting on the queue."

"This is the last requirement I have for full parole," Father rumbled. "I am required to meet with family members who are willing to speak with me. I have had seven years to review my life. I cannot change the past. What's done is done. I am not proud. I acted despicably, and I will not blame you if you want me to leave. I can only offer my sincerest apologies. I am aware of the terror and shame I caused my family, and I regret that. I wish I had been able to stop before it got out of control."

The massive shoulders shrugged. "That's it. That's all,"

Dmitri digested the information. "Okay."

What was he supposed to say? *Why, of course, Father! Apology accepted! We all knew, deep down in your heart, you didn't really mean to beat the shit out of us! You never meant to snap Elizabyeta's neck, you were just too damned drunk to know what the hell you were doing! Of course we forgive you! It wasn't really as bad as you think!*

Was he supposed to cry? Was he supposed to wrap his arms around the man and say, I forgive you! Can we pleeeease be a family again? He couldn't do that. Not that fast. But a man spends seven years trying to set his life straight, you have to say *something*.

"I – accept your regret," Dmitri decided.

Father bowed his head as if accepting a blessing. "*Spasiba.*"

"You've spoken to the others?" Dmitri inquired, finding a safe topic to discuss. "How is everyone?"

Andreiev stood up from his seat by the window. "If you'll excuse me, I must check on timed data I am running." He disappeared into the back room. Granger watched him leave, glanced at the stairs, but stayed seated.

"… but he's doing fine. And Katerina – did you know she was married? Three years now. Some doctor she knew, a psychiatrist for children. She has a little boy of her own, Roman. Blond, like his mother."

"I'd heard she was married," Dmitri said. "She must be very happy."

The elder Kirushenko sighed. "Outside of Alexei, you are the last two I have contacted. I was interested to see what you do."

More bitterness and sarcasm crept into Dmitri's voice than he meant to allow. You never, ever planned on speaking to Father like that. Not if you wanted to stay in one piece.

"Maybe we came here because we didn't *want* to be disturbed. Maybe we wanted to get away from everything that reminded us of home. Do you have any idea how many years I sat up with Sarah because she had nightmares about home? Did you really think we would all forgive you and come flocking back just because you made it through a course of rehab?"

Dmitri's voice rose. Always, always, he'd been one of the peacemakers. He'd *never* raised his voice to his father, *never* given him a smart-assed reply, always did his best to keep Father calm, but a surge of white-hot fury rose within him so powerful he feared he wouldn't be strong enough to control it.

"Your showing up here has ripped open wounds that were finally starting to *heal!*"

Sasha Kirushenko shook his head hard. "No! No! *Pozhal'sta, nyet!* That was never my intent! I'm sorry you feel that way. This has been most difficult for me. I am not asking forgiveness. I can't change what's happened. I will carry that pain until I die. I guess I'm only asking for a new start. If you *wanted* to – resume contact. If you don't wish to see me again, I will understand that, too."

"I've seen you in *Hell!*" spat an icy, half-choked voice so seething with hatred Dmitri's cramped insides shriveled tighter against the chill. He knew that voice.

All eyes in the room looked up.

"Sarah! What on Earth – !" Dmitri rose to his feet. A heartbeat later everyone was standing, ready to run.

Sarah crouched on a step partway down the stairs, one of her brother's caps pulled low over her eyes. The bright-red scarf Mother used to drape over the holovision receiver swathed her head and shoulders, hiding all but her eyes. A palm-sized Allied Fleet-issue EPSAR stuck through the spindles, aimed directly at the table.

231

"Sarah! What are you doing! *How did you get that?*" Dmitri blanched. "For God's sake, put that back!"

"*Where* did she get that?" Sullivan asked, staring at the EPSAR that wasn't supposed to exist.

"Is it charged?" Granger asked. He glanced at the father, a meter or so across the table. *Not too close.*

"It has no power cell," Dmitri swore. "I made sure of that before I stored it."

"It took me a year and a half to crack the code on your safe, Dimi," Sarah confessed wistfully. She sounded – *younger*, once more the terrified child running from Father on the rampage. "I never expected to find the right combination. I didn't even *want* to know what was in there, but I did look, and this was hidden in the very back. Remember it?" She tipped the EPSAR to show him.

"You said you never wanted to get caught without a good weapon again. You were right. You're always right about things like that. All those things I never think about. I found the power cell in the same drawer you keep those little black nightclothes for your girlfriends. I know, I'm not supposed to be in there, either. I'm sorry. You can yell at me if you want.

"It's not fair, Dimi! The nightmares had stopped! They'd finally *stopped!* I was trying so hard to keep our bargains. Why did he come back? Did they call him because of the omnicomp? I said I was sorry. Did you call him because of Jaycee? You never believed he'd get us for testifying, but I warned you!"

"Don't talk crazy, Sarah! Of course not!" He hadn't heard it in a long time, but Dmitri would never forget that tone of voice, the dead, flat voice that meant horrible thoughts were bubbling up through her darkness, overriding any hope of rational thought. It was the warning siren of an imminent breakdown.

"I want him out of here, Dimi. *Please!* If it is the last request you ever grant me, I beg you! *Please* make him leave! I will not speak to him. I won't let him see me."

Dmitri pretended to be calm, hoped his failing nerves would hold. He took a step forward, hand out. "Give me the EPSAR first. It's mine, Sar, and I want it back *now*. It is *my* job to protect you."

"Stop, Dimi. Get him out of here. I'm not the one you should be stopping. Don't make me do it, Dim. I don't want to hurt you."

Dmitri took another cautious step, then leaped back cursing as Sarah scrunched her eyes and fired a short burst at his feet.

"Sin sukah!" Dmitri's toes tingled from the near-miss of electrical energy, even through his boots.

"Sarah, put the weapon down," Granger urged with professional calm. "Dmitri and I will help you, but you've got to give him the EPSAR."

Andreiev appeared in the alcove. Jack signaled with a low hand for him to stop, hiding the motion with his leg. He shook his head ever so slightly. The lieutenant stopped cold, hidden in the shadows.

Jack held still, except for a single finger held close to his leg. He pointed at Andreiev, then twisted the finger toward the stairs.

Danil flattened himself against the inside wall, then peered around the corner, shocked as everyone else by what he saw.

Sarah's thumb moved the setting.

"Get – rid – of – him!" she pleaded, emphasizing each word. "No more nightmares! No more not knowing if I'm asleep or awake, if the voices are real or only imagined, if I'm truly guilty or not. Afraid of dreaming, lest it all come back so real. So real."

Shahir shuddered behind his client. "We can't head for the door unless you put that weapon down." He poked Sasha in the back. "You're her father! Order her to put it down!"

"Sar'ina! You have every right in the world to hate me, to hold that weapon to me and wish I was dead," Sasha Kirushenko said with uncharacteristic calm. "There are many days I wish I could have done that to myself. I *wanted* to die, especially after your mother died, but I was a coward. But it is just as cowardly to shoot unarmed people." He took a step forward, only to have the EPSAR blast the floor before him.

The smell of ozone rolled heavily through the room.

Sarah moved the dial another notch.

"Sarah… " The captain drew her attention, giving Andreiev time to act. "Why should we do what you're asking? Your father can go to Hell for all I care, but I'm responsible for the safety of my crew. I need some kind of guarantee for them. What will you do with the EPSAR if your father leaves? Will you give it to your brother?"

"I… I don't know."

Andreiev used the moment of indecision to move. He slipped around the corner, tight against the wall.

Everyone spoke at once. Sarah's eyes darted speaker to speaker, her fractured mind overwhelmed by the mass of voices.

"Sar, put it down, before someone gets hurt. I can't do anything with an EPSAR pointed at me. You know that."

"Answer me, Sarah! How do I know my men will be safe?"

"Sarah, I understand your fear, but you've got to *trust* me! Give me *one* chance ..."

"Miss Kirushenko, your actions are irrational in the face of your request. To ask someone to leave, then threaten them harm if they take a single step, negates your original request."

"Sar'ina, I'm so sorry to have caused you that much ...."

"Silence!" Sarah pressed a hand to her head, as if pushing down the chaos. *"Molchitye!"* For emphasis, she fired a longer burst that exploded in the middle of the table, blackening the top. Flakes of ash floated up as the men dove for the floor, the smell of charred wood thick enough to taste.

She clicked the dial once more.

"Sorry? We're supposed to believe you're sorry?"

Tranquility settled over her, soaking up the turmoil the way a blanket of snow swallows a shout.

"Sorry that you beat a six year old until she almost died? Sorry for killing 'Byeta for interrupting you? Sorry for killing my mother through irresponsible breeding? Sorry for trying to rape my best sister, and not having the decency to *remember* it?" The EPSAR began to tremble; the tremor became a wobble.

"Nyet," she whispered from her trance. "No one can be that sorry."

Andreiev crept a third step.

Dmitri scrambled to his feet. He saw what was about to happen, knew it had to happen, hoped no one would be hurt in the process.

"Okay! Okay, Sar! I can't disagree you've got damned good reasons to do this, but you're making me *really nervous*, Sar! Why don't – why don't we *all* leave now? Okay? I – I will escort Father to the edge of the yard, and tell him never to contact us again. Then we'll pack up and move somewhere else, where no one can ever find us. If you want, you can lie about your age, say you're eighteen. I'll grant you that if you want. I did it when I was your age. While I'm outside though, your part of the deal is to put my EPSAR back in my safe, okay?" He took two steps backwards to prove his point.

"I wouldn't do that, if I were you," Granger warned under his breath.

"Don't patronize me, Dimi. You of all people. You're as much a victim as I am."

Danil eased four, five steps.

Sarah sagged forward against the posts, bending the brim of the cap upwards. Her eyes were dull and vacant, darkly purple above the red scarf. She never wore anything red. Red was the color of blood, the color of death.

"He's never really going to get out of my head, is he, Dimi." She tilted the front of the EPSAR to examine the emitter crystal.

Now! Granger mouthed to Andreiev.

"Of course he will, Sar," Dmitri said. He stepped bravely forward. "Just *give me the EPSAR* and I *promise,* he will be gone, once and for ..."

Dmitri never finished his promise. Up six of the eight steps, Andreiev lunged. Grabbing the girl with one arm, he seized the EPSAR with the other.

Sarah screamed, thrashing like a feral porshie. She knocked Danil backwards, and together they fell bumping down the stairs, her hand still clutching the weapon. Intentional or not, the EPSAR discharged upwards. A section of ceiling glowed, then vanished in a roll of smoke; clothing, papers, and the odd memento rained down from what used to be the bottom drawer of her clothing chest. Wrenching backwards on the girl's wrist, Andreiev forced her to release the weapon.

Dmitri and Sullivan rushed over. Jack snatched the EPSAR, locking the mechanism and swiftly removing the powerpack.

Granger offered a hand. "Are you hurt, Lieutenant?"

Andreiev coughed on dust. "I don't think so. I was more afraid of hurting her."

"Excellent work, Mr. Andreiev," Sullivan said. "Another moment and it might have been one of us instead of the ceiling." He turned to Dmitri, sitting on the floor among the debris, cradling his sister.

"I don't believe this! I should hold you both on interference charges! Not only illegal weapons, but weapons smuggling, breach of interstellar law, and a few others as well!"

"Charge me later," Dmitri growled from the floor. He pointed a finger beyond Sullivan to his father.

"You! Get out! Get out of *my* house! Haven't you done enough harm to our family?" He blinked back tears, unsure if they were from anger, fear, or just plain pain. "We will not be your salvation and comfort! If you carry your guilt to your grave, old man, it won't be long enough! *Leave!* Leave before I give you a piece of your own idea of justice!"

"As you wish." Alexander Kirushenko did not fear death. Such an end would have been properly ironic, worthy of an ancient epic, but such deaths were reserved for heroes, not cowards. His aide peered around the open door, using it as a shield.

"I truly am sorry." Kirushenko paused, then folded himself out the doorway. The door shut with a meek *thunk.*

Dmitri breathed a shaky sigh, and wiped his face on his sleeve.

"Oh, Sar!" He hugged her tight and gave her a peck on her head. "What ever in the universe were you thinking? I'm so mad I don't know where to start."

Since the initial tackle, Sarah had offered no resistance, eyes vacant, safe in the circle of her brother's trusted arms. The scarf hung off one shoulder, the hat lost in the rubble. Dr. Granger's instruments buzzed around her, but she gave no hint of awareness.

"I really was going to kill him," Sarah insisted faintly.

"Znayu, znayu." Dimi stroked her hair. *I know.* "But where would it have gotten you, Sar? It wouldn't have solved anything. It just would have added to your problems."

"No, it wouldn't. After I saved Vlad, I would have turned it on myself."

"That's what I was afraid of," Granger muttered.

The words frightened Dmitri more than he cared to admit. Seizing her by the jaw, he forced her to look him in the eye.

"Listen to me!" His roughness broke through her despair until she squirmed, fearful of a tone he reserved only for the most dire of circumstances.

"You are to go with Dr. Granger! If he chooses to give you medicine, you *will* take it! *Pohnimayetye?* If he asks you a question, you will answer it until you have no voice left to speak with! *Pohnimayetye?* If you don't, I swear with all I have, Sarah, I will ship you to Father in chains! *Pohnimayetye?*" He shook her chin. "I will be right here when you're done."

Sarah's fight was gone, a deflated balloon lying rubbery and crumpled and spent. *"Pohnimayu,"* she repeated. *I understand.* Puppet-like, she awaited her next instruction.

"Come on, Sarah," Granger said, helping her to her feet. "I think you'll feel a lot better when we're done."

He held the girl's arm firmly but not tight; she didn't object as they climbed the stairs and fought their way past the door to her disheveled room. Granger noted the shutters were closed; one less thing to worry about. Light flared up through the seventy-centimeter hole under her clothing drawers, making it easy to locate the lamp on her workbench. He lit it on the second try. Sarah stood where he let go of her, lost in the center of the room. Angry conversation leaked up the stairs and through the hole.

"Maybe we should use Dmitri's room," Kyle suggested. "It might be more private. We won't have to worry about falling through the floor."

Sarah didn't respond.

Shrugging, he placed her workstool near the bed, as Dmitri had done for her 'exam.' "Have a seat here, then."

The girl remained frozen, arm still bent from his escort.

"Sarah?"

Aimless eyes shifted on the blank face.

"Uh oh."

The doctor steered her to the seat. Sarah moved as if made of clay. She didn't protest in the least – Hell, she didn't even look at him.

He sat on the bed facing her – *her* bed, forbidden territory to all but relatives, her most sacred retreat – and she didn't say a word.

"Sarah? Sarah, can you look at me? Sarah?" Hoping the action wouldn't result in violence, Kyle warned, "Sarah, I'm going to touch your face with my hands. You can pull away if you want. Try and look at me." Placing a palm on each side of her jaw, he guided the chin until she faced him. He couldn't force the empty eyes to look at him, however.

"Look at me, Sarah." This time the purple-blue eyes found his, searching his face in wonder, as if he'd just appeared.

Granger took an educated guess. "Sarah, do you know my name?"

Still the confused stare, like a lost child warned never to talk to strangers.

"Do you know where you are?"

The beautiful eyes blinked, blank and innocent. They looked away, thinking, blinking, before riveting back on Granger's.

"Dimi?" she said, bewildered. "Is Dimi here?"

"Yes! He's downstairs."

"Is he – *dead*? Did something happen to him? Or to me?"

"Dmitri's alive and well. He's downstairs right now, talking with the captain and the other officers. You can see him when we're done."

The head nodded vacuously.

Granger got down to business while he had her attention. He left his perch on the bed and went to her workbench. He picked up the first notepad he came across, found blank pages in the back, and searched until he came across a pencil of sorts, then returned to his seat.

"No games, Sarah. I know it might be hard right now, but I need you to listen to me. I want only honest answers from you, and I promise that's all I'll give you in return. I don't think you realize how serious a thing you've done, but let me tell you: Jack Sullivan's got the power to have you locked up for quite a while; your brother, too, if necessary. That all depends on what I report back to him when we're through. It's extremely important that you cooperate. Can you understand that?"

The girl still looked puzzled. "Did I do something bad again? Does Dimi know? He'll go nova if he finds out. It must have been really bad if they want to lock me up. Did I hurt anyone else, or just me?" The eyes darted down to check her wrists.

The doctor stole a curious glance. Hardly five minutes had passed. "Can you tell me what you did?"

Her eyes roamed the room, looking for clues. "I don't know."

"Do you know where you are?" *An angst-ridden head-shake.*

"Are you on a ship?"

"Is this Rangler?" she asked. Rangler was the psychiatric hospital she'd spent time at.

"No," Granger replied, scribbling several lines in the back of the notebook.

"I'm sorry! I don't know!" Sarah cried out mournfully. "It will come back! I know it will!"

"I'm sure it will. Do you know what time it is?"

The eyes wandered to the closed shutters, but couldn't comprehend. "Time is artificial in space."

Nothing. "That's true. Can you tell me your name?"

The girl's forehead furrowed with concentration. "You called me ... Sss ... *ssSarah*. Sar'ina. Sarah-Irina Kirushenko, no patronymic. That's

238

it," she agreed with herself, as if not quite convinced.

"Very good! That's great, Sarah. How old are you?"

"Mother was forty when she died. I was eight. If Mother were alive today, she would be forty-eight. That makes Dimi twenty-three. If Dimi's twenty-three, then Vlad's sixteen and I'm ... sixteen," she decided at last. "Sixteen years, nine weeks, and ... And ... *I'm sorry! I'm sorry!*" She crammed her knuckles between her teeth.

Granger pushed the hand down gently. "Don't bite, Sarah. Squeeze my hand if you feel upset." He offered his fingers, but she curled her arms against her, hands clenched.

"I'm sorry!" she repeated, rocking on the seat. "I can't remember if it's four or five days. I can't be more accurate than that. I'm sorry!"

"That's more than adequate, Sarah. Plain sixteen is all I was after," Granger encouraged. "You're doing just fine. Let's try another question..."

* * *

"You realize I'm taking control of everything as of now?" Sullivan informed Dmitri.

Dmitri scraped the remnants of his dignity together. He stood and brushed the dust from his pants. "I know. I just wanted her to realize that as well. I'm still her guardian, and I don't want to see her hurt."

"No one wants to see her hurt, but there are other issues to discuss. Sit down." Jack pointed to the table.

"I bring an analysis team down to a technology-prohibited planet to investigate a potential illegal weapons discharge that breaches said order, and after a prolonged and inconclusive investigation, I find my men and myself held hostage by a psychotic child wielding an illegal weapon that you *swore* to me didn't exist! Tell me, Mr. Kirushenko. What conclusion would you draw?"

"She's not psychotic! She just gets ... *upset* now and then. And it's not the conclusion you're thinking."

"What *am* I thinking, Mr. Kirushenko? Does or does not this EPSAR belong to you?" Sullivan tossed the powerless shell onto the charred table.

Dmitri watched the EPSAR casing roll to a stop, pointing at him. "Yes, but – It's not illegal as you say –"

"The one absolute fact we've established, Mr. Kirushenko, is that weapon is illegal," Ti'onam said.

"Yyyes, but it's not *exactly* illegal. Sort of?"

Sullivan's irritation showed in the puckered anger of his face. "Would you care to inform me just how it is *not* illegal?"

"It's not a smuggled – well, it is, but it isn't – Not the way you're thinking," Dmitri sputtered. "It's not *legally* mine – I mean, I – don't have a, uh, *permit* or anything for it. It belonged to my brother Viktor, but he's dead. We used it to defend ourselves during the raid on Outpost 62. It kind of got worked into our luggage when we cleared out his things. I guess you could say we rightfully *inherited* it. After everything we went through, I wasn't ever going to be caught without a weapon again! When we got here, I disassembled it. Without the power cell in place, it didn't register in the scanners. I slipped it into Sarah's pocket, after her last check and before mine. I'll admit that much.

"But I sure regret it now," he said. "Don't you think she scared the living Hell out of me, too? I have *never* seen her like that before, never! I took precautions! I locked it up, I kept the power cell in a different place – I couldn't do more than I did! After all this time, I would have thought it would have been drained cold. I have never, *ever* fired that weapon. It's been packed away so long, I'd forgotten all about it until you started making accusations. I checked, and everything was exactly where I hid it.

"A DNA scanning trigger is the most secure safety mechanism available," Andreiev offered. "Only the permittee can fire it. A double or triple lock will also slow down a theft."

"How many others have you brought through?" Sullivan accused. He picked up the EPSAR and waved it in the boy's face.

Dmitri leaned away "None! The only one I've even *held* is that one, right there. The only other weapons I have are my knives, and Guillaume okayed those. I swear, I've never shown the EPSAR to anyone, not even Charlie."

"Why did you set those explosions?"

"I didn't! You know more about them than I do!"

The boy was earnest enough, but too many pieces didn't fit. Too many times, his stories started out one way and ended another. Despite reservations, Sullivan had trusted the man, assumed his help was genuine. He'd come to believe the stories about the girl, finally believed her innocence.

"I don't believe you're telling the truth," Jack goaded. "Four weeks we've wasted, without any hard evidence, while the key was right here under our feet. We trusted you, Dmitri! We accepted your hospitality, slept under your roof, believed what you translated for us! How far from the truth did you lead us? What's the purpose of your mission? Who are you working with? Is Dickerson your contact?" He planted his hands on the unscorched edge of the table and leaned in with intimidation.

"No one! Jan's as straight as they come! I have never lied to you! Everything I did or said was the truth. I have no freakin' idea how she got that EPSAR to work!"

"But you admit to possession and smuggling of a forbidden weapon?" Ti'onam reminded him.

Dmitri looked away. "I'm not sure I can answer that."

Sullivan glared. "You can't answer it, or you won't?"

"I won't answer it without a lawyer present! And don't you go pestering Sarah; she's been through enough."

"*I'll* decide when enough is enough. If I don't get some solid answers soon," the captain threatened, "I will revoke your travel papers, close down the research facility, and prosecute this matter all the way through the Allied Space Fleet to the Alliance itself, if I have to! *Who are you working with at the Compound?*"

* * *

"I am evil," Sarah insisted in a monotone. "I am the common denominator. Mother was dying; I was the only one home. My sister 'Byeta died because of a fight with me. I sat with Dimi when he almost died. I was there when the Outpost was raided. They butchered Viktor like a porshie."

"Everyone hits a string of bad luck, sometimes," the doctor said. "As a new intern, I once lost the first four patients on my shift, right in a row. That takes an awful big bite out of your self-confidence. I blamed myself for quite a while, even though there wasn't a thing I did wrong, not a thing I could have done different to change the outcome. But the fifth patient survived, and the sixth, and the seventh. You keep going anyway."

Sarah studied her cuticles as if she could see them growing. "I don't think I'm meant to kill Dimi. I think I'm meant to torture him for something horrible he did in a past life. First he got stuck with me, then he almost died on my account, and then I went and lied to Jaycee. Now I've gotten him into a heap more trouble. He can't forgive me this time, not even if the Moons decreed it."

"Who's Jaycee?" Granger wondered.

"Dimi's wife."

A wave of emotion surged upward. "Why? *Why?* Why did they save me when I was born?" Sarah's hands clenched to fists over the injustice of it. "If they'd just let me die, none of this! None of the pain to all these people would ever have happened! I tried to stop it! I wasn't done with that EPSAR! Why did they stop me before I could die?"

Granger's hair prickled. Coming after her previous statements, on top of a history of self-destruction and instability, her continued vehemence screamed danger. Neurotropic drugs weren't standard in a medical field kit. He had no restraints, no medications that might help beyond tranquilizers, no psychiatric diagnostic equipment, no molecular transporters to evacuate with. The best he could offer was a ready ear and a hand to hold, and he couldn't let go for a second.

"You were saved because your parents wanted you to be saved. A new baby is a precious thing, especially one that fought so hard to survive. A child like that has a very strong will to live."

The eyes remained vacant, but the girl gave a far-away smile, eerie to behold. "I'm number ten of thirteen, only nine months after my brother. The last thing they wanted was another baby. My survival was the doctor's error. And as for your latter statement …" Sarah gave a brief choke of laughter that caught in her throat like a cry. "Let's just leave it at, *strong-willed*."

The head snapped up and the eyes focused on Granger's. They weren't dull and distant this time, but crystal clear and wide and earnest. She grabbed his arm. "If I tell you something, will you promise not to take it personally? Please! I don't want you to take it the wrong way."

It was her game right now, her rules. "All right. I'll do my best to keep an open mind."

Sarah leaned to whisper in his ear. *"I'm going to kill myself."*

Granger's skin crawled. She was so absurdly fervent, as if she'd told him she was going to do something so bold and daring and benign as to purchase a forbidden style of shoes, and that was a very dangerous thing. People that bent on self-destruction were difficult to stop.

"Now, I know you are legally bound to prevent me from doing it," Sarah continued. "I know that, and that's why I don't want you to feel bad when you can't prevent it. I've thought this out; it's not a rash decision. If I do something big and flamboyant – you know, like slicing or EPSARing or throwing myself from a tree or something, you'll stop me or heal me, especially since I've now warned you, so I can't do those."

Granger took a cautious breath. "That eliminates a lot of methods. What's left? Poisoning, or drowning?"

The childish innocence turned to horror. "Oh no! I couldn't do that! Not even in desperation! I don't like deep water at all! Goodness, no!" Sarah leaned in close. "I'm going to *will* myself to die. You cannot stop someone from doing that. Old people do it all the time. Humans can do it, and the Navarans are even better at it. I learned about those things when I was there.

"You really are a nice person, despite your profession. That's why I don't want you to feel bad." She gave his arm a sympathetic pat, looking sorry for him. "Restraints and medications won't help, so please don't take it bad when you can't stop me."

It was the strangest suicidal call for help Granger had ever witnessed. He had no doubt her intentions were honest, but it took effort to keep from laughing. One part of her was desperate to avoid the agony she was currently repressing, but the infantile will to live was so strong she couldn't have begged for help any harder if she'd known what she was doing.

"What does Dmitri have to say about it?"

"I haven't told him. If he knows, he'll just get scared and order me not to. It's really for his own good. Sometimes you just have to save stubborn people from themselves."

Another message from the rational mind held hostage, projecting her needs onto her brother in a vain attempt at survival. "Okay. You're sure that's what you want? If you're really serious, and you do it right, I can't help you if you change your mind."

"Absolutely! It's the only way to prevent me from causing anyone any more pain."

'Cause my self,' Granger understood. "Well, if you're that determined, and that's your choice, then I can't stop you, can I?"

Sarah smiled in an odd, detached way, as if she were talking to herself. "I'm so glad you understand. I was afraid you wouldn't. You can't be too sure with doctors. Some get upset at that kind of thing. Did you study on Navara, too?"

Granger ignored the remark with a shudder. "Do one thing for me first." He flipped to a blank page, then handed her the pad and pencil. Taking a gamble, he instructed, "Before you start, write down for me what to do afterwards – what arrangements you want, an address to notify your family, if any of your possessions should go to anyone in particular." If it didn't make her face the finality of her solution, it would buy some time.

Sarah accepted the notebook. She sucked on the end of the pencil, contemplating. "I hadn't thought about that. There are certain things that should go to certain people, like my brother Sergei should get all my books, here and in my locker at the compound. Charlie can have the ones in Tau Cetan. Dmitri gets anything of Viktor's. We sent him back to Russia, you know. I suppose you should send me there, too. Vlad said they have a beautiful memorial for him only a short walk from their ..."

Sarah's mouth hung open, ready for the next word. The notebook and pencil flopped to the floor, forgotten, as she covered her mouth with her hands.

"Oh *NO*! No! You *Bastard!* Moons, *no!*" She slid off the stool to the floor. Arms over her belly, she rocked on her knees, hyperventilating with pain.

Granger knelt, concerned by the strange new twist. He hadn't expected a catharsis this quick. "What is it, Sarah? What's wrong? What did you remember?"

She moaned, pulling at her hair. "I can't! I *promised* him! Moons help me, *I can't do it!*"

"Do *what*, Sarah? What did you promise?"

"I promised Vlad! I promised Vlad I wouldn't die before I came home again! *I have to suffer this!*"

"You don't have to face this alone, Sarah. Dmitri will be with you. I'll help you however I can," Kyle said. "You *won't* be alone through this."

"Lock me up! Lock me away, where I can't hurt anyone ever again! Just – please – let me send a message to Vlad once a year, on his birthday. To let him know I'm still – *alive!*" She collapsed over her knees, consumed by anguish.

"No one wants to lock you up, Sarah," Granger said, but she wasn't hearing him. Against his better judgment, he rubbed the weeping back. She gave no notice.

"I'll get you through this," he promised, combing his fingers sadly through the tangled hair. "You have my word on that. It's not as hopeless as you think right now."

The words didn't register, and he watched the incoherent scene play out before him.

Kneeling, the girl clasped her hands before her face, fingers interlocked in a grip so fierce they turned dark. She turned the hands this way and that, staring at them, oblivious to anything else.

"Oh Vlad!" she mourned through her tears. "I'm sorry!" She laid a cheek on the back of one hand, closing her eyes as she caressed it. "I'm so sorry, Vlad! I ruined it! They'll never let me come home now."

She kissed the back of the hand reverently several times before pressing it once more to her cheek. "Oh, Vladimir! *Minyeh prostitye*! Forgive me! I was so, so scared! You must understand that! Please understand! Oh, Vlad, I'm *sorry*!"

* * *

"What do you make of it?" Sullivan asked Andreiev.

The weapons officer pursed his lips in concentration, the disassembled EPSAR spread across the table in front of him. "I don't know. If he's correct, and it hasn't been charged in four years, there should not have been any power at all. A full charge, dormant, will last twelve months. It then loses strength, until by two years you might get one or two weak shots, but that's all. It's dead."

"Any possible way she could have recharged it?"

Andreiev laughed. "Not out here, sir! Not unless they managed to smuggle an entire particle generator as well. She had to have help. The cover plate is gouged around the edges." He ran a finger over the roughened seams to show the captain. "Someone was so inexperienced, they missed the catch and tried to force it open. Anyone with any knowledge of a hand weapon at all would know how to replace the power cell." He demonstrated the simplicity of removing the cover from the housing – if one knew where to press and pull. "I can't see someone figuring out particle generation if they can't even open the case."

"But someone did," Sullivan insisted. "What about the unusual discharge patterns?"

"I don't have a theory for that yet, sir," the lieutenant admitted. "I can't safely analyze the waves until we get back to the ship. The omni reads a nonstandard distribution that I am unfamiliar with. I should be able to pinpoint it when we return."

Jack Sullivan sighed with frustration. "Keep working on it, Lieutenant. We'll see what Dr. Granger has been able to learn."

"One more, Sarah," Granger soothed, readjusting the instrument. "No matter what anyone else has tried, no matter what has ever happened, this *will* make you sleep. A deep, dreamless sleep, so don't be afraid of it." The aeroderm hissed against her skin before she might change her mind.

Immediately, Sarah's exhaustion seized her, and it was mostly under the doctor's assistance she stumbled the meter from the chair to the bed.

She slipped at once into unconsciousness.

After a check of the girl's vitals, Granger thumped down the stairs, three hours after he'd begun.

Dmitri jumped to his feet, crazy with nerves. All the shrieks and cries had filtered down through the ceiling hole, tearing him apart. "How is she? What's she doing? Why are you leaving her alone like that? I want to see her!"

Granger stretched and gave a yawn. "I've got her sedated. She'll be unconscious for several hours. After that, for a day or two at least, I want someone with her every waking moment."

"What's your opinion, Doctor?" Sullivan asked.

Kyle sat and handed the captain his raw notes. He rubbed his eyes wearily. "I'm a certified diagnostician with a surgeon's license, not a psychiatrist, but right now she's in deep shock. Her reality testing is completely unreliable. She knows she did something wrong, but she sat in her own room, in her own house, and didn't know where she was. There's some disintegrative dissociation going on. On a preliminary basis, I'd say it was a panic attack, fueled by a resurgence of traumatic stress, triggered by the sight of her father. She saw him, flashed back to an earlier crisis, and felt she had to defend herself or suffer further harm."

"How long until the sedative wears off? I want to question her before we return to the research base, and I plan to leave here at the first sign of daylight, rain or not. Mr. Kirushenko insists the EPSAR was under lock and key, without a usable power supply. I want to know exactly what she did, and who helped her."

"Absolutely not, Jack. I don't dare move her for at least twenty-four, preferably forty-eight hours. I don't have any heavy-duty neuroleptics with me. The best I can do is tranquilize her, which isn't much better than a tourniquet on an amputation. I had to draw up and sign a contract with her to get her to trust me even for that. I have to protect her interests to the best of my ability, and in return she pledged cooperation and promised to wait at least twenty-four hours before any attempts at killing herself."

Dmitri seemed comforted. "That's good. She sticks to her contracts, no matter what."

"I didn't know you were into hostage negotiations, Dr. Granger," Sullivan said. "I understand her upset, but she's not in a position to ask favors. I need answers, and I need them now. I want to get back to the ship as fast as possible, so I can file charges, if necessary. Is she or is she not fit to stand up to those charges?"

"Right now? Based on my notes and the interview I just finished?" In certain instances, a doctor could outrank a captain, and Kyle had stepped on heads before, friendships not withstanding. "As Chief Medical Officer of the *Triumph,* it is my best medical opinion that Sarah Kirushenko is not fit to stand up to charges on this evening's incident. Based on my findings, I fully believe Sarah Kirushenko to be medically and legally insane at the present time."

* * *

Though the day had certainly taken a major turn for the worse, Jack Sullivan didn't forget to chew out two of his officers. The precariousness of the situation demanded utter professionalism, and any further hint of personal friction would be dealt with most harshly. He waited impatiently at 25:00 hours, when his handicom chirped twice in his hand. The sudden noise in the quiet room startled him, and he answered it fast. "Raines! Status report."

"All departments report normal, sir," Jupiter's voice replied. "Dr. Bakari's patient transferred to Starbase 79 as per your orders. Return to standard orbit at 19:10 hours ship's time. Captain, there's a second ship orbiting, a Mystic-class interstellar cruiser, crew of fifteen. Registration is Altairan in origin. They claim to be chartered by the UPA Department of Rehabilitation."

"Keep an eye on it, Mr. Raines. Let me know when they transport anything. Chances are they are on legitimate business, at least as they see it. I believe I have already met their passengers. If they're not leaving orbit within two standard days, notify me at once. I'm hoping to be back to the ship within four."

"You found the cause, sir?"

"Not yet, Mr. Raines, but we found one answer, and that has become my first priority. I'll be in touch when I have more details. Sullivan out."

He upped the frequency channel and the handicom sent a signal of its own. "Sullivan to Chessorak Base."

"Chessorak, Jihan Ziva."

"Get me Commander Guillaume, Priority Red."

There was a pause. "Guillaume here, Captain. What's going on? Our sensors picked up several more bursts almost under your feet. Did you notice anything unusual? Were you able to pinpoint the location?"

"I've managed to pinpoint several things, including a breach of security in your compound!" Sullivan growled. "I'm holding two of your

247

'harmless' field associates on numerous charges, including attempted murder of Allied Space Fleet personnel. This field station is closed, effective immediately. Send me a team of at least four of your most trusted staff, including no less than two women, and at least two who can function as translators, since I no longer trust my current ones. Outfit them with whatever equipment you have to haul materials back for detailed examination. Send a magnetic containment box with them; get one from the *Triumph* if you don't have a portable. I want them here as soon as humanly possible, inhumanly if necessary, so we can transport the prisoners back to my ship. As soon as your team leaves your gates, you are to lock them and not allow anyone out until I return, not so much as an animal. Is that clear, Commander?"

There was another pause as his words sunk in. "Why, yes, absolutely, Captain!" Guillaume sputtered. "But, surely you don't mean the Kirushenkos?"

"That is exactly who I'm holding responsible right now. When Mr. Kirushenko the father arrives, I want him off the planet immediately. I have nothing against him myself; in fact, his presence was instrumental in solving one of my mysteries, but I don't need him complicating things any more than they are. In the meantime, I want you to run a check on every one of your security measures, including scanners, with particular attention on detecting weapons and metallic objects. I want to know if something was tampered with. I also want you to recall from your records all operating data from the day the Kirushenkos first arrived, including molecular transport records. Be assured, I will review everything myself when I get there."

"It – will be done," Guillaume said, disappointed. "I'll have a team on the road before sunrise. They should be there within a day and a half."

"We'll be waiting. Sullivan out."

Двадцать два
Twenty-two
Shivalavash

The Kirushenko boy woke first, and let his sister sleep. She didn't sleep well when upset, and this would most likely be her last good rest for a while. He'd eaten half his breakfast when the shriek made him swallow his tea the wrong way. He bolted from his seat, coughing, only to be stopped at the end of the table.

"Keep him down here," Sullivan ordered Ti'onam.

"No! You've got to let me up there! You're going to make things worse! You're going to scare her! Sarah!" Dmitri shouted at the ceiling hole. "I'm still here! You're okay!"

Jack rushed up the stairs, past the bright gouges on the floor from forcing the door open. Granger spoke to the girl; outnumbered, she took one look at the captain and fled to crouch against the far wall. "What's going on, Doc?"

Granger's eyes never left his patient. "I'm not really sure. She woke up, took one look at me, and jumped out of bed screaming. I didn't want to touch her, but she ripped out two handfuls of hair."

"Is she able to understand us? Can she speak?"

"I don't know."

Sullivan stepped forward, palms raised in a gesture of good will. "Peace, Miss Kirushenko. No one wants to hurt you, but we don't want to see you hurt yourself, either. I'd like you to answer a few questions for me."

Sarah pressed herself against the wall, tense and silent.

"No one will touch you. Just talk. Do you remember me? I've been staying in one of your downstairs rooms. My name is Jack."

"Where's Dimi? What have you done to him?" Sarah demanded. "I want my brother!"

"Dmitri's eating breakfast. After we talk, you can have some breakfast, too." He took a step forward.

"Get away from me!" A wary eye on the men, Sarah leaned sideways and snatched a glass of water from the table by the bed. Holding it by the bottom, she dashed it against the table. Shards of thin glass exploded onto the floor with the last of the water, but a portion of it remained in her hand, jagged and sharp. She held the weapon up, threatening.

"Better back up, Captain." Granger pulled his sleeve until he retreated. "Even if you're not a doctor, she could attack if she feels threatened. Sarah, don't move," he ordered. "You'll cut your feet."

The girl gave a chilling laugh. "I've lived through far worse than cut feet. I want my brother!"

Sullivan held his ground. "I've already talked to your brother. I want your side of things now. I want the truth, not what you think he might want to hear, or what he might want you to say. Answer my questions, and then we can talk about your brother."

"Sarah!" Dmitri's voice interrupted through the floor. "I'm right here, Sar!"

Sarah's eyes searched the ceiling, looking for spirits. "Dimi!"

"Are you covering something up? Why won't you let me see him? What did you do to him? *Why can't I talk to him?"* She raised the empty hand to her mouth and bit hard on a knuckle, seeing only what was in her head.

"Jack," Granger warned, "I think you better bring him up here. She's not strong enough for this. It's not going to help anyone if she worsens."

Sarah pointed with the broken glass. "If you hurt him, I *will* kill you! And if you harm me, I have five other brothers who will gladly take revenge! Two of them are big enough to kill you with their bare hands, and one of them would do it just for the fun. *What did you do to Dimi?"*

"Put down the glass. There's no need for violence." Sullivan took a gamble. "You like to make deals, Sarah. I'm willing to make you a deal. I will let you go downstairs with your brother, sit with him all you like, but you have to answer my questions while you do, and I expect honest answers. If you can't do it, then," he walked his fingers up an imaginary staircase, "back upstairs you go to sit in your room alone, with a guard to make sure you stay here. That's my deal."

Sarah sucked her lip, unsure. "I want Dimi," she whimpered. "No tricks! Cross your heart and hope to die, swear by your ship up in the sky! Do it!"

Sullivan eyed her with a heavy heart. Yesterday she'd been an honorary member of his crew, discussing problems and analyzing data as skillfully as any of his junior officers. Today there was nothing left but a frightened little girl, with more faith in schoolyard oaths than the people around her.

"No tricks. I swear it. Cross my heart."

Sarah picked her way around the broken glass toward the doctor, never-ever taking her eyes off the captain. She turned the unbroken end of the weapon toward Granger, allowed him to take it, and fled down the stairs.

Sullivan followed seconds later. The siblings were locked in a tight embrace.

"Enough. Sit down," Jack ordered. "I held up my part of the bargain; now it's your turn."

Dmitri wiped Sarah's eyes with his thumbs, kissed her forehead, and turned her around. She pulled his arms around her. Everything would be okay as long as they stayed together.

Sarah caught sight of the scorch-mark on the table, mesmerized by the darkness against the grey wood. The seconds passed, ten, fifteen, before she repeated, "What did I do? What did I do? What did I do?"

Dimi murmured softly and broke the fixation. He steered her to straddle the bench. He sat behind her in the same manner, arms around her, watching the captain's every move.

"Do you remember what happened yesterday? Do you remember your father paying a visit?" Sullivan asked.

"I'm not sure."

"Where did you get the EPSAR?"

Sarah sniffed and rubbed her nose with the back of her wrist. She glanced behind at her brother; Dmitri nodded permission.

"Dimi's safe." Her gaze wandered back to the burn.

"How did you get it?"

Sarah didn't answer, and Sullivan had to repeat the question. She wrenched her eyes from the tabletop. "I discovered the code on the lock. I knew the ending number, so I started at 00-00-89, and after a year and a half and 3,137 tries, I actually hit the right number."

"Why did you need the EPSAR? Why were you after it?"

"I didn't!" Sarah cringed against her brother. "I didn't even know it was in there! I was going to put it right back, but Viktor promised I could fire it, and I never got to. I just wanted my turn. I figured no one would ever know."

"So you took it outside and started shooting trees."

Trees. Some trees were grey. And EPSARs on low settings left black marks on grey bark. Scorched. Just like the ...

Sarah jerked her eyes from the table with a gasp. "No. It wouldn't fire. It didn't have a power pack."

"So you stole one."

"No. I don't steal! It was in the back of Dimi's drawer. It didn't work."

"So you pried the cover off to see if you could fix it. When you couldn't, you took it back to the research compound and had someone recharge it for you, or swapped the cell for a fresh one. Who did that for you? Dickerson? You seemed rather at ease with him. Or perhaps this Mr. Ennis who sends you things."

Confusion broke the bewitchment of the tabletop. She picked at her ragged nails. "No. I think I know better than that! If Marc or Dimi'd found out, they'd have killed me! I – I recharged it myself, upstairs."

Dmitri leaned around to stare at her. "You don't know anything about EPSARs! How could you do that?"

"How *could* you do that?" Sullivan frowned. "How did you get the equipment to recharge a power cell?

"Answer me!" he barked when she didn't respond.

Dmitri gave her a poke.

"Don't yell at me!" Sarah cringed. She twisted a lock of hair around her finger, tugging it hard every so many revolutions until Dmitri made her stop. "Isn't there some law that says I don't have to incriminate myself?"

"Yes," Ti'onam replied without hesitation.

"Perhaps, but you can complain to a lawyer when we get back to the ship," Sullivan said. "I am the law out here. I want to know how you managed to recharge a phased-particle energy weapon in a wood-fuel society. How did you get the equipment out of the compound?"

"Go on, Sar," Dmitri urged in her ear. "It's okay. I want to hear it, too."

Sarah spoke to the impartiality of the wall. "When I was in school on Navara, we had to do a project on solar energy. My group came in second, only because we overcompensated and our results incinerated. I remembered that, so before the rainy season started, I – built a kind of solar collector for it, and I powered it up that way. It took about a month to where I thought it was good enough."

Jack couldn't have heard correctly. "You recharged it – through a *solar collector*? Andreiev!"

"Understood, Captain!" The weapons specialist rushed to the back room where the EPSAR sat, and carried the power cell carefully out of the cabin to the safer location of the workshed, his crewmates giving him wide berth.

"Do you have any idea – !" Sullivan couldn't complete the sentence. "Obviously you don't, or you never would have done that! You *thought* it was charged enough? *Do you have any idea how dangerous that was?!* You could have killed everyone in this room! You never, *ever,* recharge a micro-focused fuel supply from a fluctuating energy source! The result is an unstable power dispersal that can explode without warning!"

"God damn!" Granger swore.

"Although the risk is unacceptable, I am most impressed. You were successful, even without a magnetic field relay or an Allen particle modulation tool?" Ti'onam looked shamefully surprised. "I would be most interested in learning your methodology."

The swelling stench of anger in the room overrode the compelling whispers of the scorch. "Don't yell at me! How was I supposed to know? It didn't say anything about that in the article I read." She picked at her nails, watching Sullivan through her hair. "I didn't have any of the tools or things they talked about, and I knew Marc would never give them up. I knew how to build a solar collector, so I just guessed at everything else. I scrounged substitutes as I went along, and I judged the power by the strength of the beam when I fired it."

"What article was that?" Jack demanded. "Where did you get it?"

"I don't know. Some tech manual or other. I never looked at the title page."

"I want to see it."

"I burned it. I kept the diagram, though, if that's any help."

The captain turned his back as he counted to twenty, *twenty-one*, *twenty-two*, fingers massaging the rock-hard knots of tension that formed in his temples.

He took a deep breath and turned back to the pair. "All right. Show me every piece of your creation you didn't burn or otherwise destroy."

It took two people to lift the heavy trunk enough for Sarah to retrieve the computer-printed diagram of an EPSAR and its workings, with her own rough sketches and formulas on the back. From her top drawer she pulled lengths of metal wire – the same wire she'd used on her hair, only this was wrapped obsessively with endless amounts of heavy string to insulate it. From behind her bookcase she retrieved a number of flat glass plates, as long as a boot and twice the width of her hand, inked black. From elsewhere around the room she dug out thin metal foil, the missing curved glass to the clock face, and other accoutrements. With Dmitri's approval, it took Sarah no more than ten minutes to reassemble her makeshift charging device – minus the EPSAR.

Sarah writhed with nerves, but stayed more focused away from the table and its cancerous lesion of misbehavior. "I salvaged these discarded photo-voltaic sheets at the compound; they're damaged, but enough of it still worked. I hid my collection panels among the roofing shingles. It was a slow process, but I found I could speed it up by concentrating the sun's rays using the clock glass. The wires ran along the log seam here, in through the window, under the workbench, and I secured the EPSAR on the underside here in the corner with these metal packing straps I found in a trash heap at the Al's." She squatted down to show Sullivan. "It wasn't visible unless you knew it was there. I made sure of that."

Jack shook his head, dumbfounded. "Have you ever heard of something like this, Mr. Andreiev?"

"No, sir," the officer said. "It is unique. It is possible to charge an EPSAR through an alternate energy source, but it's normally done through storage cells, or portable generators. At worst, you can rig a system to transfer power from another similar but mismatched cell source – such as an omnicomp cell into an EPSAR cell. I have never heard of it being accomplished with direct solar power. That could explain the unusual emission patterns. If that is what she did, I could believe she did act alone. No one with any knowledge of particle energy would have allowed this."

Sullivan nodded. It was as frightening as a ten-year old bringing his science project to school and discovering he'd built a working plasma weapon from a photo in an advertisement. Jack paced the floor, sequencing the events.

"So, once you felt the EPSAR was adequately powered, you ran off and shot trees with it."

Sarah shrugged. "I wanted to see if it worked. I took it out into the forest where I knew no one would be around. I'd already been there; I knew it was uninhabited. I thought I could use it for logging. I tried it on a tree, but it took so long I was afraid I would use up all the power. It didn't appear to be a practical application for such a small unit, so I just spent some time playing. When I came back to the cabin, I put it back in its cradle. The next time Dimi went out, I returned everything where it went and I didn't touch it again. And that's the absolute truth, so help me Sil'anak!"

"What about the explosions?" Sullivan demanded. "Did you also fuel those through solar-powered devices, or did you use a chemical detonator? What was the content ratio, and who helped you acquire it?"

"I don't know anything about the explosions!" Sarah swore. "I had nothing to do with them! I can be accounted for both times! I swear I had nothing to do with them! Dimi, I didn't! You *know* I didn't! I've *been* telling the truth! I *don't lie!*" She scrabbled across the floor on her hands and knees to hide behind her brother's legs.

From downstairs came a clicking and a rattle, then a knock sounded.

"Father's back!" Sarah whispered in panic. She hugged Dmitri's knees. "Don't answer it! Don't! Don't!"

<Dimi–tri, you home?> came a familiar Tau Cetan female's voice.

Dmitri's shoulders slumped with relief. "Mrs. Al. We never unbarred the door. It's her day to clean and cook."

"Not today," Sullivan said. "Tell her there's been a change in plans, you don't need her services today. And you," he took Sarah by the elbow and pulled her to her feet despite her fearful cry, "will translate every word they say for me and do it correctly, or I will order you separated again. Is that clear?"

Sarah nodded, and the group thumped down the stairs.

<Dimi-tri?> Mrs. Al called louder.

Dimi opened the door part way. He held up a hand. *<Please, it not good day for you to bother cleaning today.>*

<Dimi-tri? Why you say – That Sarrah back there?> she asked, peering around him. *<Why she look so – Dimi-tri, she sick?>*

Sarah backed against the wall, hugging herself as she eyed the table. She mumbled her translations distantly, as if talking to herself.

<Yes!> Dmitri seized on the idea. *<She sick – I sick – We all sick! That why you should not come today. Charlie, too. Is not very bad, but I not want you to get sick, too. Maybe – maybe it from something I cook, maybe it not. We will rest. Wait day or two, then come see.>*

Mrs. Al raised the end of her wrap over her face. *<I make you good food, leave it at door. I check tomorrow,>* she promised, and hurried away.

<Thank you, most kind!> Dmitri called after her, and barred the door once more.

He turned back to the room. "Happy now?"

Двадцать три
Twenty-three
Shvala Chednash

The voices grew louder as they neared the cabin, accompanied by the vociferous squalling of tired porshies and the rattly squeaking of a cart. No one was surprised to hear a knock this time.

"Find out who it is," Sullivan instructed Dmitri.

<farrash lxa?>

"It's Jan, Dimi."

Sullivan opened the door. "Thank you, Mr. Dickerson. We've been waiting for you. Please, come in."

"Tova, see to the porshies," Jan said. "The only water's in here; you'll have to carry it out in buckets." He entered the cabin, followed by a woman with long hair the same brown as her shoes. An older man followed, and a young woman in her early twenties.

"Captain Sullivan," the lieutenant-commander acknowledged with a bow of his head. "Commander Ti'onam. We hurried as fast as the porshies would go. What's going on? Commander Guillaume said you were closing the outpost."

He whistled in amazement at the hole in the ceiling. "Dmitri? You all right? What the hell happened?"

Dmitri nodded. "We're okay."

Sarah's rocking chair was turned to the wall, the better to ignore everyone, but the brown-haired woman knelt next to her anyway. "Sarah? What's happened?"

Sarah put her hands over her face and bent over her knees. "I'm sorry! I'm sorry, Nora! It's my fault! I'm sorry!"

Sullivan placed the EPSAR in Dickerson's hand. "Does this look familiar to you?"

Jan's eyes lit up, and he whistled again. He flipped it over, examining it. "Is this one of yours, Captain? It's not one of ours. This is an ARS417K. We have the ASD772X, which replaced the ARS two years ago, of which every one was visually accounted for just before I left. It feels light; is it complete?"

"Not at present," Sullivan said. "I haven't decided what to do with the power cell. It's to be considered dangerously unstable, and I can't safely drain it here. I hope you brought a containment box with you; I want it sealed in there immediately. I could detonate it, but it would destroy my evidence in the process."

"Where did it come from?"

"Perhaps you should ask Mr. Kirushenko about that."

Jan stared. *"Dmitri?"*

Dmitri hung his head. "It's mine. I had it locked away, not bothering anybody, until Sarah found it. *Crying out loud, Jan!* Who the hell let my father loose on this planet, anyway! He had no business being here! We think he's safe in prison somewhere, and bang! There he is at the door! I don't blame Sarah one bit. Whoever sent him out here is every bit as guilty as I am. It never would have happened if you hadn't!"

"I'm sorry. Commander Guillaume didn't want him out here, either, but he presented all kinds of credentials. We had no idea it would cause a problem for you."

"Yeah, well, it did."

Dickerson deferred his authority to the ranking officer. "What can we do to help, Captain Sullivan?"

"Break it all down," Sullivan ordered. "I want every last thing of theirs packed up and hauled back to the compound. We've been able to examine some things; I want the rest gone through with microscanners, just in case. We've found one illegal item; I'm not convinced there aren't more."

"By the time we do that, it will be too late to start back today," Jan said. "We drove the porshies hard; they need to rest or they'll get balky and quit on us half way back. It would be better to start out first thing tomorrow."

"That will have to do. Dr. Granger has Miss Kirushenko on a twenty-four-hour medical watch; I want at least one of the women with her at all times. He can fill you in on the details. She is not allowed outside the cabin and is to be kept away from windows at all costs. The shutters in her room must remain closed, lest she escape through them. We will take turns guarding Mr. Kirushenko."

"Like I've got somewhere to go!" Dmitri sneered. "Tell the computer to hold my calls, I'm going for a haircut and a manicure, and I'll be at the Low-G tennis finals until six. After that you can reach me in the Crystal Gardens at the Starburst Hotel, where I'll be privately entertaining the wife of the Jovian Prime Minister."

Sullivan happened to be looking in the direction of his Phy-Sci officer as Ti'onam tilted his head and frowned, the ripples of his ears twitching.

"Captain?" he said, and the rest of the room became aware of it as well: a distant, low beeping, like an automatic warning sensor. It stopped, only to start again several seconds later.

"The handicom!" Sullivan realized, and rushed through the alcove to his room. Tearing into his pack, he retrieved the chirping device and answered it.

"Mr. Raines! If I remember correctly, I'm supposed to call you. It had better be important."

"Aye, Captain," Raines said, "I'm aware of regs, but you wanted to be kept informed of anything unusual on scanners. We're picking up a sudden concentration of radioactive gasses eleven kilometers southeast of your location, including cesium, aliothite, radon, and hydrogen."

"Have Lieutenant Reese transmit the data to Mr. Ti'onam's omnicomp. How radioactive is the area?" Sullivan said as Ti'onam retrieved his machine.

"We're currently reading levels 300 percent above normal background radiation."

"Any sign of an explosion?"

"Negative, Captain. No explosions, but the center of the disturbance is about 180 degrees Centigrade."

"Keep an eye on it, Mr. Raines. We'll try and get a closer look down here. I'll keep the handicom with me; if there's any change in status or if you see signs of an explosion, no matter how small, inform me at once."

"Aye, sir. Will do. Raines out."

Sullivan closed the handicom and stuffed it in the pocket of his trousers. "Ti'onam, are you able to pinpoint the coordinates?"

"Coordinates confirmed, eleven-point-three-five-six kilometers south-east of this location. It is in a sloping area, approximately two kilometers from the nearest marked roadway."

"Are you up to a little more travel?" Sullivan asked Dickerson.

"We rode in the cart most of the way. We could use the stretch."

"Captain, what about the prisoners?" Granger said. "I'm not comfortable leaving the girl."

Sullivan counted heads. "We have enough manpower to leave them behind. I had planned on taking you with me, Kyle."

"I want to go, too," Dmitri said. "You keep accusing us of setting these explosions. It's kind of hard to defend myself when I have no idea what I'm guilty of."

"That's very well, but it makes security rather difficult. Where you go, your other half will want to follow." Jack glanced over at Sarah with her back to the room, face buried, 'hiding.' "Kyle? What's your opinion? Is she able to travel?"

Granger rocked on his toes as he thought. "She's certainly not in the greatest of shape, but if you're letting him go, I think we're better off letting her stay with him. I don't want her collapsing while I'm not here."

"It helps to have someone who knows the area, but what's to keep you from disappearing on me?" Jack asked Dmitri.

"I guess you'd have to trust my word."

"That's a bigger risk than I'm willing to take. Mr. Dickerson, find something to tie him with. Just tethered will do. I have a feeling if we keep her brother from wandering off, Miss Kirushenko will stay quite close on her own. Make haste, gentlemen."

Nora Guillaume watched in wonder. "I've never heard of anything like it. Not here."

A metallic burning smell saturated the base of the rocky hill, and sat like cold iron somewhere on the back of the tongue. Thick moisture weighted the air. The groundcover underfoot glossed with condensation; boulders on the steep hillside glistened with it, and moisture dripped down from the leaf canopy with annoying regularity. The temperature was much warmer at the base of the hill, even steamy. In places where moisture had evaporated from the more distant rocks, a greenish-white residue remained.

Sullivan watched the misty plume of gasses boiling up from the ground. Held low by the heavy humidity, the cloud was slow to rise, billowing outwards to create a foggy bank ten meters high. Less than three hours of daylight remained; whatever they did, it would have to be quick.

"Safety zone, Doctor?"

Granger adjusted his omnicomp and compared computations. "We should be able to get within five or six meters, but I wouldn't stay there more than a few minutes. If the air were drier, we'd be at less risk, as the vapor would rise and dissipate faster. Even from back here, I think it would be best if we limited exposure to a half-hour, maximum."

"Or we wind up fried like that kid?" Dmitri's nostrils flared with revulsion. "I think I'll head back right now, thank you. I've seen enough." He scratched at the rope around his wrist. The other end was tied to Jan

Dickerson.

"Not quite," Granger assured him. "I'm erring on the side of caution. You'd probably have to stand in the middle of it to get a dangerous dose, but in any case, you're better off staying upwind of the cloud."

"It doesn't matter," Sarah muttered. She stood lifelessly at Dmitri's elbow, fingers hooked into the waistband of his pants to make sure he stayed close. "They've brought us out here to die. They will tie us up and leave us here in the middle of nothing, and when that cloud blows, there will be no trace of us. Vladimir will never know."

Dmitri scowled. "Will you stop talking like that! At least that would be quick and painless. I told you what that kid looked like."

"Here's what we'll do, then," Sullivan said. "Ti'onam, Andreiev, set your 'comps to reflect different areas for data collection. You'll each go forward in turn as far as you feel comfortable, record data for four minutes and then back out, passing your recorder to the next person in line. Stay as low as you can to minimize exposure and avoid being scalded by the cloud. Mr. Dickerson, I'll take Mr. Kirushenko's leash. You will take Mr. Ti'onam's omnicomp and follow after Mr. Andreiev, then Mr. Tova, Ms. Soterios, and Mr. Khalfani. Doctor Granger, please check everyone afterwards and make sure we're still operating in the safety zone. Hopefully, that should give us enough data to make a guess. As soon as Mr. Khalfani is finished, we'll head out. Go, Ti'onam.

"The rest of us," he glanced behind at the Kirushenkos and Nora, who currently had the thankless job of guarding Sarah, "will stay out of the way."

The increasing darkness made the return trip slower and more difficult. Tired and chilled, it had been a welcome surprise to discover Mrs. Al had paid a visit, leaving a large kettle of stew and a basket of fresh rolls behind. Judging by the neatness of the place, she'd been there quite a while, waiting.

"I'd like to open the floor to discussion about this afternoon," Sullivan said as they squeezed around the table with their simple but warm meal. "Mr. Ti'onam, have you been able to make any headway on the data we collected?"

"Based on the information collected from the omnicomps and the long-range scans from the *Triumph*, we can make a reasonable hypothesis regarding today's findings," Ti'onam asserted. "Indications are the cloud we discovered was indeed a type of geologic vent."

"Like a volcano?" Dmitri asked. He tried to entice Sarah into eating some pureed fruit and half a buttered roll – at the far end of the table from the mark.

"Not exactly. There is no evidence of pressurized magma anywhere in this region, no recently dormant craters, no recognizable fault lines, no known history of sizable earth tremors. However, the hills to the west of the town appear to have been created eons ago by metamorphic forces. There may yet remain areas of super-heated gasses trapped deep below the surface of the area. When these gasses reach a certain pressure, for whatever reason – techtonics, barometrics, ocean pressure, natural decomposition, gravitational or magnetic anomalies are all possibilities bearing further investigation – they begin to press upwards, looking for the route of least resistance to the surface. What we saw today was an active vent. The dimensions of the core were similar to the ones seen at the two explosion sites. Using the long-range scanners on the *Triumph*, it was possible to trace the core of the active area to a series of vents that radiate throughout this geographic area."

"And those gasses were radioactive?" Nora Guillaume asked.

"Some of them, yes," Andreiev spoke up. "There were high levels of aliothite-346, plus radon, hydrogen, thoranium-294, and traces of fluorine. It was the aliothite that was giving off Warshan's rays."

"But we were right there in the middle of that cloud," Tova mused. "If the other areas exploded, why didn't this one?"

"Good question," Sullivan said. "Any guesses?"

"Aliothite and hydrogen, in the presence of oxygen and a few other things, can combine to make aliothite hydrolide," Granger offered, "a highly unstable, highly explosive compound. Any time you're using aliothite derivatives in a pressurized environment, it has to be in a helium or other inert gas atmosphere for safety. Even after decontamination, you're not supposed to put anyone directly exposed to aliothite in a hyperbaric oxygen atmosphere for at least a week."

"I would think gasses out in the open would dissipate enough to minimize the risk of explosion, though?" Nora asked. She knew little about chemistry; her specialty was the same as her husband's, xenoanthropology.

"The humidity of the area today registered ninety-four percent at a distance of 250 meters," Ti'onam reminded her. "Such moisture acts as a blanket, preventing gasses from rising and dissipating as rapidly as they would on a drier day. The hillside helped protect the cloud from any air currents that might have dispersed it."

"Even so, outside of spontaneous combustion, something would have to ignite it to make it explode like that," Andreiev said.

"An electrical storm, perhaps?" Sullivan offered.

"No," Dickerson said with certainty. "We wondered about lightning, too. We checked atmospheric gradients and weather patterns for those days. Both days were overcast, and one had periods of light drizzle, but both were cool and the skies were calm. No detectable shifts in atmospheric electrical charges. No incoming meteors that might have been glowing. No solar flares, either."

Sarah mumbled something to the dish in front of her.

"I'm sorry, Miss Kirushenko. I didn't catch that," Sullivan said.

"I said, 'bonfire'."

"Bonfire?" Sullivan frowned. "Why would anyone build a bonfire near a smoking vent?"

"You think like a spaceman," Sarah said with a hurt expression. "Think like a *native*! There's a group of you out in the middle of the forest cutting trees on a cold, damp day. Your clothes are sticking to you from sweat, and the wet clothes make the cold seep into your bones. Your hands become stiff and numb. You build a bonfire out of the small branches to heat up the area, at the very least something large enough to warm your hands, maybe your lunch. What if you didn't notice the vent, or thought it was just fog? Green wood gives off pops and high-flying sparks. All you need is one burning leaf or ember to be carried off and land wrong, and Boom!" she finished with open disgust. "By Mr. Granger's chemical process, one by-product of the explosion should be water. Radioactive gas up, water down, no forest fire."

"She's got something there," Dmitri agreed. He held up a finger, thinking. "We've done that ourselves on cold days outside." He pointed across the table. "Dr. Granger, didn't that Tani- boy say something about a fire?"

"Yes, he might have." Granger nodded, thinking back. "His friends were taking a break and – *and warming their hands,* he said! He wandered off for a minute, which is why he survived the initial explosion. I never thought about *how* they were warming their hands. I guess it could have been over a fire."

"I know of that as well," Dickerson added. "We have no need for it at the Compound, but it makes sense to me."

"That would lend hard evidence to the theory," Ti'onam said, "although it is impossible to prove anything from the destruction at the first site. It falls into the realm of possibility."

"Right now we'll have to accept that explanation, for lack of a better one," Sullivan decided. "Keep working on it, Ti'onam. Thank you, Miss Kirushenko, for your informative insight."

Sarah resumed her stomach-hugging position, bent so far over her forehead touched the table.

"Well, thank you anyway," Sullivan answered her silence. "Gentlemen, we've had a long hard march today, and tomorrow's will be even longer. I suggest we retire for the night and rest up."

* * *

Charlie harnessed his porshie for another try at riding. He'd worked it hard the last ten days, strapping bags of grain to its back to simulate a rider, and putting it through its paces twice a day if he had a chance. He convinced his mother it was safe to ride, and with a lot of pushing and shoving he boosted her up. They would head out early to Dimi-tri's, and make breakfast for everyone.

Mrs. Al was impressed; although porshies were obstinate, ill-natured, and known for following whatever whim entered their undersized brains, the trip down the familiar path was smooth and flawless. The animal trotted willingly at a reasonable speed, not fighting guidance. Charlie's triumph faded to the back of his mind as they rounded the corner of their neighbor's workshed. The porshie made a perfect stop as its master pulled the leads, its thick head held high, sniffing the strange scents.

Two porshies stamped their feet before the Kirushenko cabin, hitched to a cart. A strange man was arranging a mound of travel bags, boxes, the safe, and a laundry tub of blanket-wrapped bundles. Charlie recognized Dmitri's brown hiking pack, and Sarah's khaki one. Someone was taking all their things.

Mother said they were sick ... If something had happened ... Charlie's heart pained at the thought. He breathed a sigh of relief to see Dmitri exit the cabin, apparently healthy and dressed for travel, until he realized Dmitri's hands were bound in front of him. Dmitri didn't seem happy to see him.

"Dimi-tri? What here doing?" Charlie demanded in his friend's own language. "Sarrah?"

<She fine. It – it bad things happening,> Dmitri admitted.

<I go – get help?>

<No, Charlie. No. It will not help. They – from my country. We must return to that country, to see officials there.>

Sarah came out, the long wrap wound around her shoulders, followed

263

by another woman. Sarah's hair lay braided neatly back, and she wore shoes on her feet. A fast glance at her neighbors, and she hung her head.

<Why? What they doing?> Charlie slid from the porshie, forgetting his mother still sat on it, and that he'd let the reins drop.

Even the porshie sensed something was dreadfully wrong. With its unpredictable sense of timing, it dropped its back end on the ground, then settled its front half with a braying *whoosh*. It wasn't going anywhere any time soon. Mrs. Al took advantage of the move and jumped off while it was safe. One of the cart animals gave a confrontational bellow and snapped its teeth in their direction. Charlie's porshie wasn't close enough to bother responding, claiming its territory by lying on it. People filed in and out of the cabin, some of whom the Aletneshfajas had met, some they hadn't.

<It my fault, Charlie.> Sarah said with a look of despair. *<I tell you once, Father dead. He not. We just wish it. He search hard, find us here. I so scared, I try to kill him. Now these – soldiers come, take us home, make us face law.>*

Mrs. Al's feisty side overrode her shock. *<No! That Moonless! You good girl. They not take you anywhere. We settle this with Cawman Ojanikashi in town.>*

<There nothing to be done. We must return.> Dmitri said sadly. His wrists were bound, but he bent his elbows and slipped his arms over the woman to hug her. *<It be okay.>*

<No!> Mrs. Al insisted. *<Did not soldiers kill favorite brother? They will hurt you, too?>*

<Oh, no!> Dmitri made a silly face. It was impossible to describe the Burin-Jai to the Als; the word 'soldiers' had worked well until now. *<They not hurt us. Lock us up maybe, but we be okay. Thank you,>* he whispered. *<Thank you for help. Thank you for being friend to Sarah.>* He kissed her on the top of her head.

Mrs. Al burst into tears. She wrestled herself free and covered her face with the ends of her wrap.

"Captain Sullivan," Dmitri said. "In my hiking pack you will find two knives made of Denebolan steel. You've seen me wear them. Commander Guillaume knows I have them; he himself approved them. I want them given to Charlie."

"Very well." Sullivan nodded approval. "Mr. Andreiev, retrieve the knives, please."

As Sullivan turned his back, Mrs. Aletneshfaja charged with an angry

264

yell, punching the captain with her fists.

<*You!*> she screeched. <*You Moonless mad beast! You live in Dimi-tri house! I cook for you! You eat my food, you inside of lazy end of porshie! I wish I use poison!*> She spit on his shirt. <*That what you deserve! Take away good people! They never hurt anyone! They only good people! You bring shame to Moons!*>

Sullivan grabbed the pudgy fists; Mrs. Al kicked him hard in the shins, huffing and puffing until she was dangerously red in the face.

<*Please! Stop! Do not,*> Dmitri intervened, steering her back to the porshie. <*You make bad thing worse.*>

<*Moonless!*> she raged. <*Oes, Allash and Taber! May he lose eyes! May his days be dark as fresh-plowed field! Allash refuse you!*>

Andreiev returned with the knives. One was the hunting knife Charlie had long admired, the other had a blade so long it was almost a small machete. Both were shining, laser-honed Denebolan steel, guaranteed for life no matter what the task, exquisitely engraved on the blade. The handles were both artistic and functional in design, wrapped in a soft leather from an alien animal Dmitri'd never even seen a picture of, and everything so carefully balanced they could have been used for throwing in a circus act. Dmitri'd paid a small fortune for them at the spaceport where he'd bought them, half a galaxy away; here, they were one-of-a-mysterious-kind and absolutely priceless. They would last for generations. Dmitri motioned with his head, and Andreiev held them out to Charlie.

<*Dimi-tri!*> Charlie gasped, taking the weapons. <*These yours! I cannot take from you! You will need where you go!*>

Dmitri swallowed hard. <*Take them, my friend. I give to you. When you see them, you think of me. You best of friend, Charshfenaki. You take place of missing brothers for me. You will always be brother to me.*> He couldn't get his arms around Charlie, so he settled for clapping a trembling hand on his friend's shoulder.

<*Use well. Anything left in house now yours – you take! I cannot give you land or house, but you take every movable thing.*>

Charlie's hands weren't bound, and he crushingly embraced the best friend he'd ever had. <*You will not ever come back?*>

<*No. I must stay in my country now. We make it okay there.*>

"If you've settled your affairs, we need to move," Captain Sullivan announced. Dmitri nodded, and turned toward the porshie cart. Sarah's trunk had been loaded in last. One of the officers from the compound secured it with a rope.

<Take all pretty plants!> Sarah yelled to Mrs. Al.

Mrs. Al crossed the yard in a waddling rush to hug the girl to her, the closest thing she'd ever had to the daughter she'd always imagined – though her dream daughter had never been anything remotely like Sarah.

Sarah stood stock-still at the close contact. *<Thank you!>* she whispered, holding her breath against the sobs that shook her.

Tova shouted a command to the lead porshie, which squalled in protest. The second brayed in response; the Al's porshie squealed in sympathy. Tova poked the flank of the near one with a stout porshie-stick; the animals gave a mighty tug, and the loaded cart began to roll.

Mrs. Al didn't let go. Granger pulled at Sarah's elbow, pushed at the older woman. Dickerson helped, comforting the woman in Tau Cetan. Mrs. Al ran to wail against the cabin.

Sarah looked over her shoulder at Charlie, tears brimming. She pulled away from the doctor.

An infinite sadness marred her face. *<I most sorry!>* she whispered to Charlie. His eyes were a redder brown than Dmitri's, a rusty cinnamon. *<I sorry I could not be girl for you. You deserve best.>*

Breaking every rule she'd ever instituted, Sarah reached up and cradled his face in her hands. She kissed him very lightly on the lips, backing away before he might kiss her in return.

A harder sob made her squeak with a hiccup before she was able to finish, *<Thank you for being so nice!>* She stepped back until she was even with Granger. *<shanveh Shojeni! Moons light your way, for all times.>*

<Sarrah!> Charlie cried out in anguish. He stepped after her, but Dickerson stopped him.

For a moment Sarah feared Charlie would fight back. She shook her head and forced a smile through her tears. *<I write you letter, just like brother far away! Let you know we safe. Take four, five months, but you must read to mother! You wait! You see! We do okay!>*

Двадцать четыре
Twenty-four
Shtvala togant

The massive gates of the southern wall of the Chessorak Compound shut with a thud. Three of the Chessorak crew wrestled the mammoth crossbars into place. The size of small trees, no one could lift those braces by themselves. Sarah stopped to watch. The gates cut off her last view of the lush countryside, leaving nothing to remember the planet by but dull skies and muddy street. Hands pulled gently at her.

"Come on, sweetheart." Nora put an arm around the girl's shoulders. "I've seen them locked a hundred times. It's nothing to worry about. Nothing's changed."

Dickerson addressed the man who met them at the gates. "Mr. Yalut, please see to it that the items on the cart are brought directly to the meeting house for transport to the *Triumph*."

"Aye, sir."

Marc Guillaume jogged down the damp street. "Captain Sullivan! Could you please tell me what the hell's going on? Your last message was a bit ambiguous, and that rehab group brought back a whole bunch of stories that, quite frankly, we find impossible to believe. All three compounds are in an uproar. Are you merely shutting down the outpost, or the whole damned compound? I'd at least like to know why."

"Right now, just your outpost," Sullivan said. "Depending on the outcome of your security check and the one my crew is about to run, I'll let you know about your compound. Mr. Dickerson can fill you in for now. I will check in with my ship and make some arrangements, then I will return to brief you in full in ninety minutes. I want all your top people at that meeting."

"They'll be there."

Dmitri spoke up. "You know me, Marc. Do you really think this is necessary in here?" He held up his bound wrists.

Guillaume looked to the captain.

Sullivan gave a nod, and Jan released him. "You've been cooperative, Mr. Kirushenko. Please don't try anything foolish."

Guillaume lay a concerned hand on Sarah's shoulder, rubbing it. She turned her head away, visibly struggling to keep control.

"How is she, Nora?"

"Exhausted, chilled, and a bit frightened, but holding on," his wife replied.

"I'm sorry, Marc," Dmitri said as they entered the meeting house. "It was never supposed to happen. It never would have, if you'd simply told us ahead of time you had a message from our father. I'm guilty of possession, I can't hide that, but you're responsible for every other part of it."

"I'm sorry," Sarah repeated. She looked sadly at Nora. "Thank you for everything." She ran the three steps to her brother and buried her face in his neck.

"Shhh." Dmitri gave her a hard squeeze, swaying. "I'm still here. You're okay. Hey! Come on. Stand on your own. I love you, Kid, but I don't want some damned transport computer making us half one and half the other. I need my privacy now and then, you know?"

Sarah took two steps and waited while Dickerson clipped a locator signal to her clothing, since she didn't have a handicom.

Sullivan dug his 'com out. He sent a signal and waited for the response. "Have a security team standing by."

Jupiter Raines greeted the investigation party when they solidified in the isolation chamber of the transportation room. "Welcome back, Captain. Check out the fancy shirt!"

"Thank you, Mr. Raines." Sullivan and Granger stepped out of the chamber to make room for the next wave. "If you'd like, I'll send you down for one of your own. I want a security detail sent below. Have them run a full safety check – computer systems, scanners, weapons, surges, everything. I want an expert to go over their computer records for one specific date, someone who can read and decode patterns by looking at them."

"I'll have someone get right to it, sir," Raines said as Andreiev, Ti'onam, and the prisoners materialized. "I'll look into the power utilization records myself."

"I was hoping you'd say that, Jupiter. I trust your expertise. I want a report on ship's status in conference room two in ten minutes. Security: for the moment, Miss Kirushenko and her brother are to be considered detainees. Take them to the brig, separate cells. I'm sure they'd like a chance to clean up. Get them some decent clothing and something to eat while I contact headquarters as to the situation."

"Jack, given a choice, I'd rather see her under restriction to regular quar… " Granger began, but he was drowned out.

"What!" Dmitri exclaimed. "What do you mean, brig? You've got to be kidding! I've done everything you asked!" But the guards moved in around him.

The moleybeam left Sarah dizzy and nauseated. She hadn't slept more than a total of five hours in the last three days, the previous night on the trail not at all. "Dimi? What does he mean 'cells'? I'm staying with *you*!" she declared as security officers flanked her. "Dimi!"

Dmitri reached for her hand, but the detail blocked him.

"Sir, if you'll come this way, please … "

"Just a minute…"

"No! NO! Back off! Get away from me! DIMI!"

"Hold on, Sar. It will be okay. I'll get it worked out. Just hold on!"

"Don't touch me!" The girl shrieked and darted behind the massive transport control console. A security officer followed, and she gave a warning kick in his direction.

"Jack, maybe until she gets settled you could let … " Granger tried.

"NO!"

Raines blocked her, grabbed her, and held her from behind. Sarah pulled, twisted, kicked backwards, smashed her head toward his face, but he held her tightly.

"Stop it!" Dmitri struggled against the burly hands hauling him toward the door. "Stop it! Let go of her! You're scaring her! You can't *do* that! You don't understand!"

The security team closed in, four more hands touching her, pulling at her, forcing her. Sarah gripped the edge of the control console, screaming. Frustrated beyond coping, helpless to make anyone understand, overpowered by authority, she fell back on old self-destructive behaviors. Better to render herself unconscious, even dead, than to deal with the unbearable fear and upheaval she felt inside. She brought her head down on the edge of the console as hard as she could, three times, before she was pulled away.

"Sarah! NO!" Dmitri shouted, but he couldn't hear himself above the screams. "Stop it! Let her *go*!" The doors opened, and he was dragged through.

Blood now ran from a cut on the girl's forehead, but she battled fiercely against the restraint. More hands came at her. Granger dug through his carry pack to retrieve his kit. Ti'onam stepped in, reaching over a guard for the girl.

Sarah saw it coming. Four years among Navaran children, she knew what he was trying to do. *Mind control.* Navarans were touch-telepaths, a fact rarely confirmed by outsiders, but it required direct skin-to-skin contact. Sarah had been an insider. Her classmates had practiced on her a dozen times at least, until the game was discovered and forbidden. She had gotten fairly adept at relaxing her mind to allow the light, curious, childish probing, but had never been comfortable with the disembodied, itchy feel of the mental contact. Nor had she ever been in contact with a stronger adult mind. She countered the alien's attempted maneuver by the only means left her: she sank her teeth into the outstretched hand.

Ti'onam jerked back. Sarah twisted and howled, unable to break free. Granger's hypo found its mark, and the room quieted. They eased the limp girl to the floor.

"Granger to medical," the doctor barked to an intercom. "Send a litter to the moley-room, priority one." He closed the intercom and walked over to Ti'onam. "How's your hand?"

Ti'onam flexed his fingers several times. Deep teethmarks ringed the side. "Satisfactory. I believe any damage will be temporary."

"Well, the skin's not broken. It'll probably be sore for a couple of days, though I don't expect that will bother you. Follow me down to the sickbay, and I'll give you something for the bruising."

"One does not need a medical degree to care for a bruise," the Navaran declined with hostility, "nor do my present duties allow me time for such luxuries. My responsibilities are not limited to a single department. I must attend to a number of tasks before I return to the compound. Please save your attention for those patients who cannot avoid you." He left the moley-room as the medical team came through with an anti-grav stretcher.

"Take her up to sickbay," Granger ordered. "Might as well restrain her for now. Have Sundback clean the wound, and I'll be up there in a minute to take care of it."

"Maybe it would be better if you kept her in sickbay," Sullivan said. "She's been quiet, but she's obviously in need of closer monitoring. Kyle, we're approximately fourteen days from Starbase 21. I'd like you to run a full evaluation by then. I want to know exactly where she stands. Is she actually aware of what she's done? Can she understand the charges against her? Was this all willing disobedience, or just the result of some impulsive whim? Just because she's intellectually advanced doesn't mean she has the moral background to differentiate right from wrong."

"I'll do my best, Captain," Granger said as they left the transport room. "I may be a little late to the briefing, though. Leave me for last."

"Just this once," Sullivan called as they went their separate ways.

* * *

Though an investigation crew had been dispatched within twenty minutes, four hours passed before Sullivan had a moment to return to the Chessorak Compound. The meeting house swarmed with officers and compound personnel, scurrying to support various investigations.

"Status report, Mr. Lang?"

"All systems responding normally, sir," the lieutenant in charge of the security team said. "We haven't been able to find anything out of the ordinary. No signs of tampering anywhere along the lines."

"Could someone have reversed the tampering to avoid detection?"

"Unlikely, sir. We accessed the records on the last seventy-two hours; nothing non-standard has been touched. If someone did, they would have had to know how to break into the main record banks and cover their tracks. It would take a high-level tech expert, sir," Lang replied. "There's only one comptech for the entire project, and she's currently working at the Kinonah Compound. That's a seven to eight week journey from here.

"Very good, Lieutenant. Carry on." Sullivan turned to Marc Guillaume, who had been under foot the entire investigation, while Jan Dickerson kept a tenuous semblance of order through the rest of the research team.

"Well, Commander, it appears … " He stopped short as the air crackled with electricity, and the familiar glow of an incoming transport energy field appeared. A *Triumph* officer solidified, a roll of papers in his hand.

"Mr. Ti'onam," Sullivan said with a touch of surprise. "I thought you were working on the vent data?"

"I am, Captain," Ti'onam assured him. "I have found something remarkable I thought might be of interest both to you and Commander Guillaume." He approached the lone table in the meeting house and spread out the papers.

Dickerson recognized them. "Those are Sarah's maps."

"Affirmative. I was reflecting on the geology of the region in regard to the explosions, and regretted there was no previous history to compare. It was then I remembered Miss Kirushenko's forest sampling. She recorded the diameter of each tree she noted. The trees in the Vandijoc forest average three meters in circumference and 300 local years in age.

271

They themselves contain a biological record of the area – minerals, moisture, fire, blight, and more. I fed Miss Kirushenko's statistics into the computer and asked for an analysis. Upon examination of her data, I was able to confirm a possibility of previous explosions."

"You're kidding!" Guillaume exclaimed.

"Indeed, not." Ti'onam ringed several areas of data with a long finger while the officers looked on. "I have had the opportunity to review a number of Miss Kirushenko's scientific investigations, and in each case her relentless pursuit of accuracy resulted in viable conclusions. Based on her measurements, there are several circular areas on the maps in which *all* the trees are of a significantly smaller diameter, and thus ostensibly of a younger age, than that of the surrounding forest."

"As if the trees had been cleared and had to grow up again," Guillaume said.

"Precisely. I then compared this data with long-range scans made from the *Triumph* and found further evidence of mineral dispersion and geologic development similar to the three sites we examined in person. It is possible to make a strong case for similar explosions occurring in the area some forty-five, eighty-eight, and ninety-three years ago."

"So the area's actually got a history of such activity," Guillaume said. "And since people only started settling Vandijoc some twenty or thirty years ago, no one knew it. It's too bad we didn't have weather data from back then to help correlate things. I can see a need for a full-time geologist on our team. I'll alert the rangers to keep an eye out for areas of younger growth and possible vents. We could spend a year on that investigation alone. So you've officially concluded the events were natural? We're off the hook?"

"Not officially, but it certainly looks like it's headed that way," Sullivan agreed, giving the map another glance. "Your records indicated that the Kirushenkos originally transported down by means of the equipment on the *Aidan Ha*. The ship would not make note of outgoing weapons, only incoming ones. They materialized in the open street; you would have had no warning about the EPSAR."

"And without the power supply in place, it would not have registered as such on our scanning sensors." Guillaume repeated what he already knew. "So we can continue our research in peace?"

"For the time being. We will install tighter security measures that will scan for specific content; it will be up to you to keep a closer eye on your outpost personnel. Perhaps your base teams should make more frequent inspections of your field operatives' living quarters, instead of having the operatives come here."

"Depending on our complement at the time, that could be difficult," Guillaume said. "The average stay for personnel is one year. Except for a handful of dedicated people here at base, the Kirushenkos were among our oldest, most reliable staff. It's a serious setback to our program, losing them like this. Are you sure you couldn't see your way to just censuring them? I'll revoke their right to community access, make them remain here at the compound."

"If it were merely a matter of a forbidden object, I might consider it, but the other factors are too serious. Attempted murder is a hard crime. Add in the fact that one of your operatives was running dangerous, unsupervised experiments with powerful energy sources, and the problems multiply. The Kirushenko girl has severe mental health issues, and you have no supervising physician."

"I understand, Captain. We're still sorry to see them go," Guillaume said with regret. "We're taking this a bit personally; they're the closest thing to children we have. They were so young when they arrived, so blasted naïve they didn't know how to hold a broom, let alone use one. We didn't expect them to last through training. When they were actually flourishing at the end of three months, we took them under our wing. What will happen to them, Captain?"

"I'm afraid that's up to the Allied Fleet," Sullivan said. "The girl is in desperate need of treatment. Dmitri admits to smuggling a contraband weapon, but claims never to have used it. He took active steps to prevent it being discovered by indigenous personnel, so it's possible the ASF may overlook some of the charges. It's in command's hands now."

"I don't mean to make light of what you went through out there, Captain," Dickerson said, "but the team here still supports them, despite their – *error of judgment*, shall we call it? I would like to send a statement of defense for them myself, a recommendation, for all they've done for us."

"I think they would appreciate that," Sullivan said, engaging his handicom. "I'll be sure to tell them, and I'll see to it that you are informed of the final outcome."

"Thank you, Captain. We'll be waiting."

Двадцать пять
Twenty-five
Shtvala'chi

arah turned her head to see who had entered the exam room this time. That damned nurse with the molded hair kept coming in to talk to her. Nothing was worse than nurses who pretended they were your life-long friend, all sugary nicey-nice when no one was around, but when it came time to carry out a doctor's order you didn't want, you knew damned well whose side they were on; it sure as hell was never yours. The freakin' nurse wouldn't release the disgraceful straps that bound Sarah to the anchors on the bed, another specimen on display. She was all alone in the six-bed ward; there would be no witnesses to any torture.

This time it was the backstabber himself, nearly unrecognizable in a navy and red uniform instead of Sigma Tau Ceti clothing. So brisk, so efficient, so comfortable and in charge now that he was back in his own territory. Every evil now lay at his fingertips, and the legal right to use it.

"How are we doing?" Dr. Granger said, watching the readings on the diagnostic bed's screen. "Just a quick touch." He brushed the hair from her forehead to examine the work he'd done hours earlier.

"That's looking good. You'll never notice it in another day or two. You gave yourself a slight concussion there, Missy. If you have any sort of headache, let me know, and I'll order something for it."

Sarah knew better. She could *ask* for a headache remedy, but who knew what mischief might be substituted?

"What floor is this?" she dared inquire. "What's the designation?"

"Designation? This is my sickbay. Deck nine."

"Where is my brother? I can't rest until I know where he is."

"Dmitri's fine. I talked to him after I fixed your head there. He's over in the brig. That's in another section here on nine."

"So he's close by. Thank you." Sarah filed the information away. A worried crease lined her forehead. She glanced several times at Granger.

He noticed. "You look like you want to ask me something. I can't help unless you tell me."

Sarah blushed. "Is it possible to get these straps removed? I – I need to use your... *facilities*."

274

"Of course, my dear." Granger undid the arm straps, then the legs while Sarah lay calm and obedient. He helped her sit, but she pushed him away, jumping right to her feet.

"Take it easy, there, Miss! You've had a head injury; you could get dizzy if you move too fast... *Ow!*"

Granger never got a chance to finish. Free of the restraints, possessing the knowledge she needed, Sarah didn't waste the opportunity. She'd fought with brothers all her life, and studied self-defense back when she'd had the chance. She was a little rusty, sure, but she hadn't forgotten the basics of surprise. The hands found their marks with strength and accuracy. She didn't wait to see if he hit the floor. She had to free Dimi. He'd know what to do. He would protect her. She hadn't left his side in seven years; she wasn't about to now.

Out in the corridor, a klaxon sounded.

She'd forgotten just how big a Star Explorer was. She didn't care if she ran in these hallways; speed was of the essence here. She came to an access ladder long before she found the damned lift. Down a floor, down the corridor to another ladder, back up one floor, hopefully in a different location than the labyrinthine medical services corridor, ignoring the shouts and footsteps behind her. At last she saw the interstellar symbol for a lift, every running step taking her a meter closer to the doors that could bring her to the brig section, but somewhere in the run, electric EPSAR fire jolted her spine with irony, making time stand still. Fire shot down her limbs, leaving them powerless jelly, unable to break her fall. Her ears rang, her vision flashed white, then black, the twinkling-bright phosphenes dancing before her open eyes. The sharp odor of electrified air seared her nose; she recognized the scent but was unable to give it a name. Her body dropped like a bag of water, her head bounced on the cool decking, but she couldn't do a damned thing about it, couldn't hold the thought in her head. She lay immobile, unable to think at all, as a hand reached out to check the pulse at her throat.

"What happened? Sarah?" Dmitri ran forward as two security officers carried his unconscious sister through the hallway to the cell next to his, followed by Dr. Granger. He stepped back as the wavering electrical field across his doorway zapped his fingers. Dmitri would have preferred bars; at least he could grab something solid, or stick his hand out and touch someone.

"Somehow I knew that alert was for her. Is she all right? What happened?" he begged, unable to see around the corner into her cell.

"She should be coming around any minute," Granger said as the officers placed the girl on the cell's bunk. They left the cell and activated the energy barrier. "She's just stunned. I'm sorry, Dmitri. I tried to keep her out of here, but Captain Sullivan gave the order, and I think I agree with him this time. Sickbay isn't equipped for high-security measures on active patients. I'd have to keep her sedated and restrained, and I don't want to do that. She caught me off guard, nearly broke my ribs trying to find you. Even if you can't see her, you can still talk to each other. I'll look in on her every so often."

Dmitri sighed. "That's something, I guess. Thank you. You seem to know what's going on around here. Can you tell me something?" The forcefield snapped a warning as his hand skimmed too close.

"I can try. What's on your mind?"

"What's going to happen to us? I mean, is the captain really serious about sending us to a rehab facility over this, or is he just trying to scare us? What kind of things do they do to people there?"

"Right now, nothing is going to happen. It's fifteen days to Starbase 21. During that time, I have to run a full eval on your sister. The more she cooperates, the more thorough my results, the better things will go. Maybe you can help her see the logic in that. I have to run a few profiles on you as well, as a preliminary to legal proceedings."

"That's fine! I can do that!" Dmitri said. Maybe he'd get extra credit for being cooperative. Anything to stay out of prison. The degrading numbers on his father's hand replayed in his mind. He once played piano for a living. How could he ever play in public with numbers on his hands? "Whatever you need, I can do it! What'll happen to us in rehab?"

"I wouldn't go getting all worked up about that just yet," the doc insisted. "Let's wait and see what headquarters decides. They could throw the whole case out based on Sarah's exam results, or they could suspend the sentence to time already served here in the brig. Anything can happen."

"But, what if?"

"I don't know. I know there are a lot of intake exams. You'll probably spend your entire first month talking to experts. After that, depending on the program, there's all sorts of individualized rehabilitation services – job training, education, social skills networking, a lot of psychotherapy. You'll learn about yourself, where you went wrong and why, and how to avoid legal problems in the future."

"But I already *know* what I did wrong and how to avoid it again!"

Granger held up a hand. "I'm sorry, Dmitri. I really don't know. I've never worked in social rehab. You'll just have to wait and see."

* * *

Jack Sullivan jammed a thumb on the intercom switch in his cabin, only to hear the voice of his Chief Medical Officer.

"Jack, I think you better come down to the brig," Granger said. "I've got a patient with first- and second-degree burns on thirty percent of her body, who hasn't slept or eaten in two days. If you can't change your orders, I may have to override them under the auspices of humane treatment of prisoners."

"On my way."

"Custards, soft eggs, gelatins, pureed vegetable soup, pudding – chocolate pudding's her favorite," Dmitri chattered through the forcefield as Sullivan strode into the brig. "I guarantee I can get her to eat it if you let me. I'm used to it."

"Let's try that, then," Granger agreed. To one of the security staff, he ordered, "Bring me a bowl of vegetable soup, a high-protein chocolate pudding, and a raspberry-lemon fizz."

"What's going on, Kyle?" Sullivan demanded. "How can someone get second-degree burns in a holding cell?"

Granger dropped the girl's screen and motioned Sullivan in. "By insisting she was going to join her brother and trying to walk through the energy field."

"That's … ." Sullivan didn't want to say it.

"Crazy," Granger agreed. A security officer reinstated the field behind them. "I know. She came damned close to making it, too. She's not improving, Captain. According to security, she's refused all meals and hasn't slept since she came aboard, either curling up on the floor a centimeter from the forcefield, or standing there catatonic like that. I know your feelings on the subject, Captain, but it is my medical opinion that isolating her like this is putting her health at risk, and therefore violates the laws governing fair and humane treatment of prisoners. Technically, she hasn't been convicted of anything yet. I put a first wave of treatment on the burns; if there's no further tissue damage, they should heal in twenty-four hours."

Sullivan approached the girl. Flattened against the back wall of the cell, she stared through him, unseeing. Against the singed red of her face,

277

her fair hair glowed white. He picked her hand up gently by the wrist; Sarah didn't flinch, didn't make a sound. Her fingers and palms, on up to her sleeves, were covered with painful-looking blisters from repeatedly touching and testing the forcefield. The skin glistened with the healing protectants.

Sullivan released the arm. It stayed suspended until he pushed it gently to her side. "You can't tranquilize her? She's obviously a danger to herself."

"'Chemical restraint is to be considered a last resort, if efforts to reduce environmental stress fail.'"

Sullivan gave a nod to the officer at the doorway. "Let him in."

The captain stepped aside as the Kirushenko boy was brought over. It took a minute or two of coaxing before the immobile figure sprang to life, throwing herself around her brother, all but knocking him off his feet.

"Easy, easy, don't hurt yourself," Dmitri murmured, wincing at the sight of the burns. "Shhh! I'm all right, and so are you. That was really stupid, Sar." He sat on the bunk. Sarah didn't let go, climbing onto his lap. "What good did it do, burning yourself like that?"

An officer brought a meal tray. "One hour, Mr. Kirushenko," Sullivan granted. "You have one hour to make her eat something. If she eats, you may have two hours together. If she hasn't eaten everything on that tray within one hour, she will be taken down to sickbay and force-fed. Is that clear?"

"Yessir! Thank you, sir!" Dmitri said gratefully. "She'll eat for me. Won't you, Sar?"

Granger motioned the captain into the privacy of the security area's office. He touched a switch, and a monitor lit up with a live feed of the girl's cell.

"I thought my orders were clear, Doctor," Sullivan barked. "I wanted them kept separated. Now what? Every time she disagrees, she can harm herself and have her way? She knows where he is, and they have unlimited verbal communication. I think that's a reasonable compromise."

"It's not that simple, Jack. I meant what I said. She's slipping in and out of a total breakdown, and if we let that happen without taking the most obvious steps to prevent it, then we're guilty of mistreatment. That won't look good at arraignment."

"You may be right, Doc, but look at them! You can't see how distorted their relationship is? She's a sixteen-year-old girl possessed of a superior intelligence, and she deliberately burned herself because she couldn't be with her brother. Look at the monitor, Kyle! He's spoon-feeding her like an infant. You can't tell me there's a single healthy thing about that arrangement." Sullivan moved another switch to add volume.

"I happen to concur, Captain," Granger insisted, "but this isn't the moment to deal with that issue. You can't take a table that's only got three legs, kick one out, and still expect it to stand. Let's at least get a stick underneath it before we do. Sure it's an unhealthy relationship, but if you watch, you'll find out just where that stick should be placed."

On the surveillance cameras, Sarah chattered in a frenzy, the pent-up fears of two days' silence flooding out to the one person who would understand.

"Computer: translate, please," Granger ordered; captions flashed by in a scroll at the bottom of the screen as the computer translated the Russian into Standard.

"Come on, Sar!" Dmitri cajoled on the screen, holding out a spoonful of pudding. "You haven't had this in ages! It's your favorite!"

"I can't!" She started out on her brother's lap, then spun around to kneel before him, tears oh-so-very-close to the surface. "I've been through this before! They medicate the food, Dimi! It's all mixed in so you never know! You can't eat it!"

"It's fine, Sar!" He ate a spoonful of pudding. "See! There's nothing wrong with it." He licked another spoonful.

Sarah stared in horror. "Don't you get it? They'll get you, coming or going! They drug the food, they put tranquilizer gas in the ventilation system... You can't win! The cameras know what you're doing every second! They sit in some hidden place, and watch you pick your nose and scratch your underside and laugh and make comments about you and what they think you do when you're alone, and what they'd like to see you do. I'm so tired, Dimi, but I don't dare sleep! They just have to wait. Eventually they'll catch you off guard, and you're at their mercy! I don't care what kind of people the Fleet is supposed to hire, they're still men, and they still sit and make comments about me while they watch their little monitors and think I don't know it! I feel like I'm not wearing enough clothes, and I have no more to put on!"

Dmitri frowned, glancing about. "Where?"

"There, there, there, and there." Sarah pointed to the dark spots of panoramic lenses among the ceiling panels. "It was the same in the hospital, Dimi! I've been there, I know! They can do whatever they want!

If you don't like it, they tie you up and do it anyway. You have no choice!"

Dmitri looked uneasy. *"Just because there are observation cameras doesn't mean it's the same as the hospital, Sar. And you **do** have a choice: if you eat this, we get twice as much time together."*

"Didn't you hear a word I said!" Sarah shouted. "They want me to eat so they can force medications on me!"

"Justified paranoia?" Sullivan asked.

"No, the food's clean. See what I mean, though?" Granger sighed. "It's not a simple matter of who blinks first, Jack. We're up against every bad experience she's ever had, and she's had a lifetime of them. If she feels more secure in the presence of her brother, then we need to pay attention to that before we add to that harm. No matter what happens or where she winds up, she's going to go into treatment from *here*. How she responds to that treatment is going to depend on how she's treated *here*. We can either ease her fears, make her more receptive to treatment, or we can add to the bad experiences and let the next facility deal with the results."

"Were you this much of a pain in the ass on the *Covenant*?"

"Oh, and then some," Kyle said with confidence. "Why do you think Captain Maddox threw me such a big going away party?"

"You're probably right, Doc. It's hard to keep her intelligence separate from the emotional state. Let's see if we can't stop some of that right now." Jack returned to the girl's cell.

"I haven't given up!" Dmitri scrambled to his feet as Sarah screamed and clung to his leg, tearing open blisters. "I said I can get her to eat, and I will!"

"I'm sure you can." Sullivan thumbed an intercom switch. "Computer: Bridge. Mr. Reese?"

"Reese here, Captain."

"Mr. Reese, please note in the log to all duty personnel: on my direct orders, under no circumstances are medications to be administered to the current prisoners in any foodstuffs, nor are any aerosol substances to be used in the ventilation systems in the Security area, not even standard anti-virals. Also, until further notice, I want female and only female security staff to be assigned to duty in the brig. Pull women from other departments if you have to."

"Affirmative, Captain. It will be noted."

Sarah turned helplessly to her brother. "See? They were watching the entire time."

Sullivan closed the circuit. "Does that help things, Miss Kirushenko?"

Sarah watched him from the corner of her eye. "What's to stop you from rescinding the order behind my back?"

"Nothing. All you have is my word, and that's something you're going to have to take on faith. I'll make you a deal: cooperate with Dr. Granger, eat one full meal a day, and I will grant two-hour visitations with each other every two hours. Any more harming yourself, and the deal's off."

Sarah nodded immediately.

"Could you put those intervals back to back?" Dmitri thought ahead. "Four hours together, four hours apart? That way I can get her to sleep some. She really needs to sleep."

It went against everything Jack wanted to do, but there was logic to it. "All right. For the time being we'll try that, but first she eats."

* * *

"Something interesting?" Jack looked over his friend's shoulder at the monitor. He hadn't heard a word from the doctor in three duty rotations, so he stopped by Granger's cabin to catch up. The monitor was tied into the brig circuit, showing the girl's holding cell. "I didn't know you were into voyeurism, Kyle. Doesn't that make you one of the unseen masses watching her scratch from remote locations? I thought she was flinging pudding over the cameras?"

"Security washes the ceiling after meals. It's not funny, Jack. I've been keeping a close eye on her. I think confining them both to a regular cabin would reduce the stress on both of them. She might regain some functioning capacity in a more natural setting."

"I've already met you half way. They're prisoners, not dignitaries. She's extremely resourceful, physically violent, mentally unstable, has already overpowered my Chief Medical Officer and escaped once, besides attempted murder. The brig is one of the most secure areas of the ship, and she still managed to injure herself. Even with a guard at the door, that's too big a risk for confinement to quarters. You saw how fast she could escape that house, Kyle! Besides, isn't it better they wean themselves from each other in a controlled setting, than rip them apart all at once after their trial?"

"Maybe. Maybe not. You still think it will go as far as a trial?"

"At the very least, evaluation of competency." Jack watched the screen. Following his orders, the pair were in the midst of a four-hour visit. Dmitri sat against the wall, dozing. Sarah lay curled in a fetal position under his arm, head in his lap, defensive fists tucked close to her face even in exhausted sleep. She twitched and gave a soft cry. Dmitri opened an eye and ran a hand over her back.

"All she needs is to suck her thumb. She sleeping any better?"

"No." Granger shut off the viewscreen. He opened a wall panel and took out glasses and refrigerated bottles. "She only sleeps if he's there, so she's averaging four to six hours every twenty-four. It's better than nothing, but not enough for the condition she's in. Dmitri's been working with her on cooperation. We got her to bathe yesterday. She examined every square centimeter of the shower capsule, looking for monitoring devices – disassembled the showerheads and as many control panels as she could get apart. She won't trust the computers or scanners, thinks we've programmed them to fool her. Dmitri had to stand in the doorway where she could see him, and talk to her the whole three minutes she was in there. We offered her better clothing, but she refuses to wear anything but her Tau Ceti costume. She doesn't want us to think she's giving in to the 'luxury' of captivity."

"Have you made headway on the testing?" Jack accepted the beer Granger handed him, but declined the shot of whiskey, sitting down at the doctor's small table. "We're ten days out of Starbase 21. You think you'll have your evals by then?"

"I don't know." Granger sank into a chair. The whiskey went fast, but he played with his beer more than he drank from it. "She is trying. I've gone over the notes from her previous hospitalization a dozen times, and by their data I'm making rapid progress. She'll do any of the performance tests without a hitch – either she enjoys the challenge, or she's showing off. We've been working out of conference room four. She finds it less threatening than the medical offices. Getting her to cooperate with invasive things like interviews and neuroscans has been more difficult. Anxiety levels are off the scale, her blood pressure's extremely high for someone her age, her heart rate's up twenty-five percent even when sitting still, and I'm getting readings on neurochemicals that show she's slipping into depression on top of everything else. So far, everything's consistent with the old findings – measurable IQ of 180, but on the scales for emotional maturity she had an abysmal median score of nine years two months, about the age she was at her last hospitalization. A few peaks into the adult range, but the valleys fell as low as four years in one or two subtests, which correlates perfectly with the dysfunctional score on Ballenstein's Test of Self-Reliance."

"What about medication? Wouldn't that improve her functioning, or at least her comfort?"

"She has cooperated a little on that." Granger sipped his glass, thinking. "If nothing else, I'm trying to stop the slide into depression. I suggested something, but she insists she only takes Elavixor, which she was on before, so she's not afraid of it. She didn't do very well; they raised the dose four times in six months because of increasing resistance. If you're going to get any effect at all, it will be within three days. She let me try her on a moderate dose for three days without much result, so I stopped it. I went over a different medication with her today, right down to molecular analysis, and she's 'considering it' until tomorrow. Hopefully, she'll trust me enough to say yes. If that doesn't help, I've got a third one we can try. I'm trying to avoid general tranquilizers, since the idea upsets her."

"Since when have you ever let your patients dictate treatment? That's not like you, Doc."

"I don't often treat severe mental illness in extremely intelligent young girls who have enough experience to second-guess me. And I'm trying my best not to get beat up a third time. She's tough. With her background, I think she's had to be. I think she is giving us her best at this point; it's just a very slow process. I think time, patience, and understanding are the best things we can offer her right now. You can't rush neuropsychiatry."

"In an ideal world, perhaps." Jack finished his beer and stood up to leave. "I can give her understanding, even sympathy, but she'll have to rely on you for the patience. And as for time … You've got ten more days to make your case."

Granger sat on a chair at the far end of the conference table, a compad in front of him for notes. Two-thirds of the room away, the other eleven chairs from the table were lined up with obsessive perfection to form a barricade between him and his reluctant patient. Their truce was a thin one, and made no laughing matter about a doctor needing patience. This one ate up eight hours of his time out of every twenty-four, and most of that was spent in silent observation, gaining her trust simply by not doing anything. It was an uneasy peace on both sides, but for now, it worked. Granger felt the progress to be a success, despite the fact the girl ate only the bare minimum needed to survive, and her weightloss was noticeable after only a week.

"Should I repeat the question?"

Sarah hadn't acknowledged him for three minutes. Sometimes she paced behind the chairs, sometimes she sat withdrawn in the corner. Granger's patient overflowed with obsessive rituals and self-injurious tics – tugging her hair, nipping every one of the twenty-eight knuckles on her hands in a set order, biting her nails until they bled, touching her fingertips together rapidly in sets of three – the more agitated she was, the faster the rituals sequenced. Sometimes she just sat and rocked. This time she paced, touching the back of each chair in precisely the same places with each pass.

"I don't need to answer it," Sarah replied, concentrating on the chairs. "It's the same answer as the other six times you've asked it in one form or another. I told you, I will answer the same with truth serum. Without Dmitri, I would be dead, several times over. He's been there when I'm sick, he's been there when I'm troubled, he's been there for me my entire life. He has never, ever hurt me, even when he's had the will and the chance. He has always been my Savior. You can ask me a hundred times more, and I will answer the same. I will not lie to please you." *Tap-tap, tap-tap, tap-tap.*

"Very well." Kyle gave up. Either she remembered every word he said, or she believed herself. He hadn't tripped her into revealing something new in quite a awhile. "I know the crew at the compound, and I know Charlie and Mrs. Al, but the other week you mentioned someone's initials, 'J.C.' Who is J.C.?"

The finger stopped cold above a chair. "I did?"

Even if she didn't say another word, Granger knew he'd hit on something important. He circled the letters on the compad.

"You sure that was me?" The girl resumed her pacing with a casual shrug. "It's not initials, it's a name. J-A-Y-C-E-E. Jaycee was a girl Dimi knew for a while. She was very nice. She liked to do things for me, to make me happy. He liked her a lot."

"Just a girlfriend? Not his wife?"

The doors to the conference room opened unexpectedly, and Jack Sullivan entered. He paused, seeing the row of chairs. The girl ran for the farthest corner of her space and entrenched herself.

"Doctor Granger, may I speak with you for a moment?" They moved to the opposite end of the room from the girl.

Sarah watched from her corner with a merciless mistrust. Sullivan showed the doctor a piece of paper. Granger's eyes widened as he read it, and whispered words were exchanged.

They approached the flimsy barrier.

"Sarah, I want to ask you a question that's puzzling me," the captain said, unusually gentle. "Perhaps you can put it into perspective. I'm hoping it's a joke of some sort, part of a game, or a story, perhaps. Since it is written in your handwriting, I thought I should come to you first." He held out the paper.

The girl's face took on a ghostly cast. Before Sullivan finished extending his arm, she left the safety of her corner and stood against the boundary.

"Where did you get that? That belongs to Dimi! That was locked in his safe! Those are his private things. Give that back to him. You have no business with it. Give it back to him!"

"Sarah, if I read that right, that paper belongs to *you*," Granger said carefully. "Why don't you take it for safekeeping."

"NO!" the girl shouted, slapping at his hand. "Give it back! Give it back, right now! It's Dimi's! Don't lose that! GIVE IT BACK TO DIMI!"

Granger backed off. "Okay, Sarah. We'll give it back. Take a deep breath. Maybe you can explain to the captain … "

"GIVE IT BACK! GIVE IT BACK! GIVE IT BACK! FOR MOON'S SAKES, GIVE IT BACK!"

"Why? What does it mean?" Sullivan asked. "What will happen if I don't?"

With a cry, the girl grabbed a chair out of the line-up and flung it behind her. One by one, the rest of her insulating border guards met the same fate, bouncing off the conference room walls. The officers retreated several steps, but she never aimed in their direction.

"You can't do that!" she pleaded, out of chairs. "GIVE IT BACK TO HIM!"

"I will see that he gets it back," Sullivan promised, but it was too late.

Out of chairs, Sarah threw herself at the wall as hard as she could. Undamaged, she wrapped her fingers in her hair and ripped locks from her scalp. Fists pounded her head several times before she gouged her cheeks with her short nails.

Granger's directions went unheeded. Sarah dropped to her knees, screaming. She stuffed her fist into her shrieking mouth and bit down on her hand, tearing flesh before he could reach her with a tranquilizer.

Двадцать шесть
Twenty-six
Shvala'elmenan

mitri had gotten used to the little trips to Medical, and to one of the little security visitor's rooms to answer questions for one officer or another, but when the conference room doors opened and he found himself facing the entire Sigma Tau investigation party, sitting on the same side of the table like some grand inquisition, he knew he was in trouble. His security escort took up posts inside the door.

Dmitri was a firm subscriber to his mother's belief of staying positive. He'd always been too short and scrawny to be much of a fighter, and never cared to be. A cool head and a silver tongue were all he'd needed. In almost every situation, if you looked bad things in the eye with pleasantness and good cheer, the bad would wither and good things would follow. This was going to be one of those times.

"Captain Sullivan; sirs," he nodded in greeting. He'd traded his rough Tau Ceti clothes for the modern comfort fabric of the jumpsuit the security department offered him, and had his shaggy hair cut back into style. When he'd asked, Captain Sullivan allowed him his regular-world shoes from his confiscated belongings. Dmitri felt like an equal to the officers, now that he was dressed more like them.

"Is something wrong? Everyone looks so formal."

"Sit down, please, Mr. Kirushenko." Sullivan pointed to the lone chair opposite. On the table before it sat a piece of portable equipment.

As he complied, the captain continued, "In the process of pursuing weapons charges, several rather disturbing facts have come to our attention. I have called this meeting of the investigation team so that, as a group, we can go over these questions with you and hopefully arrive at some answers."

"Okay," Dmitri said, ever cooperative. He clasped his hands on the table. "Fire away."

"Do you recognize the device in front of you?"

The square box was no bigger than a dinner plate. Its dark glass top gave no clues to its function. "No."

"It's a portable scanner to measure biophysiologic stress reactions.

It's more than ninety-percent effective in detecting when a person is telling the truth."

Dmitri's bubbling cheerfulness fell a notch. "I've told you the truth all along. I haven't lied about anything – especially about the EPSAR."

"It's not the EPSAR we have questions about," Granger said.

"As a group, we've agreed there is enough evidence to charge you with neglect of a minor," Sullivan said. "We want to clarify if we should add abuse to that charge."

Dmitri threw himself back in the chair and rolled his eyes to the ceiling. "Oh, *man!* How can you possibly say that! I told you, I've been with her day and night! There's never been a single moment when I've been negli ..."

"The fact that you allowed her to be placed on a drug that could have seriously damaged her health as an alternative to proper psychiatric treatment, then hiding her on a planet where she couldn't get care if she needed it, was extremely negligent," Granger reminded him.

"Coupled with poor accountability of her whereabouts and her activities, it presents a questionable picture," Sullivan said. "She could have been selling secrets to an enemy armada and you wouldn't have known."

Dmitri straightened up. "I think you're exaggerating just a little. I didn't start Sarah's problems. If anything, I've taught her how to deal with them."

"Place your hand on the scanner, please," Sullivan asked.

"What the... !"

Ti'onam asked, "Please state your name."

Dmitri gave a sour sigh. He'd been through this routine three times with three different officers. "Dmitri-Mikhail Kirushenko, no patronymic." The plate under his hand glowed green.

"Place of birth?"

"Jerusalem City, Israel, Earth." *Green*

"Date of birth?"

"Earthdate, 18 March, 2246."

The scanner gave a squawk and turned red.

"Inconsistency," swore a computerized voice.

Dmitri pulled his hand up in disbelief. "That's my birthday!" he argued with the box.

"The truth, Mr. Kirushenko!" Sullivan ordered.

"That is!"

Ti'onam's face remained impassive, but he laced his long fingers over each other as if settling in for a lengthy wait. "That information is consistent with your identification and your interstellar passport. However, when the computer ran your educational and medical records, an inconsistency was found. Please replace your hand and state the correct date."

Dmitri gave a hard sigh. He placed his hand on the scanner, but several seconds passed before he answered, "Eighteen March, 2247."

The scanner lit up green.

Sullivan pursed his lips. "Twenty-two forty-seven. Then by the dates on your guardianship documents, you were only *sixteen* when you gained responsibility for your sister. Are those documents falsified as well?"

"No, *sir!*" Dmitri swore with confidence, and was happy to see the scanner agree with him. "They were legally signed in a court of law in Kar Kuomi, Navara."

"Under false representation? By being a year older and having yourself certified as an independent teen, you could then legally apply for guardianship."

"We were *abandoned*!" Dmitri pressed his right hand on the scanner with his left, trying to make the computer see his way. "Ask Sarah! Valeria had it in for both of us ever since she took charge."

Sullivan seemed disappointed that the scanner continued to glow green. "Very well. Do you recognize this document?" He passed a paper across the table, covered on both sides with Sarah's fine, perfect script.

Contract of Understanding
25 October, 2268

*1)I, Sarah Kirushenko, do formally acknowledge that Dmitri Kirushenko is a full-fledged adult with all the legal, moral, and human rights guaranteed therewith, including but not limited to the right to carry on consenting adult relationships in the **PRIVACY** of his own home without having to consult anyone else about it. I agree to respect these rights.*

I, Dmitri Kirushenko, realize that in this process, I do not have the right to display explicitly lewd, erotic, or carnal behaviors in open areas of the house or in the presence of my sister. I have the right to be granted reasonable, uninterrupted privacy, and I must extend and respect that right to others.

ÐMK *SJK*

2) *I, Sarah Kirushenko, do hereby acknowledge that Dmitri Kirushenko, being a ~~fairly~~ responsible adult and legally my guardian, is hereby qualified to make all final decisions regarding my care and I am honor-bound to respect and obey any and all reasonable decisions made by him in that regard, whether or not I like them or approve.*

I, Dmitri Kirushenko, being in full charge of my sister, agree to involve her in any major and/or life-changing decisions whenever possible. I agree to take her views and desires into consideration before making my final decisions. I will not abuse my power of guardianship by making decisions that are intended to harm, humiliate, or mistreat my sister. I cannot and will not resort to violent measures to enforce obedience to my decisions.

SIK

DMK

3) *I, Sarah Kirushenko, hereby acknowledge that I need to develop more interpersonal skills with non-family members and agree to make a <u>visible</u> <u>effort</u> in developing those skills necessary to help me function in society, with a long-range goal of making friends of a similar age of <u>both</u> sexes.*

I, Dmitri Kirushenko, agree to aid and support my sister in pursuit of this goal. I agree not to push or place her forcefully into social situations that she may not be ready to handle, or abandon her in situations that she finds herself uncomfortable in.

SIK

DMK

4) *We the undersigned agree that this contract is made null and void in the face of emergency situations, alcohol intoxication, chemical influence, or personal violence.*

Dmitri M. Kirushenko

Sarah~Irina Kirushenko

"Yes. That's our current contract," Dmitri acknowledged. "Those are the rules we currently follow.

Sullivan eyed him critically. "Four rules for behavior? You don't list the consequences if either of you violate those rules. What would happen?"

Dmitri shrugged. "I don't know. We never had a problem. We write the rules together, and we stick by them. We take our word very seriously. It's never failed us yet."

"I'm concerned about the first rule, Dmitri," Granger said with apprehension. "This contract is only two years old. Generally, rules like this are made *after* a problem has already risen, in an attempt to correct it. Your entire first rule of conduct concerns privacy and sexual behaviors. Can you tell us why this rule came about?"

"Hand on the scanner, please," Sullivan reminded him.

"It goes back to that subject I don't talk about. Sarah had some … *difficulties* with my marital status. You've seen how she has a habit of appearing places when least expected. Well, she had a habit of doing that every time I tried to get some private time with my wife, if you know what I mean?" He rolled his free hand to carry the insinuation a step further. "I mean, she didn't even want me *kissing* Jaycee. The rule was meant to stop her interruptions."

The scanner agreed, and Granger nodded. "I can understand that. She's so absolutely dependent on you, any type of competition for your attention must have seemed catastrophic."

"If there was such perfect harmony with your rules in place," Sullivan said, pushing the smaller cream paper to him, "how do you explain this?"

Dmitri felt his hair rise. "Hey! Be careful with that! You shouldn't have that! That was in my safe! Whatever you do, don't lose that! If you destroy that, Sarah will – I'm not sure *what* she'll do, but I know she'll never be mentally of this world again."

Granger glared. "I have little doubt of that. When we asked her about it, she became so upset I had to tranquilize her for the first time since coming aboard. That alone tells me how much she believes what's written there."

"This a receipt for a *soul*, Mr. Kirushenko," Sullivan said coldly. "If there were no consequences for misbehavior, what crime could a young girl possibly commit that would make her feel obligated to give her soul to her brother as repayment?"

"That was all her idea! I *never* asked her to do that. I'm only the keeper of the receipt."

"But you willingly accepted a paper your sister believed constituted her soul?" Ti'onam clarified.

"Yes, I did."

"I want it returned immediately," Sullivan ordered in a tone that forbid defiance. "Dr. Granger believes that by doing so, you may ease some of her discomfort."

Dmitri studied the table, lost in thought. At last he said, "I can't do that. I'm not ready to give that back yet."

The officers stared at him.

"What could she do that was so terrible she felt she had to pay you back with her *soul?*" Sullivan repeated, astounded.

"That's a private matter between my sister and me. We don't discuss it. She understands."

Sullivan's jaw set in a hard line. "In the twenty-two years I have worked for the Allied Fleet, I don't think I've ever seen such a blatant abuse of power. You know your sister is suffering, you know how to ease it, and you refuse to even discuss helping her. And you don't think that's abusive? You disgust me, Mr. Kirushenko! I want the truth, and I will have it. Guards, hold the prisoner. Dr. Granger, please administer an appropriate compound to make Mr. Kirushenko comply with my request for an answer."

"Aye, Captain." Granger reached for the hypo case clipped to his belt. He loaded the instrument with the proper hypnotic that would reduce the boy's inhibitions.

"Now wait a minute!" Dmitri struggled as the guards seized his arms. "That's not fair! All right! All right! I'll tell you!"

The captain allowed a reprieve. "I'm tired of your incessant lying, Mr. Kirushenko! This is your last chance. Place your hand on the scanner and answer the question."

Dmitri pulled away from the guards and adjusted his clothing. It took a lot to get him boiling, but the Kirushenko temper ran hot and true. *To Hell with a silver tongue!* He pushed the scanner aside and leaned over the table at the men.

"Fine! You want to know what neither of us will talk about? You want to know the power I hold over my sister? It's called *guilt,* Captain! Sarah's as guilty as the Devil himself, and she knows it! That little shit you've got locked up destroyed my marriage! For five months, she carried out tactics designed to drive my Jaycee away, and despite everything I could do, it *worked.* She deliberately destroyed the one happiness I ever had, because she was so impossibly jealous of a sweet girl who wanted nothing more than to be her friend. *That's* the key to my power!

"I could have killed her at that point! I wanted to see her burn at a stake, but instead I did something much, much worse: I ignored her. She's not stupid! She knew she'd crossed the line between being mean and doing real harm. I *couldn't* speak to her until some of the anger faded, or I *would* hurt her. I accepted her offer, and we declared a truce. Now if I get trouble out of her, I simply remind her of the situation, and she pulls herself together."

"No." Dmitri shook his head firmly, shadowed by a haunting sadness that made his story seem more recent than two years past. "I am still too angry over how she tormented the sweetest, kindest, most beautiful person I have ever met. Do what you want to me, but I won't do it. Even if you give it to her yourself, she won't accept it. It must come from *me*, and I can not do that yet. Put it back. You had no right to touch it in the first place. It is *you* who will cause her more suffering if you mess with that paper."

The panel of judges remained unmoved.

"*That paper* declared a break in the hostilities!" Dmitri insisted, thumping a finger next to it. "*That paper* ended her fear I would walk away and leave her there alone! *That paper* helped ease my overwhelming urge to choke the living breath out of her every time I saw her. If that paper makes me guilty of anything, Captain, it's of *preventing* abuse! Until you arrived, her mental health was pretty damned good. If anyone is guilty of abusing her, it's *you*!"

Passion spent, Dmitri slammed himself into the chair, furious at the indignity and injustice he was up against.

Andreiev glared at him. "You had family back on Earth that she missed. If you hated her that much, why didn't you send her home to live with them?"

The change in topic eased some of Dmitri's hostility. "I told you, we take our word seriously. I signed a paper saying I'd take care of her to the best of my ability, and I meant that. I was supposed to send her back to the people who abandoned her in the first place? Where's the sense in *that*? Just because we had a falling out over something, I'm supposed to throw her away as well? I'm not Valeria!"

"This lack of abuse you claim – did that include chaining her to a wall?" Sullivan charged.

"Who the hell told you that? She told you that?"

"No, she didn't," Granger acknowledged. "In fact, she's denied any sort of abuse by you at all. But considering the fact that she believes you control her living spirit, I find her account highly questionable."

"Mr. Andreiev?" Sullivan gave the floor.

Danil's eyes held an anger that rivaled Dmitri's, and he didn't attempt to hide it.

"When we first arrived at your cabin, you were arguing with her in Russian, asking if she understood something. I distinctly heard a metallic noise, like coins clanking. When we cleared out your cabin, we found a metal chain in the closet under the stairs, the kind used to chain animals. It made the exact same noise I heard that day. We found a hook imbedded in the wall behind your chair, about the same distance from the ground as an ankle."

"You heard a squawk, you found an egg in my cupboard, and you brilliantly assumed I'm keeping chickens," Dmitri sneered. "Review your logic. *We worked on a farm.* There is nothing illegal about owning a chain or having a hook in a wall. In fact, we had several. We hung our clothes and lamps from them."

"Do you deny having ever chained your sister up, for any purpose whatsoever?" Sullivan demanded. "With your hand on the scanner, Mr. Kirushenko!"

Dmitri refused to be intimidated, but knew he had to answer. If he didn't, they'd force him, or worse yet, separate him even more from Sarah, and that would only upset her further. For better or worse, they'd been a team for almost seven years. Yes, at times their relationship had strained to the very last thread, but that frayed thread had held. He couldn't let this break them apart, either. Sarah understood the risk.

He eyed the scanner with distrust. He knew how those things worked. They couldn't read minds, only biometric reactions. His blood pressure was already high, his heart revved, his palms slimy with nervous perspiration.

Good! Let them be!

With a self-righteous air, Dmitri squashed his palm firmly on the plate, increasing the contact. He held his breath while the scanner adjusted to his biometrics, and replied, "No, I haven't." He let the breath out slowly, allowing his body to relax.

The scanner read green.

* * *

"I can understand that. So, even though you weren't that mad at your sister, you felt you had to side with your brother, because he was in trouble for protecting you." Granger repeated Sarah's words back to her.

The girl was calmer today, pacing the far end of the conference room in short, fast laps. The wall of chairs had gone, but she made sure the table was always between them. She wasn't talking as much today, just yes's or no's or neutral shrugs, but many of the compulsive rituals had died down. Kyle was happy with the improvement.

"When did you realize she actually meant to leave you?"

"I don't want to talk about that stuff."

"All right." Granger changed direction. "How are the meditation sessions with Commander Ti'onam working out? Are you finding it easier to relax?"

"Yes. No." Sarah shook her head irritably. "Yes, his instruction has helped me restrengthen my skills, but no, I still cannot relax enough to clear my mind."

She slid into a chair behind the table. "May I ask you something?"

"Absolutely."

"Mr. Ti'onam said we are allowed independent counsel to address this matter."

"That's right."

"In order to acquire independent counsel, I would have to inform a lawyer I require their service, correct?"

"I suppose so."

"I cannot inform counsel if I cannot contact them. Am I correct in assuming that I am allowed to make a hyperspace call to request said counsel?"

Granger thought for a moment. "It makes sense to me. I don't see why not."

"May I, then? I wish to place a call requesting legal aid."

"Did you have someone already in mind, or do you need a public defender?"

"I have someone already in mind. I know the link address already. I would like to call immediately, if I may."

"Okay," Granger agreed, impressed that she was thinking about the future. Maybe it was her, maybe it was the medication, maybe he was getting through to her, but she was stabilizing. "Let me run it by the captain just to be sure, and I'll set it up for you."

She was alone in the security office, but a guard stood outside the door, and Sarah knew she was no doubt being monitored by a camera somewhere. "Hyperspace connection established," the voice on the intercom announced.

"Thank you," she replied to the unseen woman, hoping against hope, all the way to her toes, that the someone at the other end of the link would be able to help. She'd ground her teeth over the idea since she'd first thought of it two days ago, afraid to call in case the answer was no. She hadn't placed a direct call to Earth in ... four and a half years? Maybe they didn't want to hear from her. Maybe they were too busy right now. What if they weren't home, and her message got deleted? What if Valeria answered and refused the call? Dimi would rage against it, but this was for his own good. It wasn't *exactly* lying to him. It came up during a therapy session. She'd been encouraged to place the call immediately. They'd helped her clear it with The Man Upstairs. She didn't have time to ask him. It didn't matter what happened to her anymore, she didn't care, but she'd done Dmitri a terrible wrong again, and this time she sure-as-hell was going to make it up to him. It *wasn't* his fault.

"Ivanov Galactic Corporations," said a woman. "How may I connect you?"

Huh? Sarah didn't recognize the woman on the screen. "I – I'm sorry," she said, crestfallen. "I was – trying to reach the Ivanov home connection. Has it been changed?"

"This is Mr. Ivanov's reception service. He is currently unavailable to take calls. If you will leave a message, I can have him reply in ... four hours."

"That could be too late! I don't want to speak to *him*! I am trying to reach Vladimir Kirushenko! He lives at the Ivanov residence. It is an *emergency situation*! Tell him it is Sarah Kirushenko who requests to speak to him, and I know he will accept the call. I must speak to him immediately!"

"One moment, please."

Sarah fought to breathe. *They had to allow the call! They HAD to!* She tried to bite her nails, but couldn't find a single place where they weren't chewed and torn to the quick. She picked furiously at her cuticles instead. An endless minute ticked until a new face appeared on the screen.

"Sarah? What's wrong?" said a man who appeared to have just woken from sleep.

"Uncle Tomas?! I'm so sorry! I did not think to check the time first! I asked them to connect me to Vlad. I did not mean to disturb you."

The disheveled man on the screen smiled affectionately. "We're happy to hear from you *any* time, Little Ghost, day or night. After midnight, the only incoming line open is here in my apartment. All calls go through me first. You look upset, Sarah. What's happening? Can I help in any possible way?"

Sarah fought a sudden surge of tears. "I think we're in terrible trouble, Uncle Tomas! I don't know *what*'s going to happen! I really need to speak with Vlad!"

"Hold on, Sarah, let me connect you. If you don't mind, I'll join you in his room. Sometimes two minds can solve a problem better than one." The man spoke to an intercom. The viewscreen changed.

"Sarah! Sarah, is it really you?" A teenaged boy clawed his way into the screen, blinking his sleeping eyes into focus. He resembled a smaller version of Dmitri.

"Vlad?" Sarah stared at the image. She touched the image converter with one hand and the screen with the other; the youth did the same, and through the viewscreens it looked as if their fingers were touching. "Oh, Vlad! You don't sound like you! You look so *different!* You grew up without me!"

"I'm sorry! I waited as long as I could, but it happened anyway. You've grown up, too! Look at you! We're the same age again you know, at least for another few days."

"I never forget the Magic Weeks!" Sarah choked down the horrible homesickness for her brother. For ten and a half weeks a year, they were exactly the same age. "I forgive you! It wasn't my idea to stay away this long."

Uncle Tomas appeared on the viewer alongside Vladimir.

"Oh, Vlad! I'm afraid it's going to be even longer until I can come home!" Sarah lost her battle and burst shamefully into tears. It was a horrible thing to do. She *never* cried when she was at home, ever.

"Shh. Tell us what's happened, Sarah," Tomas said, ever gentle. "Last we knew, things were quite steady with you."

Sarah sniffed hard, gave a lung-wrenching cough, and regained some composure. "Vlad? Father's out of prison!"

"I know. I saw him. Valeria and Galina met with him, and they made the rest of us go, too."

"Why didn't you tell me!"

"Because it wasn't that long ago, and you only get your mail every three months. I wasn't sure I *should* tell you. I didn't want you to worry until I knew more about it."

"Worry? Vlad, I tried to *kill* him! In a roomful of Allied Fleet officers, I tried to kill him! Now they're charging me with attempted murder. I need help, Vlad! I'm so scared! I guess I only threatened to

shoot him, but they're counting it as the same thing. Dimi is completely innocent, but they're charging him, too.

"Vlad said you know a lot of important people," Sarah told the older man. She'd never met Uncle Tomas in her life, had only spoken to him twice when he'd intercepted her rare calls to Vladimir, but he'd always seemed very nice. Vlad insisted he was. "I thought – I was hoping that – maybe you knew a really good lawyer who would be willing to take our case. I promise to pay them as soon as I'm able, though it might take a while."

"As good as done, Sarah. Where are you?" Dmitri forbid Sarah from ever discussing their location, but Tomas was so widely traveled, and Sarah dropped so many hints, that he usually had an unstated, general idea where she and her brother were hiding.

"We're on a Star Explorer – the *Triumph*."

Tomas nodded. "I've heard of that one. That's a good ship."

"We're on our way to Starbase 21, where they plan on prosecuting. We're scheduled to be there in … five more days," Sarah counted in her head.

"Your lawyers will meet you there," Tomas promised with confidence. "What are you charged with?"

"I took Dimi's EPSAR – it's not even his, it was Viktor's – and I broke into his safe and took it without asking and I … "

"Shah! Sarah, stop. Don't tell me the details," her uncle warned. "This is an unsecured channel. Anything you say could be recorded and used against you. Don't say a thing to anyone until the lawyers arrive. All I need to know is the charges, not what actually happened. What are we up against?"

Sarah took a deep breath. "I am charged with six counts of attempted murder, misuse of a weapon, violation of Independent Destiny, and one or two other little things. I don't remember exactly. I wasn't listening too well at the time."

"What about Dmitri? How's he holding up?"

"He's okay, I think. They keep us separated as much as possible, so we can't collaborate. That's the worst part. I think he's charged with illegal possession, theft of a weapon, theft of Allied Space Fleet property, weapon smuggling, and a whole bunch of other things, none of which he's guilty of!"

"No details, Sarah," Tomas reminded her. "I will make arrangements immediately. In the meantime, I want you to rest up and not worry about a thing. Your lawyers will be waiting for you when you get to the starbase and they will already have a plan of action in place. Tell Dmitri not to worry, too."

Sarah glanced off screen, as if listening to another person. "I'm on a sixty-second countdown 'til they cut my transmission."

"Go, Sarah! Let me work on this from here," her uncle ordered. "Demand a hard copy of your legal rights in the matter, and make sure they're followed to the letter. Call us again, if you're allowed."

"Please, Sar!" Vlad whispered. "We miss you!"

"Not half as much as I miss you! Thank you!" she squeezed in before the transmission ended.

* * *

Tomas changed the screen immediately and gave a list of orders to his answering service. While waiting for the proper information to return, he told his nephew, "Go, wake your sisters! We have a lot of work to do, and no time to do it. If I remember right, it's at least four days to Starbase 21. It's two hours to Moscow Interstellar, and I want to be on a flight by six a.m. at the latest."

"Is this it?" Vladimir asked, afraid to hope. "You think you can get her back this time?"

"Should I wait until Mercury freezes over? It's now or never, Vlad. What do you think I should do?"

"I thought you left yesterday!" Vladimir disappeared down the hall in a flash.

Twenty-seven
Shivala Jombass

No sooner had the *Triumph* received assignment for orbiting space at Starbase 21 than Commodore Enwright hailed Captain Sullivan. It was not unexpected. Such a call would have been a courtesy between starbase and starship, but the *Triumph's* purpose for visiting required advanced preparation. The commodore would need to be updated on the situation as soon as possible.

Enwright wasted no time on idle chat. "Captain Sullivan. We've been expecting you. You still have your detainees aboard?"

The speed with which the commodore came down to business took Jack by surprise. "Yes, Commodore. They're still aboard. I assume … "

Enwright cut him off. "Good. I have representatives here from the Ivanov Corporation who want to speak with them as soon as possible, but I'd rather you kept them on your ship until we have a chance to discuss this matter in person. This station is public property. Why don't you meet me in reception seven on the executive level at 1500, and we can converse at length."

"Of course, Commodore. Fifteen hundred hours." Sullivan understood: Enwright smelled trouble. The station was public property; everyone aboard had equal rights. The *Triumph* was military property, off limits to the public. Prisoners would remain inaccessible.

"It seems someone else has in interest in the case. I've never heard of the 'Ivanov Corporation.' Have you, Jupiter?"

"No, Captain, but you can bet I'm about to find out." A dark finger tapped several commands to the computer. "Ivanov, Stroganoff … You think that ends with a 'V' or a double-'F'?"

"Start with 'V', Mr. Raines." Sullivan rose from his command post on the bridge. "If you need me, I'll be getting the latest update from Dr. Granger."

Trinkets and details festooned the executive level, located in a secluded section of the starbase reserved for dignitaries. Ornate trims framed artwork and interfaces; real flowering bushes adorned empty corners and framed the lifts; plush furniture filled the nooks at the upgraded refreshment stations, inviting lingering conversations.

"This is certainly a change of pace," Sullivan said to Raines as they found the corridor. He eyed the ten-meter mural stretching down the hallway, a far cry from the dull utilitarian walls of the ship. "It's the first time I've ever had a briefing in the first-class section before. Did you find anything on this Ivanov Corporation? I'm assuming they're the legal representation the girl contacted."

"It's a strong possibility, Captain," Raines said, "seeing as her call connected to a state in Russia. I think you said she had family there. If it is, we may be dealing with something we didn't think about."

"Like what?"

"Like powerful connections, or perhaps that secret government affiliation you were hunting for. The Ivanov Corporation is an Earth-based parent conglomerate consisting of several smaller companies, including Ivanov Galactic Imports, the Ivanov Financial Group, Ivanov Research Partnership, The Ivanov Foundation, and Ivanov Industrial Investments Incorporated. Makes a pretty logo, the four 'I's like that. The Foundation is a charitable trust, donates money to all kinds of needs. The Research and Industrial branches are privately owned by an Andrea and Tomas Ivanov, a mother and son team based in Minsk, which, in an amazing coincidence, is in one of the Russian states. Of the remaining branches, fifty percent is publicly owned. Last year's posted corporate profits for all four companies combined totaled some thirty *billion* credits."

"Well, I'd certainly call that a decent profit. Entire planets could be bought for less. That's something to keep in mind. You don't think they're trying to buy Sigma Tau, do you?" The decorated doors of reception seven opened to his presence, and he stepped through.

Commodore Enwright turned away from a group of people. "Ah, Captain Sullivan. We've been waiting for you. I believe you already know Admiral Wang?" He waved a hand in the direction of a dignified man in full dress uniform, who bowed his head slightly in recognition.

"Mr. Ivanov, may I present Jazak Sullivan, Captain of the Star Explorer *Triumph,* one of the finest ships in all the Allied Fleet. He's a witness to the incident in question, and is acting as the chief prosecutor against the defendants. Captain Sullivan, this is Tómas Ivanov, CEO of the Ivanov Corporation," the commodore said. "He is here with his legal team to discuss your case against the Kirushenkos."

"Captain! A true honor to meet you, sir!" Ivanov said heartily in a voice that bore only the slightest trace of accent. He gave Sullivan's hand a firm shake. "I read about your travails with the Gorath Assembly in *Galactic Exploration Quarterly* last year. Absolutely fascinating!"

Sullivan raised an eyebrow to Raines. Someone had done their research. The man before him looked like an advertisement come to life, perfect and polished from his flawless brown hair to the tips of his spotless white shoes. The friendly smile was so warm and sincere it was unnerving to see it on a total stranger. His face bore only the faintest of lines, either leftovers from exquisite plastic surgery or the hallmark of very favorable genes. For a man who, taken alone, was so average in stature and physical appearance, he was an imposing figure.

"Thank you, sir," Jack said. "It was a learning experience, to say the least. This is my First Officer, Commander Jupiter Raines."

"Pleased to meet you, sir." Ivanov shook the dark hand with the same enthusiasm.

Raines returned the greeting. "Mr. Ivanov. All the way from Russia?"

"Straight from Moscow Interstellar itself. This is my legal team," Ivanov indicated two men and a woman nearby, "from the firm of Bestwood and Shu of New York City. Please, gentlemen, sit down." He waved an arm toward a circle of cushioned seats. There was no conference table to hide behind, just a cozy ring in which people were forced to speak face to face.

"How can I be of help, Mr. Ivanov?" Sullivan began as he sat. "I wasn't aware this was a matter of corporate interest. I didn't think Sigma Tau Ceti had been licensed for exports yet?"

"It isn't," Admiral Wang admitted, "but based on preliminary work, that could change at any time. They don't have much to offer at the moment – artisan crafts, produce, lumber, some textiles. There are still two years left on the ban on flora and fauna."

Ivanov sat forward on the sofa, hands folded on his knees, a thick wedding band on one hand and a gold signet on the other. "Well, I will certainly keep it in mind the minute it opens, though the distances involved would make costs rather prohibitive, unless certain tariffs on Class-Four worlds are lifted." He turned to Sullivan. "As captain of such a prestigious ship, I'm aware your time is most precious, and I thank you for taking the time to speak with me in person on this matter. I'm hoping that by meeting this way, we can both avoid a drawn-out court battle that would no doubt be a further waste of time for both of us. I'm asking you to dismiss the charges against your prisoners. I've come to take them off your hands."

"Impossible!" Sullivan sat up with sharper attention. Next to him, Raines managed to swallow a sarcastic hoot. "There are numerous charges against both of them, not the least of which is six counts of attempted murder."

"Now, now, Captain," Enwright drawled. "Let Mr. Ivanov finish talking."

"Sir, that girl's a world-class tiger in disguise," Raines said politely. "You can't just set her loose on the street. I wouldn't walk her to this meeting without a four-man security detail armed with stunners."

Ivanov looked so at ease, as if he hadn't heard the refusal or the seriousness of the charges. "Captain, the boy and his sister are my nephew and niece. They disappeared nearly seven years ago after a bitter sibling dispute. They were scheduled to arrive at my home two hours after the rest of their family; they never did, and we've been searching for them ever since. Several times we've been close to cornering them, but they slipped away before we could act. There is no doubt the girl wants to return home; I have numerous written statements from her in my possession that will support that. Until I can speak with Dmitri, I don't know his view on the subject."

"That's a very nice thought," Sullivan replied. "Personally, I think increasing their family contact is a good idea, but sudden family visits seem to evoke, shall we say, catastrophic reactions. I'm not ready for a repeat of the other week. I don't think they are."

"That is precisely why I did not bring other family members," Ivanov agreed. "I am only an uncle; I've never met either of them face to face, though I have spoken with them over hyperspace. Their brothers and sisters live with me, and have for the past seven years. I knew of their father's release; I had no idea he would attempt to locate them like this. I'm sure it was an incredible shock to have him appear without warning. Given the circumstances, I can't say I wouldn't have reacted the same way.

"I have gone over the testimony you filed. You have every right to be upset over what occurred, but I'm asking you again to drop your case. They have no criminal histories. They are young, extremely frightened, and still running from an argument that ended two days after they vanished. They have experienced a number of aversive events in their lives, lived through an untold amount of fear. How could they do anything *but* panic? Surely you don't think they ever really meant to hurt anybody?"

"Their intentions are not my concern. Their actions are," Sullivan emphasized. "The EPSAR pointed at me and my crew was set to kill, Mr. Ivanov. That fact remains. No matter what they've experienced in the past, it doesn't dismiss the fact they willfully disregarded regulations they swore they would uphold."

"Excuse me, sir," a lawyer spoke up, "but the girl was only twelve when that contract was signed. She was not legally bound by it, then or now."

"But her alleged guardian was, no matter which ID you looked at. That is why the majority of the weapon charges are directed at Dmitri, and the attempted murder at his sister," Sullivan pointed out. "There is a long-standing court summons on Dmitri for failure to show for a guardianship review. In the process, it came to our attention that his identification papers were falsified; at the time he gained guardianship of his sister, he was still a minor himself. If he cannot prove his claim that he and his sister were abandoned, he could be held to charges of kidnapping. The girl suffers from severe mental disturbance and requires around-the-clock intensive care. I'm sorry, Mr. Ivanov. I realize they are your relatives, but I cannot release them back into the galaxy at large. The charges will stand. An administrative review board is scheduled two days from now. The final decision will rest with them."

"Let's not be too hasty, Captain Sullivan," Admiral Wang said. "That's what this meeting's for, to discuss options. There are more people out there with false documents than legitimate ones. It's a misdemeanor, solved with a small fine."

"I can get a notarized statement from Valeria Kirushenko within the hour, attesting to the abandonment charges. There are statutes of limitations on falsifying documents, and even a common-law guardian has certain legal rights. You will not consider even a reduction of the other charges?" the uncle pressed. "A written warning, a long probation, perhaps ban them from anything less than a Class One passport?"

"Not at the present time. No."

"I'm sorry you feel that way." Ivanov's smile slid into a sorrowful line of regret. "You understand my lawyers are prepared to fight you, charge for charge?"

The man was perfect, too perfect, as if he'd just stepped out of a video program. No one was that perfect. Sullivan distanced himself, unsure what lurked behind the smokescreen. He stood up to leave. "If you feel that's what you must do, you're free to do it. We will see you at the court review."

Ivanov stood up as well. "Captain? May I please have your

permission to speak with Dmitri? I would like to know his opinion on returning home."

Ivanov had brought the lawyers to represent the pair; Jack couldn't deny them private counsel. "I don't see where that should be a problem. You may have a one-hour visit every twelve with each of them, on the *Triumph*, beginning tomorrow morning."

"Thank you, sir." Ivanov's smile returned to a level of politeness. "That's quite fair."

Timing was everything, and in typical bureaucratic fashion, the timing was poor. Jack Sullivan had been asleep only two hours when Reese paged him on an urgent basis. The captain wrestled himself awake, ran his hands over his hair, and pushed the reception switch.

"Admiral Brancourt. What can I do for you?" Sullivan said to the viewscreen, trying to exude more enthusiasm than he felt. "This wouldn't happen to be about the launching of the third Paladin-class destroyer, would it?" The last thing Jack wanted right now was to be a decoration at a ceremony.

The admiral sighed. "No, Captain Sullivan, I wish it was. I understand you were involved in an incident that took place out near the border on Sigma Tau Ceti."

"Yes, we happened to be there when it took place. I didn't realize it was making the rounds at Headquarters."

"Unfortunately, it's creating a bit of a stir. I understand you are prosecuting the suspects. I'm asking you to reconsider your position, Captain."

"Admiral, three of my men and I were threatened and fired upon with intent to kill by a weapon that was not only in violation of constitutional statutes, but had been dangerously modified. There are a considerable number of charges against the subjects, from smuggling to falsifying court documents. One of the suspects is certified incompetent. I'm afraid I don't understand."

"Captain, I've seen the list of charges. While they may appear serious in print, they are minor in the grand scale of things. If the suspects had a criminal history, we could throw away the key, but they don't. Outside of minor property damage, there were no injuries tied to the incident. I have six recorded statements from personnel at the Chessorak research base begging for leniency, and Commander Guillaume has offered to take full responsibility. If anything has been damaged by this incident, it is the program on Sigma Tau Ceti."

304

"I understand how Commander Guillaume may feel responsible, but a crime was still committed, Admiral, by a second-rate con man and a criminal genius. If we allow one weapon to be smuggled without recourse onto a prohibited planet, what guarantee dowe have tomorrow it won't be a cargo shipment?"

The admiral dropped formalities. "Jack, you of all people should know when it's time to stop playing by the book. Had Marc Guillaume discovered the weapon first, he would have handled the whole thing internally, and no one would think twice. Have you ever heard of the Ivanov Corporation?"

Sullivan rubbed his chin. "Not until today. I met with a Tomas Ivanov. I explained the situation and assured him I was not about to change my position. I don't approve of allowing mentally disturbed children to play with loaded weapons."

"And I am calling because the president of the Alliance was bombarded by the ambassadors to no fewer than twenty-three different planets, screaming about the Allied Fleet's abuse of power on Sigma Tau Ceti, which, I remind you, *isn't* a member of the Alliance. They demand to know why a star explorer, an arm of interstellar law, is involved in a local planetary incident, and why children are being held prisoner without proper representation. Imagine the president's chagrin when he had no idea that an incident took place! We've had to place the research teams on standby, in case some independent planetary government heads out there to start trouble. The president has asked me to help defuse the situation," Brancourt said. "We cannot allow a negligible mishap to turn into a political scandal that could destroy the peace we've tried so very hard to maintain."

"Admiral, I assure you we are following protocol to the letter, especially the laws about fair and humane treatment. One of those 'children' is a fully responsible twenty-three years old," Sullivan said. "Surely, that's hardly worth bothering the president?"

The admiral gave a frustrated sigh. "This is dirty pool, Captain Sullivan. There's no other word for it. The suspects are directly related to Mr. Ivanov. Ivanov Corporation has threatened to pull their business out of those twenty-three planets if this trial results in full prosecution. They're small, weaker worlds, but still with important ties in the UPA. If the corporation pulls out, it could feasibly crush the economies of those planets. They jumped us on the rumor market and they hit us hard; no matter how truthful a counterbite we respond with, the Alliance is going to look bad. I-Corp is fiercely opportunistic. They *think* they smell a profit, you can bet they're the first in line to check it out, and they're not above marketing at a loss just to win the contract. They supply mining equipment here, agricultural stock there, fund all types of research and development – including a few programs for the Alliance that we can't afford to see disappear. If they're not supplying the merchandise, they're supplying the ships to transport it. The Alliance is not prepared to deal with this major a crisis overnight, especially if it can be avoided. It could take weeks, even months, to fill that many gaps in interplanetary trade, with untold economic devastation as a result."

"What you're speaking of is blackmail." Jack had never yet bought into such a scheme, and he wasn't about to now.

"That is one way to look at it," the admiral conceded, "but at the moment, it's also legal. Ivanov is one cagey sonofabitch. He has hundreds of lawyers working for him, always making sure he's just inside the law, and always making sure he never has more than a forty-eight percent share of anything, so he can never be accused of being a monopoly. Never more, but never less. He has the right to take his business anywhere he wants. It's the scale of the problem that has many politicians holding their breath. It may not be ethical to you or me, but it *is* legal. It would be in everyone's best interest if this matter could be put to rest as quickly and quietly as possible. It's not a direct order, Captain Sullivan, but it's a strong suggestion I'd like you to consider very carefully. I need to know what to tell the president so he might have a chance to intervene, if necessary."

"In light of the information you have given me, I will give further consideration to Mr. Ivanov's request for leniency." Sullivan sighed, seeing his last great hope for a decent night's sleep evaporating at lightspeed. "I will update you within the next six hours."

Admiral Brancourt nodded. "The sooner the better, Jack. I'll await your call. Brancourt out."

Sullivan swore foully for several seconds, knowing his instincts had served him well yet again. He relayed the message to his first officer.

"Well, Mr. Raines? What do you feel like doing? Shall we speak once more with Mr. Ivanov, or shall we wipe out the livelihoods of twenty-three worlds in a single 'no?' Now, that's just a suggestion, Commander, not a direct order. I don't want to put any pressure on you. It's your choice."

"Looks like we got more than we bargained for," Raines grinned on the screen. "They didn't say which worlds, did they? I mean, can we buy enough time to swap our own investments around and make sure we don't get fried?"

"Investments? Where do you manage to get money for investments on your salary, Jupiter? I thought you were supporting three wives?"

"Don't remind me, Captain. Shall I inform the base you're on your way?"

"Send a message to Mr. Ivanov to meet with me immediately, and don't be overly polite about it. Get a Tech to the moley room on the double, then page Dr. Granger and have him meet me there in five minutes. We seem to have reopened our negotiations."

"Captain Sullivan! I didn't expect to meet again so soon." Ivanov stood up, flanked by his lawyers, as the ship's team entered the meeting room. He wore casual attire this time, loose pants and a custom-tailored athletic shirt, but the jewelry remained. "Please forgive the way I am dressed, Captain; I mean no disrespect. Your time constraints didn't allow me to assemble a more polished appearance. I don't believe I've met your officer … "

The doctor gave a nod. "Ship's Medical Officer, Kyle Granger."

"Personally, I don't care if you're wearing swim trunks," Sullivan said with false courtesy, ignoring the outstretched hand and taking a seat. "I don't care what corporation you're in charge of, or the amount of your net worth. I don't take lightly to blackmail."

Ivanov sat down. He leaned back in the chair and crossed his legs, unhurried. "Blackmail? That's a rather ugly accusation, Captain. I'm afraid I pride myself on never resorting to dirty games like that. In fact, I believe you're the first person to accuse me of it."

"You deny threatening to pull your business out of twenty-three Alliance planets if your demands are not met?"

Ivanov's eyebrows crawled toward his thinning hairline. "Really! That's the first I've heard of it. I'm afraid that would be a very foolish move on my part. I currently have contracts with thirty-one different planets; to lose twenty-three of them would destroy me. You can check the outgoing hyperspace records of the starbase, Captain. Since we last met, I've placed two calls to partners who are covering for me in my absence, one to a hospital, and one home, asking for advice and support. If this is how those people choose to support me, I cannot be held responsible."

Neither could Pilate, Sullivan thought to himself. Gall! This man had endless gall, and he did it without so much as a drop of sweat or an unpleasant word. "I am willing to reopen discussion on this matter under *my* terms: One: You will contact the same people and have them remove any threats to the planets in question, no matter what the outcome. Two: I will not back down on my prosecution. Whether it goes to a jury review or not, someone is going to be held responsible for that weapon. Three: You can make any case you want, but both sides will agree to let a Fleet Court have the final word."

Ivanov's pleasant line of diplomacy disappeared, and a well-seasoned negotiator leaned across the table. "*By your own medical officer's findings*, the girl was not rational at the time of the incident. She *cannot* and *will not* be held responsible. If I had known the man was going to head out there, I would have made sure someone warned them, but *I didn't know*. I have never met him; I do not involve myself in his relationship with his children. I will not leave this starbase without the girl," Ivanov said firmly, dark eyes sharp with determination. His manicured finger thumped the table just once. "*That* fact is non-negotiable. My lawyers are prepared to discuss terms on the boy."

"You're her physician, Dr. Granger. Opinion? Should she be released?"

The doc hesitated, cautious of the venom flowing across the table. "I can't just release her like *that*," he snapped his fingers. "That would be completely irresponsible. If you're asking if I think she should be locked up in a penitentiary, no, I don't. Mentally, she's quite fragile at the moment."

"And I will take her *home,* to her family, who desperately *want* her home, and I have no doubt she wants to be there as well," Ivanov insisted. "It is the perfect caring environment for her to recover in."

"That would be a good start, but without some sort of reassurance she will get the psychiatric care she needs, I won't release her. As her current physician, that's my final opinion."

"Give me a copy of your findings, a list of your requirements, and I will have a qualified child psychiatrist with whom she is comfortable contact you within one standard hour," Ivanov vowed. "If all your questions can be met to your satisfaction, will you release her into my custody?"

"It's possible," Granger said. "If Miss Kirushenko feels comfortable with the arrangement."

"And with a court's approval," Sullivan added.

Ivanov's face broke out once more into his sincere and inviting smile, belying the cold, calculating entrepreneur Sullivan now knew lay underneath. "*Now* we're getting somewhere!"

Двадцать восемь
Twenty-eight
Shtvala'shen

Bright and early, Dmitri sat in the small conference room, alone save the guard at the door. He was to meet with someone for the next hour, that's all he knew. *A lawyer? A hangman? His father again?* He sweated out his nerves in the barren room for five minutes before the doors opened and a man breezed in. Dmitri jumped to his feet.

The man approached, exuding a confident liveliness. He was dressed in white pants and a black, Cossack-style shirt. Decorative gold buttons ran across the left shoulder; all were plainly polished except for one at the collar, which bore an engraved *И*.

"Dmitri!" The man grabbed his hand and shook it energetically. "So good to meet you at last! You don't look like you remember me? I am Tómas Ivanov, your mother's brother. I believe we spoke once, very briefly, several years ago. Sit! *Pozhalsta!*" He gestured toward the chairs, taking a seat opposite his nephew. *"Vi predpochitayetye govorit na russkom ili angliskom?"*

"It doesn't matter. English is fine. It saves security from having to translate everything." Dmitri sat, the man's energy and enthusiasm serving only to drain his strain-weary body further. He sort of remembered the man. Sarah had pictures of him, but what the hell was he doing *here*? The friendly smile left him uneasy. This uncle looked so much like Dmitri's deceased brother Viktor it was painful – the buttery-soft brown eyes, same hair combed in the same style, the attentive manner that made you feel the man really *was* listening to what you had to say, and *did* care about it. The height was about right, but this man was of a smaller, thinner build than Vik's brawny frame, much more like Dmitri himself. The jaw was similar, not exact, but it was that damned smile – the inviting, good-natured smile that made you feel better about life without even knowing why – that was absolutely the same. It was Vik's smile, it was Mother's smile, and Uncle Tomas appeared to have it as well.

"Yes, sir. I believe we did speak, a long time ago," Dmitri managed to say. "I – I don't understand, though. How did you know where we were? Did the Fleet inform you? Did Valeria send you to mess with me? I never asked for help. I thought I made it clear to Val that we're well aware of her kind of help, and we prefer to decline any more of her 'assistance.' "

The smile squished into a sorrowful line. "Dmitri, I've heard numerous sides to the story as to why you left your family, and why you harbor ill feelings toward Valeria, but I will tell you this from the start: I am not involved in, nor interested in being involved in that situation," Ivanov swore. "I can tell you it is still a very raw wound on Earth as well, and one that I refuse to take sides in. Therefore, please believe me when I say Valeria had nothing whatsoever to do with my presence here. Do let me say this: there is no shame in asking for help when it is truly needed. There is a line of people clawing each other to be the first to help you, but you refuse to see who's at the door. Thankfully, it was Sarah who had enough foresight to let them in."

"Sarah?"

"Sarah placed a call to Vladimir, asking for help. We've been waiting for that invitation for almost seven years. Vlad asked me to help her. I sent the best people I know. I'm helping her by helping you. I came myself to make sure the help is adequate, and you don't need more."

"She never could pass a comm line without calling him," Dmitri grumbled. "I thank you for your trouble, sir, but I would've gotten things straightened out eventually. I'm sorry she put you through so much bother. They probably used the call as means to get her to cooperate, and she fell for it."

Ivanov lost his unflagging optimism. "No, you *wouldn't* have gotten out of this, Dmitri. I don't think you realize how serious the charges are against you. You're looking at five to ten years in Rehab on weapons charges."

"But I'm *innocent*!" Dmitri's fists banged the table noisily. "All but maybe possession!"

"You were responsible. That *makes* you guilty. They have the original documents you signed, saying you understood the rules and agreed to uphold them, and you understood the penalties involved if you violated those rules. That was your signature, correct?"

"Probably."

"In all honesty, Dmitri, if you walk into tomorrow's trial without my deal, you will be arraigned, the documents presented, and you *will* be found guilty. The sentence is cut and dried, predetermined and calculated by the charges at hand, and the fact you admitted your guilt. Your file is already being processed, and as we speak your name is being placed on a door at some rehab center, right next to Peter the Pirate's."

Dmitri rested his forehead on his fist. He could imagine what Peter the Pirate looked like, and it wasn't a pleasant picture.

But he was *innocent!*

Ivanov saw the words sinking in, and spoke in gentler tones. "It took a lot of intricate footwork, and a lot of sweet serenading; I called in a lot of high-level favors, and owe many new ones. I nearly started an interstellar incident, but here's your deal." He laid out his trumps with an authority not used to hearing dissent, as sure of his position as the captain, but without the arrogance.

"You will plead guilty to reduced charges, and the sentence will be commuted to ninety days in a minimum security facility," Uncle Tomas informed him. "Captain Sullivan revoked your custody of your sister three days ago. In addition, there is an investigation as to additional charges of fraud and kidnapping in your claim of guardianship in the first place – and before you ask, Valeria had nothing to do with that. The warrants appeared when your name was run through a criminal history check, filed as a matter of routine by a family court on Navara after failing to make a mandatory review of custody. That charge should be nolled.

"The charges against Sarah will be dropped on the grounds of insanity at the time they were committed. She will be under a court-supervised treatment program until the age of eighteen, when she will come under review to determine if she continues to be a danger to herself and others. That includes chemical and psychodynamic therapies a minimum of ten hours per week."

Dmitri shook his head, morose. "She won't do it. She hates medication. She won't be institutionalized like that. She'll kill herself first."

"She doesn't have a choice. But I never said she'd be locked away," Tomas said. "*I* will take custody of her, bring her home to your family, back with Vladimir. Everything is already in place, waiting for the court to give approval, which I'm confident they will. When you are released, you may reapply for her custody, and if that is what you both wish, I will make sure she is returned to you. I won't fight you on that; you have my word. You might not know me yet, but you have my permission to contact any of my business associates and ask them what they think of my word."

"No, sir. I'll take you on your honor. But, *three months!* I don't want to do *any!* I told you, I'm *innocent!* I *never violated* the orders. No one native ever saw that weapon, and I never fired it!"

Tomas lost any remnants of cheer. "That is precisely why you're only getting three months. It's an interpretational loophole, but we're stuffing you through it with as much power as we can."

Dmitri stifled a somber laugh into a snort. "Sarah will never let you take her over. No disrespect, sir, but she doesn't know you from Ivan the Terrible, and she doesn't take well to strangers. She'll rip you apart before you know what hit you. She won't leave me voluntarily on a good day, and she's not exactly thinking too well right now."

"I'm aware of her past difficulties. I haven't spoken to her yet, but if necessary I have an excellent specialist in adolescent psychiatry lined up in Minsk who is familiar with her case and is willing to - "

"Porshie shit!" Dmitri couldn't stop himself. "I was really starting to believe you, but now I know you're full of shit! There's no doctor in the universe that knows a goddamned thing about Sarah's '*case*,' because she refuses to see them! *None!* For seven years, I've killed myself keeping her straight and *out* of the medical eye. And you know what? I think she did damned fine without them. You think you can tell a story or two, maybe have Val give her brilliantly warped interpretation of events to some over-eager pill-pusher, and call that being familiar with Sarah? You don't know a goddamned thing about her!"

The man absorbed the hostility with no more than a contemplative tip of his head. "I'm sorry you feel that way. I apologize if I am in error. My sources told me John Carver had been her psychiatrist during a previous crisis."

Dmitri choked. "Doctor *Carver?* You found – ! *How?* He left Starbase Four years ago! How the hell did you get him to come to Earth?" John Carver was the only doctor that Sarah had ever trusted. He'd managed to straighten her out before, and if anyone could pull her out of this mental mess, he could. Dmitri would not have been half as stunned if the man told him Sarah was presently in command of the ship.

"I'm afraid I had nothing to do with it," Ivanov admitted. "He married my niece a few years ago, and she wanted to stay in the area. Katerina sent you an invitation, but you never sent a response. She'd been saving the name of her intended as a surprise."

Dmitri's face burned scarlet; the animosity evaporated. He sagged backwards in his chair. "Yes sir, she did. Father said she'd married a doctor. I didn't realize. Sir, I'm afraid I owe you one hell of an apology. I am most very sorry for shooting my mouth off and calling you a liar. It was wrong of me, and I do apologize. You're right. Sarah'll go back to him in a nanosecond. She trusts him like nobody else, maybe even better than me. How did Katya manage to marry *him*? I thought you had to be really old to be an established doctor? Kat's my age!"

Tomas' familiar smile softened his features once more. "They shared a common interest in someone they both cared about, and through that interest they discovered they shared a common interest in each other. He is a bit older, but not unreasonably so. They both seem rather happy with the arrangement."

"Good. I'm glad to hear that. Kat deserves some happiness for a change. I'm sorry." Dmitri apologized again, scrubbing a hand over his eyes. "Thank you for coming out here, and for your help. I'm – a bit upset over the whole situation, and I'm sorry if I seem ungrateful. I guess I'm not. I've had an awful lot on my mind."

"I'm sure you have. And Dmitri? Just in case you feel an overpowering urge to disappear after your time is served, I have volunteered to be your parole sponsor. If you do not return to Minsk to serve out your parole, you will be rearrested and serve a mandatory sentence of five years. Do you understand?"

"Yes, sir." Dmitri sat lost in silent thought. "Have you told Sarah yet? She'll go crazy, wanting to leave last year already."

Tomas chuckled. "She can't possibly beg any harder than Vladimir did, wanting to accompany me."

Dmitri joined in the laughter, remembering what a pest his little brother could be when Sarah wasn't there to guide him. It felt good to laugh, even for a brief moment. "You don't know Sarah."

"Then let's call her in, and let me meet her at last." Ivanov spoke to the guard, and a page was sent to the brig.

Fifteen minutes of uncomfortable silences and polite generic conversation passed before the room's doors opened, and several seconds more before Sarah appeared, fighting all the way.

"DO IT!" she spat as a guard managed to propel her into the room. She fell to the floor, but rolled to her feet almost before she landed. "You have the authority! Someone had the nerve to do it before! You're going to execute me anyway." Failing to get a response from the harried young ensign, she dove for the EPSAR weapon at his hip. He blocked the grab, but Sarah was quick and her hands were fast, feinting punches to his stomach and groin when he tried to stop her.

She stepped away, head back, arms out, as wide as she could make herself. "Don't they give you target practice? You won't miss! No one's *that* lousy a shot! *Shoot me!* You know you want to! Come *on!* Push the damned trigger and *shoot* me! *Please!*"

Tomas and Dmitri rose to their feet. *"Sarah!"* Dmitri burst out, frightened by the force of her antagonism.

Sarah spun around. Her waist-length hair, never a high priority, had not been washed or combed in days. She still wore Sigma Tau's native clothing, a heavy green jumper of a style not common in Russia in at least two hundred years. She was barefoot, having thrown her shoes at her escort two corridors before. A cry stuck in her throat as she hurled herself at Dmitri. He braced for the impact.

"Shhh." He rocked her in return. "Stop. You're okay. Hey! Next time you go calling in heavy artillery, how about warning me first, huh?"

The girl peeked out cautiously, jaw dropping as she recognized the face.

Tomas gave her his best welcoming smile. "Vladimir's Little Ghost! We meet in person at long last." He extended his hand across the table. "I have wanted so long to -"

"Vlad?" Sarah interrupted. "Did you bring Vlad? Where is he? Is he safe?" She released Dmitri, the mention of Vladimir too strongly alluring for caution.

"He's very safe. He couldn't … "

Tomas stepped back as the girl lunged across the table, seizing his hand. He paused in his retreat, giving Dmitri a confused, questioning glance.

Dmitri held up a hand. *Let her be.*

Tomas held still as the girl lay belly-down on the table, uncurling his fingers. She ran her nose over them, sniffing each finger closely, one at a time, his jewelry, then the palms, turning his hand back and forth to search every millimeter.

"When! When did you last touch him?" she demanded.

"About five days ago."

Sarah wailed, staring at the hand with such total despair Tomas looked sad as well. "It's no use! You wash too much! He's not there!" She pressed the hand to her cheek, and closed her eyes. Sensuously, she moved his fingers to caress her cheek, her chin, up her other cheek, and back again.

"Oh Vlad!" she mourned. "So close! So very, very close!" She took the hand from her face and pressed her fingertips to those of her uncle as he watched in puzzlement. Her hands were the exact size as his. A sob shook her as she stared at the pressed fingers, oblivious to all else.

Still possessing the hand, she pulled the fingers back to expose the palm. So very slowly, so very, very gently, she pressed her lips to the base of the fingers, held it, then lifted her head. She folded the unresisting fingers over the mark and kissed the back of the knuckles to seal it. Sarah glanced up, releasing the hand.

Tomas gazed deep into the wild eyes, eyes so dark a blue they seemed purple. Eyes that seemed to be looking only on the inside, as if everything outside were too terrifying, eyes glazed with agony and sadness and fear.

"Sir – *please,* sir! Give this to Vlad? Please see that he gets it, tell him it's from me. I have nothing else to send him."

"Of course I will, Sarah," Tomas said, heavy with sympathy. "Absolutely. I know Vlad will be most …," but the girl slid off the table.

Sarah poured herself into her brother's lap. "Oh, Dimi! I can't do this! I *can't!*" She leaned back against him, straddling his knees as if she were a child. Her face twisted in a pained grimace, hands writhing and twisting on restless arms. Every few seconds she pressed a fist to her head or her mouth, unable to stifle the infantile whimpers that slipped out.

Dmitri's arms held her tight. "Shhh. Yes, you can. You're okay."

"No, I can't! They won't leave me *alone.* Make them stop, Dim? Make them stop these drugs? They won't listen to me. I can't sleep at all, and I'm so *tired,* Dimi! I can't *do* this. Why won't they shoot me? I just want to rest. Just five minutes? I'm sorry, Dim. I'm so sorry I did this. I didn't know this would happen."

"Shhh. Don't be stupid, Sar. They're not going to shoot you. I'll talk to Doctor Granger about the meds. We'll get them changed. Relax.

"Come on, sit up now." Dmitri pushed her off his lap. He guided her to the chair next to him. "Enough! Mr. Ivanov here was kind enough to … "

"Lawyers!" The word hurled from Sarah's lips as if she were spitting out poison. The head snapped up, and she looked the older man in the eye with a shrewdness that said not only was she aware of his presence, but he'd offended her as well. "Did you bring a lawyer?"

"Yes! I brought some very good ones…"

"I should hope so! Bad ones would be a gross mismanagement of resources. I could have gotten a bad one on my own."

"Sar, Mr. Ivanov thinks … "

A shriek of agony cut Dmitri's reply. Sarah jumped to her feet, pointing in horror at the uncle. "He dropped it! He dropped Vlad's kiss! *Dimi!*" she screeched. Her fingers wrapped in the tangled hair and began to pull. *"He threw it away!"*

Ivanov leaned back, wary. Dmitri took to his feet and tried to force her back into the seat. "No, he didn't, Sar. He wouldn't do that."

Sarah grabbed the edge of the table and resisted. "Yes he did! He doesn't care! He doesn't care about Vlad at all!"

"Of course he does — "

"No he doesn't! *You* never did! Then he hates *me*! He hates me, and that's why he threw it away, and Vlad will never-ever know I sent it to him!"

Dmitri resorted to shouting. "I said *stop!*" The effect was instant; the girl folded into the chair and resumed a tucked-in, head-down position. "Don't be stupid! He doesn't hate you, and he doesn't hate Vlad! Crying out loud! He – put the damned thing in his pocket for safekeeping!"

Tomas seized the cue and patted his shirt. "I have it here in an inside pocket, Sarah," he said, though he didn't actually have a pocket on him. "I'm keeping it warm, close to my heart. I know Vladimir will treasure it dearly."

"See? Now settle down and stop it!" Dmitri dropped in his chair with an exhausted sigh.

The writhing returned. "I'm sorry, Dim. I can't think. I can't take this much longer."

"As soon as we're done, I promise, I'll take care of it, but for now, you have to listen! Got that? Sit quiet and listen to what Mr. Ivanov has to say. He has a good plan."

Ivanov summoned a weak smile. "At home I'm Uncle Tomas to everyone. If you're not comfortable with that, just Tomas is fine. I'm here as a member of the family, and as a friend. Let's leave Mr. Ivanov to the officials."

Dmitri nodded. "Yes, sir."

Sarah took the pressure off. "What happens to Dimi?" she whispered, seriousness and sanity pausing on her face. Her eyes were beautiful in their startling depth, but they looked so achingly sad and old.

Tomas braced for a reaction. "He has to serve three months in a low-risk rehab center, then he'll be on probation for five years."

The white-blonde head nodded, accepting. "I guess that's not so bad. We can do that, Dim. Three months seems like forever at the start, but by the time you think you can't take it another day, there's only two weeks left. We'll live through it. We've lived through worse."

Dmitri braced himself. "Um, Sar? I – I don't think you're allowed to come with me."

Her face clouded. *"What? Break up?* No! *No!* Where will I go? What will I do? You're in charge of me! You can't leave me alone!"

Dmitri saw the panic rising faster than light. He shook her by her shoulders. "Stop! Listen to me!" He moved his head about to keep the frightened eyes focused on his. When he knew she heard him, he continued, softer.

"You have your wish, Sar!" Dmitri made himself smile, but the more he laid on the cheerfulness, the sicker he felt. She was free, she was going home to friends and family who would greet her and comfort her and take care of her, and he was going ... to be alone, truly alone for the first time in his life, and he was going to be alone ... in *prison.* He forced the smile wider in a hopeless attempt to counteract his own emotions, tried to make the tears seem like happy ones, the trembling from excitement.

"You hear me? You're going home! You're going *home.* Uncle Tomas came to take you home. Vlad's been waiting an awful long time to hold your hand. Don't you think it's time?"

"Vlad?" Sarah sniffed for the deceit before it could trick her. "Please don't lie to me like that. That's very cruel."

"It's truth," Tomas swore. "I will be calling him later to tell him how you're doing. If you'd like, I will ask if you can make that call with me, talk to him yourself."

The head nodded, not yet daring to believe. "That's not very fair. I caused the trouble, but Dimi's going to prison, and I go free."

"Not – exactly," Dmitri said.

Tomas caught the cue, and took a cautious breath. "You're being exonerated on the grounds of ... insanity. As a result ... the courts will oversee you until the age of eighteen, with probation until the age of twenty-one. You are required to undergo mandatory psychiatric treatment – medication, therapy, training. I have applied to be your custodian in Dmitri's absence; if that is granted, it will keep you on an outpatient status. If the court denies it, I'm afraid there is little I can do beyond appeal, and bring everyone for daily visits."

"And guess who your doctor is going to be!" Dmitri interjected before Sarah could protest. "Uncle Tomas found John Carver! Can you believe that? Your very same Doctor Carver! You can find it in you to work with him again, can't you? Remember how he helped us on Navara? I know you'll work hard for him again. Think of all the new stuff you can talk about! And he has a big surprise for you – I won't tell you what it is, but I know you'll go absolutely *nova* when you find out! It's *really* big. You can handle that, can't you?"

317

The stoic blankness of the girl's face attested to her overwhelming strain. "That's all too good to be true. It's too much to believe."

"Start believing it, because it's true. I'll come back to see you the minute I'm freed, I promise. Hey." He poked her in the side. The false cheerfulness in his smile melted into sickly fear, and he swallowed hard against his emotions.

"You won't forget about your big brother while I'm gone, will you? You'll write me the same way you wrote Vlad? Let me know what it's like? Let me know what Val really thinks about me, see if she'll let me in the house yet, you know? Scout it all out, report back. We did enough of that in Vandijoc to know what to do, huh?"

The nodding head might have been about to say something, but the meeting room doors slid open without warning. Sarah grabbed him with a yelp.

"You *are* here," Dr. Granger said. "Security said I could find our Little Miss down here. I don't mean to break anything up, but I need to steal her for a few last procedures."

Sarah hid behind Dmitri, who rose to his feet.

"That's fine," Dmitri said, "but before you do that, I want you to change whatever medication you have her on. I don't care who thinks they're in charge, or who has what authority, *I'm* telling you they aren't right. She's much more irritable on this stuff, and neither one of us is happy. Change it, and don't give it to her again."

"I can certainly look into that," Granger said. "How much cooperation can I expect, or should I not bother to ask?"

Dmitri pulled Sarah out from behind. He held her chin until she looked directly at him. "If you want the meds changed, you *will* cooperate. Uncle Tomas just gave us a high-stakes deal. Play it right, you get to see Vlad and work with John. Keep thinking about that, and nothing else. Hear me? Count the cards and don't blow the hand. *Behave.*" He gave the girl a quick kiss on the forehead and turned her toward the door.

Sarah squirmed, eyes pleading to stay put. A bare foot gave a warning tap, but Dmitri tipped his head toward the door. "I'll see you in two hours. Go."

After hesitating, the girl ran and attacked the security guard by the door, trying for his weapon. The guard caught her hands.

"Let go of me!" Sarah shrieked, thrashing and kicking.

"Get her to the sickbay." Granger took the girl's arm himself and assisted the guard out the door.

The noise diminished as it moved down the hallway, plunging the meeting room into awkward silence.

Tomas spoke first. "Please tell me she's not always like that. Even if I hire qualified staff around the clock, Mamá won't stand for that. She won't have long-lost relatives screaming from the attic."

Dmitri shook his head vehemently. "*No!* I swear to you, she's not like that. That's a really bad crisis. She doesn't get much worse than that, and if you bring up how she acted, she'll be so damned embarrassed you'll never get her out of hiding. It'll take her time to adjust, but you shouldn't have any trouble after that. Just give her some space."

"Has she changed at all since you left?"

"In some ways. She's a lot more cautious. Keep her away from Valeria; that's just asking for disaster. The boys should know how to handle her. They're really close. Whatever you do, don't get between her and Vlad. Just let them get their fill of each other, because I think they'll kill anyone who tries to separate them again. And Kat." Dmitri remembered to include their favorite sister. "Katya knows her, inside and out. If she can't cry on Vlad's shoulder, Kat's your best bet."

Tomas nodded, relieved. "Thank you; that's good to know. Do you think she … "

"Sir, your time is up," interrupted the remaining security officer by the door. "Mr. Kirushenko must return to the brig."

Ivanov tipped his head. "Of course." To Dmitri, he said, "If I cannot arrange to speak with you again tonight, I will see you tomorrow. I am confident my proposals will be accepted."

"Thank you, sir. I sure hope so." Dmitri stood and shook the man's hand with grace this time. "You've gone to a great deal of trouble, and I do appreciate it, believe me. Sarah will, too, once she settles down. Give her time. It'll take me the rest of my life to pay you back for this, I'm afraid."

Tomas clapped him on the shoulder. "As long as you return home, you've incurred no debt of mine. What's the phrase your family uses? 'We take care of our own'?"

Dmitri grinned, remembering. "Yes, sir. Thank you again, sir."

He walked toward his escort, then turned back to his uncle. He bent and scooped something from the floor, wiped it off on his shirt, and held it out to Tomas.

Tomas put his hand out, curious, but when Dmitri released it to his palm, there was nothing there.

"I suggest you keep a better hold on that," Dmitri told him with a wink. "And whatever you do, make sure Vlad gets it, because Sarah *will* ask him. She doesn't forget something like that." Tomas didn't seem to understand, so as he walked out the door, Dmitri touched his fingers to his lips and threw a kiss in the man's direction. Comprehension dawned.

Tomas Ivanov, CEO of the multi-billion-credit Ivanov Corporation, stood alone in the conference room staring at his hand, which sure as hell looked empty to him. He closed his fingers around the 'kiss' before he could 'lose' it again, searching the empty room for guidance. What was he supposed to do with – *this*? Where did one keep it? How could Vladimir possibly know if he received an invisible, intangible item?

What in Hell had he gotten himself into?

Двадцать девять
Twenty-nine
Shtvala dossan

Oh-nine-hundred. For some, it was an early hour. For Sarah, unable to sleep, unable to eat from the nerves twisting her stomach, it was cruelly late. Oh-six-hundred would have been late enough. She'd played her last card, waved her white flag, prayed on her knees to her brother in the Afterlife for someone to rescue her. The cavalry charged through the skies, but even they didn't know if the battle had been won. Never had strangers been able to call all the shots, arrange her life against her wishes. This wasn't like a hospital stay; no one mentioned a release date, and if there was one, it wasn't going to be just three months away. And this time, Dimi couldn't save her. He couldn't save himself.

Oh, how she'd screwed everything up!

They were brought to the starbase separately, Dmitri under male escort and Sarah under female, but they met outside the conference room.

"Hey, don't look so grim!" Dmitri grinned cheerfully, but Sarah knew the anxiety in his eyes.

Her arms squeezed the breath out of him. Instantly, three pairs of hands gripped her.

"Come on! Thirty seconds!" Dimi pleaded, drawing as much strength from the touch as he was giving. He lifted Sarah's chin. "Listen to me! No more scenes! You will be strong! No one keeps a Kirushenko down, you know that! You go in there, you tell the truth, and we'll win this. You can be brave. Be brave for me. Be brave so Uncle Tomas can go home and tell everyone how strong you are, how nothing can keep us down! Not Father, not the Burin-jai, not some star captain. Let's see your face."

Sarah kept the tears in her eyes, and hinted a faint smile.

"You can do better."

The false smile doubled to small.

"That's better." Dmitri made a fist and gave her an affectionate brush to the chin. "Now go," and they entered the room that would decide their fate.

The starbase's conference room was larger than the meeting rooms on the *Triumph*. Admiral Wang, Commodore Enwright, Captain Ishwae Ja of the science vessel *Linnaeus*, and Commodore Theodora Blaine, Chief of

Allied Space Fleet Medical for the Epsilon quadrant, headed the judicial team at the front of the room. The *Triumph* investigation team sat at a table to the left, looking more uncomfortable in stiff dress blacks than they had in Tau Cetan costume. At the right-hand table sat the formidable Kirushenko defense team, from the respected firm of Bestwood and Shu, of New York, Tokyo, and London, Earth, and Hellas Colony, Mars. A handful of chairs were taken up by Allied Fleet spectators. In the farthest back corner, hidden to most of the room, sat the bargain-driving Tomas Ivanov, dressed in a conservative blue suit, every stitch sewn to perfection by the four-handed tailors in Porrima City. He'd paid for the very best in legal counsel; it was now up to them.

Granger left his group as Sarah entered the room. "How are you feeling?"

"How do you expect me to feel?" she snapped. "I've been dragged here to have my throat cut with legal measures, and these ... *Ursans* won't let me breathe!" She motioned to her guards.

"Would you feel more comfortable if I sat with you? For today, at least, I'm still your physician. You feel yourself about to go under, I can order you removed, or perhaps give you a different medication."

Sarah considered the idea – the sitting part, not the medication. "If it would make you happy."

Granger steered Sarah to the front row, directly in front of the review panel. There was nothing to hide behind, nothing to protect her, an open target for sharp words and accusations. Dmitri took the seat directly behind. She slipped a trembling hand back between the seats; he gripped it as tightly as she clung to his. They could make it through this part. They'd been on a witness stand before. It didn't look like this, but some of the procedure was the same.

Admiral Wang picked up a decorative hammer and struck a chime on the table, three slow *ding*s.

Key of D, snapped nervously through Sarah's head.

"This hearing will come to order. This administrative panel has been called to decide whether or not there is enough evidence against the accused, depending on plea, to warrant a full jury trial. Miss Kirushenko, will you please rise."

Sarah's heart fell over inside her chest. Granger's current potions helped, but they didn't eliminate the hopeless terror chewing up her insides. The doctor's hand prompted her to stand, but it wasn't until Dmitri patted her on the back that she found the strength.

"Miss Kirushenko, you are charged with six counts of attempted murder, illegal discharge of a firearm, willful violation of the law of Independent Destiny, and unsafe use of a weapon. How do you plead?"

Sarah opened her mouth, but her tongue had cemented itself to the bottom.

A lawyer stood up. An expert in medical law, he was the member of the team handling her specific case. "Admiral, on behalf of Miss Kirushenko, I am authorized to plead 'Not guilty, by reason of mental disorder.' In accordance with legal policy 462, section 31A, the medical review file supporting the plea of mental disorder was filed at 1330 hours yesterday, Unified Date 640645."

"Commodore Blaine?"

"Received and reviewed, Admiral," Blaine replied. "The original test battery was completed 640639 by Commander Kyle L. Granger, Chief Medical Officer of the *AFS Triumph*, who was also a witness to the incident in question. Secondary battery was run by Dr. Musa Bakari, also of the *Triumph*. I observed the accused personally at 1800 hours yesterday for one hour, and attempted an interview for another hour. As Chief of Medical for the Epsilon Quadrant, it is my opinion there is ample evidence to allow such a plea."

"Thank you, Commodore. Miss Kirushenko, you may be seated. Mr. Kirushenko, please rise."

Sarah collapsed onto the chair as Dmitri stood up. She folded her arms over her knees and buried her face in the crook of an arm.

"Mr. Kirushenko, you are charged with willful disregard of the Constitution of the United Planetary Alliance, theft of a weapon, illegal possession of an energy weapon, unsafe storage of an energy weapon, weapon smuggling, interference with an investigation, falsification of identity, willful endangerment, neglect of a minor, and child kidnapping. How do you plead?"

The last three charges had been unexpected, and they hurt. Against what he was told, Dmitri altered his plea. "On the charges of neglect and kidnapping, I plead Not Guilty!" With subdued reluctance he added, "On the remaining charges, on the advice of legal counsel, I plead 'Guilty,' sir."

Dmitri's lawyer was quick to stand. "Admiral, I have a notorized video statement by a Valeria Alexandrovna Kirushenko, witnessed at 23:00 hours last night in Minsk, Byelorussia, Earth. The statement attests to the fact that both of the accused were formerly wards of the undersigned and were indeed abandoned by the undersigned near Kar Kuomi, Navara. There is no legal ground for a charge of kidnapping."

"So noted," said Admiral Wang. "We shall confirm that statement later. Captain Sullivan, as prosecutor, do you wish to make an opening statement?"

"Yes, sir, I would," Jack Sullivan replied. He stood and tugged at the silver-trimmed collar of his dress blacks. "The Kirushenko's legal team and I met extensively to discuss appropriate procedure in this most unique case. Alexander Kirushenko, although the intended target for the attempted murder, refused to press charges, dropping the charge to five counts. With approval by this court, I am willing to abide by the prosecution bargaining agreement filed at 1400 hours yesterday. Under the terms set forth in said document, I accept Miss Kirushenko's plea of insanity, and will drop all charges in exchange for the treatment program outlined therein. While I still feel their relationship has many problems, in the six weeks I have known the Kirushenkos, at no time have I known Mr. Kirushenko to have anything but the utmost consideration and patience for his sister, whether he was legally bound to or not. I withdraw the charge of neglect. I will drop all but three of the charges against Mr. Kirushenko. Illegal possession, falsification of personal documents, and smuggling cannot be ignored, and will remain as charged."

"I have received and reviewed that document," Admiral Wang said. "Everything appears to be in order. Captain Sullivan, will you please take the stand and relate the facts to the incident in question as you remember them … "

Sarah sat through the testimonies, drawn so completely into herself time stopped. Blackness filled her mind, a mental hidey-hole devoid of emotion, devoid of fear, devoid of the illusion of hope.

"Sarah?" Granger prompted several times. "You all right?" He dared to take her hand from her lap and squeeze it.

Sarah poked her mind out of its hole long enough to look at him, and pull her hand back. She understood the contact was meant to give solace, but she could not force herself to reply more than a single nod. She slipped back into her hole and pulled a lid over it.

In, out. In, out. There is no fear. There is no fear. In, out. All is One. My mind is empty. Energy flows around me, through me. I am at One with the Universe. In, out.

Sarah concentrated on her breathing, nothing but her breathing, making sure each breath was exactly the same length and depth as the one before it. Her breathing in control, she clutched at the salvation of academics, reciting long Navaran meditation chants to herself, then translating them into Russian. They didn't sound as elegant in Russian, and some of the concepts had no direct translation. For practice, she translated them into Tau Cetan, but the concepts involved were so foreign to Tau Cetan culture and experience, she soon found herself bogged down in long, hyphenated descriptions to take the place of nonexistent words, and she gave up. The chiming of the court bell to announce the meal recess broke through her self-hypnosis like an EPSAR shot, spooking her so she nearly fell off the chair.

"You don't like chocolate, Sarah?" Tomas Ivanov inquired during the break. "You haven't touched your drink. Perhaps there's another flavor you like more?"

Sarah clung to Dmitri as if she'd grown there. She hadn't responded to Tomas' first three attempts at conversation, either.

"Chocolate's her favorite," Dmitri had to explain. He forced another sip of the high-calorie protein drink between her lips. "She hears you, she's just not able to answer right now. Don't take it personally. You're better off letting her concentrate on holding it together."

"I see." Ivanov's cheer faded. "How long does that generally take?"

Dmitri snorted. "When the Devil ice skates."

Dr. Granger visited several minutes before the hearing reconvened. "Just checking in," he said to Sarah. "Are you able to manage on that dosage, or do you want something stronger?" He ran a scanner down her side.

Sarah slid onto Dmitri's lap. "No."

"It's not good," Dmitri translated over the top of her head. "I mean, it's good she's able to be in control of herself, it's a lot better than the last thing you gave her, but I think the situation is still kind of critical."

"Okay. Let me know if you think she's about to worsen," Granger said. "I won't be far."

"She'll be okay." Dmitri sounded confident, but his smile was too wide to be honest.

Dr. Granger took the witness seat for much of the afternoon. He reviewed test after test – more than thirty different measures, from blood components to brain scans to personality profiles to psychiatric history, before the Board adjourned to meet privately.

Time seemed to stop as Admiral Wang entered the room and took his seat with authority. The review board filed in behind him, faces unreadable. A lifetime seemed to pass before he spoke.

"Based on the evidence presented here today, the Administrative Review Board supports and accepts the proposed bargaining agreement." Wang tapped his chime after each statement.

"Sarah Irina Kirushenko," he decreed, "you are hereby declared not guilty of the charges against you due to overwhelming mental disability at the time of the incident. (*ding*) You are hereby rendered to the custody of your maternal uncle, Tomas Fedorovitch Ivanov, for a period of not less than ninety days, or until a court deems otherwise. (*ding*) You are hereby ordered to undergo psychiatric treatment for your mental disability with a qualified psychiatrist no fewer than ten hours per week until the age of eighteen. If you demonstrate significant improvement via psychometric examination, you may, upon medical and court approval, be released from direct medical treatment at that time. You will remain on probation until the age of twenty-one. (*ding*) If you do not demonstrate significant improvement, your treatment will be continued until such measure is achieved. (*ding*) You are required to meet with a Court Systems Manager on a quarterly basis for the court of the city in which you will be residing to ensure compliance with this order. Failure to comply with any portion, on your part or that of Mr. Ivanov, will result in the termination of Mr. Ivanov's guardianship rights and your placement in a residential psychiatric facility that will ensure compliance with the court's decision. (*ding*) You are hereby released into the custody of Tomas Ivanov. Case transferred to the Minsk City Counseling Center for Youth, Minsk, Byelorussia, Earth." *Ding* went the chime one final time.

Sarah heard the words, felt the damned chime jolt through her body, every sharp clang as final as a nail in a coffin. She was being legally buried alive, fully aware of the fate that awaited her at the end of the ceremony, and unable to make someone realize it. Every one of the Admiral's words froze in her mind; she could recite his entire speech from memory after hearing it only once, but at the moment her mind was unable to comprehend it.

Admiral Wang continued his countdown of doom. "Dmitri-Mikhail Kirushenko, you freely admit to falsifying identification for personal gain, smuggling a weapon, and illegal possession of an energy weapon. (*ding* jarred the death-bell again) This court accepts the extenuating circumstances regarding the other seven charges, and agrees to drop them. (*ding*) You are hereby sentenced to ninety days in a minimum-security rehabilitation facility for intensive social and civic re-education, to be followed by 360 hours of community service in the city in which you will reside, followed by five year's probation. (*ding*) Violation of this order will result in a mandatory five-year incarceration. *(ding)* Upon successful completion of your rehabilitation program, Mr. Ivanov has agreed to be your parole sponsor and will coordinate your productive return to society. Case transferred to Gandron Rehabilitation Facility, Prima Vega. I wish to thank everyone involved that this matter was solved so quickly and cooperatively. Court dismissed."

One final *ding* hammered through the room. An eternal moment of silence elapsed before the sighs and coughs and whispers broke out. Chairs rattled, and people stood up to stretch.

A security guard approached Dmitri. "Sir, if you'll step this way, we'll prepare you for transfer."

As if from a great distance, Sarah heard the request, and it snapped her back to reality.

"No!" She sprang over the chair. "No! You can't! You can't take him! He can't go with you!"

Dmitri caught her in his arms. A guard grasped her. Sarah hung on, kicking the orderly row of chairs apart.

Granger almost assisted the separation, but instead turned to the board. "Admiral, with your permission, I would ask that the Kirushenkos be allowed a few minutes to say good bye. As Miss Kirushenko's physician, I feel it would be in her best interest."

"Agreed," said Admiral Wang. "Security, please allow the prisoner ten minutes before transfer." The hands released their pull.

"NO! I STAY WITH HIM!" Sarah screamed, arms around her brother's knees. "He's in charge of me! We're a TEAM! You can't split us up! YOU CAN'T! I WON'T!"

Memories flooded back, another time, another parting against her will, one that had bled continuously for almost seven years. She couldn't separate them in her head, didn't care to try. It didn't matter if this was now or then, if this was Dmitri or Vladimir, if this was a starbase or the baking wastelands of Navara. She was being torn from someone she loved. She couldn't let it happen. She couldn't bear that kind of pain again.

"Back off! Like I can really run anywhere with her hanging on me like this! Just give me a minute." Dmitri waved the crowd back; the doctor sided with him, helping give them space.

He pried himself loose. "Hey! Hey! Stop! Sar! Hush! It's me! It's only me! Listen!"

A whimper replaced the screams. The hands scrabbled up to his neck, locking in, and he knelt there on the floor among the scattered chairs, holding her, stroking her hair as he spoke to her in Russian.

"It's gonna be all right, Kid. You're scared, but I know you can be brave, too. You can be real brave when you have to."

"You can't go! You promised you'd take care of me! I did the bad thing, not you! I'm coming, too!"

"You can't, Sar. They don't mix girls and boys in prison. I put off my promise way too long, but I'm finally keeping it. We're going home. Remember that. I know it's hard right now, but keep thinking of Vlad. He's probably worn out the floor, waiting for you."

He pulled her teary face from his neck, waiting with oft-practiced patience for the reluctant eyes to focus on his. *"Look at me, Sar. Look at me. It won't be long, just ninety days. I order you to behave for them. You will go with Uncle Tomas. He is in charge until I get there. You will follow his directions, better than you follow mine. He's a good man, Sar. He's family. Trust him. I trust him with you. Vlad trusts him, and that should tell you something. Go back and show everyone I took good care of you. Show Val I did do a good job, in spite of it all. Tell them how good we had it. Make me proud."* He clenched his teeth to keep his chin up, but the muscles weren't working very well.

"I don't want to! I'm going with you!"

"But you'll do it anyway. I will be there in three months to get you, I swear on Viktor's grave. You'll be okay, Babe. Where's my handshake?" Dmitri held his arm up; she twisted hers weakly around it until their hands met in the secret handshake only the bigger boys had used. Not even Vlad had been allowed to use it.

He gave her one last trembling hug, and kissed her on the head. *"I have to leave now. You will go with Uncle Tomas. You will obey him for ninety days until I get back. Understand?"*

"Da," Sarah whimpered, trying to be strong for him when every molecule screamed out *nyet*.

He stood up, holding her hand. Sarah remained kneeling, motionless, afraid to move lest it break her last tiny shred of control. Dmitri gave the hand a final squeeze and shook his free, backing up until he stood with his escort.

"I love you, Kid," he sniffed as he placed his arms behind his back. A security officer locked transfer restraints around his wrists, then placed gait-limiting electronic cuffs around his ankles. He couldn't run; he couldn't defend himself.

"Write me! Send me hyperspace feeds if I'm close enough. I'm counting on you! I'll be there in ninety days. Be good for me!" Dmitri called as he was led out of the room. The doors slid shut.

He was gone.

Sarah fell forward as the doors closed, nose to the floor. She locked her hands over her head and let loose a wail of anguish.

"I'm sorry, Sarah," Dr. Granger said nearby. "I know what your brother means to you. Why don't you come with me for a little while? Maybe we can talk about it."

"Sarah?" said another voice, almost in her ear.

Sarah held her breath at the closeness, at the unfamiliar scent of a stranger, but she didn't care what happened to her right now. Dimi was gone. She was alone. She was going to crawl down a dark, deep hole, and she wasn't ever going to come out.

"Sarah, please? Please look at me?" said the unsure voice. "I know you're very upset, but please try. I don't want to touch you without your permission. I know you don't like that."

The consideration caught her attention. No one ever respected her rules without constant reminders. Sarah peered at the speaker with one red eye.

Uncle Tomas, in all his finery, knelt next her, hand outstretched, copying her position right down to his cheek on the floor. He smiled warmly when she looked at him, a smile that reminded Sarah of her brother Viktor. Viktor had been a patient soul, kind and gentle and caring. Sarah couldn't remember the last time someone had been self-assured enough to reach out on her level like this. Certainly, no one on the *Triumph* had. Vladimir swore Uncle Tomas was very nice. He never got mad, he never yelled, and he never, ever, hit them, even when they screwed up. She turned her head to see with both teary eyes.

"Thank you," Tomas breathed. "I'm very sorry you had to separate. I'm sorry I couldn't prevent it. If there's anything I can do to help, anything I can get for you, please don't hesitate to ask. Anything at all, night or day. We're free to leave, Sarah. I understand you might not want to talk to me yet, but, perhaps we could walk around the base and get acquainted, unless you have another idea. Can you do that, or do you want more time?"

All Sarah really wanted to do right then was curl into a ball and cry her eyes out for the next month or two, uninterrupted. Then she might get something to eat, curl back up, and cry some more until she decided enough was enough, but she knew she'd never be allowed to do that.

Damned doctors!

Her heart was too heavy to think, her brain too dull. She was no longer a prisoner; she had nowhere to go, nowhere to be. Freedom had never been so frightening. Uncle Tomas seemed to be trying very hard to be nice. Dmitri said he trusted him, and she should too. Vlad did, and if Vlad did, that should be good enough for her. After all, Tomas had brought her lawyers when she'd asked, never even mentioned the price, and flew out here himself to make sure all went well. He'd even offered to pay for a hyperspace video account once, if she'd wanted to talk with Vlad more often than Dmitri could afford. It wasn't like she had much choice. The court said he was in charge. Dmitri said she had to obey him, and Dmitri hadn't released her from their contract.

Tomas' hand was waiting. Sarah gave a shuddering sigh, and reached out to take it.

"Thank you!" Uncle Tomas smiled wider, holding her hand very lightly. "Come on. I hate courtrooms. Let's get out of here." He helped her to her feet.

"Nice work," Granger said. "Call me if you hit trouble."

* * *

"Dr. Granger?" Commodore Blaine called him back to the front table. "Could I speak with you for a moment? I have a few more questions."

"Of course, Commodore."

Blaine glanced over the notes she'd made. "Have you done any preliminary studies for genetic manipulation?"

"No, Commodore, I hadn't considered it. It's my understanding that genetic manipulation is reserved for intractable schizoid psychosis. I haven't seen anything to date that would warrant such an extreme plan of treatment."

"Perhaps not yet, but if we are still seeing repetitive aberrant behavior patterns eight years later, as difficult as it may be, we must accept the position that we may be dealing with a disintegrative psychosis that may not ever resolve."

"With all due respect, Commodore, I think it's a little premature to make that statement," Kyle said. "While I have personally witnessed a profound distrust of authority figures, dissociation, suicidal ideation, and severe panic, I have not seen any instances of psychotic behavior since the original incident, nor were any indicators found on three separate

330

four-hour brain scans. At this time, I feel Miss Kirushenko's needs can be met through a secure, stable environment, neurochemical blockades, and psychotherapy to decrease the severity of her panic attacks and give her more control over herself and her environment."

"But according to your own reports, Doctor, you have yet to find a neurochemical combination that has been effective in stemming these behaviors."

"I've tried three, *with* limited success each time," Granger reminded Blaine. "I didn't have much faith in the Elavixor, but it was the drug my patient was most comfortable with. The second, Neuroxin, reduced the norepinephrine overload, but produced a side effect of insomnia and profound irritability. She's currently receiving a combination of Beta Thiotropine, Antivox, and Lexovore, which does have some therapeutic effect in familiar settings. Insomnia is still a concern, but it is highly likely this may be due to environmental factors."

"What about a neurotransmission feedback pump?"

"I was more concerned with stabilization. I was leaving long-term therapy to her psychiatrist on Earth."

Blaine frowned, thinking. "Given the patient's history of non-compliance with drug therapy, a neurofeedback monitor will provide the most optimal treatment for non-permanent long-term therapy. I would like to see one in place before release. Even at Davies power six, it will still take a week for her to reach Earth. That will ensure drug compliance during that time, and make the transition easier for her."

Granger nodded. Fair enough. "I can do that."

* * *

Tomas Ivanov sat in the café, watching his new ward take the tiniest taste of the Delphinian custard before her. She touched the spoon to the candy-pink dessert, lifted a minute bead of custard onto the tip, turned the spoon upside down and touched the custard to the tip of her tongue, never letting the food or even the spoon touch her lips. For the past four hours she'd been virtually silent but not uncommunicative, offering nods and shakes in reply to his one-sided conversation. The offer of dinner brought out heavy conversation – *no sir, yes sir, thank you, sir.* At least he knew she wasn't ignoring him.

For the first hour he didn't speak much himself, the silence between them so heavy it made even walking difficult. Then, between the long pauses, Tomas told her about his house in Minsk, about her family, about

Minsk itself. He brought her up to date on her old psychiatrist, the one she would return to, now a founding member of a treatment center for children with difficulties. She accepted the information with the same blank expression she wore when he wasn't talking. Several times he thought he saw tears in the lifeless violet eyes, but they never fully materialized.

At least she wasn't screaming over imaginary objects.

Sarah declined his offer for dinner, but after three separate tries Tomas was quite hungry, and asked if she wouldn't mind just sitting with him while he ate. She agreed to that, but looked frightened when he ordered her the custard.

"If you don't like it, you don't have to eat it, I won't mind," Tomas insisted, "but Dmitri said you like custards, and Delphinian is a very good one; one of my favorites. You haven't eaten anything since breakfast. You need at least one meal a day to keep up your strength."

"Thank you, sir," came the monumental answer – three words in a row! It took five full minutes of poking and dabbing before she tasted the light dessert.

"Do you like it?"

Her face registered no opinion. Another fast glance, then a nod. "Yes, sir. Thank you, sir."

Five! Steady progress!

That had been almost an hour ago. Ivanov ate slowly, giving her time, but he was still done long before she finished just half.

"Would you like more time, or would you like to leave?"

Sarah put down her spoon. "I'm finished, thank you, sir."

"It's getting late. Why don't we head back to my rooms and get you settled. Your ship doesn't arrive until tomorrow, and it won't leave until the day after. I'm waiting for Captain Sullivan to release your things to me."

The head shot up and stayed there for the first time that day, the purple-blue eyes wide with fright. Tomas feared she might snap. He wasn't ready to handle that, especially in public. *What did he say?* After a moment the eyes returned to the table, but the face was no less tense.

She spoke timidly to the half-eaten dessert. "Sir? I do not wish to seem ungrateful for the efforts you have made for me, for you have been beyond kind, and I *will* abide by your final decision, but, if I may, sir, I – I would like to return to the sickbay on the *Triumph* for the night. I – I am not certain I am well enough to be away from prompt medical care just yet."

Ivanov hadn't expected that answer. He felt somewhat rebuffed, true, but his knowledge of medicine could be summed up by the label on a can of antibiotic healing spray. If she were afraid she might need assistance, he wasn't about to argue.

"Okay," he agreed amicably. "If you feel you the need, that's fine with me. Come on. I'll take you there now."

Kyle Granger greeted her as the doors to the sickbay opened. "Sarah, just the person I wanted. Why don't you bring your uncle into my office over there. We have some things to discuss. How did your afternoon go?"

"Very well, I think," Ivanov said, preceding Sarah into the office. No matter how he tried, she would not walk in front of him, not even side by side. "We had a long, pleasant stroll, and a light dinner afterwards. I offered her the use of my suite at the starbase, but Sarah felt she might be better off staying in your medical area tonight. She feared she might have difficulties that would require your attention."

Granger sat at his desk. "That's a change of pace, but probably not a bad idea. It'll make things a little easier on me."

"Why did you wish to find me?" Sarah blurted in a rush.

"I had a meeting with the review board," Granger said. "They suggested a course of treatment, to be implemented before I can release you for good." He reached into a cabinet behind the desk and withdrew a white case. From it he removed a tiny device.

Sarah braced, ready to run. "What is that? What are you going to do to me?"

"If you wait five seconds, I'll explain it. I'm not exactly happy with the decision, but it's not the worst plan, either. Sending you off on a long trip right after implantation doesn't allow time to ensure there won't be complications."

"Implantation!"

Granger held up the mechanism, an egg-shaped device no bigger than the tip of his thumb, sprouting several infinitesimal hairs from both ends. "The court is insisting on the implantation of a neurofeedback monitor. Do you know what the adrenal glands do?"

"They're involved in the production of adrenaline, a cortisol hormone involved in the regulation of fight-or-flight behavior," Sarah recited warily. "Sympathetic nervous system, if I recall."

"Exactly. What I'm required to do is surgically implant the device near your adrenals – "

Sarah took two steps toward the door. "Absolutely not! I won't allow surgery!"

"Sit down, please, Sarah. Hear him out first," Tomas said. He reached out, caught himself, and pulled his hand back before he might touch her. "I don't know anything about this. I need to learn." He motioned to the doctor to let him examine the device. Sarah took another step toward the door, arms crossed defiantly.

"I'm not removing anything," Granger assured her. "You won't feel it, you won't hear it, you can't see it, and no one will know it's there. I make a small incision on your back and encapsulate the sensor housing among the interior fascia. I then implant the sensor filaments into the inferior vena cava, and the transmitter delivery microfibers into the abdominal aorta. When the sensors detect elevations of specific neurotransmitters beyond a certain point, they signal the pump to release chemicals in appropriate amounts that will counteract the overload and put you back in control within seconds."

"So I'm never allowed to feel *anything*? If someone tickles me, I can't laugh? If someone threatens me, I stand there and get pulverized? I won't be made into an android like that!"

"If it's working right, that shouldn't happen," Granger said. "It shouldn't affect personality or functioning at all. It kicks in only when levels reach a preset limit, and it should kick out when the levels fall below that. It can be adjusted through a medical communication wave, and if necessary replenished through a microlette; no other surgery is required except for removal. If anything, you'll be known for being able to keep a clear head in an emergency."

"I don't want it."

"Unfortunately, refusal is not an option. I have orders."

"What side effects will that have?" Ivanov inquired. "What should I be aware of?"

"If it's underreacting, she won't feel much difference at all. If it's overreacting, she might feel sleepy in tense situations, maybe experience a fall in bloodpressure enough to make her dizzy. Some people are sensitive and get transient tics – muscle spasms in an eyelid, maybe a tremor on one side. They pass quickly, and lessen with time. It's really a very safe method of maintaining a therapeutic level of neurochemicals."

"Try it, Sarah," Tomas urged, handing back the device. "Give it a week. If it's not right, John will remove it when you get back."

Sarah remained unconvinced. "I want to be awake through it."

"Also not an option," Granger said. "This is microsurgery. I can't risk you coughing and severing a nerve in the process. The surgery shouldn't take more than a half hour, and you should be on your feet again in two. If you'd like, your uncle can stay and make sure I don't do anything I'm not supposed to."

"No! That won't be necessary."

"What I do won't leave a scar. I make sure of that, especially on my female patients. I've been through your records, Sarah," the doctor said gently. "Dmitri told me you have one or two old scars that are painful. If you'd like, with your uncle's permission, I can remove those while I have you under."

"Absolutely," Tomas agreed. "Whatever she needs to make her comfortable."

Sarah's face burned with shame, and she turned away from the men. Her face twisted and grimaced until it was almost possible to see the raging argument taking place in her head.

"Okay," she agreed with a tremendous pout. "But only *you* are allowed in the room."

"I'll need at least a nurse."

"One nurse, that's ALL!" Sarah ordered, stomping a heel with a finality that threatened violence.

"All right," Granger conceded. "We'll do it first thing in the morning."

"We can't do it *now*? I could change my mind twelve hundred times by then!"

"I've been on duty for the last fourteen hours. I think you'd rather have a neurosurgeon who's a little more rested than I am," Granger admitted wearily. "I know I certainly would."

Тридцать
Thirty
Chednala

"Here it is," Tomas said as he and Sarah entered the workroom on deck 19. Here her belongings had sat for two weeks, picked through piece by piece until the captain was certain no further contraband materials were present. On the floor sat her packing trunk, complete with hand-hammered metal edging and latches, two weary travel cases covered with destination-tag souvenirs, and a beat-up oversized desert-tan backpack. A worktable in the center of the room held an assortment of transport cartons, and two worn travel cases without tags. Dmitri's safe squatted doorless against the back wall.

"Do you see anything missing?"

Sarah gave a soft squeal and rushed to the trunk like a child at Christmas, running her fingers lovingly over the top. She knelt, flicked open the latches and raised the lid.

"Look at this!" The trunk was packed neatly, largest and heaviest items on the bottom, smallest and lightest on top, with cushion wrap folded under and over breakable items. "Everything! They went through *everything!* Someone has touched every one of my things! They had no right! These were *mine!*"

"The Allied Fleet can be very thorough when they want. I'm sorry if it upsets you."

"It's a violation of *me!*" Sarah sifted the neatness, disrupting it. She snatched a small striped child's shirt and held it to her face, sniffing.

She held it up proudly. "This is Vlad's! I'll bet he can't wear it anymore."

Tomas played along. "No, he just might not. We kept him in the greenhouse all last winter, where he actually managed to grow." He watched with delight when the girl smiled – really smiled! – at his humor, a beautiful shy smile, too full to be her mother's, showing straight, perfect teeth. Maybe the neuro-pump *was* the best thing for her. Maybe things were going to work out well after all.

The girl placed the shirt on the the now-jumbled belongings and lunged for a travel case, hugging it. "These are my *real* clothes!" She opened the case and snatched a sparkling gold shirt, something the height of fashion several years before.

"This is my favorite!" she said, only to be disappointed. Even if the fabric stretched, it didn't look nearly large enough. "I guess *I've* grown in the last four years."

"I'm sure you have. We'll get you some new things you'll like just as much. Come sit, Sarah." Tomas pulled a chair out at the table. "We have much to discuss." Sarah stuffed the shirt in the case, choosing to sit around the corner of the table instead.

She gave a melancholy glance at the boxes on the table. "Those are Dimi's things."

"And they will be again. They'll be shipped home with you, cargo. If you think Dmitri won't mind, you may arrange his room, so he'll feel at home when he arrives. In the meantime, the *Pride of Polaris* is docked at the starbase. You will be boarding at 1700 hours for an 1800 departure."

He opened the seal on a folder he carried, and pushed a computer card across the table to her. "This is your boarding pass. Please do not lose it. You will be in the ambassador class section, suite nine. Two rooms, in-room refrigeration and replicator facilities, full environmental controls, in-room direct hyperspace connection, entertainment span, everything. You should be fairly comfortable there."

Sarah stared at the card in awe, reading the big red words AMBASSADOR CLASS over and over. She opened her mouth to speak, but a tic started somewhere hear her right eye. The spasm spread, became a hard shiver, then a tremor, traveling down her face to her neck and shoulder and arm, until it ended at her fingers. Her hand flew to her cheek when the seizing stopped several seconds later. She looked helplessly at Tomas, embarrassed to the core.

"It's over," he soothed, laying his hand on hers. Sarah jerked her hand into her lap, and Tomas sat back just as fast. It was hard to remember all the rules. Her brothers were very physical, slapping hands, wrestling, punching or squeezing everyone affectionately. The girls were full of hugs and little kisses and gentle caresses. The youngest siblings were as eagerly affectionate as puppies. Sarah was … different.

"Doctor Granger said it's only temporary. It will lessen as your body gets used to the neurotransmitters. Are you okay?"

"Yes. Thank you, sir. I don't mean to belittle your thoughtfulness, sir, but, I'm used to traveling fourth-class economy. I – I couldn't handle cargo class without Dimi," she remembered with a shudder, "but fourth class is fine with me, sir. Such luxury is unnecessary."

"I do not send my mechanic fourth-class," Ivanov informed her with a tinge of disdain. "You are family; Ambassador class it is. I want to be able to contact you at any time."

Sarah frowned. "What do you mean, contact me? You won't be with me?" She grimaced as a tremor started near her mouth, spread to the eye, and marched down the same side again.

"Unfortunately, I must make a few brief business stops. Meeting your clients face-to-face helps breed good will and business loyalty. My ship departs at 1500, and I should arrive home the same time you do." It wasn't the right thing to do; Tomas knew that. He'd sat up half the night thinking of alternatives, spent several hours on the expensive hyperspace frequencies talking to her 'new' doctor, but he didn't have much choice.

"I don't travel alone! I don't even walk to town alone! It isn't safe to be alone! What if something happens? Who will be there?" She pressed her hands to her face as she twitched again.

"*Nothing* will happen. You are sixteen years old. That's plenty old enough to make a simple spaceflight on your own. You will be escorted to your ship, the ship will fly directly to Earth, and you will get off there. Even if you board the wrong orbital shuttle and wind up on the wrong continent, we can moley-beam you into Minsk if we have to. If I cannot be there, John has agreed to meet you at the spaceport. Your medication administers itself, outside of the vitamin complex and the Lexovore, which I'm trusting you to take on your own. You should be responsible enough to do that. If you aren't, please tell me now, and I will have a ship's officer dispense them. I will be in contact with you at least twice a day, and I have no doubt the family will be calling you as well."

"But...! But...!"

"No buts." Ivanov was firm. "I would not ask you to do something I was not absolutely certain you could do. You can do this, and you will. Now, do you have enough traveling money?"

Sarah tried to find her wits. "*Umm.* Dmitri has our money in an account, but the Rehab department froze the balance until he's released. I have about a hundred interstellar credits, cash, that Dimi kept on hand in his locker."

"Cash?" Tomas smiled with amusement. "I haven't seen cash credits in years! They're still good, of course, but you'll need more than that for expenses." He pulled a green card from his folder. "That's a voucher card. It will draw up to one thousand credits from my personal accounts. Use it for whatever you need – clothing, amusements, restaurants, souvenirs. I don't care. It's yours."

"Sir! I can't accept that!" Sarah scrunched her eyes tight as the tremor started. This time it stayed confined to her face. "It's far too much! *Please*, sir! I really don't want it!"

"You cannot be without funds, Sarah. This is nonsense." He placed the card on the boarding pass. "Use what you need, and if you feel it is too much, you may return the remainder when you get home." He placed a third card on the growing stack. "This is your new passport. You were denied your Class Four; you are limited to a Class One until you are through your probation."

"I can't travel to less than a Class-One technology planet for *five years*?"

"You broke the rules," Ivanov reminded her. "That's what happens. Now, here's an updated copy of your ID card ..."

* * *

"Can you believe that, Ti'onam? Ambassador Class accommodations on a Hermitage-class starliner." Sullivan shook his head as they waited near docking hatch G of the starbase. "I think I was a commander before I ever saw that kind of luxury, and that was only because of the person I was escorting. I'm not sure I could even swing that for myself as a captain."

The Navaran's hands were clasped behind his back, holding a sealed envelope. "It is intriguing, the emphasis placed on environment by which to judge personal value. While desiring a temporary place to store personal items during travel and ensure safety during sleep, many travelers insist on accommodations that far exceed the style, class, and manner to which they are accustomed."

"There's nothing wrong with being king for a day. It doesn't mean you want to be king all the time," Jack explained. "If you're used to that kind of luxury, you might not consider a long space flight to be as much of an inconvenience as it is. If you're not, it can make a rather uninteresting trip more memorable. In a way, I'm almost glad to see it. The Kirushenkos have been living without most of the daily conveniences we take for granted; I think it's a rather nice gesture to welcome them back to civilization this way."

Down the corridor Sarah appeared, escorted by two female guards from the *Triumph*. She carried a new silver travel case in one hand, and over her shoulder hung her khaki backpack, bulging with cherished items. She still wore her Sigma Tau Ceti costume, a clean jumper of dark burgundy and a pale yellow blouse. Her long hair was combed smooth, held back by a black metal band. She eyed Sullivan unhappily, but the terror wasn't there, kept in check by the implanted neurochemical pump.

"Making sure I make it off your ship?"

"Extending you the courtesy of saying, 'Goodbye.' "

"And good riddance?" Sarah let the heavy pack slide to the floor, and placed the travel case next to it.

"I didn't say that. You ascribe more animosity to me than I feel."

"Why, then? Why did you do this to me and Dimi? We were happy. We were good at what we did. We weren't harming anyone. Until Father appeared, we felt safe. Why did you have to destroy that on us? You go crazy trying to prosecute us under the auspices of Independent Destiny, but you have no problem interfering with other people yourself."

"Because ignoring a problem and hiding from it only makes it worse," Sullivan said. "Independent Destiny is designed to protect cultures that are developing of their own accord. The relationship between you and your brother was stagnant, and had been for years. It was unhealthy, and over time it would only continue to worsen. Dmitri knew that, but he hadn't gotten up the courage yet to act. All I did was give things a push. He'll only be gone three months. In that time, I think you'll learn a lot about yourselves. Life is constantly changing. You can't be afraid of that change. It's a major part of growing up."

"I'm not afraid," Sarah insisted. She glanced at Sullivan from under her bangs. "Is there a word that means more than 'terrified'?"

Sullivan smiled. "I have every faith you'll survive, if not thrive."

Ti'onam held out his envelope. "Miss Kirushenko, this is yours. It is the results of your educational exam. I congratulate you on achieving a Basic Education certificate, one year ahead of schedule."

"Not as impressive as if I'd done it seven years ahead," she said, accepting the envelope, "but I thank you anyway. May I inquire as to my score?"

"Ninety-eighth percentile."

"Only ninety-eight?"

Sullivan coughed. *"Only?"*

"Your scores on general knowledge and history were one hundred percent correct. However, your score on the elective Navaran language sub-test was only ninety-four percent correct," Ti'onam said.

Sarah grimaced. "I guess that's not bad for a language I haven't heard spoken in seven years and didn't have time to really brush up on. Not the selfish glory I wanted, but I guess that's what I get for taking it with a hangover. It will have to do."

"Nonetheless, it *is* an impressive score," Ti'onam praised her. "I urge you to continue your scientific pursuits. It would be most foolish to allow such a promising talent to go undeveloped. I will expect to see your botanical study published within the coming year, and I look forward to reading papers on your future scientific endeavors."

"You give me deep honor, sir," Sarah replied, bowing her head. "I would be most pleased if that can occur."

"Sarah Kirushenko?" A uniformed woman with a compad approached from the docking port. "The *Pride of Polaris* is boarding now. If you'll follow me, I'll escort you to your cabin and help you get settled." The woman picked up Sarah's tired, travel-weary backpack, the very first thing Dmitri had ever bought her.

Sarah snatched it back. "That's mine! *I* will carry that!"

"Of course, Miss." The woman took the travel case instead.

"Good-bye, Sarah," Sullivan said. "May you have a safe and pleasant trip home."

"Without Dmitri, that is not possible," Sarah said bitterly, lost and frightened once more. "Goodbye, sirs." She followed the woman through the docking hatch without a backward glance.

Jack Sullivan stopped at the sickbay on his return to the bridge.

Granger looked up from the stack of shipping crates in front of him. The *Triumph* had picked up supplies at the starbase; he was checking and unpacking the new inventory. "She's officially gone? I can put away the whip and chair?"

Jack hooked a hip over the corner of a table. "Yeah. I think I expected more enthusiasm out of her. She was so dead-set on escaping the ship; she seemed just as reluctant to leave it."

"She's on her own for the first time in her life. It takes a lot less courage to stay with a familiar evil than to break away into the unknown, even if you know it's for the best." The doc tossed a compad at the captain. Jack caught it at the last second, fumbled it, turned it over to look at the screen. "My discharge report on the Kirushenko girl. You might as well sign it while you're here."

Sullivan glanced over the computerized form, scrolled it, then gave it a quick scribble. He put the pad on the doctor's desk, but twiddled the stylus in his fingers. "What's your prognosis, Kyle? Eight years later, she's still fighting the same demons that dragged her down before. Do you really think she has a chance at rehabilitation, once and for all?"

Granger peeked in a carton, removed a sample jar, and logged the acquisition with a scanner. "It's possible. She's still young. With the proper medications and therapies, she should move forward. She's stuck with at least two years' worth of intensive treatment, whether she wants it or not. I spent some time yesterday talking with her uncle; for all his ruthless reputation, he seemed honestly concerned about her. He's raised the rest of her family these last several years, so he's no stranger to the ins and outs of teens with issues. A structured family life, a formal education program, appropriate medical treatment, a chance to make friends – you'd be amazed how fast she might make progress. She never wanted to leave her family in the first place. The time apart will give Dmitri a chance to get his life in order, figure out what he might want for himself. In his entire life, he's never had a time when he wasn't responsible for at least one other person, never had time to think about who he really is, and what he wants out of life."

"It's regrettable neither one of them ever had a real childhood."

"It certainly didn't help matters. They did the best they could."

Sullivan pointed the pad stylus at his friend with a wry gleam in his eye. "I heard a rumor you ate dinner with Ti'onam last night. Don't tell me you're going soft on Navarans? I won't have anything left to kid you on."

Granger's reply was an icy glare. He returned to his inventory. "Don't get your hopes up anytime soon. It wasn't my idea. I was already eating when he asked if I would mind answering his questions on neurochemistry."

"I'm shocked you didn't tell him to look it up for himself."

Kyle sighed. "You ever break a horse that was born wild?"

"I petted a horse in a zoo once. Does that count?"

Granger wasn't amused. "We were allowed to cull six horses a year out of the wild herds, if we caught them on our land. We'd have to tame them and train them before selling them. If you look in the eyes of a horse like that, really stare deep into them, you can see what he's thinking. That horse knows he's smarter than you; he's had to be to survive. You just have to let him know that you know he's smarter, and that's all right. Watching the Kirushenko girl these last few weeks, I realized she was nothing but a free-range filly. I approached her the way I approach my horses, and I'll be damned if it didn't work. It got me thinking about it in terms of psychology.

"Now, the biggest sonofabitch I've met yet on this ship is that damned Navaran…"

"Moreso than the Mensans in Life Systems?"

"Even moreso than the Mensans. So I said to myself, Kyle, if you can tame a wild girl who was half-Navaran by upbringing, it might just work around Ti'onam, who's a whole Navaran by birth. I figure the Navarans are exactly the same; they just haven't been tamed yet to human ways. Without having to suffer that planetary inferno, I can give the job my close and careful attention. I can't compete with Navaran arrogance, but if you give me time, I'll bet you cold cash I can tame that Navaran."

"Knowing you, Kyle, I'll bet you can."

The End
Book 3

It's been a dream for seven years. Seven long, agonizing years since Sarah was ripped from her family, and now she's actually coming home. A new home, a new guardian, a new chance at happiness - or is it? A lot of water went under the bridge in her absence, and nothing is the same. Little Nikky is a rambunctious eleven, Katya is married, Galina about to be, Valeria is involved, and even Vlad turns his head after girls. Sarah's the lonely one who can't seem to grow up.

Burning with old guilt, smothered by unforgiven shame, emotionally strangled by horrors in her past, Sarah's being forced to learn new rules, forge new relationships, accept new standards to live by, but first she has to dare to trust herself. And just when she feels it might be safe to come out of hiding, guess who's coming back to his family?

Best
of
Everything

The Best things in life are worth waiting for

The final installment of *Best Intentions*

Susan Staneslow Olesen

Overview on
Pelonishala Region
Sigma Tau Ceti IV

There are 22 written consonants and 5 vowels in Pelonishalak, the dominant language of the Pelonishala region of which Vandijoc is a town. Printed Pelonishalak resembles a cross between the Arabic and Burmese writing systems on Earth. Most letters have one equivalent sound, that's all. Of course, Pelonishalan towns are small and spread apart, so local dialect may put different edges on them, such as slurring Vandijoc (Vandijoke) to *Vandijawk*. **Accent is on the syllables in bold print.**

Roman-letter equivalents to Pelonishalak phonemes:

$\mathcal{M}$ - *mem*, as in more, many

$\mathcal{A}$ - always says *ah*

$\mathcal{B}$ - *bay*, as in *ball*

$\mathcal{V}$ - *ev*, as in vacuum, valiant, verve

$C/\mathcal{K}$ - *kee*, always hard, as in <u>c</u>ake or <u>c</u>at. In the Eastern Fijanishak district, from which the Pelonishalak language evolved, there is a differentiation in the 'kuh' sound of the 'C' and 'K' symbols (a 'khuh' vs. a sharper 'kuh'), but this has been lost in Pelonishalak, and the symbol/sound is virtually interchangable.

Ch - *chen*, the hard ch of <u>ch</u>air, <u>ch</u>icken, <u>ch</u>ur<u>ch</u>

$\mathcal{E}$ - *eh*, always short, as in *egg* or *elephant* or *extra*

Sh - *sheh*, Sh! Lots of soft sh'sh's

$\mathcal{G}$ - *ghah*, always hard, as in girl or glass. **Never** soft like a J, but gargle it a bit, so it sounds like you're either choking or clearing your throat. Closer to a Russian *X*. A hard *Hah!*

ι - *ea* - always like a long E, as in *pilaf* or *ski*.

$\mathcal{F}$ - *feh*, as in *feather* or *phish*

$\mathcal{P}$ - *apeh*, as in paint, pepper

$\mathcal{J}$ - *jiuh*, as in jump

$\mathcal{L}$ - *lo*, as in lamp

$\mathcal{T}$ - *toe*, as in turtle

$\mathcal{W}h$ - *wha*, as in what, where, why

$\mathcal{D}$ - *du*, as in Dmitri

$\mathcal{S}$ - *sah*, as in snake

$\mathcal{Z}$ - **zin**, as in zipper

$\mathcal{Z}h$ - **zhen**, the soft j sound found in plea<u>s</u>ure, mea<u>s</u>ure, lei<u>s</u>ure

$\mathcal{O}$ – **aw,** usually a long O, as in <u>o</u>we and t<u>o</u>tal, but occasionally a softer *aw*, as in Vandijoc.

$\mathcal{U}$ - **oo**, as in moon or broom

$\mathcal{R}$ - **reh,** as in rabbit. Rolling it is not uncommon.

$\mathcal{N}$ - **nah,** as in Newton

$\mathcal{T}h$ - **thi,** a voiceless th as in <u>Th</u>orazine, weal<u>th</u>, <u>th</u>ought, never voiced as in this, those.

$\mathcal{K}$ - **ka** - as in kite

$\mathcal{X}$ - **ksah**. Yes, you can say this. The same *ks* as in a<u>x</u> (aks) or loo<u>ksy</u> or Tur<u>k's</u>.

7 pronouns:

Ima (I, me)

Imarak (We, us, specific to you and me and him, a "local" we)

Imarakashi (a global We, as in We the People, All of us here at home, everyone at school, those of us in town, etc.)

Ahn (you, meaning just you)

Ahnax (You, plural, meaning both or all of you and your whole family, too, or a very respectful you, as in you, your body, mind and spirit included.)

Ix (He, she, or it; there are no genders, no differentiation)

Ixo (they, them)

Pronouns or subject nouns receive the primary stress in a sentence, no matter where in the sentence the word winds up.

Articles don't exist in Pelonishalak. There is no *an, the, a*, etc. Example: "*have You good porshie,* (it) *go far before* (it) *stop at* (the) *river to have* (a) *drink.*" Intonation will tell you if the words are a statement or a question.

In written language, sentences do not start with capitals. Pronouns can be capitalized, but most often, the main noun of the sentence is capitalized. Pronouns can start sentences, but most often they fall somewhere in the middle of the sentence.

Known Pelonishalak words and phrases: (Bold print shows accented syllable)

Pelonishalak names: names tend to be long
Charshfenaki Aletneshfaja
Alwhulida Aletneshfaja
Jaycelani Sivalaxa
Alikinashta Tanishwahdani
Chelikonash Ojanikashi – elected lawman of Vandijoc

Pelonishalak towns, cities, villages:
Arvijicanti - between Vandijoc and Ezoshala, pop. 400.
Chanchi - village nearest Chessorak Research Compound, @ 3 miles north, pop. 300
Chartaiga - Northwest of Otaiga, pop. 700
Chessorak - continent of Sigma Tau Ceti where Pelonishalak language is spoken, location of an Allied Fleet Research Compound, complement of @ 50 people.
Demorak - village southwest of Vandijoc, east of Sharfaxil, pop. @ 400
Ezoshala - east of Vandijoc, pop. 300
Fithma – the largest Allied Fleet research compound on Sigma Tau Ceti IV, the one with the evacuation transport equipment. Fithma is on another continent, approximately 4,000 miles from the Chessorak base. Complement @65 people
Kinonah – Another Allied Research compound, located on an island approximately the size of Greenland, but with a climate resembling that of the Gulf coast. Approximately 1200 linear miles from the Chessorak camp.Complement @ 40 people
Lozintal - south of Vandijoc, pop, 376
Otaiga - town in Pelonishalak district, half way between Vandijoc and Chessorak Compound, population @1500
Rizoshanti - around 50 miles due east of Chessorak Compound, pop 2,800
Sharfaxil - southwest of Vandijoc, in high hills, pop. 330.
Vandijoc - forest town in Pelonishalak district, approximately 40 miles from Chanchi, population @ 5-600

Moons of Sigma Tau Ceti: Moons are important to the native population. Three dominate the night sky: *Oes* (**Oh**-ays) (the little yellow one), *Allash* (the biggest, with a red hue to it), and *Taber* (the big silver one). Oes and Taber chase each other at the same speed, appearing in the sky at roughly the same time. Allash moves in a different plane, and takes twice as long to wax and wane. When in the right phase, Allash can be faintly seen during the day due to its coloring. Pelonishalak religion and folklore put great emphasis on the moons, giving them omniscient, God-like powers. The blood-red rays of Allash are said to heal the sick and give strength to the weak. Taber gives comfort and lights the way for travelers, and Oes is supposed to answer prayers and give insight to those who seek its help. Because of all the moons, many Tau Cetans are avid night-sky watchers, though when all three moons are full, it's hard to see any stars.

Common animals:
porshie - large draft mammal with a body somewhat like a small elephant, hair like a yak, but a neck, head, and tail more like a brontosaurus. Strong as a freight train, they're vicious, independent-minded, and far beyond obstinate in character. With great patience, a strong arm, and a hard club, they can be trained to pull carts, logs, plows, etc. A gelding can be taught to carry a rider, but most Pelonishalak women don't have the strength to control the strong neck. Porshies prefer fresh grasses and grains, but will eat just about anything they come across - small animals, crops, laundry on a line, farmer's backsides, etc. They are also raised for meat and hides. Hair is rough, usually buff to rust in color, but grays and dark browns are not usual (black is rare, pure white never seen). Hair can be spun and woven into coarse, water-resistant yarns. Porshies are mammalian in nature and give birth to single live young weighing @ 70 kilos, after a gestation of @ 10 months. They nurse for approximately five months, but are not sexually mature for 18 months.

galishnixa (plural, galishnixan) - a ground-dwelling rodent half-way between a squirrel and a prairie dog, with no tail and big black eyes.

urpinta (pl, *urpintan*) - a small goat-like herbivore, but more delicate, like an antelope. *Urpinta* means 'hardy little bugger." Raised as meat, for milk, and for soft leather.

joubash - a domesticated land bird used for food, as fat as a duck but more like a chicken in character. Joubash eggs are pink speckled with brown, and highly flavorful.

chirfana - a rare wild herbivore, the size of a large jackrabbit, highly prized for its soft fur and resulting pelt.

tuturina - cross a kinkajou with a possum; a common tree-dwelling animal with a waddling gate and golden fur, eats plants and insects. Pesty if they get in barns because they'll eat grain.

kupu – small, timid mouse-like rodent, often hiding in barns.

Words and phrases:

Aggenta -sanitary facility, toilet, outhouse *(polite form)*   *aggit (slang, very rude; lit. shithole)*

Ahniosh tessali jo Ima - I love you

Aj, aja, No

Akixshra - floor

Attwor - spoon

Axa, yes

Banati, Bata - father, dada

Banatishi - Uncle

degsha - table

Dimi-tri, joladi Ixi regavish chudaka? Dmitri, Friends they, you know before? (They are old friends of yours?)

Elistri – sister

Enab – a unit of measurement, equal to 1.84 cm, or a hair less than three-quarters of an inch.

Farrash Ixa? - Who's there? (Arrives who?)

Filash - local currency

Ganai- stop

Gash ix dira meralon - Please pass the salt."

gelatna, Niu ta bishnet porshi, lepivash Sarrah? Ride do you wish the porshie, adventuresome Sarah?

i Joso mas "PIGS" - All men are pigs

Imad Ahn risak - I love you

Ispa - Please

jenacha firat, Ahn! sorrat via Ahn Ixi! "You did it! You rode him!"

ki – and

koffo-ti shanweh Shojeni lorach stirinas Ahnaxin: May the Light of the Moons Brighten Your Way *(short form: shanweh Shojeni/*Light of the Moons : Have a Good One/See ya round/Good Luck!/Peace be with you/Good Night!

Mangato / esa mangato, Ahnax - Blessings (thanks) / many blessings (thanks) to you/ Thank You

navichet – hacking tool, similar to an adze.

"**Ho**hai! **Ho**hai! Hai! Hai! *Hai, vovorash porshu!*" Whoa! Whoa! Slow! Slow! Slow down, you dumb-ass porshie! (The 'H' sound doesn't exist as a separate written character; it is often implied by the consonant that precedes it. In a forceful initial vowel, the word may be translated with a Standard H before it for clarity, but the actual spelling remains with an initial 'O' (Oai! Oai! Ai!).)

"olashana, kirich, to uma Imarakashi nagosti gis privashak. Imarakashi, nagosti, lajafashto!" Gentlemen, tonight we are forbidden to discuss work. Tonight, we party!

Ombiri - bench

shagshwe - lamp

shamweh Shojeni! – Light of the moons (be with you); a farewell blessing, akin to *God be with you.*

shilak - spotlessly clean

Shojai/shojen – Moon/Moons

Shojen noti! Moons Above! (mild invective/ Holy Cow!)

Shojen ki Chaven! Moons and Stars! (mild invective/ Oh my God!)

tavana, Tata - Mother, mama

tavanishi - Aunt

tintima, Ispa – repeat, please

"to Aja tuxna," I don't speak [the language]

"...to, migaris dosh chynopradesh Ixo satti!" - ... if you slice them thin enough!

"torach Ix?" Is it safe?

to tuxnu Ahnax Pelonishalak? Do you speak Pelonishalak?

"tozhto Ahnax ti kappera!" It is pleasure to see you.

"uzhavad Ixan." - That is (They) backwards.

Vonash – Go! (away yourself)

Zappirash - an intoxicating beverage

Susan Staneslow Olesen is a graduate of Chase Collegiate School and studied psychology and writing at Wells College. She is a special-needs foster parent with more than 20 years experience in autism. In addition to working at her public library, she currently juggles six kids, six cats, four dogs, and an eight-foot-tall mystery plant in her garden. *Broken Trusts* is her third novel.

For info and trivia, follow along at
Best Intentions book series on Facebook.com